"IMPRESSIVE . . . A feat of sto...
—*Chicago Sun-Times*

"Those who enjoy intelligent, provocative science fiction will be highly rewarded by reading Benford's latest effort."
—*San Francisco Chronicle*

ALONE AGAINST THE UNKNOWN

Killeen sighted on the flickering image of the moving Mantis while his left index finger pressed a spot in his chest. In his left eye a sharp purple circle grew, surrounding the volume where the Mantis image oozed in and out.

He fired. Sharp claps in the stillness.

Legs blew away. Antennae slammed to the ground.

Killeen could see the Mantis's blue-green electric life droop and wink out. He ran.

"HARD SCIENCE FICTION AT ITS VERY BEST. . . . What's most notable about Benford is that behind the brilliant speculative frameworks that he constructs, behind all his ability to send the imagination soaring, behind the gripping adventure stories that he tells, his chief interest is the nature of humanity."
—*St. Louis Post-Dispatch*

"PROFOUND AND ORIGINAL . . . Probably Benford's best since his award-winning *Timescape*."
—*Newsday*

"Benford's well-deserved reputation as a star producer of hard science fiction should climb a few notches higher with this one. . . . Benford's writing flows like electrons along a copper wire, and his concepts and images are clear and insightful."
—*The Tampa Tribune*

*ALONE AGAINST THE UNKNOWN

Fanny lay tangled, head lolling. Her lined face stared blankly at the sky and her eyes were a bright, glassy white.

"No!" He couldn't move.

The Mantis had somehow interrogated Fanny's nerves, her body, her very self—all in moments. The Mantis had invaded her, read all. Until now, a marauder mech had to capture a human for at least several uninterrupted minutes to do this kind of damage. That had been a small advantage humanity had over the roving, predator mechs.

If this Mantis was a sign, that thin edge was now lost. . . .

"GRIPPING, STIRRING, Sometimes horrifying work, packed with glowing detail and astounding extrapolation."
—*Kirkus Reviews*

"DON'T MISS THIS ONE. It's a masterful job."
—*Analog*

GREAT
SKY
RIVER

Gregory Benford

BANTAM BOOKS
TORONTO • NEW YORK • LONDON • SYDNEY • AUCKLAND

To
Lou Aronica and David Brin
two knights of the Sevagram

GREAT SKY RIVER
A Bantam Spectra Book
Bantam hardcover edition / December 1987
Bantam paperback edition / October 1988

Library of Congress Cataloging-in-Publication Data

Benford, Gregory, 1941–
    Great sky river.

    (A Bantam spectra book)
    I. Title.
PS3552.E542G7 1987   813'.54   87-47584
                ISBN 0-553-27318-3

Published simultaneously in the United States and Canada

PRINTED IN THE UNITED STATES OF AMERICA

O   0 9 8 7 6 5 4 3 2 1

PROLOGUE

The Calamity

Killeen walked among the vast ruins.

Exhausted, he kept on through a jumble of shattered steel, caved-in ceilings, masonry and stone and smashed furniture.

His breath rasped as he called his father. "Abraham!"

A cold murmuring wind snatched the name away. Smoke seethed from crackling fires and streamed by him, making the air seem to waver and flow.

From here the Citadel sprawled before him down the broad, knobbed hill. Intricate warrens were now squashed into heaps of stone and slag. Legs stiff from exhaustion, eyes stinging with smoke and grief, he paused above a shattered plain of marble-white rubble—the caved-in shards of a dome that once rose a kilometer above the Citadel arboretum. Places where he had run and played, loved and laughed . . .

"Abraham!" He had seldom spoken his father's name and now it seemed strange and foreign. He wheezed, coughed. The acrid bite of smoke caught in his throat.

The lower ramparts of the Citadel burned fiercely. The mechs had penetrated there first. Black murk hung over the larger districts—the Broadsward, the Green Market, and the Three Ladies' Rest. Soot coated the jagged teeth of broken walls.

Beyond, lofty spires had been cut to blunt stubs. Their stumps radiated gorgons of structured steel. The shifting breeze brought him the crunch of collapsing walls.

But the wind carried no moans or shrieks. The Citadel

lay silent. The mechs had taken lives and selves and left nothing but emptied bodies.

Killeen turned and moved along the hillside. This was his old neighborhood. Tumbled-down blocks and twisted girders could not wholly conceal the paths and corridors he had known as a boy.

Here a man lay, eyes bulging at the bruised sky.

There a woman was split in two beneath a fallen beam.

Killeen knew them both. Friends, distant relatives of Family Bishop. He touched the cold flesh of each and moved on.

He had fled with the remnants of Family Bishop. They had quickly reached the far ridgeline and only then had he seen that his father was not among the survivors. Killeen had turned back toward the Citadel, wearing powered leggings for speed. Like lean pistons, his legs carried him within the slumped defensive walls before anyone in the Family noticed that he was gone.

Abraham had been defending the outer ramparts. When the mechs had breached those, the human perimeter had fallen back in a mad scramble. The mechs poured in. Killeen was sure he had heard his father's voice calling over the comm. But then the battle had submerged them all in a rushing hot tornado of death and panic.

—Killeen!—

He stopped. Cermo-the-Slow was calling over the comm. "Leave me alone," Killeen answered.

—Come on! No time left!—

"You head on back."

—No! There's mechs still around. Some comin' this way.—

"I'll catch up."

—Run! No time left.—

Killeen shook his head and did not answer. With a flick of a finger he dropped out of the comm net.

He climbed among tumbled stone. Even in his powered suit it was hard to make his way up the steep angles of ruined walls. Though the mechs had gouged gaping holes, the massive bulwarks had stood for a while. But beneath the incessant pounding blows even the heavy foundations had finally yielded.

He walked beneath an arch that had miraculously survived. He knew what lay ahead but could not keep himself from it.

She was in the same position. The heat beam had caught his wife as he carried her. Her left side was seared raw.

"Veronica."

He bent down and looked into her open gray eyes. They peered out at a world forever vanquished.

He gently tried to brush closed her rebuking eyes. Her gummy, stiff eyelids refused to move, as if she would not give up her last glimpse of the Citadel she had loved. Her pale lips parted with the half-smile she always made just before she spoke. But her skin was cold and hard, as if it had now joined the unyielding solidity of the soil itself.

He stood. He felt her eyes at his back as he made himself walk on.

He scrambled over slumped piles that had been homes, workshops, elegant arcades. Fires snapped in the central library.

The public gardens had been his favorite spot, a lush wealth of moist green in the dry Citadel. Now they were blasted, smoking.

As he passed the smashed Senate, its alabaster galleries groaned and trembled and slowly clattered down.

He moved on warily, but there was no sign of mechs. "Abraham!"

Around him lay the exploded remains of his boyhood. Here in his father's workshop he had learned to use the power-assisting craft. There, beneath a lofty corbelled vault, he had first met a demure, shy Veronica.

"Abraham!"

Nothing. No body. It probably lay beneath collapsed bulwarks.

But he had not covered all the rambling complex that men had built through generations. There was still some chance.

—Killeen!—

It was not Cermo this time. Fanny's voice cut through to him sharp and sure, overriding his own cutoff of the comm.

—Withdraw! There's nothing we can do here now.—

"But . . . the Citadel . . ."

—It's gone. Forget it.—

"My father . . ."

—We must run.—

"Others . . . There might be . . ."

—No. We're sure. Nobody left alive here.—

"But . . ."

—*Now*. I've got five women covering the Krishna Gate. Come out that way and we'll head for Rolo's Pass.—

"Abraham . . ."

—Hear me? Hustle!—

He turned for one last look. This had been all the world for him when he was a boy. The Citadel had made humanity's warm clasp real and reassuring. It had stood resolutely against a hostile universe outside, strong yet artful. Its delicate towers had glistened like rock candy. Returning to the Citadel from short forays, his heart had always leaped when he saw the proud, jutting spires. He had wandered the Citadel's labyrinthian corridors for many hours, admiring the elegant traceries that laced the high, molded ceilings. The Citadel had always been vast and yet warm, its every carefully sculpted niche infused with the spirit of the shared human past.

He looked back toward where Veronica's body lay.

There was no time to bury her. The world belonged now to the living, to fevered flight and slow melancholy.

Killeen made himself take a step away from her, toward the Krishna Gate. Another.

The blasted walls teetered past. He had trouble finding his way.

Fog and smoke swirled before him. "Abraham!" he called again against empty silence.

The Citadel's high, spidery walkways now lay broken in the dust, sprawled across the inner yards. He crossed the ancient, familiar ground in a numbed daze. Craters yawned where he had once scampered and laughed.

At the edge of the smoldering ruins he looked back. "Abraham!"

He listened and heard nothing. Then, distantly, came a quick buzzing of mech transmissions. The rasping sound narrowed his mouth.

He turned and ran. Ran without hope, letting his legs find the way. Stinging dust clouded his eyes—

A jerk.

Intense, blinding light.

"Hey, c'mon. Wake up."

Killeen coughed. He squinted against the high glare of harsh yellow lamps. "Huh? What—"

"C'mon, gotta get up. Fanny says."

"I, I don't—"

Cermo-the-Slow loomed over him. The big smiling face was weary but friendly. "I just pulled the stim-plug on you, is all. Got no time, wake you up easy."

"Ah . . . easy . . ."

Cermo frowned. "You been dreamin' again?"

"I . . . the Citadel . . ."

Cermo nodded. "I was 'fraid that."

"Veronica . . . found her."

"Yeah. Look, you don't think 'bout that, hear? She was a good woman, won'ful wife. But you got let go her now."

"I . . ." Killeen's tongue was raw from calling his father. Or was it from the alcohol he had gulped last night?

This was morning, early morning. He felt the stiffness in him from the night's sleep. Peering upward, he could make out the shadowy bulk of alien machinery. They had bedded down for the night in a Trough, he remembered. Around him, Family Bishop was waking up.

"C'mon," Cermo urged. "Sorry I pulled the plug so quick. Snap up now, though. We're movin' out."

"How . . . how come?"

"Ledroff spotted some Snout comin' this way. Figures it's headed into this Trough for supplies."

"Oh . . ." Killeen shook his head. An ache spread from his temples into his clammy forehead. A bead of night sweat dripped from his nose as he sat up.

"You better stay off the stim-tab awhile," Cermo said, frowning. "Gives you bad dreams."

"Yeah." Killeen nodded and started groping for his boots. They were the first thing you put on and the last you took off.

"It's been years, after all," Cermo said kindly. "Time we let it be."

Killeen frowned. "Years . . . ?"

"Sure." Cermo studied him a moment, plainly worried. "Been six years since the Calamity."

"Six . . ."

"Look, we all like it, gettin' a li'l stimmed now 'n' then. Not if it takes you back into bad times though."

"I . . . I guess so."

He clapped Killeen on the shoulder. "Get on up, now. We're movin' quick."

Killeen nodded. Cermo-the-Slow went away to awaken others. His large frame slipped quickly among the shadows of the alien vats and machines.

Killeen's hands pulled on his boots but his mind still wandered among memories. His dirty clothes, the worn boots, the calluses and stains on his hands . . . all testified to what had happened since the fall of the Citadel, the Calamity.

He stood slowly, feeling his chilled muscles stretch and protest.

The Citadel was gone.

Veronica.

Abraham.

He had left now only Toby, his son. Only a fragment of Family Bishop.

And finally, he had left before him now the endlessly stretching prospect of flight and rest and flight again.

PART I

LONG RETREAT

ONE

Something was after them.

The Family had just come straggling over a razor-backed ridge, beneath a pale jade sky. Killeen's shocks wheezed as his steady lope ate up the downgrade.

The red soil was deeply wrinkled and gullied. Cross-hatching was still sharp in the tractor-tread prints that cut the parched clay. There had been so little rain the prints could well be a century old.

A black-ribbed factory complex sprawled at the base of the slope. Killeen flew over the polished ebony domes, sending navvys scuttling away from his shadow, clacking their rude dumb irritation.

Killeen hardly saw them. He was watching spiky telltales strobe-highlighted on his right retina.

There: a quick jitter of green, pretty far back.

It came and went, but always in a new place.

There, again. Far behind.

Not directly following them, either. Not a typical Marauder maneuver. Smart.

He blinked, got the alternative display. The Family was a ragged spread of blue dabs on his topo map. He was pleased to see they kept a pretty fair lopsided triangle. Cermo-the-Slow was dragging ass behind, as always.

Killeen saw himself, an amber winking dot at the apex. Point man. Target.

He grimaced. This was his first time ever as point, and here came some damn puzzle. He'd tried to beg off when Cap'n Fanny ordered him to the front. There were others better experienced—Ledroff, Jocelyn, Cermo. He'd much rather have stayed back. Fanny kept giving him extra jobs like this, and while he'd do whatever she said without protest, this had made him jittery from the start.

Fanny knew more than anybody, could see through Marauder tricks. She should be up here. But she kept pushing him.

Now this. He dropped from the air, eyes slitted.

Killeen came down on a pocked polyalum slab, the old kind that mechs had used for some long-forgotten purpose. Packing fluff blew in the warm wind, making dirty gray drifts against his cushioned crustcarbon boots. Mechmess littered the ground, so common he did not notice it.

"Got a pointer behind," Killeen sent to Fanny.

—Snout?— she answered.

"Nossir noway," Killeen answered quickly to cover his nerves. "Think I'd sing out if was that same old Snout, been tagging us for days?"

—What is, then?—

"Dunno. Looks big, then small."

Killeen did not understand how his retinal area scan worked, had only a vague idea about radar pulses. He did know things weren't supposed to look large on one pass and small the next, though. Habit told you more than analysis.

—'Quipment's bust?—

"I dunno. Flashes okay," Killeen said reluctantly. Was Fanny joshing him? He didn't know which he liked less, something that could come up on them this way, or his gear gone flatline on him.

Fanny sighed. She was a nearly invisible speck to his right rear, wiry and quick. Killeen could hear her clicking her teeth together, trying to decide, the way she always did.

"Whatsay?" he prodded impatiently. It was up to her. She was Cap'n of the Family and had a long lifetime rich in story and experience, the kind of gut savvy that meant more in dealing with Marauder mechs than anything else.

She had been Cap'n for all the years that Family

Bishop had been on the move. She knew the crafts of flight and pursuit, of foraging and stealing, of deception and attack. And through terrible years she had held the Family together.

—Comes closer?—

"Looks. Dodging fast."

Fanny clicked her teeth again. Killeen could see in his mind's eye her wise old eyes crinkling as she judged their positions. Her warm presence suffused his sensorium, bringing a sure, steady calm. She had been Cap'n so long and so well, Killeen could not conceive how the Family had done without her before, when they lived in the Citadel.

—We make the fist, then,—she said with finality.

Killeen was relieved. "Goodsay."

—Sound the call.—

He blinked. "Won't you?"

—You're point. Act like one.—

"But you know more about . . ." Killeen hesitated. He did not like admitting to his own doubts, not with Ledroff and others probably listening in. He liked even less the prospect of leading an attack.

"Look, Ledroff has done this before. Jocelyn, too. I'll drop back and—"

—No. *You.*—

"But I don't—"

—Naysay!— She was abrupt, biting. —Call!—

Killeen wet his lips and steadied himself. He sent over general comm, —Heysay lookleft! Fist!—

Most of the Family were over the ragged ridgeline now. That would provide some shelter from whatever was coming from behind. He watched as they came spilling down the ruddy, gorge-pocked hillsides. They were a slow tumbling fluid, their individual tinny acknowledgments coming as thin insect cries.

Killeen did not consider for a moment that the voices he heard were carried on radio waves, for he had lived all his life in a sensory bath provided by the linking of acoustic and electromagnetic signals. The distinction between them would have demanded more science than he had ever mastered, ever would master. Instead he heard the gathering peppery voices as scattershot ringings, carrying long

and remote across the hot still silence of dusty late
afternoon. Though each Family member glided in beautiful
long arcs, the Family itself seemed to Killeen to hang
suspended in the middle distance, so gradual was its
progress, like thick dark down-swarming molasses. Gravid
and slow they came, this worn and perhaps only remaining
remnant of humanity: eagering, homing, tribing.

Killeen caught fragments of talk from Ledroff.
—Why'd Cap'n put *him* . . . Damfino why he's up
there . . .—

"Cut the chatter!" Killeen called.

—Couldn't find his ass w'both hands . . .—

"I said *quiet*!" he whispered fiercely.

Killeen had heard Ledroff's muttered jibes through the
comm before. Until now he had ignored them. No need to
provoke a faceoff with the big, self-assured man. But this
time Killeen couldn't let it pass. Not when it endangered
them.

—Seems me he's jumpin' at spooks,— Ledroff got in,
then fell silent.

Killeen wished Cap'n Fanny had come on full comm
line and cut off Ledroff. A mere disapproving click of her
tongue would have shut him up.

The Family skimmed low, using savvy earned through
hard years. Wheeling left, they seeped down among the
knobby, domed buildings of the manufacturing complex.

Factory mechs wrenched to a stop as the Family
skipped light and fast through their workyards. Then the
blocky, awkward-looking machines hunkered down, with-
drawing their extensors into marred aluminum shells. Such
mechs had no other defense mechanisms, so the Family
gave the slope-nosed, turtlelike forms no notice.

Still, the humans had to be fast. They knew if they
stayed here long these slow-thinking drudges would send
out a call. Lancers would come. Or worse.

Killeen pondered for a moment the possibility that the
thing trailing them was a lone Lancer, summoned by a
minor pillage the Family had made a few days before. He
checked the faint, flickering tracers behind.

No, nothing like a Lancer. Something smaller, certainly. It gave off hardly any image at all. Still . . .

"Yea!" he called. Tapping his right temple twice with a forefinger, he sent his scan topo map to the entire Family. "We're bunching up!"

With muttered irritation they spread out, dissolving their moving beeswarm triangle. They formed the traditional concentric rings, ragged because the Family numbered a mere 278 now. And some of them were achingly slow—gimpy, or old, or wounded from past scrapes and fights and blunders.

Fanny saw the problem and called, —Show the wind our heels!—

The old saying worked. They began to run faster now, a keen unspoken fear at their backs.

He sent the latest topo to Fanny. It showed a muddle of bluewhite tracers behind them.

Fanny sent, —Where's it?—

Killeen admitted, "Dunno. Looks to be some kinda screen."

—Deliberate confusion?—

"Don't think so. But . . ."

—Situation like this, your topo's no good for figurin' size. Go by speed. No 'facturing mech moves quick as a Marauder.—

"This one's slow, then fast."

—Must be a Marauder.—

"Think we should stand 'n' wait for it?"

He felt her assessing regard like a cool wedge in his sensorium.

—What *you* think?—

"Well . . . it might just be reconning us."

—Could be.—

She was giving nothing away. "So'd be best if we keep on, make like we don't see it."

—Long's we can keep track of it, sure.—

Killeen wondered what Fanny meant by that, but he didn't want to ask, not with Ledroff listening. He said guardedly, "It keeps jumpin' 'round."

—Might be some new mechtech.—

So? he thought. *How do we respond?* He kept his voice flat and assured, though, as he said, "I figure we don't give away that we see it. If it's just checkin' its 'quipment, it'll go away."

—And come back when we're sleepin',— she said
flatly.

"So? Our watch'll pick it up. But if we take a shot at it
now, when we can't see it so good, maybe it gets away. Next
time it comes back with better mechtech. So then we don't
pick it up and it skrags us."

Fanny didn't answer for a long moment and Killeen
wondered if he had made a fool of himself. She had coached
him in the crafts and he always felt inadequate compared
with her sure, almost casual grasp of Family lore. She could
be a stern Cap'n, a shrewd tactician, firm and fast. And
when they had fought or fled, and again gathered around
nightfires to tell their tales, she could be warm and
grandmotherly. Killeen would do anything to avoid disap-
pointing her. But he had to know *what* to do, and she was
giving him no easy answers.

—Yeasay. That's best, long as this's a reg'lar
Marauder.—

Killeen felt a burst of pride at her approval. But a note
of concern in her voice made him ask, "What if it's not?"

—Then we run. Hard.—

They were out of the foothills now. The Family
sprinted across eroded flatlands.

Fanny asked as she panted, —See it yet?—

"Naysay."

—Should've climbed the ridge by now. Don't like
this.—

"Think maybe a trap?" Killeen cast about for possibilities as he searched his topo display. Again he wished
Jocelyn or even goddamn Ledroff had this job. If an attack
came he wanted to be near his son. He scanned ahead and
found Toby in the middle of the moving Family formation.

Fanny dropped back, scanning the ridgeline.

Killeen searched again for the elusive pursuer. The
topo danced in his eye, speeding ribbons of light.

More cloudy tracers.

To the right came a dim speckling of pale blue.

Killeen realized too late that it would have been better
to hold the ridgeline. They were exposed and had lost the
enemy. He grunted in frustration and sped forward.

They were partway down the broad valley when he

looked right and saw first the overlay winking green and then the far rocky scarp. It was fresh rock, cleaved by some mining mech, its amber faces gouged and grooved.

But the clear bare cut hadn't been there moments before. Killeen was sure of that.

"Bear on my arrow!" he shouted to the whole Family. He cut toward a low hill. "Fanny, you'd—"

Killeen heard a sharp crackling.

He saw Fanny fall. She gave a cry of surprise. Then her voice sharpened, riding an outrushing gasp of startled pain.

He turned and fired at the distant carved hills, where stood half-finished blocks of rhomboid stone.

Back came an answering echo of snapping, crisp circuit death.

A hit. Probably not enough to drop the thing dead, but it would buy some seconds.

He shouted, "Max it!"

With Fanny down, he'd have to get the Family away, fast. Killeen blinked, saw the blue dots of the Family swerve toward broken terrain that provided some shelter. Good. But where was—?

"Toby! Hug down in that stream bed, see?"

A klick away, his son hesitated.

"To your right!"

—and for a moment that seemed balanced forever beside a harrowing abyss, Killeen was sure his son's gear was blown or overloaded, making it impossible to hear the warning. Or that the boy was confused by the scramble of electronoise. Or weary from the run. And so would remain standing while on the dry rutted plain no other simple unmoving target would leap into the fisheye lens of the unseen Marauder mech. His son's frozen indecision would recommend itself as a target.

Hanging there on the instant, Killeen remembered a time when he had been on a scavenging expedition with his father, a mere short foray for needed chip-parts, so easy his mother consented to her son's going along. And there a Marauder had chanced upon them as they looted an isolated ramshackle field station where navvymechs labored in mute dumb servitude. Killeen had been on a small side trip to snag servos from a dusty storage shed, and in the attack the Marauder (a Rattler, old but fully armed) had seen him and run him down. Three men and a woman had blown the Rattler to spare parts, catching it two steps away from Killeen's frantically fleeing form. He had been scared so badly he shat his suit. But what he remembered now was not the embarrassment as the shitsmell got out, and not the taunts of his friends. Instead, he recalled in a spirit-sucking instant his own father's look: eyes burned into the sockets, deadwhite. Eyes that had drilled into him with their desperation. And Killeen knew his own face now locked into the rictus of foresighted horror as his own son stood, unmoving, for one solid thudding heartbeat of immutable lost time—

"Toby!"

—Uh, yeasay.—

The distant figure scrambled down an embankment, into the fossil snaketwist of an ancient waterway.

Killeen could not breathe. He realized he had gone rigid himself, a perfect target.

"Hunch 'n' go, boy," he called as he swerved and dodged away.

And felt something go by—*tssssip!*—in the still air.

He saw quick darting orange sparks in his right eye. That meant something was poking, trying to find a way into him. But *fast*, faster than he'd ever known.

A prickly coldsweat redness skittered through him with a grating whine.

Killeen dropped to the ground. "Fanny! How you?"

—I . . . auhhhh . . . can't . . .—

"This thing—what *is* it?"

—I . . . haven't seen . . . years . . .—

"What'll we *do*?"

Ledroff tried to cut in on the narrow-cone comm line. Killeen swore and blanked him out.

—Don't . . . believe . . . what you . . . see . . .—

"What's—"

She coughed. Her line went silent.

Fanny knew more than anybody in the Family about the rare, deadly mechs. She'd fought them a long time, back before Killeen was born. But Killeen could tell from her sluggish voice that this thing had clipped her solid, blown some nerves maybe.

No help from the fine, wise old woman, then.

Killeen looked back at the warped, worked shapes of stone on the far hillside. There were contorted planes, surfaces carved for purposes incomprehensible to humans. He thought of them not at all, had long ago learned to look past that which no man could riddle out. Instead he searched for the freshness of the cleavecuts, the telltale signs of autochisel.

Which weren't there.

"Jocelyn!"

The scraped stone surfaces thinned. Shimmered. Killeen had the dizzying sensation of seeing through the naked rock into a suddenly materializing city of ramparts and solid granite walls. It hummed with red energy, swelled as he watched.

"Damnall what's that," he muttered to himself.

The city shimmered, crystal and remote. Plain rock melted to glassy finery.

And then back again to chipped stone.

Jocelyn called, disbelieving, —The whole hillside?—

Killeen grunted. "Mirage that size takes a big mech."

—Or new kind,— Jocelyn said.

She came in from his right, bent low and running with compressors. Behind them the Family fled full bore, their pantings and gaspings coming to Killeen in proportion to their distance. They were a constant background chorus, as though they all watched him, as though all the Family was both running for safety and yet still here, witness to this latest infinitesimal addition to the long losing struggle with the machines. He felt them around him like a silent jury.

Jocelyn called, —You hit somethin'?—

Killeen ducked behind an outcropping of ancient, tortured girders. Their thick spans were blighted with scabs of burnt-red rust. "Think so."

—Solid?—

"Naysay. Sounded like hitting a mech circuit, is all."

—It's still there, then. Hiding.—

No chance to try for Fanny yet. He kept a safe distance

from her crumpled form, sure she would by now be a well-found target point.

—I can smell it.— Jocelyn's alto voice, normally so cottonsoft, was stretched thin and high.

He could, too, now that he'd calmed a fraction. A heavy, oily flavor. His inbuilt detectors gave him the smell, rather than encoded parameters; humans remembered scents better than data. But he could not recognize the close, thick flavor. He was sure he had never met it before.

A fevered hollow *whuuung* twisted the air. It came to Killeen as a sound beyond anything ear could capture, a blend of infra-acoustic rumble at his feet and electromagnetic screech, ascending to frequencies high and thin in the roiling breeze.

"It's throwing us blocks," he said. "Musta used a combination on Fanny, but it don' work on us."

—She got old 'quipment,— Jocelyn said.

"It's prob'ly sweeping keys right now," Killeen said, breathing hard and wanting something to do, anything.

—Looking for ours.—

"Yeasay, yeasay," Killeen muttered. He tried to remember. There had been some mech who'd done that, years back. It broadcast something that got into your *self*, worked right on the way you saw. It could make you believe you were looking at the landscape when in fact the picture was edited, leaving out the—

"Mantis," he said suddenly. "Mantis, Fanny called it. She'd seen it a couple times."

The Mantis projected illusions better than any mech ever had. It could call up past pictures and push them into your head so quickly you didn't know what was real. And behind the picture was the Mantis, getting closer, trying to breach you.

—Figure to run?— Jocelyn called. She was a distant speck and already backing off, ready to go.

"Not with a big green spot on my back."

Killeen laughed crazily, which for this instant was easier than thinking, and he had learned to take these things by the instant. Any other thinking was just worry and that slowed you when you needed to be fast.

His problem was the topo and mapping gear, which he

alone carried in the Family. He backpacked his on his lower spine.

Legend had it that the topo man was the first to fry. The story was that hunter mechs—Lancers, Stalkers, Rattlers—saw the gear as a bright green dot and homed in on it. They could bounce their low hooting voices off the stuff, get some kind of directional sense from that. And then hoot louder, sending something that invaded the topo man's gear and then slithered into his head.

—What do then?—

"Got to shoot."

He heard Jocelyn's grudging grunt. She didn't like that. For that matter, he didn't either. If this Mantis thing was half as good as Fanny'd said, it could trace your shot and find you before your defenses went up.

But if they didn't kill the Mantis now, it would track them. Hide behind its mirages at night. It could walk up and pry them apart with its own cutters, before they even laid eyes on it.

"Wait. Just 'membered something Fanny said."

—Better 'member fast.—

Fanny's way of teaching was to tell stories. She'd said something about the Calamity, about how in the midst of humanity's worst battle some Bishops had found a way to penetrate the mirages.

He tapped his teeth together carefully, experimentally—one long, one short. That set his vision so the reds came up strong. Blues washed away, leaving a glowing, rumpled land seething into liquid fire. The sky was a blank nothing. Across the far hillside swept crimson tides of temperature as his eyes slid down the spectrum.

—Fanny's hurt. Think we should try for her?—

"Quiet!"

He shook his head violently, staring straight ahead, keeping his eyes fixed on one place. What had Fanny said . . . ? Go to fastflick red, watch out of the corners of your eyes.

Something wavered. Among the sculpted sheets of wintry-gray stone stood something gangly, curved, arabesqued with traceries of luminous worms. The image merged with the rock and then swam up out of it, coming visible only if Killeen jerked his head to the side fast.

The illusion corrected quickly but not perfectly, and for fractions of a second he could see the thing of tubular legs, cowled head, a long knobby body prickly with antennae.

—Gettin' much?—

"Lessee, I—"

Something punched a hole in his eye and went in.

He rolled backward, blinking, trying to feel-follow the ricochet of howling heat that ran in fast jabbing forks through his body.

Molten agony flooded his neural self. It swarmed, spilling and rampaging.

He felt/saw old, remembered faces, pale and wisp-thin. They shot toward him and then away, as though a giant hand were riffling through a deck of cards so that each face loomed sharp and full for only an instant. And with each slipping-by memory there came a flash of chrome-bright hurt.

The Mantis was fishing in his past. Searching, recording.

Killeen yelled with rage.

He fought against a grasping touch.

"I—it got in—" and then he felt the pain-darter clasped by a cool quickness in his right leg. He sensed the roving heat-thing sputtering, dying. It was swallowed by some deeply buried, spider-fine trap, fashioned by minds long lost.

Killeen did not consider what had saved him. He understood his own body no more than he understood the mechs. He simply sprang up again, finding himself at the bottom of a crumbling sandy slope which his spasms had taken him down. In his sensorium strobed the afterimage of the pain-darter.

And his directional finder had followed the telltale pulses to their source.

"Jocelyn! I can get a fix," he called.

—Damnfast it, then.—

"It's moving!"

In the glowering ruby twilight the Mantis jerked and clambered toward Fanny's sprawled body. Killeen heard a low bass sawing sound that raised the hair on the back of his neck.

Like yellowed teeth sawing through bone. If it got close to Fanny—

Killeen sighted on the flickering image of the moving Mantis while his left index finger pressed a spot in his chest. In his left eye a sharp purple circle grew, surrounding the volume where the Mantis image oozed in and out. He tapped his right temple and Jocelyn got the fix.

—Wanna frizz it?— she called. She was a small dot across the valley. They would get good triangulation on the Mantis.

"Naysay. Let's blow the bastard."

—Ayesay. Go!—

He fired. Sharp claps in the stillness.

The two old-style charges smacked the mech fore and aft.

Legs blew away. Antennae slammed to the ground.

Killeen could see the Mantis's blue-green electric life droop and wink out, all its internals dying as the mainmind tried to stay alive by sacrificing them. But mechanical damage you couldn't fix with a quick reflowing of 'tricity, he remembered grimly.

The mechs were often most vulnerable that way. Killeen liked seeing them blown to pieces, gratifyingly obvious. Which was the real reason he used charges when he could.

He bounded up, running full tilt toward the still-slow-dissolving Mantis. Popping ball-joints let the legs go. Its trunk hit the ground rolling. The mainmind would be in there, trying to save itself.

Killeen approached gingerly, across sandy ground littered with mechwaste jumble. He kicked aside small machine parts, his eyes never leaving the Mantis. Jocelyn came pounding in from the other side.

"Booby trap, could be," he said.

"Dunno. Never saw anythin' this big."

"I'll yeasay that," Killeen murmured, impressed.

All splayed out, the Mantis was longer than ten humans laid end to end. For him the heft and size of things went deadsmooth direct into him. Without thought he sensed whether something weighed too much to carry a day's march, or if it was within range of a given weapon.

Numbers flitted in his left eye, giving the Mantis dimensions and mass. He could not read these ancient squiggles of his ancestors, scarcely registered them. He didn't need to. His inner, deep-bedded chips and subsystems processed all this into direct senses. They came as naturally and unremarkably as did the brush of the warm wind now curling his faded black hair, the low electromagnetic groans of the Mantis dying, the dim irk that told him to pee soon.

"Look," Jocelyn said. This close he heard her through acoustics, her voice a touch jittery now from the exertion and afterfear. "Mainmind's in there." She pointed.

A coppery cowling was trying to dig its way into the soil, and making fast work of it, too. Jocelyn stepped closer and aimed a scrambler at it.

"Use a thumper," Killeen said.

She took out a disc-loaded tube and primed it. The disc went *chunk* as she fired it into the burnished, rivet-ribbed cowling. The carapace rocked from the impact. Steel-blue borers on its underside whined into silence.

"Good," Killeen said. Nearby, two navvys scuttled away. Both had crosshatched patterns on their side panels. He had never seen navvys traveling with a high-order mech. "Hit those two," he said, raising his gun.

"Just navvys—forget 'em."

"Yeasay." He ran to Fanny. He had been following Fanny's long-established rules—secure the mainmind first, then look to the hurt. But as he loped toward the still, sprawled form his heart sank and he regretted losing even a moment.

Fanny lay tangled, head lolling. Her leathery mouth hung awry, showing yellowed gums and teeth sharpened by long hours of filing. Her lined face stared blankly at the sky and her eyes were a bright, glassy white.

"No!" He couldn't move. Beside him, Jocelyn knelt and pressed her palms against Fanny's upper neck.

Killeen could see there was no tremor. He felt an awful, draining emptiness seep into him. He said slowly, "It . . . blitzed her."

"No! That fast?" Jocelyn stared up at him, eyes fevered and wide, wanting him to deny what she could see.

"Mantis . . ." The realization squeezed his throat. "It's damn quick."

"You hit it, though," Jocelyn said.

"Luck. Just luck."

"We've . . . never . . ."

"This one's got some new tricks."

Jocelyn's voice was watery, plaintive. "But Fanny! She could protect herself better'n anybody!"

"Yeasay. Yeasay."

"She knew *every*thing."

"Not this."

In Fanny's half-closed, .fear-racked eyes Killeen saw signs which the Family had been spared for months. Around her eyes oozed pale gray pus. A bloodshot bubble formed in the pus as he watched. The bubble popped and let forth a rancid gas.

The Mantis had somehow interrogated Fanny's nerves, her body, her very self—all in moments. Mechs could never before do that swiftly, from a distance. Until now, a Marauder mech had to capture a human for at least several uninterrupted minutes.

That had been a small advantage humanity had over the roving, predator mechs, and if this Mantis was a sign, that thin edge was now lost.

Killeen bent to see. Jocelyn peeled back the hard-webbed rubbery skinsuit. Fanny's flesh looked as though thousands of tiny needles had poked through it, from inside. Small splotches of blueblack blood had already dried just under the skin.

The Mantis had invaded her, read all. In a single scratching instant it had peeled back the intertwined neuronets that were Fanny and had learned the story of her, the tale each human embeds within herself. The ways she had taken pleasure. How she had felt the sharp stab of pain. When and why she had weathered the myriad defeats that were backrolled behind her, a long undeviating succession of dark and light and swarming dark again, through which she had advanced with stolid and unyielding pace, her steady path cut through the mosaic of worlds and hopes and incessant war.

The Marauder-class mechs sometimes wanted that: not

metals or volatiles or supplies of any sort. Nor even the tiny chips of brimming 'lectric craft which mere men often sought and stole from lesser mechs, the navvys and luggos and pickers.

The suredeath. Marauders wanted information, data, the very self. And in questioning each small corner of Fanny the Mantis had sucked and gnawed and erased everything that had made her Fanny.

Killeen cried in confused rage. He sprinted back to the fragmented Mantis and yanked free a leg strut.

Chest heaving, he slammed the arm-length strut into the wreckage, sending parts flying. Ledroff tried to call to him and he bellowed something and then shut down his comm line entirely.

He did not know how long the smashing and shouting lasted. It filled him and then finally emptied him in the same proportion, expending his rage into the limitless air.

When he was done he walked back to Fanny and raised the strut in mute, defeated salute.

This was the worst kind of death. It took from you more than your present life, far more—it stole also the past of once-felt glory and fleeting verve. It drowned life in the choking black syrup of the mechmind. It laid waste by absorbing and denying, leaving no sign that the gone had ever truly been.

Once so chewed and devoured, the mind could never be rescued by the workings of men. If the Mantis had merely killed her, the Family could probably have salvaged some fraction of the true Fanny. From the cooling brain they could have extracted her knowledge, tinted with her personality. She would have been stored in the mind of a Family member, become an Aspect.

The Mantis had left not even that.

The suredeath. Tonight, in the final laying-low of Fanny, there would be no truth to extract from the limp hollowed body which Killeen saw so forlorn and crumpled before him. The Family could carry none of her forward and so it was almost as though she had never walked the unending march that was humanity's lot.

Killeen began to cry without knowing it. He had left

the valley with the Family before he noticed the slowburning ache he carried. Only then did he see that this was a way that Fanny still lived, but all the same it was no comfort.

TWO

Shadows stretched long and threatening, pointing away from the hoteye of the Eater. Its harsh radiance cast fingers across the stream-cut plain, fingers reaching toward the onstruggling human tide.

Each windgouged rock, though itself dull and worn, cast a lively colored shadow. The Eater's outer ring was smoldering red, while the inner bullseye glared a hard blue. As disksetting came and the Eater sank to the horizon, it drew from the least rocky upjut a tail of chromatic ribbons. Shifting shadows warped the land, stretching perspectives. The seeing was hard.

So it was a while before Killeen was sure. He blinked his eyes, jumping his vision through the spectrum, and barely picked up the wavering fern-green pip.

"Heysay," he called. "Ledroff! Give a hard lookleft."

The Family was spread through a canyon shattered by some ancient conflict. No one was closer than a klick. They slowed, glad to pause after the hours of steady, fearful flight.

"For what?" Ledroff called.

"See a Trough?"

"No."

Killeen panted slowly, smoothly, not wanting the sour sound of his fatigue to carry to the others. Ledroff's response was slow and minimal. Killeen knew that if Fanny had been speaking, Ledroff would have been sharp and quick. By Family tradition, they would choose a new Cap'n as soon as they found safe camp. Until then, Killeen was point and called their maneuvers. Ledroff understood, but that didn't stop his grumbling.

They had paused to conduct a quick service for Fanny, concealing the body in a hastily made cairn. Then they had run long and hard. They could not go much farther. Killeen had to find shelter.

"Jocelyn? See anything?"

"I . . . maybe."

"Where?"

"A little thing . . . could be a mistake . . ." Strain laced her thin voice.

"Can you cross-scan with me?"

"I . . . . here . . ."

A quick picture flared in Killeen's right eye. Jocelyn's overlay showed a sputtering blip.

"Let's find it," he said.

"Naysay," Ledroff said sternly. "Better we sack in the open."

"And shut ourselves down?" Jocelyn asked, disbelieving.

"Safer. Mech will naysay it's us."

"We're too tired," Killeen said. He knew Ledroff would have been right, if the Family wasn't played out. Mechs usually couldn't find a human in a powered-down suit. They scented circuits, not skin.

"Trough? Found Trough?" Toby sounded fuzzy from daze-marching.

"Could be," Killeen said. "Let's look."

Ledroff shouted, "Noway!"

But a chorus of assent drowned him out. Ledroff started arguing. Which was what you'd expect when a Family marched without electing a new Cap'n. They all needed to rest and think.

Killeen ignored Ledroff and loped in long low strides over the nearest hill. It took teeth-gritting effort to achieve the flowing smoothness but he knew the following Family would take note. Without thinking about the matter clearly he understood that, worn to a brittle thinness, the Family needed some display of strength to give confidence, to regain their vector.

Ledroff came up behind. Killeen's eyes automatically integrated Jocelyn's display and picked up the sputtering slight promise-note again. He surged over rumpled, scarred hills and realized he had overshot only when the signal faded.

"It's buried," he said.

"Where?" Ledroff asked with a cutting, impatient edge.

"Under that old factory."

Tucked into a dimpled seam were sloping sheds of wrought rockmetal. Navvys clucked and rolled and labored around them, carrying out the endless production that had given mechs their steady dominion over humanity. Such sheds were erected wherever the land offered a rich seam of weather-collected minerals. This was a neglected station, far from the lands where mechs chose to build their majestic woven ceramic warrens. Yet the endless succession of such minor stations had flooded this world with mechlife and soon, Killeen reflected, might end the long battle between the mechs and all else.

"Nosee! No is," Sunyat called from far away. She was always the most cautious of the Family. "Maybe trap."

Killeen made a show of ignoring her, same as he had done to Ledroff. Most times that was the best way, rather than talk. "Trough's buried. Navvys've built on top of it."

"Troughs're *that* old?" Jocelyn asked.

"Old as mechs. Old as men," Killeen said. He landed beside a navvy and followed the half-blind thing as it rolled into the factory. Sure enough, the navvys were refining some ceramo-base extract from the rocks, oblivious to the large rusted door that formed one whole wall of their little world.

Within moments the Family had converged on the factory. They sapped each navvy, powering them down enough to pry out some portable power cells, but not so far that the navvy would register a malf. At this they moved with accustomed grace. This small place had no supervisor mechs to confront, no dangers. Navvys were easy pickings. The fact that the Family was like rats stealing crumbs from a back larder did not concern or bother them.

Ledroff went into the Trough first, Killeen behind. It was a vast old barn, ripe with scents Killeen savored in the air. The Family conducted its entry automatically, each darting forward while the others covered, exchanging not a word. Killeen and Jocelyn crept carefully along rows of leaky vats, boots squishing in the slop.

Nothing. No navvys came to greet them, mistaking them for mechs. That meant this Trough was tended poorly, expected few visitors. Its navvys were loaned to the factory outside.

"Out of business," Ledroff grunted, sitting down on an iron-ribbed casement. He started shucking off his suit.

"Food's good," Jocelyn said. She had already stuck a fist into an urn of thick syrupy stuff. She licked it with relish. Long brown hair spilled over her helmet ring, escaping. Her bony face relaxed into tired contentment.

Killeen listened as other Family prowled the long hallways, sending back the same report: nobody home. He went back to the entrance and helped swing the big moly-carb hatch closed. That was it, for him. They were in safe haven and now he let himself lie down, feeling the quiet moist welcome of the Trough envelop him.

Around him the Family unsuited. He watched them lazily. Jocelyn shucked her knobby knee cowlings with a heavy sigh. Mud had spattered her shin sheaths; she had to pop their pinnings free with the heel of her hand. Her slab-muscled thighs moved gracefully in the dappled light, but inspired no answering in Killeen.

The Family removed their webbed weaves and tri-socketed aluminum sheaths, revealing skins of porcelain, chocolate, sallow. Their flesh had red, flaky areas where insulation bunched and rubbed. Many carried ruddy seams of forgotten operations. Others showed the blue-veined traceries of old implants. These were add-ons from the days when the Family still knew how to work such things. Glossy slick spots spoke of injuries soothed. But nothing could shore up the sagging flesh, the pouch-bellies of inflamed organs. The Family carried a wearying burden of slowly accumulating biotroubles, unfixable without the technology that they had lost with the Citadel.

Jocelyn had found a bubbling caldron of sweetyeast. Killeen ate some of the foamy yellow head with the single-minded ferocity that the years of wandering had taught each of them. It had been four weeks now since they'd last found a Trough. They all had been running on hardpack rations and bitter water hand-scooped from tiny, rare streams.

Troughs were all that kept them alive now. The dank, dark places had been made for the Marauder-class mechs, and of course for the higher mechs for which humans had no names because men never survived a meeting with one.

Marauders—like Lancers, Snouts, Trompers, Baba Yag-gas—needed bioproducts. Roving, they sometimes stopped in at the randomly sited Troughs to refeed their interior, organic parts.

"Think this's better?" Jocelyn asked quietly. She displayed her hair, now washed. Killeen realized he had dozed off for a while.

"Looks different, yeasay. Fine."

He could never think of anything to say to her these days. She was finger-curling her hair into a tide of tight whorls that seemed to rush away from her high forehead. Cermo-the-Slow carefully combed her side panels down from the crown. Jocelyn had already parted and smoothed Cermo's bushy blond growth, which sloped over his ears with streamers of white and yellow. A blue elastic gathered his thick tufts into a firm knot at the base of his skull.

Killeen dreamily squatted, watching Cermo groom Jocelyn. A life of running had given all the Family legs which could squat for days, ready to move instantly. It had also given them helmets for protection, which in turn messed their hair. In the years when humanity dwelled in the Citadel, those who went out to forage among the slowly encroaching mechworld had been treated to a ceremonial cleansing upon their return. This ritual expanded from a mere efficient scrub into a prolonged bath and hairdressing. Those brave enough to venture forth deserved a marker, and their hair became their badge. At each return they would sculpt it differently, whether men or women, affecting elaborate confections. They wore lustrous locks lightly bound by a jeweled circlet, or thick slabs parted laterally, or two narrow strips with a blank band between; this last was termed a reverse Mohawk, though no one could recall now what the proper name meant.

Killeen liked his hair done as finely as any. It was long, with rumpled currents working into unmanageable snarls at his neck. Undoing the damage of the march would take patience.

He decided that this was not the right moment to ask Jocelyn. He had paid little attention to her of late, had little feeling for her beyond the simple, automatic brotherhood he gave any other of the Family. They had slept together—

fitfully, as all things were now—for years. But a hundred days ago the Family had decided in Whole Council to numb the sex centers of each member.

It was a necessary move, even overdue. Killeen had voted for it himself. They could not squander the energy, psychic and physical alike, which men and women expended on each other. It was the firmest measure of their desperation. Sex was a great bonding. But alertness and single-minded energy rewarded the hunted with survival. The Family had learned this sorely.

There was far more to the transcending magic between men and women than the chip-controlled sexcen. He felt this whenever he spoke to Jocelyn. Old resonances rang in him, coiling pressures unfurled.

But it was never with Jocelyn the way it had been with Veronica. He knew now that it never would be. That had passed from his life.

Still, they could share the pleasures of grooming. They moved continually, every frag of packmass weighing on the tip-edge of survival, and hair had become their sole remaining mirror of self pride. They combed and slicked and pigmented themselves, against the raw rub of their world. Plucking beauty from a tangled, smelly mat brought some small refuge.

The sweetyeast had finished its work. Cermo had dropped a pinch of primer into vats as soon as the Family entered. Long ago, the mechs had converted their organic proteins, made the molecules helix in the sense opposite to what humans could digest. Cermo's precious primer—a dwindling legacy of the Citadel—coiled the helix back, to human use.

Cermo and Killeen popped the release valve on a big vat and portioned bowls of froth out to the eager Family. To force the valve, Killeen used the leg strut he had taken from the Mantis. It seemed right to use a trophy as a pilfer tool.

When Killeen felt the sugary sap working in him, bringing an emberburn of interest, he lurched to his feet again and went to pace through the Trough. Its long, inky corridors reeked of coarse full grain, of buttery soup, or ripe tastes unnameable.

It could have been a thousand years since a Crafter or Stalker came here, seeking food. Yet the Trough murmured and cooked on. Its repair displays still offered themselves, articulated arms yawning for the embrace of a mech. Electrical auras buzzed, trying to entice vagrant machines with indecipherable crackling promises of renewed energies. The worn or damaged mechs who wandered into a Trough might know only dimly what they needed, or that they needed anything at all. The Trough seduced them with sensuous lubrication, with fresh clip-in components, with rich mechwealth humans could tap only fractionally.

Killeen found a huge cavern in which blue-green lichen hung in strands, fluttering in the passing almond-rich breeze. Trompers liked those, he knew. A mere tongue-lick would kill a fullgrown man.

In a side passage were stacks of grease-paste. Some said mechs ate the slimy nuggets, while others thought it was a lubricant. Killeen slashed open cases, watching it shower out, cursing under his breath. If humans starved, so would mechs.

Another cavern offered great mossy black slabs. Snouts used those to replace living polybind joints. Killeen's father had shown him all these things, knew their function. But now the Family could use only what it could carry.

"Dad?"

Killeen was startled. "Naysay!" he called softly, swiftly. "Bear on my spark."

"Why?" came Toby's stillsoft voice, all electrical.

"Naysay!"

Toby came flitting through the pools of shadow, between vast vats of fuming vapors. The boy automatically moved to take advantage of light's inky confusions, as twelve hard years had taught him.

Toby reached his father and gazed up at him in the amber halflight. His face was unmarked by fear, dark eyes open to a world of endless new adventure. "Why be so quiet?"

"If there're defense mechs, they'd hide far back in here."

"Jazz! You think there might be?"

Killeen didn't, really, but anything that made the boy cautious was useful. "Suresay, I would."

"I naysaw any," Toby said breathlessly. As did all members of the Family, they grasped and patted each other in the dark, hands speaking, trusting the human press of flesh over all other signatures.

"They carry cutters. Slice you spinewise in the dark." He cuffed Toby slightly, grinning.

"I cut *them*."

"Noway nosay."

"I *will*."

"With what?"

"This."

Toby produced a forked circuit-choker. It had long prongs that could wriggle into any mech's input hole. Some said the sensitive tips were living-tech, organic.

"Where'd you get that?"

Toby smiled impishly. His bright eyes danced merrily as he read his Dad's puzzlement. "Junkpile."

"Where?" Killeen tried not to let his concern show. "C'mon."

Toby was starved for playmates. In the years since the Calamity, the Family had been forced to wander, never spending more than a few days in a single place. Any longer and some silent alarm might bring Lancers or worse.

So the boys and girls of the Family had never known permanence, never paused anyplace to build a play fort or learn the intricacies of shared, invented games. Watching Toby bound away into the veined halfdusk, Killeen wondered if Toby needed games at all. To him their long flight from the Calamity was like a play of endless pursuit. Life was a game.

Toby had seen dozens die, but with the effortless immortality of the young could shrug it off. The Family's blighted history was still only a talked-about backdrop, weightless. And Toby was too young to understand the Aspects, though he knew that in some way the dead still lived through them. That was apparently enough.

Ahead, Toby disappeared down a gloomy passage. Killeen had to stoop to follow, his nose filling with the musk of moldering grease.

"Here," Toby whispered.

Killeen felt a chill steal over him as he poked at the

pile of debris. Carbs, axles, sprocket drives, plugs and caps and tanks. Parts he recognized without understanding.

All from a Marauder-class mech.

All the latest designs.

All burnished with use, but still showing silvershine where they'd been protected from the grit outside.

"Good stuff," Killeen said casually.

"Yeafold, eh-say?"

"Ummmm . . ." But parts of what?

"Can I use it, then?"

Killeen hefted a crosshead block. It was big enough to fit on a Stalker. "Uh, what?"

Exasperated, Toby said, *"This,"* holding out the circuit-choker.

"Oh. What for?"

"Kill navvys!"

Killeen looked around, studying the pools of shadow. If a Stalker was in here, had heard the Family come through the hatch, and decided to bide its time . . .

"Well?"

Speculations. And a fidgety feeling. That was all.

Killeen looked at his son and saw there the open testament of all that he could hope to pass on, the slender thread of his posterity. Yet Toby would not be fully what a human could be in this harsh world if he had his childhood stolen from him. He needed a sense of security, of certainties. And if Toby became fearful now, he would sleep poorly. Tomorrow he would be less swift.

"Come on, we'll go back, hit the food vats. Have some more chow."

"Awwww . . ."

"Then we'll go outside, maybe, nick some navvys."

Toby brightened. He was the last child in the Family. Mechs and accident and racking disease had stolen all the others. "Jazz!"

Killeen got the boy to play a kind of hide and seek, with Toby leading the way back. This let Killeen rear guard without seeming to do so, ears pricked. He sensed nothing strange. The caverns rang hollow, empty, waiting.

When they reached the vats Toby was winded. Killeen found him a glob of sticky foam stuff that smelled of leather and spice. Then he went to Ledroff and described the mech parts.

"So? I checked the whole place," Ledroff said. "Had Jake-the-Shaper do it, too."

"Those parts weren't old. Latest stuff."

"So a mech left 'em."

"And might be back."

"Might not, too." Ledroff squinted at Killeen. His luxuriant black beard grew up to his eyes and hid his expression, but the cutting edge of Ledroff's voice was clear enough.

"You wanted we sack down in the valley, 'member?" Killeen said evenly.

"So?"

"Maybe you were right."

Ledroff shrugged elaborately. "Different now."

Something had changed since arriving here, something to give Ledroff assurance. Killeen shook his head. "It's damnsight odd. Why're parts left in a pile? Usually navvys take 'em."

Ledroff grinned, showing broad yellow teeth. He looked around at the few Family members within earshot and raised his voice. "What's got you so jumpy?"

"That Mantis today."

"Whatsay of it?" Ledroff demanded loudly.

"Fanny said once that a Mantis, it works with others."

"What others?" Ledroff's bushy eyebrows lowered, encasing his eyes in shadow.

"There were a bunch of navvys in that valley."

"Near where the Mantis was?" Ledroff's lips lingered on the words, turning them over for inspection.

"Yea. Ten of 'em at least—"

"Those can't hunt us," Ledroff said scornfully. "You're getting addled."

Killeen smiled grimly. "You ever see a Marauder-class mech travel with navvys?"

"I'd vex on mechs, not navvys." Ledroff laughed loudly. The rhyming's slight taunt confirmed Killeen's suspicion. Ledroff was playing to the audience. But why?

"A mech who has navvys can have other mechs. Stalkers. Or Lancers."

"You can be night guard, then," Ledroff said mildly. "Put your vexings to good work."

He unstuck a gobbet of organic paste from his belt and offered it to Killeen. The Family nearby nodded, as if some point had been made, and went back to digesting their motley meals. Killeen only dimly sensed what Ledroff wanted with such talk, but decided to let it go. Fanny's death had fair well unhinged them all.

Killeen took the food and ate, an age-old sign of comradeship. Ledroff smiled and walked off. Toby came from seeking more sweet and thumped down beside his father, gesturing at Ledroff. "What wanted?"

"Talk of the laying-low," Killeen said. No reason to bother the boy with his own misgivings.

"When'll it be?"

"A while."

"Time for some more of the sticky?"

"Sure."

Toby hesitated for a moment. "It's okay, the sticky. But when're we finding a Casa again?"

"We'll start looking tomorrow."

Toby seemed content with that stock answer, and went scampering off. Killeen found some rank but nourishing stuff that tasted like metal filings mixed in cardboard. His thumbnail chemsensor assured him it wasn't poisoned; Marauders did a lot of that.

He picked at the gummy stuff, thinking. He couldn't remember how many months it had been since the Family had stayed in a Casa. A year, maybe—only he had no clear idea how much a year was. He knew only that it was more months than he could number on both hands. To know exactly would mean calling up one of his Aspects, and he did not like to do that.

Unbidden, taking advantage of Killeen's distraction, his Arthur Aspect spoke. The small, precise voice seemed to come from a spot just behind his right ear. In fact, the chip that carried Arthur and many more Aspects rode high in Killeen's neck.

Our last stay in a Casa was 1.27 years ago. Snowglade years, of course.

"Uh-huh."

The Aspect was irritated at not having been called up for so long. This showed in the clipped, prissy exactness of its voice.

The Family does not use the week or month any longer; otherwise I would speak in those terms. Such short time scales are artifacts of a settled people, adjusted to priorities of agriculture. In my day—

"Don't get on that," Killeen snapped.

I was merely pointing out that even a year ceases to have meaning now, since the mechs have obliterated the seasons.

"Don't wanna hear talk 'bout the old days."

He forced the Aspect back into the recesses of his mind. It squawked as he compressed it.

Killeen listened to his Aspects less and less now. He'd had the Arthur Aspect only since the Calamity, and had consulted it seldom. Aspects had lived in eras when the Families dwelled in Citadels or the larger, ancient Arcologies. They knew damn little about being perpetually on the run. Even if they had, Killeen disliked their talk of how great things had been. Killeen always smothered Arthur's techtalk. No matter how they phrased it, Aspects always came over as rebuking the Family for having fallen this low.

Killeen didn't want to hear that, or anything about the Mantis attack. Their long flight from it had let him keep his grief bottled up. But he could feel the press of it, and knew it had to vent.

Ledroff was moving among the crouching figures of the Family, arranging the nightwatch. Soon the Witnessing would begin. They'd discuss Fanny's death, and sing, and then choose the next Cap'n.

Killeen got up, his legs stiff from hard running, back tight and aching. But he would have to dance his respect to Fanny, sing the hoarse cries of farewell.

"One good thing for that," he muttered to himself. He

had not been thinking of it, but now his nose caught the thick, swarming savor of alcohol vapor from a nearby vat.

Troughs produced it as a side effect of their endless chem-cycling. An old story held that mechs got high on alky, too, though there was no evidence of it. Come to think of it, there was no proof that mechs got high at all, Killeen thought.

He didn't like alky as much as the sensos you got in a Casa, nobody did. But alky would get him through the laying-low. He needed it. Yes. Yes. He followed his nose.

THREE

Killeen woke with a technicolor headache.

Ledroff's voice came booming down from somewhere high in the air. Killeen rolled over and blearily realized he had fallen asleep on his watch.

"Lazeball!" Ledroff shouted at him. "Up!"

"I . . . what . . ."

"Naysay you *any*thing. Up!"

Killeen got to his hands and knees, feeling every muscle stretch tight and stingsore.

Ledroff kicked him in the butt. Killeen yelped. He sprawled. A damp moldering smell rushed up into his nostrils, sharp and biting.

Ledroff grabbed his collar and jerked him to his feet. Killeen staggered forward, pushed by the rough, callused hands of other men. His legs were wooden stumps. The hollow cavern swerved eerily. Women hooted, rebuking him. A hand cuffed his cheek. A muttered curse found strident echoes. The Family formed a grumbling circle in the dappled gray light. Ledroff marched Killeen to the center of it and booted him again in the ass.

"Watchdrop," Ledroff said simply, a plain indictment.

"Drunk, he was!" a woman accused.

Jack-the-Shaper, whose word carried far in the Family, said disgustedly, "Coulda got us raided."

Ledroff nodded. "Whatsay punishment?"

The family didn't hesitate to answer.

"Three fullpouch!"

"Naysay, four!"

"My thermpack!"

"Mine too!"

"Let 'im carry my medkit."

"*And* canisters."

"*All* the canisters."

"Yeasay. He slept, let him stagger now."

Killeen kept his head bowed. He tried to remember what had happened. The alky, right. He'd had some. Done some dancing. Started sobbing, he remembered that. Drank some more . . .

The Family bickered and joked and hooted. Idle rage, frustration—Ledroff orchestrated them to vent their feelings. Anger diffused into mere irritation. They finally settled on a penalty load for Killeen to carry: one fullpouch and the medkit, relieving two of the older women of a good third of their burden.

"Take you it?" Ledroff demanded ritually.

Killeen coughed hoarsely. "Uh, yea. Doubly yea."

Killeen then recited the sorrow-giving, letting the words trip out through swollen lips without having to think about them. Silence followed the ancient sayings.

Ledroff laughed, breaking the remaining tension around the circle. His lips twisted in an unreadable expression, Ledroff made a joke about the stains on Killeen's overalls. The Family chuckled. Killeen didn't even look down to see. He knew he had fallen asleep on something sticky. He welcomed the laughter. To be the butt of a joke was nothing compared with the humiliation of not handling the alky, of falling asleep on watch.

He didn't look up to find his son's eyes as Ledroff cuffed him aside. He felt a smarting in his eyes, perhaps from tears, but the roaring ache in his head made it impossible to cry. He would've liked to slink away, humiliated, but his mouth and throat were parched from the harsh malty alky. He walked unsteadily down an alleyway shadowed by a row of vats, away from the Family, until he found a spring of processed water. Someone had popped a feeder line, creating a frothing geyser. He slurped it up, stripped, washed himself in the bitterly cold spray. As he stood in the warming air, letting the breeze of a yawning duct dry him, Toby came from the inky recesses of a forging machine.

"Dad . . . what . . . ?"

Killeen looked into the upraised, trustful face. "I . . . the laying-low. Guess I let it get me."

"Looked like alky," Toby said sardonically.

"The alky was a way out."

"Thought it was . . . Ledroff, maybe."

Toby was trying to comfort him, Killeen saw, and thought that being direct was the best way. Or maybe Toby simply wasn't old enough to know how to talk and say nothing at the same time.

Killeen nodded slowly, so his head didn't ache so much. It was all coming back. "Ledroff . . ."

"After the laying-low songs," Toby said matter-of-factly, "he talked some."

"I remember . . ." A blur.

"Decided we'd head for a Casa."

"Great. He got any idea where one *is*?"

Toby shook his head. "Hesay lots, but not that."

" 'Cause he dunno."

"Family liked how he talked, though."

"He make sense?"

Guardedly: "Some."

"What'd I say?"

"Nothin' that went over real well."

"Oh." Killeen couldn't recall any of this. "I get much support?"

"Some. Paid off lots better for Ledroff."

Killeen shook his thick hair free of droplets, wrung it in both hands. "Huh? How come?"

"They made him Cap'n."

Killeen stopped, dumbstruck. "*Cap'n?*"

"Yeafold, the voting was. Ever'body but you."

"Where was I?"

Toby shrugged, a silent way to say that Killeen had been insensible by then.

"We got better than Ledroff. Why, Jocelyn's—"

"He talks good." Toby didn't have to say *better than you, drunk,* but he didn't need to. Killeen knew the Family thought he was good but unreliable, and not really old enough to be Cap'n anyway. Even if Fanny had been training him, same as Ledroff and Jocelyn.

Until now Killeen had been glad to have them think that way, too. It kept them from always coming to him with disputes to settle, intrigues, the rest of it. Every Family had that, and on the run everybody whined more and sought shelter in the casting of words around their problems.

"Well, maybe Ledroff will have some ideas after all," Killeen said lamely.

"Uh-huh."

"I got look after you, anyway."

"Uh-huh."

Something distracted him from his son's guarded, puzzled expression—a small warning somewhere in the back of his mind. He brushed it aside. Time to scheme later. Right now he wanted to gain back some of his son's respect.

"You don't really believe that," Toby said solemnly, accusingly.

"Well, let's give him a chance." Killeen climbed back into his overalls, scratching where the water hadn't taken all the scum from his skin.

"You figure he's any good?" Toby persisted.

"Well . . ." There was an obligation not to badmouth the Cap'n. Boys didn't understand that.

"Dad, you could've talked sense into them."

"Look, son, I don't want to mess in that. Got enough just lookin' after you." Killeen sat and began drawing on his hydraulic boots.

"You *could've.*"

"Yea . . . well . . ." Killeen had no words. Ledroff had made him look stupid before he'd started drinking, he remembered that now. The man had been playing for support. Calculating that Killeen would drown his grief in alky. So Ledroff had held up the Witnessing until Killeen was thick into the sauce.

"Well, I know I . . . I had a problem. . . ."

"Sure did."

"Guess I let it get away from me."

Toby swallowed with difficulty. "Y'shouldn't *do* that."

"Yeasay . . . it's just . . ."

"Fanny. I know."

"Fanny." Last night the full weight of it had come in on him. He would never see that weathered, crusty face again. Never hear the gravel-voiced jokes. Never.

Killeen rummaged for a way to deflect the talk. "Come on, let's go outside." He pulled on his helmet, secured it.

Suspiciously: "What for?"

He reflected wryly that Toby could see around him pretty easily, and only twelve years old at that. Even better evidence that he wasn't cut out to be Cap'n. Everybody would guess his moves before he knew them himself. "Have a look at the land, now we're not so tired."

"If Ledroff *lets* us," Toby said sarcastically.

"Don't be so—"

A faint tinny sound, high up.

"Huh?" Toby asked.

"Naysay!"

Toby didn't hear the sound. The boy opened his mouth to say something more, eyes serious and adamant. Killeen clapped a hand over the mouth and sent a whispery red Mayday to the Family.

Something coming. But not on the floor.

Through the long hollow bay Killeen heard the Family furtively snatch weapons from clips, shuffle across the tile deck, fade into hiding places. Quick, unhesitating, almost instinctual.

Killeen pushed Toby into a hollow beneath a steaming sulfurous vat. The boy protested, wanting to see what would happen. Killeen kept a firm hand on the boy's chest as he listened, figured.

Anything downlooking in the IR would see the vats ripe in red. Hard to pick out humans, then. Adequate shelter for the moment, but the Family would be pinned down. Once the ones up above were spread widely, each human who emerged would be a ripe moving blob, target-simple.

Killeen activated his boots. He stepped clear and leaped for the rim of the nearest vat. He landed unsteadily on the narrow steel ledge, felt his balance going. If he was lucky his IR image blended with the vat vapor. He wobbled, trying to see above, inhaling a rank biting lungful.

A tinny clank to his left.

He hesitated, starting to get scared. His arms wind-milled to keep steady.

Another clank.

He leaped. Off at an angle this time, vector chosen more by his toppling than by his plan.

He soared into the high arching vault. A sudden coldness invaded his chest and he felt a thousand hostile eyes probe him. He did not know the smooth curve he followed was a parabola but sensed immediately that he would hang too long at the apex, too warm and radiant against the cold ceiling. So as he passed a broad girder he lunged and grasped it. He hauled himself onto a rough shelf deep in rust flakes.

He rolled, lost his grip, almost fell off the other side. The dust of ages prickled his nose. The slumbering dark seemed shot through with flashes of yellow and ivory. Killeen got to his hands and knees and blinked to let his eyes adjust.

He was staring into the face of a mech. It was a three-eyed navvy, with skin of burnished organiform and blunt brass seize-and-draw hands. It wasn't a fighter but it lunged at him, face coming up fast in Killeen's still-speckled vision.

He jerked a ramrod launcher from his belt and held it forward and the navvy—knowing nothing of fighting and obviously commandeered by some higher form, enlisted for this—slammed into it. The sharp point sensed the mech coming and darted sideways to the softest spot. Killeen held it firmly and felt the point go in, just beneath a thin ceramic slitvent. The point found a circuit, worked its magic, and the mech abruptly froze.

But this was just a simple navvy. Killeen rolled left to see around it. Across the chasm were further webbed girders, solid black lines scratched in gray gloom. Something skittered along one. No, three. Opalescent forms moving in quick little rushes, surefooted.

And beyond, in gathering muskgloom, were two more. They had traction clasps which clamped them to the girders and permitted easy movement. Long bodies, a feathery quality to their gliding gait. And between the wedgelines of girders, smaller forms prowled among the knobby iron struts.

Killeen's tongue touched his farthest back tooth a certain way and he sent *Stay still. They're up top.* on a low-frequency channel he would never understand but had used throughout his life.

His only advantage was the navvy body. He pulled a pulse pistol from his belt and awkwardly leaned around the lifeless hulk. The nearest target was coming his way, perhaps curious but more likely following a search pattern.

Below, the vats fumed covering vapors. Killeen flashed a quick look in the IR and saw a mottled haze, pinpricked by bright sources which might be human. As soon as this bunch of mechs scanned the floor, they would select targets, he knew.

He shot the first one clean. Its fore-eyes flared blue and then it died. The next target started to turn his way. He kicked hard at the navvy body. It rocked unsteadily. That would make it look active. Immediately something smacked into it, delivering crackling blue webs.

All right. That would tell them that this mech was dead and the real target had to be elsewhere. Good enough. He kicked it again and it teetered. A second bolt hit it and blew a tread off the far side. The navvy wrenched sideways and fell, exposing Killeen.

He was ready and fired quickly at anything he could see. Already an illusion of misty orange leaped into his right eye. He knew they would blind him if they could find the right key into his nervous system.

Two more dim profiles shot at the mech as it fell. He traced them by their sudden spurts of emission in the radio. He thought he had hit them. Then the mech struck the deck below with a splintering crash. It roared in his ears, which had enhanced themselves without his thinking of it. The crash brought cries of surprise in his inner ear, from the Family.

A bright green volley glared at his right. A crisp sputtering answered, bringing the descending *hurrriiii* of a wounded mech.

A hoarse shout of *Got 'im!* and more firing.

Killeen felt the odd *whoooom* of passing bolts. If one struck it could wriggle into his circuits, seize his nerves or worse. He fired back at the source. The mechs were of a class he could not tell, but they moved quickly in the gloom and were not mere scavengers. They did not aim to kill, but to probe and subvert.

There! Up!

Crossin' to you, Jake.

Trackin'. Watch—

A white glare.

Jake!

The sudden brightness blinded Killeen for a moment. He kept his head down while his systems adjusted and when he looked up again there were fewer mech-signatures in the IR.

In his inner ear hoarse voices shouted.

Ledroff gave cool commands.

Someone was counting dead mechs but Killeen paid no attention. He was looking for movement among the vats.

Down a shrouded lane below came something slick. It had a narrow, ferret head and oblong body. Killeen recognized it: a Crafter.

The Crafter slipped among repair modules and threaded its way quickly through a spare-parts bin. Spindly legs jerked and found purchase.

A Crafter was not a fighter or forager. They were smart, though, able to organize navvy teams. Surely this one would not usually care about a band of scavengers which had blundered into its resting station.

But it had organized the navvys up here as a diversion while it crept below. That meant that the Crafter either felt itself threatened or else had an injunction specifically to act against humans, even if that was not its main job.

And it was only meters away from the cubby where Toby crouched.

Killeen knew he could not penetrate the Crafter's upper body with a bolt. Only his ramrod could.

He got to his feet, crouched low, and judged distances. A beamed message to Toby would alert the Crafter. He perched to jump and—

—*whooooom*—a blurring, clawing cloud flooded him

with brittle images of crisp yellow deserts, gritty sand, sicksweet smell of roasting flesh—all scrambled and coming fastfurious into him. He lost his balance, felt his hands and feet go coldhard numb.

He jumped anyway.

The deck rushed up at him and he leaned forward, sensing nothing in his body but able to direct his sawdust hollow hands to thrust forward on the ramrod. Wind whistled. The Crafter gleamed metalpure in pale descending light. The ramrod quivered into life, its head turning as its minute sensors sought and savored. The Crafter's ceramic sheen beckoned it.

Killeen hit the Crafter boots first and rocked forward. The ramrod point plunged in and he felt it snake and seek and bite hard. A fast jolt of electricity shot through him and shorted to the self-ground of the Crafter, its power source exhausting itself in a snapping prickly surge.

It whined and froze.

Killeen lay on it for long moments, unscrambling his senses.

Something strong had hit him just before he dived. He listened to distant silky shouts and tried to tag the voices with names. They were all saying something about Jake but for a while he could not untangle the mingled threads.

Only as he stiffly picked himself off the curved carbochrome back of the Crafter did he understand: Jake-the-Shaper was dead. Not just killed, but suredead. Something up among the halfdark girders had found Jake, sucked him of self, and was now gone.

Toby swam into his vision, leaned him back against the Crafter cowling. His son popped a drink into Killeen's mouth and spoke to him anxiously. Killeen muttered something, his voice a dry croak. Slowly, the world came back.

Ledroff came clumping down the sky, bounding among the now-ordinary girders, torchlit in orange. Ledroff was in a pureblind rage, eyes glowering. Five women searched the struts for the things that had attacked, but there was nothing left. Ledroff saw Killeen leaning against the Crafter's ceramo-shank and landed a few steps away, his legs wheezing with the impact.

"What'd you *do*?"

"Heard 'em coming. Went up top." Killeen squeezed fingers against his eyesockets, trying to make them trigger over to normal vision.

"You shoot first?"

"Sure." Killeen felt his eyes click back to normal. The world leaped toward him, then steadied.

"I naysayed shooting."

"Wasn't time to ask."

"Damnfool! These're ordinary mechs. They wouldn't've left us if you hadn't—"

"Belay the noughtsay, Ledroff. They were directed."

Ledroff's face bunched into a grimace of disbelief. "By what?"

Killeen slapped the Crafter.

"This's a *laborer*," Ledroff said dismissively. "It wouldn't hunt us."

"It did. Way I figure, we surprised it while it was laid up in this Trough, getting fixed. Toby found the parts, 'member?"

"Coulda been left here anytime."

"Navvys woulda picked up the parts. Crafter dropped them and finished up its repair job quick, once it heard us comin' in."

"Took its navvys with it?"

"Looks like. Those mechs up there, you give 'em a look. Modified. Crafter's good at that. It heard us, backed off. Thought things through. Built a little raiding party while we were resting up last night."

Ledroff scowled. "Maybe."

Killeen sighed. "Hasta be."

Toby put in, "That's what *happened*."

Ledroff smiled at the boy. "I'll decide that."

Killeen was about to spit back a sharp reply when Jocelyn came up hurriedly and said, "Cap'n, we tried with Jake. Couldn't save even a scrap."

Ledroff nodded soberly. Hearing Ledroff addressed as Cap'n startled Killeen. He was going to have to take orders from this man.

Ledroff already carried the mantle of the Cap'ncy with unconscious gravity. He said, as though to himself, "Point is, what'd the Crafter want?"

"Kill us," the boy said with horrible simplicity.

"Crafters make things, Toby," Ledroff said. He lifted an extruder arm from the burntout carcass and hefted it. "They don't hunt humans."

"Till now," Killeen said. "Till now."

FOUR

Two dead in two days. Suredead. Gone.

The Family was thus diminished more than through the loss of three or even four to the ordinary death. Centuries had piled upon them this injunction: that while the shuddering final gasp of the body was a tragedy to the person, it need not hurt so deeply those who loved the vanquished soul.

If Fanny or Jake had lingered there would have been time. A few Family members carried the small intricate gear which could extract vital fractions of the near-dead— quickly, deftly, gathering up threads of pastlife and personality.

But something in the rafting girders had aimed at Jake the most awful of weapons. The suredeath was, until now, encountered only in the Marauder mechs.

The thing above had escaped. If it was a mere navvy, or even another Crafter, that meant the mechs had added another hateful ability to their riverrun of innovation.

Two suredead. So deep a wound made it impossible for the Family to leave the Trough that day. Wisdom would have forced them out, away from such a betrayed trap, but wisdom comes only from reflection. The Family mourned and hated, both acts sapping them of purpose.

In vengeance Killeen fell upon the Crafter. He kicked in plates, ripped away whipwire antennae. The Family gathered and in pureblind rage they stripped the Crafter clean. They yanked free the parts and servos, booty used to maintain their own suits. Over the finely machined carcass they crawled, pillaging the finest workmechship of factories men had never seen and never would.

Mourning Jake-the-Shaper, women savagely ripped

away delicate finetuned components, slashed through orchestrated constellations in copper and silicon, and tossed aside what they neither recognized nor could use. This was almost all of the Crafter, for none in the Family knew how such things worked. The most able of them could only connect modular parts, trusting her eye to find the right element. Of theory they had little, of understanding even less. Long eras of hardship and flight had hammered their once-rich heritage of knowledge into flat, rigid rules of thumb.

In place of science they had simple pictures, rules for using the color-coded wires which carried unknown entities: Volts, Amps, Ohms. These were the names of spirits who lived somehow in the mechs and could be broken to the will of humanity. Currents, they knew, flowed like water and did silent work. Clearly, the shiny wreaths of golden wire and perfectly machined onyx squares somehow bossed the currents. Electrons were tiny beasts who drove the motions of larger beasts; such was obvious.

In the days of the Citadel there had been men and women who knew crude electrocraft. The years of long retreat had eliminated them. And there was no time to patiently learn anew from the Family's Aspects.

The Family scavenged with a vengeance, tearing the Crafter apart brutally. Cylinders bled oil on the tile deck. Optical threads snarled up and tripped the plunderers, only to be stamped flat and kicked into dark corners.

Killeen slowly let his rage seep from him. He had known Jake-the-Shaper all his life, a rather distant man of hangdog eyes and a thin, perpetually exhausted mouth. He mourned him. But the implications of the attack would not leave his mind. He left off the looting and instead probed its inert entrails, lured by curiosity.

He found the inboard mainmind by accident. A frosted aluminum panel suddenly popped free. Killeen blinked, startled out of his reflective daze. He knew he had only moments to act. He had assumed the Crafter was already dead, but the encrusted mass inside hummed with muted energy.

He could call for Sunyat, ask her what to do. She might

know and she might not, but in any case the time it took her to arrive would narrow their chances greatly.

So he mentally braced himself. He made the few twists and taps at his skull and called up his Arthur Aspect.

You have been very busy.

"Arthur? Look—"

Perhaps you do not recognize me? Six times you have summoned me in, I believe, some several years.

"Yea, yea." Damned if Arthur didn't bring up a gripe, right in the middle of— "Look, how I disarm this one?"

Why do you want to? I doubt you can fathom it.

"Dammit, no backtalk! *How?*"

Very well. See that yellow relay? Pull it up.

An overlay winked in Killeen's left eye, a ghost image of the relay rising, disconnecting. He followed the picture.

Now use the pliers. Tweak the blue cables free.

He did. An ominous buzzing began.

Quick! The spring clip!

Killeen cut it with a slicer bolt set on max. The mainmind rasped nastily but did not show signs of dying. "Ah," he sighed.

Quite satisfactory. Ever since I have known them, the higher-order mechanicals have had quite good defenses against theft of their memories.

"Uh-huh." He stripped away lightpipes to find the cluster-core.

A simple evolutionary development, really. This Crafter does not wish its expertise stolen by a competing class of machines, or by those serving a foreign city. So it is taught to fry itself before it can be interrogated.

Killeen half-listened to Arthur's lecture running through his head as he snipped away the leads to the cluster-core. He never did understand much of what Arthur said, but when he was doing some job like this it was handy to have an Aspect up and running, ready to give advice. The trouble was getting them to shut up. Arthur had lived centuries before and ruminated endlessly about the old times. Killeen seldom had the patience for such talk. But he did like the chromatic emotional halo around Arthur's Aspect, a cool distant certainty that insinuated into Killeen's way of thinking.

Yet we caught this one. Odd. Probably there is some delay before they suicide. Elsewise, a sudden accident could convince it that it was being attacked. That would make it suicide unnecessarily. So this delay period when we caught it must mean that Crafters are programmed more against accident than against attack. Yes, I'm sure that's it. I—

Killeen had his pliers near the core. He felt first a flash of heat in his hand. Then a quick rattling spurt jarred him. It was so loud he did not feel it as sound but as a force, like getting hit in the ear by a fist.

He staggered away. Numbed fingers dropped the pliers. Family members howled and covered their ears. They came tumbling off the Crafter body, scampering away with offended yips.

Killeen breathed deeply, dazed. His sensocenters were momentarily blitzed. He sucked in amplified musk and oil and rank sour chemwaste. Through a near-silent gray world he called, "Damn! What exploded?"

Nothing. That was not sound, though I admit
your/our nervous system does not distinguish
these very finely any longer. (A necessary adapta-
tion, I fear, but one which loses a certain delicate
thread of sensibility.)

"What the *hell* . . ."
A baying of complaint sounded through the cavern.

It was a powerful electromagnetic signal. I
caught a dab of it. I gather it has the typical
signature of the Crafter's personality, its accumulated (though finely processed; trimmed of
excess; admirably well edited) knowledge.

Killeen blinked. "Wha . . . Why?"

The Crafter was broadcasting to its home. Saving
its heritage, I'll wager. Now it can die.

Killeen staggered back to the Crafter carcass, his head
ringing. His tongue felt fuzzy, his eyes kept trying to cross.
He picked up the pliers and poked at the cluster-core.
"Hey! It's got no power."

The dead take their secrets with them.

"All?"

Anything that a competing mech civilization
might find useful. Data on this territory, or on
variant machines this Crafter has encountered.
Skills it has acquired, perhaps. And of course a
fragment of the personality this experience has
generated in as advanced a mech as this.

Killeen followed almost none of this, but he didn't
bother to ask. A question would just bring more endless
yammer winding through his mind. He could hear Arthur's
original voice, rather prissy and refined, but moving faster
than real people could ever talk. When he called up an
Aspect, it sat in the back of his mind like a monkey on the

shoulder. It could chatter on, give technical help, and Killeen got a character-scent of the person behind the seated knowledge, like someone in the same room with him.

"Anything we can salvage?"

Let's see . . . try that stimclat there.

Killeen had no idea what a "stimclat" might be. Arthur sensed this as he formed the word, and so provided a dancing green dot beside a flanged metal part. Killeen attached leads and did as Arthur's green simulation said. In a moment he felt a quick darting pleasure-pain sensation behind his ears.

"What's that?"

Some of the Crafter's recent memory, I daresay. We might mine it for information.

"Heysay, I'm kinda tired."

Actually, he was bored. Arthur would know that too, but something made him keep up a polite manner with the Aspect. After all, Arthur was an ancestor.

Rest, then. I'll translate from mechspeak and show you results later.

Killeen did not rest, though he seemed to. He reclined on a mossy cushion of brown organo-refuse and fished forth a small slab of memorychip. It was ancient and showed cracks and gouges of use, though the pale polylithium was said to be surehardened.

He had been thinking of this for days. And especially he lusted for it in the chilled nights when the Family had to sleep on rough ground beneath the star-spattered sky. He would then look up into the orange and green and bluehot points of light, hundreds of thousands of them scattered like jewels in oil, wreathed by radiance that came from halos of dust and gas. Ample light streamed down, enough to walk and even read—if any of the Family could have read more than simple numbers and a few directions coded on mechs.

This was the only night he had ever known, a welcome halfdark after the blistering doubleday cast by the Eater and their own planet's star, Denix. Yet he fled from it, too, when he could. Into the realms of the old dead times.

He found an output current plug in an autorepair slot. The cage walls were scarred and smeared from centuries of casual use by passing mechs. He spliced in the extra Amps and laid back and was at once in a gossamer finespun holotime of delight and transfigured brassy radiance.

It came to him as a shuddering series of exaltations and shimmering potentials. Ruby. Tingling. Pepperhot. Slow-building. Raspbreathed.

Spinning forever in a humming gyre . . . slicksliding grace beyond time or process . . . halfsleep and half-wake . . . this inner world filled his lungs with cottony pleasure. Brought him again and again to the longthrusting ecstasy yet did not let him pass over into warm oblivion. Sweet resurrections . . .

Stark light. Rough swearing.

Killeen blinked. A hand grabbed his collar and lifted him. "Didnja hear? There's a transmech outside."

It was Cermo-the-Slow, his porepocked face orbiting against the overhead glare of the Trough. Cermo had disconnected Killeen from the power feed.

"I . . . was just . . ."

"I know whatcha doin'. Jes' don' let Ledroff catch you, is all."

Cermo-the-Slow let go. Killeen dropped back into the acrid moss. He had an impulse to jack himself back into the wall, snatch a few minutes before somebody else came by to muster him. . . .

And forced his hand away from the cable. That somebody might be Toby. Too many times the boy had already caught his Dad slacksack on the tether, volted out.

Slowly, slowly, Killeen put away the jack-tab. He had to remember that Fanny was gone. Everybody needed some refuge from the world's rub, she'd said. She'd let him get away with some time on the jack. Some drinking, too.

Not anymore. Ledroff was decent, solid, but inexperienced. Until now, Killeen had devoted himself to looking after Toby, begrudging the time spent on Family business. That would have to change. But it would be hard.

Getting up, away from temptation, took all his blurred concentration. As he got creakily to his feet he heard Ledroff barking somewhere at Family who still lounged or slept. Killeen hurried to pull on his hydraulic boots.

He fidgeted clasps into fittings, making himself suit-ready. And Arthur broke in with:

I've analyzed that scrap of memory from the Crafter. Quite interesting, I think you'll find.

"Uh?"

See? Views the Crafter had gathered.

His eyes filled with yellow-green still-lifes: a journal of repairs made and things shaped. There were closeups of complex machine parts. Tangles of circuitry. But beyond, as needless incidental background, were hills of florid green and even windblown silver-yellow growths that Killeen recognized. Trees.

"These . . . they're not from the oldtimes?"

No. From the Crafter's encrypted data, I gather these are recent. They are from sites only a few days' march from here.

"Great!'"

Abruptly the lush still-life switched off. Arthur sensed an approach even before the still-fuzzy Killeen could. Ledroff loomed before him, the thick black beard like a shield to hide the man's true expression.

"What's great?" Ledroff demanded. "You near ready?"

"Uh, yea . . . Cap'n." Killeen made himself say it. The word was hard to get out. "Look, I was just processing some quickgrit from that Crafter."

Ledroff shrugged. "Crafters dunno nothin'." He turned away.

"Naysay! This one attacked, didn't it?"

Ledroff turned, hands on hips. "It made a mistake."

"It organized those navvys. Took Jake."

"So?"

"I think it's something new."

"Programmed to recognize us?"

"Yeasay, if it chances on us. And then not just call for a Marauder and wait. It recruits some navvys and strikes."

Ledroff frowned. "Yea, so I've thought as well."

"I sliced a frag from its memory."

Ledroff looked guarded, as though Killeen was lying. "You've been downdoggo."

Killeen answered sheepishly, "Just a rest, that's all."

Ledroff was a big man but seemed now curiously insure of himself. He did not welcome new information, but instead distrusted it. Killeen realized that the man had finally gotten what he wanted for so long—the Cap'ncy—but had no clear idea of what to do next. And feared that his fact would come out. This was in his voice, a mere shade of defensiveness. "So?"

"Can read some."

Gruffly: "Do."

"Have."

Suspiciously: "And . . . ?"

"Big green valley. Three-, four-day march."

Ledroff looked startled, then beamed with sudden relief. The Family had been without good maps or sure direction ever since the Calamity, when all humanity's orbiting satellites were destroyed. They had wandered, using only old maps and surveys. Their only certain guide was the need to avoid the mech cities, where surely they would be killed. Yet the ever-shifting weather of their world, Snowglade, had by now confused their remaining maps. They had no true vector any longer.

Ledroff thought out loud, "A transmech just came in at the factory outside. If we can redirect it, override its routine . . ."

"This greenland, it could be a fringe of a Splash."

"Yeasay, yeasay." Ledroff looked relieved.

Killeen smiled, glad to be for once not the layabout he knew Ledroff had always thought him to be. "Let's go. Come on!"

FIVE

Jake-the-Shaper's laying-low had taken a while, and then the grumbling of the Family took more as they got ready to move again. Voices rose in fatigued dissent. Tired, sun-browned faces knotted. Eyes narrowed, considering hangdog resistance.

The Family was only beginning to shake off the dust of the last several weeks. Legs ached from the long shuffling march. Bellies growled for more of the vatsoup, the protein cakes, the spongy sourbread. They hungered for the Trough's moist illusion of security and wanted to cling to it.

Ledroff showed some leadership then. He had stopped several from trashing the Trough itself, after the Crafter attack. Such fever-blind revenge might well have raised an alarm, brought a Marauder to answer it. Ledroff calmly disarmed the alky-soaked few, set them to useful work.

He also tolerated no mean, spiteful talk. In the years since the Calamity the Family had learned that aimless jawing had to be carefully controlled. In a crisis—slow-coming or quick, no matter—it was always better to run than to talk.

Someone had to cut off the winding jabber that passed for discussion. This Ledroff did, using his booming voice to override.

The Family meandered to their gear and reluctantly figured how much they each could carry away from the Trough. They dallied, ate some more, took every chance to stop and sit and fidget with their harnesses, their 'matics, their carefully tended boots. Ledroff's voice boomed again then, cajoling them to resuit and pack away foodstuffs for a march of uncertain end. Killeen nodded, still smarting from his humiliation, but he saw what had to be done.

There were jobs. Ledroff assigned some to covering their tracks in the Trough. The worst task fell to Killeen and Cermo-the-Slow: disposing of Jake. There was no place to bury the carcass, a stiffening, stilled clockwork whose skin was a patchwork of blotchy browns and oblongs of stark

48

white. As he hoisted it, Killeen felt Jake's deadweight as a thing more solid and bulky than the living Jake had been.

They had to feed Jake slowly into one of the vats, letting the flesh dissolve into a ruddy mucus. It was wrong to waste flesh in the soil, that they knew and felt deeply. What went into a Trough could someday come out of it.

Still, watching Jake blur and bleed, the ghostwhite bones first poking up through translucent papery skin, and then splitting it, the peeling parchment curling away—

Killeen's heart had climbed into his throat. His hands were slippery on Jake's ankle. The harsh fumes that rose from the waxy vat scum found their way high up into his head and fogged his eyes, leaked tears from his eyes.

Yet it was Fanny he wept for, not Jake.

Time ticked on. The smell cut sharper. At last he could let Jake go. As a foot and spindly calf sank into brown, crusted mire, Killeen said goodbye to Fanny as well. Then he stumbled away.

He helped Toby suit up, carefully sealing his son's pullpoints, letting the details of preparation fill up his mind.

Only when they were moving again did he think.

Across the sloping valleys they came. Killeen carried his punishing penalty load on upper and lower back. He huffed in air as he took long strides, letting his percussive landings exhale it.

He had long since learned from his father the effort-saving, forward-tilted stride. In Snowglade's low gravity the muscles of humanity, augmented with servos and cobbled-together suits, made them stride like giants. The parts were filched from mechs and hand-wrought to human calves and shoulders. Shapemetal blended and smoothed like a soft chrome clay, when it was triggered with the right de-poly signal.

This was the principal craft the Family still retained—indeed, would die without. Jake-the-Shaper had been best at it. Jocelyn, Cermo, and a few more knew the shaping art. The talent lived mostly in the hands, so the Family carried it as an ongoing dexterous art. Many of the Aspects which rode in the backminds of the Family members knew as much. But mere talksay was not enough. Aspects could not work your muscles. You had to have the feel of it, or else seams would pop, burrs would rub at bunching muscles, servos would clog and freeze.

Killeen listened with a fraction of his mind to the hum and work of his suit, letting his senses range over the land ahead. Tawny scrub bushes dotted the hills, life persistent and uncrushed, though the orange clay was crosscut by myriad mech treads.

"Looking damper," he sent.

—See any streams?— Jocelyn answered.

"Those gullies southward look fresh."

—You suresay this is the right vector?—

"Dead on."

Arthur came in unbidden:

I'm recalculating every ten minutes. We are heading at the bearing I judge appropriate for the data the Crafter carried. Of course, the Crafter might have been confused, or erred—

"Beggin' off now, uh?" Killeen muttered irritably.

I am not. I simply said—

Ledroff broke in, —You checking the route?—

Arthur was inaudible to anyone except Killeen, of course. It was uncanny, though, how Ledroff could gather what Killeen's Aspect was saying. Maybe Killeen had been muttering over the comm. "Yeafold. See those green spikes? There were some like it in one of the Crafter's pictures."

—Huh.—Ledroff was a distant speck, his voice tinged with skepticism. Killeen could tell it would be a long while before Ledroff forgot the alky-drinking. The Cap'n would use it as a handy way to undercut Killeen. Already he was favoring Jocelyn, to keep Killeen in his place.

"Let's go that way."

—Might's well.—

Killeen could hear Ledroff click his teeth together, which meant he hadn't any better idea. Ledroff skip-

walked, kicking up dust plumes. Beyond him chugged the
transporter mech they had commandeered.

The older Family members rode on the copper-ribbed
sides of the big hauler, clinging with slaptabs to the buffed
aluminum tank walls. They swung like boughs of motley
fruit, bobbing as the transporter lumbered with dogged
persistence over the bumpy terrain. Iron-gray massifs
towered on the far horizon like unreachable fortresses.

Killeen didn't like jouncing along on the transporter
and had given away his rest turns on it. He preferred to be
in the open. If a Marauder chanced to intersect their path,
it would see the outlying men and women first. It seemed
to Killeen only right that he should be the most visible,
while Toby walked closer to the transporter.

To a Marauder its barrel-shaped fellow mech would
not be a target. Only on close inspection could a Marauder
tell that the dull-witted transporter had been hijacked,
redirected, and no longer dutifully carried cargo from the
little factory to a regional depot.

—Heysay, Dad.— Toby waved from far away.

"Time to eat?"

Toby laughed. It was an old joke, from the time when
the boy had wanted an extra snack every few klicks. That
had been during the hard times after the Calamity. None of
the Family had been truly prepared. None had imagined
that their lot would be one of endless fleeing.

—Noway,— Toby said. —I'm no porker.—

"Whatsay then?"

—I'm just getting tired of running alongside this fat-
pack on the 'porter.—

Nobody in the Family had a scrap of fat on them any
longer, but their talk was full of references to carrying
excess mass, to indulgence, to unsightly bulging clothes. It
was a wan vestige of a time when fat had been possible, and
valued as insurance against hard times. But now all times
were hard, and the Family used the words of opulence with
a certain longing, a hollow bravado, as if to keep the words
alive was to preserve the promise that someday they could
again amass an ample centimeter or two of girth.

"You'll pick up the porkers when they fall off."

—They'll just go *splat* if they do.—

"Keep your eye peeled all the same."

—I want be out with you.—

"Too dangerous."

—Isn't!—

"Is."

—Isn't! Nosay noway! Lookit the greenery sproutin'.—

"A damp patch, is all."

—Isn't! Ever'body knows mechs don't like green.—

"Maybe."

—They're *'fraid* of it. Can't see so good in green light.—

"Where it's green there's water. Which helps rust."

—What I said, right? So lemme walk with you.—

The plaintive warbling note in Toby's voice touched Killeen. As he opened his mouth to tell his son to stay put and safe near the transmech, he instead found himself checking the blue-dabbed overlay in his right eye. A good firm forward-pointing triangle stood out against the topo map of the rumpled valley.

"Okay. Cover on my left."

—Hey jubil!— Toby leaped twenty meters into the clear, bright air and landed on the run. He yelped with sudden energy and in moments was alongside his father.

In his son's voice Killeen had heard a treble of Veronica. Though he had recordings of her, he never called them up from his longstore chip at the base of his spine. Thus, the slightest trace of her could spear him bittersweetly. Toby was their full child. They had used no other genetic components in making him. Which meant that Toby was Veronica's entire legacy.

For Veronica had perished in the Calamity and was suredead.

Most of the Clan had fallen then, scythed down by the deft cut and thrust of a mech onslaught against the Citadel. For hundreds of years before, the mechs had slowly claimed parts of Snowglade, and humanity had watched warily. Snowglade had been a cool, water-rich world with winds that stirred the moisture in great towering cottony clouds. Mechs did not like such planets, which is why humanity came to be there, to prosper in their own humble fashion.

So went as much of history as Killeen had ever heard—though in truth he cared little for it. History was tales and tales were a kind of lie, or else not much different from them; he knew that much. Which was enough. A practical man had to seize the moment before him, not meander through dusty tales.

Family Bishop had lived in rugged rockfastness and splendor in the Citadel. Killeen remembered that time as though across an impassable murky chasm, though in fact it had been only six years since the Calamity. All years before that were now compressed into one daybright wondrous instant, filled with people and events which had no substantial truth any longer, had been swept away as if they had never been.

Since then the Bishops were swept forward not so much by a victorious horde behind, but rather by the mounting tide of the names of battles lost, bushwhacks walked into, traps sprung, Family members wounded or surekilled and sometimes even left behind in a disheartening white-eyed dishonorable scramble to escape, to save the remnant core of the Family, to keep some slender thread of heritage alive.

The names were places on a map—Sawridge, Corinth, Stone Mountain, Riverrun, Big Alice Springs, Pitwallow—and maps were not paper now but encoded in the individual's memorychip. So, through the six years of pursuit, as members of the Family fell and were swallowed up by the mechmind, the Family lost even the maps to understand where their forebears had stood and fought and been vanquished. Now the names were only names, without substance or fixity in the living soil of Snowglade.

In retreat the Family could carry little, and cast aside the hardcopy maps and other regalia which had once signified their hold upon the land. So a string of dropped debris stretched across years and continents.

Killeen's father had vanished at the Citadel, gone into chaos. Veronica had been hit standing right beside Killeen. He had dragged her body with him, seeking a medic who could repair the damage. Only when he had fallen exhausted into a muddy irrigation ditch did he see that a burst had taken her sometime as he carried her. He had been too dazed and tormented to notice. Her eyes had bulged out, shockbright and with the pus dripping from them. Sure-dead.

Until the Calamity he had known countless cousins, Family that had seemed boundless. Now he had only Toby.

—Looksee. A navvy,— Toby called. He pointed and went bounding off.

"Heysay!" Killeen shouted. "Check that thing first." He leaped forward and overtook his son.

The navvy seemed innocuous. Its bright crosshatched carapace was freshly polished. Its stubby arms rummaged among scabbed mechwaste—cowlings, rusted housers, worn gray biojoints.

Killeen approached. The mech spun its lightweight treads. They caught and clacked against an eroded spur of peppery, chipped granite. Fore-lenses swiveled to study Killeen. It paused a long moment, seeming to think. Then it turned away, uninterested, and started off downhill, raising fine dust that hung in the low gravity like shimmering fog.

"Guess it's okay," Killeen said reluctantly.

"Can I 'vest it?" Toby said acoustically, landing with a wheeze and thump on the crumbling grainy granite.

"Harvest it? Thought you were full up with servos."

Toby shrugged, jangling. Small spare parts dangled from staylines at his waist.

"You look like a walking scrapheap."

"Guy needs 'placements," Toby said defensively.

"Not more'n slow you down."

"Aw—lemme! I got room." Toby's face screwed into a laughable mask of pretended pain.

"*No.*" Killeen was himself surprised that he said it so sharply.

"But I—"

"No. Just no. Now get out on your point."

Toby wasn't striding point, but using the word made his position seem larger. That pleased the boy and he shrugged, eyebrows knitted wryly. He bounded off, ignoring the navvy that jounced away downslope.

Killeen had long ago learned to listen when something nagged at him. He stood still for a long moment. He let his augmented senses sweep out, covering the slowmotion flow of the Family, the retreating navvy. Voices slurred and nipped, the steady background roundtalk of the Family.

They were making good time down the valley. The transporter mech bumped along the bed of a sand river. Killeen selected the viewpoint of an old man, Fowler, who swung on a basket tether aboard the mech. He heard Fowler's querulous questions—*When'll we stop? Got any that soursap from the Trough? Whatta mean, is gone? Suresay we had jugsful!*—and the pebbles spitting from under the mech treads.

The valley lay quiet. Mechtrash dotted the rock-knobbed hills. Some rotted bioparts tainted the air. These random clumps of old parts littered all Snowglade, so common that Killeen barely noticed them. In outlands such as this, scavenger mechs did not bother to pick up rusted cowlings or heavy, broken axles for the long transport to smelters and factories. Over centuries the mess had gathered. As the mechs worked their changes in Snowglade's weather, ice retreated, revealing even older junk from a time when mechs had run unknown things amid the old cold ages. These jumbles too blighted the land now, rust-red spots freckling the soil.

Among this plants struggled, a welcome sign. For hours now they all had been pleased by small signs of ripening, of spreading grass, of tawny growth.

Denix had set an hour before, and now the Eater was half-gnawed by the ragged hills. The shifting colors confused Killeen, making the least crag and gully brim with light-ripe illusions.

The Family moved stolidly and with a dogged rhythm that expected little. As they breasted each rise, talk ran and swirled, words forking in the grouptalk. For months they had followed an unmarked trek through exhausted, bleached-dry valleys. Only Troughs had succored them. The slowsmelling promise ahead gave spring to their pace.

Yet Killeen felt nothing awry, but the crosshatched navvy was odd enough to warrant remembering. He watched his son carefully and often rechecked their route. In the middle of a topo survey, Arthur said:

I am enjoying the sight of greenery again.

Killeen was surprised. This Aspect was usually distant,
factual, a cool savor in Killeen's mind.
"Yeasay. I've tasted only Troughslop for so long. . . ."

I doubt you could eat these. They are tough,
fibrous growths.

"Must be ground water here."

I suspect we are entering a Splash site.

Killeen brightened. "Yeasay you? It'll get wetter?"

Perhaps. A Splash is the fracture zone surrounding a meteor strike. The cracked rock permits an
upwelling of permafrost which has eluded the
mechs' efforts to dry out the planet. Sometimes
there is even glacial ice buried beneath the
shifting sands. Meteors are the only feature of
Snowglade's weather which the mechs do not
appear to have mastered. Given our star's orbit
about the Eater, which is quite elliptical, I find it
unsurprising that we encounter many meteors.
We are plunging nearer the Eater now, and a
standard Gaussian distribution for the density of
small, meteor-sized debris would predict that we
shall receive strikes at an exponentiating rate.

"Better weather?" Arthur had to truthsay, but sometimes the Aspect used a muddy, longtalk way to do it.

Again, perhaps. The mechs seem to be altering
the orbit of IR-246.

"Huh?"

Sorry. You call our star Denix, am I correct?

"That's not what we *call* it, that's what it *is*."

To me this star is the 246th infrared source
positively resolved near the Galactic Center. The
catalog made as we approached the inner zone
of the center specifically assigned—

"Heysay, that stuff sucks like a bucket of ticks. I—"

An interesting expression, that. I remember it
had its origin in an ancient Earthside civilization
now enshrined solely in the holorecords—

"Stuff the oldsay, heysay? I don't understand—Denix is
the *sun*, that's what Denix's name *means*."

You call it such, yes. It is a simple star like the
millions you see when neither Denix nor the
Eater is in the sky. As now.

Killeen looked up, startled. The Eater was guttering
into bloodred sleep beyond sawtooth peaks. High above in
the darkening, pinpoints glowed in ambers, hard blues,
opulent greens. Fine wisps threaded between the twin-
klings. Never had he thought they might be like Denix.
    "All . . . those?"

There are approximately a million stars within a
light-year of the Eater. Many have entered late
stages of their evolution and display varied
colors. Some vent streamers from their chromo-
spheres. Advanced—

"Cut the jabber! You mean they're all *big*?"

Some are larger than Denix—which after all is an
M1 type, selected by your forefathers not for its
beauty but rather because this planet was deep
in a glacial age, and apparently of no abiding
interest to the mech civilizations—while
others—

Killeen let Arthur lecture away, unheeded. For him the sky was suddenly a vast bowl of unimaginable depths. Those were other *suns*. His whole life—of earnest childhood, of love and labor and lost hopes, of ravaged retreats—he now saw as abruptly dwarfed, as tiny motions on a bare scratched plain, beneath a night filled with eyes.

SIX

They marched on through the halfnight. Snowglade never saw true darkness, for the million pinprick fires above conspired to seed the sky with a dim, persistent radiance. There were no solid, certain shadows.

Yearly, distant blobs and swirls of twilight gas swept across the sky. Constellations of glowering stars changed in the span a boy took to grow to manhood. But stars were minor actors in the ruby-rich, storm-racked sky.

Killeen's ancestors had adapted eyes, able to scan on a scale stretched further than the normal human logarithmic response. He could see the stars as glowing torches and then, by screwing tight one eye, wreath them in a murky shroud of ink. Mechs could see in any dim radiance, so humanity had long ago aped the machines by tailoring their eyes.

Toby sent, —Mech hive over that hill.—

Killeen vectored right and in a moment landed beside his son. "Mechtypes?"

Toby's voice skittered high and excited: "I pick up three them fact'ry luggos."

"Whatdoing?"

"Workin'."

"Mining?"

"Looks be 'facturin'."

"Manufacturing what?"

"Dunno. See that transporter they're unloadin'?"

"Um. Bundles of . . ." Killeen amped up his eyes to max. He scanned the pale recesses for telltale tracks of large mechs.

"Plants," Toby said excitedly. "They harvestin' plants."

Killeen squinted, still couldn't pick up enough detail. He wondered if his eyes were losing their edge, going fuzzy on him. A man had to keep watching his 'quipment. Let it go awhile and it could kill you in a minute. Angelique, a young Bishop woman, could run some kind of internal program, unglitch eye trouble. He'd have to get a run-through and checkout. He frowned, distracted by this annoyance.

"Naysaw that before," he said.

"Nosee mechs usin' plants?"

"Saw some cut trees, back when—" and he stopped, because that led to *back when the Citadel held firm and my father went out on raids, when humanity held forests and crops and all the lost legacy,* and that was something he didn't talk to Toby about just casually, "—when there was any."

"Wonder what they're makin'?"

Killeen watched the five blocky buildings clustered together in a side arroyo. Two dust devils marched down from the hills. They swirled and glided near the brown clayformed buildings, upsucking cones of fine sand.

"Can't say. Longtime back, mechs'd chop down crops the Clan tried grow, in the valley near the Citadel. They just left 'em, though. Didn't make anythin' from 'em."

"Let's *do* 'em!" Toby said brightly.

Killeen looked at his son's thin face, splotched with the mossybrown suit-rub growths that everybody got now and then. He cuffed him on the shoulder and laughed. "We got a mechscourge here?"

"Yousay!" Toby laughed, too, and Killeen saw his mirth came in part from the fact that the boy could show his bravado and have it respected in a joshing way, without having it mean anything.

The Family would decide on any attack. Boys ran with the rest, of course—the Family was never split while in dangerous action. Humans now feared more than anything a division, a loss, a fractioning. Still, the youngers ran far back on any assault, and so their word carried little weight. In that there was some remnant of childhood freedom for Toby. Killeen instinctively tried to keep that alive. He knew how quickly the hardness of the world would come in upon the boy and make him finally no longer a boy.

Some Family arrived, coming down in low sloping curves, landing with pneumatic *chuuungs*. Ledroff conferred, talking with his helmet cocked back. A dozen Family clustered around him.

Toby waved a gloved hand at Ledroff. "Think he'll go?"

"Dunno," Killeen said.

"Lookit his beard, hey."

The matted black hair was crimped in a curved line. Toby giggled. "Got it caught in his helmet ring."

Killeen smiled. "Bet that yanks when he runs."

An old tradition allowed mild joshing of a Cap'n, and Killeen felt a sizable pleasure in the joke. He still smarted from Ledroff's adroit maneuver into the Cap'ncy.

Killeen imagined Ledroff thought the beard made him look older. Maybe the smelly, helmet-tangled mass had helped make him Cap'n. Toby said, "Ugly bush."

But Killeen said, "Keeps down the sunburn."

"When *I* get one, won't let my suit grab it."

"Naysay, *I'll* do that—" and Killeen chucked Toby under the chin playfully.

Ledroff sent on general comm: —Situation still the same?—

Already Ledroff's voice was acquiring a certainty of command.

There was no sign of interest or changed routine in the far-distant factory. Killeen eyed Ledroff and wondered what the man would do. This could be the first real engagement since he'd become Cap'n. The man looked wary, his eyes slitted, studying.

Scattershot talk laced Killeen's sensorium. He murmured only to Toby, the two of them keeping track of the minute profiles of the mechs as the distant forms carried out tasks. Since Killeen's dumbdrunk on watch, he had shied away from having much voice.

Ledroff broke into their twofold comm: "Those buildings look new."

Toby said matter-of-factly, "Fused clay, looks to be."

Killeen was mildly surprised; the boy picked up information everywhere.

Ledroff nodded. "Mechs using plants? Might 'facture something we could do with."

Killeen called up Arthur and asked silently, *How you figure it?*

This Splash zone is perhaps a decade old. There surely has been time for mechciv to exploit the organic raw materials growing here.

"Let's hit it," Jocelyn said.

"Yeasay," Cermo called, already edging downslope.

Killeen could feel the quickening in the Family. They felt stronger from a mere night in a Trough. Were Jake and Fanny forgotten, caution trampled? No. The Family did not truly need supplies badly, but something stirred in them, something ageold—a lust for clean victory, for revenge. They'd gutted the Crafter, but Ledroff had not let them vandal the Trough. Their blood still rang of retribution, and this could serve. Letting them go might be the best idea. At least it would get the sliteyed meanness out.

Ledroff glanced around, saw their impatiently shuffling feet, their thindrawn lips. Killeen felt the tide rising in them and knew it could either be seized or else would take a major clash to stop.

"Form the star!" Ledroff called.

"Yeasay!"

"I'll frontline!"

"I'm point!"

"Hoyea! Hoyea!"

They downvectored on the factories, coming in along four axes to confuse any defenses. Nothing rose to meet them.

Orange firenets crackled from their shoulders, finding navvys. The mechs went into demented throes of indecision, driven into cyberclash.

The Family rushed through the construction yards, over racks of ceramo-tubing, down sheetcarbon assemblies. They kicked in partitions, searching for manager mechs. Killeen and Jocelyn split off and sped through a long hall crammed with vast machinery. Speed was the best tactic humans had. Labor mechs were made to be sure and steady. They reacted a bit slowly, unless they were alerted to go to quick-time.

They came panting into an open bay. A manager mech rushed at them, clacking its recognition codes over the broadband comm lines. It turned an owlish set of glazed lenses on them and realized a fraction too late that they were not simply mechs wandering mistakenly where they were unneeded. The manager spun away, retreating. A copper panel snapped aside and something protruded, found Killeen as target—

Killeen leaped sideways. A rasp jarred him. He hit the deck before he sensed that the savage grating sound came to him electromagnetically. An acrid smell pricked his nose.

Jocelyn laughed, covering her mouth. "It was just tryin' tough-talk you, is all."

The rasping had been Jocelyn frying the manager with a crackling storm of microwave noise. It was frozen in a rigid, comic posture. Arms akimbo, one lone surviving sender bleated a symbol-call to NOTINTRUDE NOTINTRUDE NOTINTRUDE.

"Clothes!" Jocelyn called. She stepped over Killeen, obliviously sure he was unhurt. He got up, ruefully rubbing a shoulder. He had slammed against a big steel-sheathed machine with enormous axle-rollers. He saw it was some kind of press. Fiber entered it at the far end of the factory. Whirling cylinders tugged and wove and mixed in acrid chemicals—and out the near end came glossy sheets of amber-gold tightweave.

Jocelyn tore some off admiringly. He left her to her rooting and found Ledroff nearby. Killeen tuned in to the comm. The Family crowded in, reporting.

Supervisors numbed. No higher mechs in the 'plex.

Factories secure. Some much-needed servos found.

The supervisors had not sent out a mayday signal. The 'plex was transmitting no raidcry, as near as anyone could pick up.

The older men and women were safely in. Guards posted.

Ledroff listened, nodded. He grinned, showing stubbed brown teeth. His first raid as Cap'n, and it had gone well.

Killeen checked for Toby, found him tinkering with a manager mech. "I gutshot a navvy," Toby said forlornly, sorry he'd found nothing bigger. Killeen showed him how to make the manager spin on its rotors, whirring madly, its arms ratcheting. Toby laughed, banishing his frown. He was so taken with the mad mech that he forgot to cover his gaping, cheerful mouth. In the Citadel this had been impolite, a symbolic revealing of the coarse inner self. Killeen thought to remind him, but figured there was time enough for manners later. If ever.

Ledroff ordered the navvys uncyberlocked and set back to labor. The Family could learn more of what went on here that way. Killeen watched the slow but powerful mechs as they kept on. They ignored the humans, since their supervisors had had no time to send out a formup call. Their dull cowlings bore designs that only manager mechs could read, and no human had ever deciphered.

One had the same brushed, crosshatched alum carapace he had seen earlier, something new in navvy design. Killeen noted it and thought no more. Mech assembly was a subject of utter indifference to him—he could no more uncoil an axle housing, using fourwrench and screwdriver, than he could reprogram the biochips in his own head—but it was essential to know ordinary navvys from the higher-order mechs.

Usually a cosmetic feature worked its way down from the smarter mechs to the navvys, but this crosshatched aluminum, coming first in the navvys, apparently had some purpose. The navvys who had helped the attack on the Trough had borne no special markings. Still, any change could mean danger.

Once the factories were secure, the Family fell on the stacked wealth. Tightweave was a rarity. It responded to electrical touch-commands, splitting where a current-carrying fingernail sliced.

A dozen of the Family called up Aspects and began using the old skills to cut and plan and fit fresh clothes. Laughter rang down the long ranks of still-spinning machinery. The Family liked labor when they could see clear result. New shirts, vests, and leggings to wear beneath their suits would improve everyone's spirits.

Killeen roved with Toby, inspecting. "Lookit," the boy said, pointing to a huge mound of the tufted, dryleaved plants. Navvys were unloading small carts that brought the harvested stems and boughs. "How they make tightweave from *that*?"

"Some kinda mechknow."

Killeen shrugged. He had long since given up trying to figure how mechs worked their routine miracles. But Toby was young and thought he could understand everything in a world which had long since passed human comprehension.

"These leaves got *scabs*."

Unbidden, Arthur's cool, exact voice rippled at the back of Killeen's mind:

Those have a layer of silicon-boron to protect the plant from the Eater's ultraviolet. It captures the hard photons and converts them through a phonon process into useful—

"Naysay," Killeen muttered, and Arthur fell silent. The Aspect's departure left a faint tremor of pique, an irksome note strumming through Killeen's sensorium.

"Huh?"

"Just shutting up some Aspect lingo."

Toby fingered the tough, glassy leaves. "Naysay such."

"Must be . . ." Killeen had an idea he didn't like. "Figure they're mechmade?"

Killeen nodded, his lips twisted aside in thought. "Could be. Look awful funny."

"If they use 'em, maybe they plant 'em?"

"Never heard such."

"Sure rough, these. Like no plant at all."

Toby didn't see the implications. Killeen said casually, "Search around some. See if the navvys've got seeds."

"Yeasay." Toby was happy to be sent off on his own. He strode away through a rank of navvys which were carrying hexagonal plastibrass containers. The navvys were of the dumbest sort. They did not register Toby as more than a passing obstruction, a detail that temporarily clouded their route and then disappeared without their having to call up outside intelligence to pattern-recognize it. Major problems would be relayed to the manager mechs.

Which meant, Killeen knew, that the whole 'plex would slowly shut down as navvys met difficulties, called to the managers for help, and got none. That would eventually send out a mayday to the central cities.

Raids were always bracketed by that. The true art of them was guessing how long you had until some midmanager mech showed up. Those could be microwavefried, too, but it had been a long time since Killeen had seen one answer a mayday. The mechs were getting smarter. Or maybe they were just devoting a fraction more attention to their pest problem.

For years now the Family had lived this way—as nomads raiding isolated navvy factories, holing up where they could, following a wanderers' path through a landscape of increasing desolation. The ravaged hills offered no shade from the Eater's glaring hammerstroke. What food they could scavenge and carry was compacted, portable cubes—chaws—that drove the muscles but burned the tongue with their power. Several in the Family still knew how to make chaws from the resources of Troughs, and several times the fate of the entire Family had turned upon those sourbrowns. The Family had run for long damaging times amid ruined canyons, driving forward only by chaws and stale mouthfuls of water that seeped from mechmade rockslides.

Killeen remembered this as he treaded through shadowed corridors, beneath drumming clacking machinery. He was looking for Ledroff, but the 'plex was vast and filled with strumming long warrens of endless energetic 'facture. He explored, idling, curious.

The strange, glassy plants gave forth more fruit than tightweave. From tirelessly spinning belts and presses came fibrous sheets, toughgrained and sturdy. Killeen felt some, tried to tear it without result. There were small stonehard devices, too, with connector jacks and cogs he did not understand. In all he counted a dozen or more intricate things that spilled from the factory, few of any meaning, and only the tightweave of any use to humanity.

And warehouses nearby bulged with still more inexplicable 'factured devices, skinwrapped and enameled for shipping.

His interest was purely practical. He no longer marveled at what could come from the incessant engine of mechcraft. Such bounteous wealth spewing forth now seemed to him as inevitable as the rich, organic world had appeared to his ancient ancestors. It was simply an enduring facet of the way things were, fully natural.

His world was divided simply. He lived—as well as he could—among things green and soft and pliant, which had limited use and from which humanity had once sprung. But food came mostly from the vats of Troughs, or the rare damp warrens of the ancient, human-made Casas. Remnants of the once-rich Snowglade ecosphere bloomed in spots, mostly grasslands and desert-tough vines. This realm grew wild only in the outlands, beyond the cities and pathways of the mechs.

On the other side of a hazy division lay most of his planet. The mechs pressed against the shrinking green oases. Most of Snowglade was now open, barren wasteland, used for resources. Dotted around Snowglade were ceramo-sculpted mechwarrens. Killeen had glimpsed one once, when the Family blundered over a mountain range and paid the price of six lost members. It was a glassy, steepled thing that crackled with electromagnetic crosstalk. Its deep, upwelling voice had rung through Killeen's sensorium, immensely threatening.

Killeen accepted as simple fact that those distant and feared zones were an entirely natural way for intelligence to go forward. The humming, rotating processes around him were unremarkable, obvious. No one in humanity doubted this, for they came from a heritage rung down through centuries, in which mechs had bested the Families in every way. Once Snowglade had been a chilly but greenfilled world. Now the dryness grew, the very air sucked moisture from the throats of men. And mechs seemed to have done it all.

They most certainly did.

He was numbed by the incessant drumroll of mechwork around him. Arthur's intrusion at first seemed a
vagrant thought of his own. "What means?"

The mech civilization undertook centuries ago
to change the ecology of Snowglade. They do
not function well in the warm, wet world it was.

"What's so bad about it?"

Moisture and heat quickly bring rust. Snowglade
had Alpine woods once, and vast grasslands that
stretched from horizon to horizon. The mechs
came to see if the planet was useful for their
projects, and seem to have decided that it was,
though of course it needed what they would call,
I quite believe, improvement.

Killeen stopped beside a carboglass device that was
milling what looked like large spheres of matted, chromed
sponge. "How you know?"

I was *there*. We were first aware of them as
simple explorers. The Clans had set up their
Citadels—

"There were more than one?"
Arthur's smoothcoursing voice paused only momentarily in surprise:

Oh yes, I forget so readily now. You are young.
We once had *glorious* things. When we came to
Snowglade we were under no illusion that we
were safe from mechlife. But we could scarcely
cover an entire planet, protect every—

"Yeasay, get on with it." He had never heard of
anything truly manmade other than the Citadel, only of
things fashioned from mechcraft or stolen outright. The
Aspect frequently talked of things which Killeen knew did

not exist and so he thought they were lies or brags or else tall tales to hold Killeen's attention. The contrast of these past accounts with their present condition had made the Family seldom consult the Aspects.

> The mechs did not confront us directly. Some felt that the mechs scarcely noticed us, or else thought we were local lifeforms of no real consequence—a view which I suppose history has confirmed, with sad consequences for us all. At any rate—

Here Arthur obviously sensed Killeen's impatience. His voice speeded up until the images and thoughts came in bursting bluebright clots, vivid pictures delivered without explanation, letting Arthur's remembered experience explode directly into Killeen:

> We noticed first that winters deepened and there was less rain. Our crops dwindled. We had to undertake some extensive breeding and genetic alterations to harden them against the warped seasons.

"You savvyed weather?" Killeen was impressed, but wished there was some way he could keep Arthur from knowing. There wasn't, of course. He felt the Aspect's pleased aura.

> Understood, yes—or so we confidently thought. Only slowly did we realize that the mechs were deliberately bringing clouds of gas and dust into Snowglade's planetary path. They even used fineground asteroids. This brought the duststorms we thought were a passing feature of the changing weather, but were in fact causing that weather. The dust smothered our equatorial regions. Somehow, the mechs contrived to evaporate a great deal of the icepack at the poles. This drove Snowglade toward a dryer,

cooler climate, using processes I cannot guess. Obviously the mech civilizations have worked this kind of planetary engineering before, and they well understood the thousands of small side effects one must calculate. It was a feat of awesome power, and one carried out so gradually we had no intimation of truly fundamental change until centuries had passed. By then our crops had withered and we were eking out an existence at the Citadels, planting more and reaping less with each passing year. We were innocent, thinking the mechs at best had not detected us, or at least would ignore us. More the fools, we!

Killeen picked up one of the chromed balls and tossed it to the floor. It shattered into a thousand strands of delicate spooling fiber, each glinting in the harsh fluorolight. He concentrated on Arthur's fastpassing talk. Such ancient knowledge he had always ignored, figuring that Fanny would tell them what was useful. Ledroff, he knew, was similarly ignorant. "The Splashes're still left," he said.

So paltry were our imaginations that we did not at first recognize the significance of the Splashes. Snowglade follows a near-circular orbit around Denix. Denix itself loops about the Eater in a long ellipse. All our time on Snowglade had been spent in the warm middle portion of its orbit—after the glacial stage, but before Denix approaches the Eater. Here:

A three-color 3D diagram strobed in Killeen's left eye. An iceblue dot circled a flame-red globe. Then point of view telescoped and the globe looped around a hotpoint swirl of colors: the Eater. Numbers and words Killeen could not read gave slide-sheets of data.

"Yeah." Killeen rummaged for something to say. "Pretty."

I do not work out such intricate aids for your
artistic appreciation.

Arthur's voice was stern, piqued. Killeen dutifully shut his
right eye. The diagram swelled, showing Snowglade as a
mottled dry disk. Sandy blotches blended into gray, ribbed
mesas.

The view was time-sped. Centuries flickered by.
Glinting sheets of ice dwindled. Clouds dispersed. Deserts
gnawed at the flanks of flinty mountain ranges.

This is what they have done to approach the
climate which mechs desire. And then—

Three notes piped in his right ear, an assembly-call.
"Look, gotta go," Killeen said with relief.
Into his right eye popped a 2D map to guide him to
Ledroff.

SEVEN

Killeen could see Ledroff was holding a meeting as he
approached. Five Family were sitting on a big brassglass
machine at the end of a tin-roofed assembly shed.
"—since we silenced the managers quickstyle, there's
prob'ly no mayday, no outbound screamers, nothing,"
Ledroff was saying as Killeen dropped down on a polished
rampart.
"Ummm," Jocelyn said doubtfully, fingering a stray tuft
of glossy hair, coiling it around her thumb. "Right, we *used*
get couple days clear ride. But now?"
Ledroff said, "Our strike was *good*. The best."
Killeen thought it was pretty routine, but he said
nothing. Let the new Cap'n crow.
Cermo-the-Slow blinked owlishly. "Could use the
break."
Killeen asked, "What's on?"
Ledroff made a little dramatic pause out of putting his

helmet on a nearby lever. He was sitting on top of the blocky, alum-edged pyramid-machine, and control levers sprouted around him. "We're discussing holing up here," he said down to them.

Killeen snorted. "We got a step or two still in us."

"I think we're still tired," Ledroff said reasonably. "In the past, no higher mechs showed up 'n' checked a deadheaded factory for three, four day. I say we *use* that, rest up."

Jocelyn said, "Mantis might've called some Marauders, try trackin' us."

Ledroff nodded, his bushy beard like a frothy explosion beneath the severity of his stiffhaired ridge. Killeen noticed that the scalping around Ledroff's backchopped hair was fresh. The slick, walnut skin stretched tight and shiny. He was paying more attention to his appearance now. "Yeasay—in the open. Here they not look."

"Whosay?" Killeen demanded as he climbed up a tier on the big silent machine. From there he got a view of the whole 'plex. Navvys still went about their mutedumb rounds. A perpetual machine hum bathed the area. Among the steady, efficient trajectories of the mechs, Family moved on their own paths, taking whatever they could find.

Ledroff eyed him. "Isay. Is custom! Family hangs out after a raid."

Cermo-the-Slow nodded, his big eyes amiable and warm. "We need time, do some 'sploring. Might find more servos, even maybe stimjacks."

Jocelyn laughed. "Cermo, no stimjacks in a *fact'ry*."

Cermo shrugged. "Could be. Dunno till you look."

Something in the middle distance caught Killeen's eye and at first he did not understand.

Ledroff smiled. "Yeasay you, then? Isay we bed down in the big fact'ry, post—"

"Wait. See that?" Killeen pointed.

Jocelyn squinted. "Navvy. So?"

"Ever see one like it?"

Cermo said slowly, "Maybe once. Can't be sure."

Jocelyn said, "I 'member one somewhere. . . ."

"Earlier today. And I think it was near where the Mantis hit us, too," Killeen said.

Ledroff eyed the navvy as it approached on crawler treads. It had crosshatched side panels and, though it veered aside to a factory entrance, its fore-eyes peered at the brassglass pyramid until it vanished. "So?" he said.

"I think it's a scout," Killeen said.

Ledroff squinted down from his perch. "Could be different navvy each place."

Jocelyn said flatly, "Could be not, too."

"New kind navvy," Cermo said. "Maybe there're lots."

"Scout for what?" Ledroff asked.

Killeen said, "Marauders."

"Marauders not use scouts, I know of," Cermo said.

"So what?" Jocelyn asked sarcastically. "Just 'cause you dunno, don' mean *isn't*."

Cermo bristled. *"Fanny knew."*

"Yousay. We got no Fanny Aspect to ask," Jocelyn said sourly.

"Gotta go by 'perience!" Cermo spat back.

"Gotta use heads!" Jocelyn said.

Ledroff said, "I believe we have to use both."

Killeen frowned and said, "Listen to Jocelyn, Isay."

Jocelyn acknowledged this with a curt nod, its energy revealing a contained tension. She had learned Fanny's ways, too, but had not missed the old woman's central and hardwon lesson: *Anticipate*. Savvy the mechthink before it savvys you.

Killeen saw in her slow-smoldering eyes a resentment of Ledroff. Surprised, he saw that Jocelyn had wanted to be Cap'n. He had been too meshed in himself to see that.

"Navvys *could* be backpackers for a Marauder," Jocelyn insisted. She had started finger-curling her hair again. Then she smoothed it back carefully, getting the curls set in the right overlapping waves behind her ears.

Cermo shrugged. "That navvy wasn't carryin' anything."

"Not now, no. Could've dumped it," Jocelyn said.

"For what?" Ledroff asked.

"See what we're doing," Killeen said.

"Fanny naysay anything about such," Ledroff said. Then, hearing how lame the words sounded, he added,

"Marauders too fast for navvy. They'd clean leave 'em 'way behind."

"Mantis might be slow," Killeen said. "We never saw it move much."

Ledroff frowned. Killeen had seen Ledroff on long marches and in battle and knew him to be a cautious, savvy man. Now suddenly Cap'n, Ledroff was trying to balance the views of the others and find a communal consensus. Maybe that was the right thing to do. But Killeen felt in Jocelyn and even Cermo a slowbuilding irritation. Ledroff would have to defuse that fast. A Family should not march or rest while it brewed an anger.

Ledroff was now beset by the inevitable legacy of any Cap'n: the whines of the Family, swirling about him as a natural vortex. They were a small, steady drain. The pressure of this rain of complaint was always to rest, to allow the older and less hardy a respite. And any Cap'n, seeing the incremental damage that the Family's constant forced marching exacted, was prone to listen to these well-meaning and in fact almost pitiful voices. It was a kindness to let the Family knit up its soreness and strains. But it was often not smart.

Ledroff said slowly, "I was hoping you'd all be of one mind."

"Jocelyn and me, we saw that navvy with the Mantis. We're sure," Killeen said sharply, half to let out steam and half to signal to Ledroff that he, as Cap'n, had to do something.

"Your memory's alky-fogged," Ledroff said cuttingly.

"That's past." Killeen felt himself redden.

Cermo teased, "Killeen, you should be on our side. We stay here, you slurp some more tonight."

"I don't have your honeyroll fat, sop up the alky with, is all," Killeen said sarcastically. Cermo carried a slight roll at his belt, visible through the silver tightweave. No matter how hard times were for the Family, Cermo's meager bulge stayed, and was in fact a source of some pride for him.

"Marchin', this honeyroll'll leave you eatin' dust," Cermo said with a harsh edge.

"Not so long's you run like your boots are tied together," Killeen retorted.

"You boys mooded for rankin'?" Ledroff said evenly.

This was a signal that only the Cap'n could give and that no Family ignored. Killeen realized that this was what he had half-wanted. They needed to free the vexings that had mounted since Fanny's loss.

"Heysay," Killeen began the ranking. "Smells like you converting that honeyroll to gas."

Cermo responded, "Then 'least I got some art in my fart."

"Gas bomb the Marauders, then, let me stay with the old folks," Killeen said.

Ledroff came in with, "Only thing you blow up is your belly," directed at Cermo.

"Blow up your mother real good, you watch," Cermo answered.

"She couldn't find it, dribblin' down under that belly," Ledroff spat out, picking up the rhythm.

"It telescopes out, fella. *Way* out," Cermo said. "Next time I'm gonna show it off, you stick 'round, hear the joints pop."

Jocelyn smiled at this and came in. "I think I can see through that telescope, easy."

"You can look for free!" Cermo cried with glee. He remembered to cover his mouth, but even such basic politenesses weren't required in the ranking.

"You mean *micro*scope, it's so small!"

They went through more rounds, each throwing in a quick dash of cutting humor. The Cap'n could always order a round of ranking to defuse the tensions that perpetually came up and, if carried, would fester. The quickshot talk could abuse or amuse—ideally, both. As the jibes laced across the group, each person performed and the others responded with answering barbs or releasing hoots of applause.

"Can't tell Cermo's fart from his talk."

"You mean he can *talk*?"

"His ass knows more words than his mouth does."

"Pronounces better, too."

"Don't drool as much either."

"It's your *mother* can't talk, when I'm telescopin' her."

"Heysay, 'least I'm kind. I give your mother somethin'
nice and fresh to eat."

"Soundin', you are!"

"Your wife, she like a doorknob, ever'body gets a
turn."

"Damnsight right!"

"Your father never try. He so ugly, he crawl up to your
mother, she think it's a navvy."

"Yours, he got so many wrinkles in his head, he has to
screw his helmet on."

"Well, 'least he can screw *that*."

"Sad man, screw his helmet."

"You rankin' right!"

"Your dad, he so ugly, when he cries tears run down his
back."

"Oooooo!"

"Heysay! Heysay!"

If the rounding did not channel the aggression of a
particular pair, the group would force the two to confront
each other. By using passing-phrases, or encouraging calls,
they could finesse competition onto the pair. This time the
anger Killeen felt for Ledroff—suppressed and slowbuilding for days—came out in a few moments of flashing jibes,
ending with Killeen's holding his hands up, palms forward,
and shaking his head wisely.

"Let's get off the subject of mothers, Ledroff . . .
'cause I just got off yours."

"Oooo-ee!"

"Rankin'!"

"*Drive* that nail!"—and they all got up, chuckling and
slapping one another on the shoulder in a bittersweet calm
of aired troubles. Family members who had drifted in to
witness said nothing. They embraced others in turn,
laughing and joshing still, the chatter now aimless and
merrily undirected in purpose yet no less effective in
healing. The Family could not afford unaired anger. The
ranking round, once a pleasant social convention in the
Citadel, was as unremarkable and vital in the Family as a
handshake.

When Ledroff came to Killeen in the embracing, he

said easily, "Could be you're right. Let's get clear this
'plex."

Killeen nodded, grinned, slapped the man hard on the
back, and for the first time honestly thought of Ledroff as
his Cap'n.

Killeen found it easier to talk to Ledroff, once they
were on the move.

—You think that fact'ry means the mechs're using the
Splashes now?— Ledroff asked as they puffed along, skip-
walking with a low line of hills between them.

Toby was on Killeen's right, holding one space in from
the edge of the moving triangle. They were crossing a
brown plain of dried mud. Giant flakes of it reared up,
curled by the searing glare of the Eater overhead. The
great clay-red fans were thinner than a man's wrist, yet
reared taller than a building. Killeen had the sensation of
walking over a brown, storm-shredded lake, somehow
frozen as it tossed. He came down on one huge mud sheet
and it crumbled around him like a rotten leaf. He spilled
through the dissolving cloud and landed with a thump,
boot-deep in cloying dust.

He sneezed violently and called, "Arthur says everything we saw in that 'plex was made from plants." He
leaped out of the dust-hollow into clear, thin, dry air.

—And I found some navvys loading seeds,— Toby
broke in. —'Member that.—

Ledroff's voice sounded troubled. —So maybe
mechs're moving into the Splashes, too?—

"Looks like."

—Damnall! Why can't they stay in their fart-fat
cities?—

"Arthur thinks they plan take over all Snowglade."

Ledroff said, —Yeasay, one my Aspects been sayin'
that, too. Damn Aspects worry 'n' talk, worry 'n' talk, that's
all they got time for.—

Killeen sent an agreeing grunt. "Mechs may be just
gettin' ready for when the Eater gets closer."

Toby asked, —Closer? Will it stay in the sky?—

"Remember the orbits I drew?" Killeen reminded
him.

—Some.— The boy was not used to his interior world of projected images, lines and curves hanging in air, cascades of once-intelligible data bequeathed by forefathers who had never imagined that their descendants would see it as nonsense. Toby preferred the grip of the real.

"Arthur says things're changing. Eater'll get bigger."

—So?—

"The mechs're changin', too."

Toby laughed derisively. —Aw, that Arthur's an old fart.—

Killeen chuckled. Let the boy stay that way for a while. No harm.

Since leaving the looted factory he had been telling his son Arthur's information. Better to put it in simple terms than to have Toby get it in the stilted talk of the Aspects. That would come soon enough.

Killeen did not want Toby to carry an Aspect yet, though he was of an age when the Family would permit it. Aspects rode a young mind harder. In the old Citadel days, the Family would have waited until Toby was fullgrown. Now every adult carried the maximum Aspect load. These living presences kept their covenant with the past, made them the heirs of a grand race, and not merely a ravaged, fleeing band. This now loomed as the practical opening to past lore and crafts. Continuity with humanity's prouder days meant more, since few Family had time to learn from their Aspects and Faces while on the run.

Ledroff panted as he kept up their long-leaping, trotting pace, —If we knew what they're doin', why . . . aghhh!—

The wordless grating sound that came from Ledroff needed no interpretation for Killeen. The Family had never known why the mechs suddenly destroyed the Citadel, just as in earlier ages the Clan had never suspected what the mechs planned for Snowglade.

All attempts to reach the higher levels of mechs, to talk, to negotiate, had failed. Few humans knew how to communicate with mechs in even crude fashion. Moase, an old woman now riding on the transporter mech, had done some translating while a girl. The Family had not had

opportunity to use her craft for a long time; they were too
occupied with the simple task of running and eating and
running again.

Killeen had an older presence, a Face named Bud,
who had been a master translator long ago. But Killeen had
never used Bud that way, relying on the ancient engineer
only for simple tasks. He called up the Face and asked,
"You know anything 'bout weather changes?"

The Bud Face's reply came in stubby units, since Faces
had only limited chunks of the original personality.

1. **In my day air warmer.**
2. **I translate once for Crafter.**
3. **Crafter say Snowglade get cooler.**
4. **Need me translate again?**

"Naysay, sorry," Killeen answered the Face gently,
touched by the plaintive small voice as it volunteered. He
had not called on Bud for a long time. It was hard to release
even a simple Face and remain alert, while on the move.

He pondered Bud's question. He called up Arthur and
got a rapid summary of ancient methods of talking to
mechs. Much of it was incomprehensible.

When humanity had been forced from the sprawling
Arcologies, it had tried shrewdly to market its scavenging
skills among the mech cities. Teams would raid far cities,
then leave the best loot outside a nearby mech enclave.
Done regularly, such peace offerings enticed the neighbor
enclave to stop assaulting the human Citadels. This policy
worked for a while. Humans thought their Citadels, smaller
and less conspicuous than the large Arcologies, were safe.

Some Family Citadels built upon this, specializing in
talking to mech envoys and arranging trades. Family King
had been best at it, but even their expert translators had
been betrayed and killed at times. It was a risky life.

1. **I would do again though.**
2. **Let me work.**

Killeen noted wryly that it would be his skin risked
this time. Bud caught this and retreated, cowed. Aspects

nd Faces had a curious isolation from the consequences of
heir advice, since they did not feel Killeen's pain or
aardship. But they would die if he did.

Undaunted, a biting, ascerbic Aspect piped up. Kil-
een gritted his teeth.

> *The unholy trafficking with mechs met the fate it
> deserved. Compromise with the unliving is im-
> possible. Surely history has taught you that!*

The Aspect named Nialdi forked through Killeen's
sensorium like yellow storm lightning, releasing its years of
pent-up frustration. Nialdi was truly ancient, from the days
when humanity had spread effortlessly over the temperate
zones of Snowglade. He had been a famous priest of that
era's religion.

"I'm tryin' think of ways savin' our ass, you old
bastard!" Killeen blurted out loud. He mentally grasped at
the Aspect but it slipped away, fanning out like a flock of
angry orange birds.

> *You reject the Word? Has not the savage mech
> fury taught you at last that there can be no
> staying of our hand? The Grail speaks through
> me!*

"Get back in!" Killeen shouted. He snatched after
flapping threads of Nialdi. The Aspect kept hurling religious jargon at him, fluttering through his sensorium.
Killeen was so intent on snaring the Aspect that he himself
stumbled. Fell. His curved helmet plate was thrown back
and he got a mouthful of sand. He came up swearing.

—Can't keep your Aspects down?— Ledroff sent
derisively.

—Man's got feet like rocks,— Jocelyn jibed.

Irked, Killeen forced Nialdi back into a far cranny of
his mind and slammed the hornet's buzz into a silencing,
encapsulating crack. Aspects were getting harder and
harder to control for everyone in the Family. Another
reason not to burden Toby with one, he thought sourly.

* * *

They left the mud plain and mounted an eroded ridgeline. Denix and the Eater cast their stark, separate glares on the land. Bushes dotted the shadows. They were pushing farther into the Splash. Creekbeds were damp, as though rain had come within the last few days. Occasional puffball clouds skated high up, pushed by fast winds. Great fans of smoothed pebbles and sand spoke of torrents which had once rushed down from the slumping clay hills.

The Family was well dispersed. Even if a mech flyer spotted them and dropped an explosive bomb or a jammer, only a few could be within range.

"Lookleft," Ledroff called to Killeen. "See somethin'?"

The landscape leaped into bright focus as Killeen landed atop a rust-riddled hulk. It had been a crawler. Ancient in design, stripped of ore-rich parts, it rattled like a forlorn drum as he studied the far horizon.

"Looks to be mechs, only . . ."

"What's your Far-Ranger say?"

"Mechmetal, sure plenty that. But I'm not smellin' mechthink."

Killeen's sensors had a library of typical mech electronic signatures, and they sampled the tiny sputterings of unshielded emission ahead. Killeen could neither have read nor understood a graphics display detailing which signals were mechlike. The data flowed to him as cloying scents, laced with crisp darting odors.

"Could be they're downwindin' you?"

Killeen bristled. "I can tell a mechfart faster'n any," he said. This was not true—Cermo-the-Slow had a better nose. But the big man lacked judgment and speed.

Killeen reluctantly called up Arthur and asked for help.

You ask if mechs could hide like this? No, I doubt they could fully shield their transmissions. Nor could they fully elude the sensors we carry.

"You sure?"

I participated in the development of these techniques, I'll remind you.

"If we let that many get within scannin' distance . . ."

I assure you—

—Dad, I hear talking,— Toby called.
"What kind?"
—Some kind strange voices, I dunno who.—
Ledroff sent, —Could be a mech trick.—
Killeen was confused. His instincts said *Run!*—and he
automatically bent down to check-tighten his boots, run-
ning gloved fingers along glassy fiberseals. He turned his
head. A small shift in the capacitance of his sensorium
brought him a tinny chime of talk. He froze. Overlapping,
garbled, human voices:
—They're comin'.—
—Too many. Can't pick 'em off.—
—I say we cut right now.—
—Checkleft. Any sign they're surroundin'?—
—Might just be navvys.—
—Naw, they step too high.—
—I smell plenty mechmetal in 'em. Stinks powerful.—
Toby cried, —They're people!—
And here they were, a thin wedge straggling across the
deep-rutted plain. Killeen's mouth formed an incredulous
O.
A distant ringing voice demanded, —What Family?
What Family?—
Ledroff answered, —Bishop! Six years from the Cita-
del!—
A woman's voice answered, —We're Rooks.—
—We have kin here, kin of yours.—
—Cousins and uncles and aunts!—
Boots dug into timeworn sand and the two triangles on
the plain rushed at each other. Pellmell running, shouting.
Questions about lost relatives yelled into the sensorium,
and hoarse answers calling back. Windmilling of legs at the
high point of high leaps. Then the tips of the spearpoints
met and men and women flung themselves at each other.
Behind scratched helmets were faces half-remembered,
people who were until a moment before only faded images

from a wondrous life that had ceased to be. The faces carried furrows and brownscabbed rashes, sewn-up cuts and even hollowed-out eyesockets where no replacement parts could be found. Mouths showed ruined gray-stubbed teeth, blood-rimmed lips. They barked and called to one another, even though most of them in fact knew only a few of the bobbing faces coming across the broken plain. The Citadel had held thousands. They had gone so long in their own close and knotted company, their memories had been overladen by such a weight of daily terror, that any face was a sudden reminder, undeniable and fleshy, of the collectivity of their kind. Lost friends embraced. Shouts laced the air. Abruptly they saw themselves as far more than a straggling band of hunted creatures. Their yelps and startled joy celebrated humanity itself.

Toby found immediately a boy and two girls, who came bounding out in front of even the fleetest of running men. They embraced and jabbered and capered and even wrestled in their unthinking frenzy, while about them the two Families collided, two long-separated fluids flowing in a throughstreaming torrent of bodies and talk and simple mindless whoops and cries and sudden tears.

Killeen found a man he had known, had worked with in the fields: Sanhakan, heavybrowed and cleanshaven still, eyes dancing in a net of webbed, sunburned wrinkles. Sanhakan clapped him on the back, swore, swung Killeen off the ground in a bear grip. They both laughed wildly, peering at each other through filmed helmets, as if to be sure the other was in fact substantial and not a fever dream. They popped helmets, just as everyone was doing around them, and kissed in incredulous greeting. Only taste and touch were trusted now, the human press of warm and pungent flesh. Killeen breathed in the rank running-smell of Sanhakan. Then the slightly muskier odor of a woman who was suddenly at his elbow, heavy lips outthrust. Another woman, old and weathered and smelling of salty exertion, white hair, and something indefinably sweet. Slapping and patting and hugging, he made his way through the welter of closepressing bodies that knocked him about in their lurching joy. Faces, scabbed and furrowed. Sobbing. He came to an old man with eyes slitted nearly closed, but whose teeth sparkled with lustrous youth. Killeen embraced him, unable to hear what the man shouted over the babble-river around them. Then Killeen was passed by eager hands on to the next, and in turning away from the old man heard a sudden *spang* that sprang up from his lower spine and hurled itself through his head. Red filmed his vision. Something hit his nose, bringing the instant thick taste of blood into his mouth. He licked at it in wonderment. His tongue rasped on sand. His vision cleared slightly, clouds blowing away, and he saw he was facedown. He moved leadened muscles and rolled over. Next to him lay the old man, legs and arms stretched full out. The tongue protruded and there was a certain look to the face that struck a sudden coldness into Killeen, the awful twisted look that Fanny had.

He struggled up onto an elbow. The streaming talk around him now had a harsh high register. Screams. Bodies falling. Killeen tried to push the edge of his sensorium outward, find what was happening. It was thick, clouded, muffled, like swimming in dust. He got to his knees and saw that some of the Families were down, sprawled. Others fled. Some were frozen with shock.

Toby.

Brittle pain shot through his arms. Killeen groped around.

And saw his son lurch up uncertainly, a bare short distance away.

"Toby!" Killeen got to his knees. "Get behind something!"

Toby saw him. "Which way?"

"Come on!"

Teetering unsteadily on feet of wooden weight, Killeen stumbled toward an outcropping of jagged boulders.

"Get . . . there." They both dropped weakly behind the largest stone. Then Killeen realized he did not know which direction the attack came from.

Toby stared at the running figures, eyes white. "What . . . ?"

"It's the Mantis," Killeen said.

EIGHT

Twenty-two bodies. His subsystems counted them automatically as he carefully surveyed the far hills.

Twenty-two, all sprawled like loose bags. Suredead.

They had been hit by something firing from long range, something with remarkable aim. To do that took size, to get good triangulation.

Something big should be easy to spot. Even in the excitement, they should have seen it coming. As far as Killeen could see, there was nothing obvious, no crinkling play of sandy light.

Mantis.

Killeen heard/felt a thin, high, cold *skreeeee*. He ducked automatically. A passing fringe field. The Mantis could be behind him, could be anywhere.

Toby was down, left leg stuck straight out. The boy pushed with both hands and rolled himself partway up the side of the boulder. He grimaced and almost lost his balance.

Killeen reached for Toby's arm. "Come on!"—and they went hobbling toward the nearest gully, crouched over.

Running, Killeen felt:

Low mutter of acousto-electro noise, like a Marauder strobe-searching.

Crackling hotstink.

A hard thump in the lower spine—

Skreeeee.

Toby gasped in pain, "What was . . . what . . ."

"Went over our heads. We caught the backwash."

Killeen remembered scrambled, spike-shot cues like this. They came when you were in the secondary emission lobe, where side-angling waves interfered with each other to build a small, fast-moving peak. Killeen's father had explained it to him once and all he could remember to counter it was to shut down all your senses except vision, go numb.

Killeen blotted out sound, smell, touch—and was

instantly in a silent, numb world. He stepped down his vision. Color drained from the world.

All the while he was half-carrying Toby, lunging forward awkwardly.

He fought to keep his balance. His feet sent back only dull drumbeats.

He cradled Toby close, trying to shield him from unknown vectors.

Skreeeeeee—

They crashed down the slope of the gully and ended in a tangled pile.

Family were crouched all along the shelf of broken stone. Killeen and Toby lay panting, watching. Killeen let his senses ease back to full.

The Families fought back defiantly. Some would jerk their arms up and fire off a humming round of electronoise without aiming. If your head wasn't exposed, there was no easy route into your sensorium. But of course they had no good idea of what the Mantis could do. And this time it had them neatly pinned, bunched together.

Killeen touched the boy's knee carefully. "Feel this?"

"Ah . . . ahhhh . . . it's okay."

"You sure?"

"Musta clipped me, going by."

"How's this?" Flexing the leg a little.

"All ri—ow!"

"Let it rest. Prob'ly come back in a while."

"Ahhhhh . . ."

"How bad's it?"

Toby's eyes rolled up. His face paled. Killeen gripped him in blind fear. "Toby!"

Inside the boy a struggle snarled through embedded metal and augmented brain and parts for which Killeen had no name. His fists clenched in impotent despair. His face twisted hopelessly. "Toby!"

"Ahhhh . . ." A long sigh. Toby's legs jerked.

"Lie still."

"I . . . no . . ."

It was always this way, complex surges running faster than human thoughts could follow. They were spectators to their own feverquick interior zones. To buried ancient crafts.

The boy's lips moved numbly. They reddened. The inner battle ebbed.

Toby gasped, coughed. To Killeen's astonishment he sat up, gloves digging into gray sand. A whisper: "We got it . . . yet?"

"No, look, lie back—"

Toby's green eyes leveled, cleared. "Lemme . . ."

"Now you just—"

"Lemme shoot!" Toby demanded, voice strengthening.

"Keep down. Dunno where it is yet."

"I heard somethin' that way." Toby pointed shakily at a distant rockslide. From this low in the gully they could see only the uppermost jagged rubble of it.

"What'd it sound like?"

"When people started fallin'," Toby said wanly, "I heard metal tearin' apart. Real loud. My leg wouldn't move and I fell down and I heard that sound again, comin' from over there."

Killeen sensed as a shifting haze the random cries of the two Families, bleeding humanity blending together. The wounded grunted. Some sobbed. A woman called *Alex Alex Alex Alex* in a brittle, thin panic.

A few shouted for orders, plaintively seeking their Cap'n. Ledroff needlessly called for return fire but no one seemed to have a fix on what had happened, where to look.

They were all strewn through gullies in the plain, unable to maneuver. With almost no shelter, the Families would have to crawl out. But the Mantis could keep the high ground and follow them.

Killeen drew a long filament from his shoulder pack and hooked it into a steel eyelet at the tag end of his shirt cuff. It was a sensepipe his father had given him and its mico surface was scarred and yellowed. He snugged it into the eyejack in his temple.

Toby asked weakly, "Whatcha . . ."

"Looking."

Killeen closed his eyes and the sensepipe took over. He saw/heard quick snatches of his surroundings. Then he angled his arm up and poked it over the pebbled rim. He searched the far horizon, working the point of view down.

He regularly twitched his hand, to mix up the data inflow. That would help find mirages.

"Catching anything?" a deep woman's voice asked behind him.

"No. Leave me be."

"Can find, I hit."

"Can find, *I'll* hit."

"No. Better."

He didn't open his eyes. The distant ruined hillsides jumped and melted and flashed through the hotpoint, overloaded spectrum of his search pattern. He inched up the slope to get a lower angle and started searching the bottom fan of the rockslide.

A whisper of something metallic went by him, trailing away into a nervous rattling. A ranging shot, maybe. He kept riffling through his righteyed filters and was about to give up when he saw something move.

It was gone in an instant but he brought it back. A gangly body. Tripod legs. An intricate pattern was nestled into the rocks, its antennae swerving in jerks.

Killeen unjacked and rolled down the slope, warm sand trickling at his neck and into his suit. "Okay, let's see—"

Beside Toby, hands cradling the boy's calf muscle, knelt the woman. She wore faded gray tightweave. It clung to an exoskeleton which clasped her like a many-fingered fist. He had seen such before, but never so finely made. The exskell ribs wrapped around her long thin body and shooting down her legs in a cross-laced spiral. At her throat the black ribfingers tapered into flexible strands that coiled in at the back of her neck. They twitched slightly as she looked up at him, her muscles pulled and bunched by them. The bluegray eyes were level and assessing.

"—see what you've got," he finished, in the heartbeat's pause taking in her worn backpack stuffed with lumpy gear, her bony black exskell, her coiled and pin-tucked ebony hair.

"That you see now." As she said it she sent two signals: A rawboned hand came up to pluck from the scuffed backpack a slender pressed-plastic rod. And she gave him a wolfish grin, all sharpedge and strungwire.

"I . . ." he gestured vaguely over his shoulder, "found it. What's that?"

"Bird," she said curtly.

Toby was watching her peacefully with a wobbly smile, as if her touch had calmed him. Killeen guessed the boy was starting to feel the afterrush, as sensation flooded back into the leg and the muscles went slack.

She stuck the rod into a shiny cylinder which lay at her feet. Killeen recognized these parts as scavenged Marauder parts, fitted ingeniously into a weapon different from any he had ever seen. As she hoisted it up at the sky the exskell flexed and purred and corrected a momentary imbalance in her legs.

"Sure you don't want . . ."

The eyes glinted proudly. "I can."

"Okay."

She duckwalked partway up the tawny sandstone slope. Stiffly she sprawled forward, the exskell grinding against stones as it stretched. The black-sheened ribs kept her real ribs from jagging into the stubby rocks. She cradled the rod forward, the end of it heavy with the copper-jacketed cylinder. Her right hand popped a molded handgrip from the stock of the rod. Cradling the rig, she sighted along it. She had two eyejacks, like cosmetic pimples set just outside her dark-rimmed eyesockets. Both snugged into the mounts on the upper dowel of the stock.

Killeen wordlessly sent her his own short-time stored image of the Mantis. In the frame was a notation RANGE 2.3275 ZONE KM but he did not know what that meant.

She nodded slightly, her eyes closed. She fired.

The copper bird seemed to spin off its rod and glide away. It accelerated with a rush and before Killeen could stand up he heard a muffled *crump*.

A low tone vanished from his sensorium. He realized that the whole time since the attack he had been in the scan-fan of the Mantis, feeling its persistent probing.

The woman got slowly, achingly, to her feet.

"Damnfine weapon you got there."

Her dark, heavy-lidded eyes blinked languidly. "Killed."

With a releasing sigh he said, "Yeasay, yeafold."

* * *

The Mantis was a jumble at the foot of the rockslide. Parts had sheared off from heavy steel lug nuts and crashed among tumbled boulders.

Killeen said slowly, "Could be the same's hit us a few days back."

The woman raised a thin, jetblack eyebrow. "Is?"

"Mantis. But we drilled the mainmind with a thumper!"

"Sure?"

"I *saw* it."

She whirred and clicked as she walked, her exskell giving her a strange stiff grace. Her face angled down to a pointed chin which was covered by a red rash. To Killeen she seemed like a lattice, even her bones simply calcium rods in an onworking machine. Yet something tugged at him when the cool bluegray eyes studied his face.

"This piece here"— he poked at a rivet-ribbed steel ellipsoid—"I thought was the mainmind."

She swung her head swiftly, yet in short jerks, as though taking pictures of each piece of the shattered Mantis.

Borers spun at the base of the Mantis's central, glass-jacketed ellipsoid. The thing was trying to burrow into a sandy spot it had found. Killeen pressed his scrambler against the access lobe of the ellipsoid and fired. The thing shuddered and stopped.

"Hiding now," she said, and with surprising speed loped back toward the distant gully where the Families still crouched. Killeen followed, not understanding. He felt seeping gray fatigue as he crossed the bleached plain.

Toby hadn't moved but was testing his leg, thumping it against the ground to bring back feeling. "Heysay! Got it?"

Killeen nodded. "Must be 'nother those—"

"Watch!" the woman called.

Killeen peered back at the sprawled carcass of the Mantis. Over the far brow of the hillside came four navvys. They picked their way down, stopping often for long moments. All of them had crosshatched side panels, much like the one Killeen had seen back at the 'plex.

"Damnall!"

The first navvy to reach the base encountered a piece

of the Mantis and hoisted it aboard, fitting it securely atop the carryrack.

"Assemble," the woman said.

"What?"

She said nothing. They watched silently. Killeen helped Toby up onto the brow of the gully and a few others joined them. There were dozens of Mantis parts and the navvys carefully dealt with each one.

Killeen studied the navvys with eyes slitted against the combined glare of Denix and the Eater. Too late now he understood that the Mantis had taken advantage of the two-star glare. Even augmented as they were, a heritage handed down from centuries before, humans could not see as well as mechs in either dark or searing bright. Against the Mantis's illusions they were blind.

And the Mantis had caught them when they were least guarded, most open and humanly vulnerable. Killeen clenched his jaw regularly, as though chewing on this fact.

He did not want to walk back onto the plain behind them, to see who had fallen. He had seen too much of it in the last few days. The sensorium carried skittering wails of despair, of horrible surprise.

There would be time for that. He watched as two navvys met and mutually put their loads on a bare rock platform. It would make as good a workbench as they seemed to require. One navvy sprouted a set of finepointed tools and began to take apart a chunky, half-ruined segment of the Mantis.

"They're fixin' it," Toby said wonderingly.

"Seen before?" the woman asked.

"Naysay, nothing like," Killeen answered. "But the mainmind—"

"Not one mind."

"Howcome?"

"Easier heal."

Toby put in, "Easier bring it live again, too."

"That, yeasay." The woman pursed her lips, as if tasting a possibility she didn't like.

"Looks like they've found a way to disperse the mind into different parts of the Mantis."

"One stupid, many smart?" she asked distantly.

Killeen saw what she meant. If intelligence could be made up of many dispersed pieces, each of low level, but each contributing a vital fraction of what was needed for a much smarter mech . . . "Maybe. Then the navvys come in, fix it up. Maybe replace one of the small minds if it's dead."

"Then waking again. Thinking. Hunting." Her ebony hair was arabesqued in coils that had a blue sheen. It made a woven pattern almost like looking at tightweave with a close-eye.

"A new kind Marauder?" Killeen asked.

The woman arched her bushy eyebrows and said nothing.

"We can't kill it?" Toby asked, hobbling around to test his leg.

"Not unless you skrag the whole works," Killeen said, starting to figure in his head. He estimated without numbers, just judging by the feel of his memory. Answers popped into his head and he didn't stop to wonder whether they came from Arthur or some other techAspect he carried. He simply said, with assurance, "We barely got enough ammo. Maybe could pound each piece of that Mantis. Be real close though."

Toby said, "I'll help!"

The woman frowned. "Too much."

Killeen agreed. "We skrag it, we'll use up most our armament."

"Dangerous."

Killeen looked questioningly at her and saw she meant not immediate threat but rather the challenge that Marauders like this represented. A new mech idea.

Toby scrambled away, looking for weapons, his leg working like a stiff rod but well enough to carry him. The woman said nothing, just watched the navvys slowly dragging parts together. Her breathing was so shallow it did not flex the exskell. Time-softened gray tightweave clung to her body. She was thin but her supple curves stood out against the unavoidable rigidities of her armor-web exskell, making her seem a feminine prisoner in a black cage. He wondered how she powered it. Then he noticed the back of her shirt zipped down; she must have opened it while she loped back from the Mantis. Photovoltaic eyes turned as she moved, following the ultraviolet mana of the Eater.

All to drive a shell which brought her muscle power up to the level of others. In her, the genetic pruning for greater strength had failed. Her metabolism converted food less efficiently into power. She needed this ribbed husk to keep up with the rest of her Family. Their rules were harsh. A member who fell behind died.

He asked, "Think we should skrag it?"

"Must."

"I'll get Ledroff, some others. Those navvys're funny-actin', too. We'd better plan on taking them out from a distance. No simple disconnect."

"Time."

"What? I figure hours before they've got all the parts—"

"No. We mourn first."

He nodded. It had been better to stand here and think about the Mantis than to go and find the friends hurt or dead or even suredead. But now he had to.

"You're . . . ?"

"Shibo."

"Family Rook?"

"Family Knight."

"This isn't your Family?"

"I meet them. My Family gone."

Her eyes regarded him flatly, giving nothing away. She had not come from his Citadel, for there had been no Knights there. So the other Citadels had been destroyed, too.

Killeen had come to feel that his loss was as great as anyone's, but this woman before him had lost her entire lineage and faced as well the insurrection of her own weak body. He had myriad questions to ask her, but the wan and pensive gaze she turned on him erased all thoughts in the enormity of its unstated implications.

"Let's go. The Families'll need help."

He helped her surmount the gully and cross the bleak landscape strewn with the newfallen dead.

PART II

THE ONCE-GREEN WORLD

ONE

He came awake but did not come alive. He heard and saw nothing.

Killeen had to guide him only a seeping perception of gradients in temperature. He was lying on his belly and felt a thin chill steal up into him from the dank ground. It was as if the soil itself struck upward into him, slow and methodical, spreading through his jumpsuit, into groin and hip, creeping across his chest and into his shoulders. His arms were crossed, his forehead resting over them. In his nostrils the chill sank upward into his oozing sinuses. The sharp bite of it kindled spatterings of rosy heat in his eyes.

He turned his head. No sight, no sound. The shredded heat-spurts dwindled. As if in reply, crosscut sensations of bitter cold lashed over him. He felt crisp warm waves ripple his still-numb skin. Elusive traceries of dulling cold fought across his face. Thermal battles mixed the two in whirling knots he felt as pinprick flares, darting in hard vortices, sputtering. To his surprise the flux resolved not into minute threads of hot and chill but instead into what they had been all along: voices. The tiny, mingled, raucous speech of his Aspects.

The Grail will brook no mealymouthed stalling now, Arthur. We have got to force these people to move and right quick, too.

1. **Got to get shelter.**
2. **Mantis—don't understand it.**
3. **Can't take these losses.**

Of course, I feel quite as threatened as the rest of you by the reckless way they have been squandering opportunities. They could have followed the path we advised back at that place— what was it?—Lost Mother Ridge, that was the name. If they had, we would almost certainly have reached a Casa. I distinctly remember a Casa near there. Nialdi, your memory for the grand old days surpasses mine. What was that Casa called?

It was Oasis Godstone. I blessed the site myself at its consecration to our cause.

Ah yes, a lovely event, I'm sure. There were so many in those fine centuries, when we had proportioned way stations between the Citadels. What wealth! We traveled without fear nipping at our heels, never bothering to carry water or provisions, for we knew they lay a mere short-march away, in Casas or Citadels where—

1. **Stick to topic.**

Very well, Bud. You needn't be snippish. As I see it, with the remaining maps, we could still retrace our steps and search for Oasis Godstone. Spotty and dated as the maps are, of course I cannot be sure, but my calculations—

They've erred far more, Arthur, by ignoring the words of our Fellowship. The vouchsafed command we carry from the first days here—nay,

*from the Providential Truth made known unto us
from aeons immemorial!—definitely shows that
this wandering in a mechmade wilderness is a
wrongful path to the eventual resurrection of us
all. My halfdead brothers, if we are to walk the
land in strength and fullness, we must pull
together.*

I take offense at your hectoring, Nialdi. Your
medical skills I respect and do not deny, but—

*I am a spiritual guide to the Family, as well! I was
encased as Aspect for my moral sense, not
merely—*

1. **Pulpit-pounding not same as wisdom.**
2. **Stick to what we can do now.**

*What we must do, my stunted little Face friend, is
exert leadership. This blighted desolation where-
in we so humbly lie is an abomination! Our dwin-
dled-down Family still carries our honorable
name and is still capable of attaining the heights
humanity once harbored—*

1. **How we go?**
2. **Anyplace better than this.**
3. **Maybe build ship.**
4. **Lost lastship 269 years ago.**

You are leaping too far ahead, Bud. I am quite
aware of the mech atrocities which resulted in
our losing the last of the starships which bore us
to this hive of gargantuan—

*Mech devils! Use no other nicey-nice word for it,
Arthur! These are unholy—*

1. **Hard to build ship.**
2. **Have to make Citadel first.**
3. **Nobody knows shipcraft now.**

4. Don't talk so fast you two.
5. I'm only a Face you know.

All this went by in a shredded heatpricked blur.
Killeen lay motionless.

Somewhere in him sentience and volition were un-
joined, wires trying to snugfit again. The heat-spilling
voices blended with chilly tremors in his eardrums. Their
tangential argument resounded in sweeping thermal bell-
notes—vexed, rambling, incoherent.

He focused himself and wrestled back command of his
sight. A square in his left eye filled with dawn-gray radiance
and a fuzzy rounded edge of a stone.

He felt the voices shrinking, talking even more rapidly
now. His blunted, part-blinded sensorium translated their
speech into waning thermal codes. Rude dashes of hot and
cold rushed over his chest and neck, blaring. Arthur and
Nialdi and Bud didn't want to shrink back into their
cramped cells. They called to him.

> *Penitent you be who jostles into silence the word
> and wisdom of and from your forefathers! Dare
> you not—*

I believe you could benefit from this discussion
yourself, Killeen. I fully grant your need to arise
and see what is happening, but I suggest you will
find much of what we say germane to the
situation now faced by both Families. We need
to work out a strategy based on careful assess-
ments of potentialities and risks, including—

1. Listen, Killeen, I can figure for you.
2. You give me time I could take apart that
Mantis.
3. See how it works.

He swept them away, squeezed them toward their
crannies.

Into Killeen's eyes leaped angular blocks of light. His
blindness fluttered away. The outside world rushed at him.

He turned his head and saw the dry plain surge and twist, stretching away. The Family was sleeping. The Eater was a hazy violet whirlpool squatting above a distant mountain peak.

As his Aspects relinquished his perception-processing space, he caught the dusty savanna scent, mingled with fragrant human musk. His ears crackled, letting in the wind-whisper.

Aspects needed time to sense the world directly, not as mere leftovers. That kept them from becoming dry, husk-like embodiments, slow to respond, little better than an ancient library book. When Killeen was awake, they got snippets of the world, sitting behind his consciousness. As he slept, they could raise his eyelids, catch glimpses that gave them a gratifying sliver of experience. Such thin gruel was all they got. They listened through his eardrums, savored his sensorium—while also providing the service of isolating him, ensuring deep sleep.

Aspects craved the rush of perception, for it was all they now knew of life. As he awoke, Killeen could not hurry matters. He had to let them withdraw slowly, yielding up chunks of his sensorium sadly, one at a time, as they retreated into their bleak cells of chipstore.

This last night, Killeen had let out two Aspects, Arthur and Nialdi. They were his strongest and needed the most airing.

Bud, the Face of an engineer killed by a Snout centuries ago, was a powerful presence despite his limitations.

Faces were partial recordings of the dead. A brain deprived of oxygen, or whose nervous system was badly shocked by death, could not be fully Aspected. Personality was far harder to extract from a mind sliding into the swarming dark. The Family saved only the dead's expertise and craft.

Such a recorded Face gave some dim aura of the original person, trimmed and slow-thinking. Bud had been a fine translator of mech signs. He had even mastered some mech languages, back when humanity had contact with renegade mechs. Killeen had grown impatient with the Face's slowness. Sometimes he thought Bud was not even a

Face, and belonged with the lowest personae, the Analogs.
Still, Bud proved useful for finding an entry into a mech or
figuring the arcane designations on mech parts.

Killeen got up, feeling muscles knot. Yesterday's
terrors had become morning aches. He blinked his left eye
and called up the Bishop Family topo. Toby's orange icon
said he was still sleeping, halfway up a sheltering arroyo.
Good. The boy needed his rest.

Killeen walked stiffly toward a distant knot of Family.
They had all dispersed for the night. The two Families were
spread down a ridgeline and a sloping valley, an hour's
hardmarch from the destroyed Mantis carcass. Any hunting
Marauder-class mech would stumble on at most a few of
them, and alert the rest. Killeen switched on his functions
as he walked, bringing himself back to full sensorium.
Sleeping in the open, their best defense was to shut down
any inboard systems that the mechs could sniff. As he
rounded a wind-worn rock jut he felt the reassuring *ping* of
his abilities returning.

He was startled when a form unfolded from an
impossibly narrow crevice. It was Shibo.

"How you get in there?"

"Curl. Safer." Her eyes were red from crying but her
face bore no memory of it.

"Any trouble last night?"

"No."

"The watch see anything?"

"No."

Killeen wanted to talk to her but his mind whirled,
empty. Her one-word replies didn't help.

"Wakin' up, I'm always 'fraid I won't get all my
'quipment up and running."

"Yes."

"Always has so far, though," he said lamely.

"Yes."

"You ever have any go bust overnight?"

"Yes."

"Fix it?"

"Face did."

Without even an extra *Um-hmmm* to help he found it
hard to go on. Yet something about her made him keep

rummaging for things to say. Her finely made weapon bespoke abilities unknown to Family Bishop. And her cool, self-contained certainty was intriguing.

He gestured at his left eye. "What's your count?"

Shibo blinked, one eye gazing distantly at her Family scan, and a moment later she said, "Eighty-seven."

From the pause he knew she relied on an Aspect or subself to give the number, the same as he. "Family Bishop's down to one six six in number. We lost twelve yes'day."

"Family Rook, twenty-six."

He paused as Arthur did the arithmetic for him. "Thirty-eight gone in all. Damn!"

"Together now two five three."

"Yeasay, sadsay. And of two five three we got maybe a hundred really workin'. Rest are hurt or old or kids, like Toby."

She nodded and then said, "Good. Children."

Killeen saw what she meant. "Yeasay. Least the Rooks got children. We had nine babies born since the Calamity. Two were stillborn. Rest were feeble or deformed or died on the march."

They walked for a moment in silence. To be born on the march with any shortcoming meant the mothers killed them. Killeen did not want their conversation to end there. He was breathing a little deeper with the exertion of keeping up with her. She moved with a quick, efficient scissoring of muscled legs. Her exskell whirred like a strange mechanical pet.

He tried again. "Wonder why the Mantis didn't hit any kids yes'day?"

Whereas Family Bishop had lost all but Toby, the Rooks had, through luck or some intuited skill, kept some young ones from the Marauders. But they had no babies.

"Smaller target."

"Don't think that's it."

"Puzzle." Shibo shook her head at this further unfathomable facet of the mechs. The Mantis had surekilled the oldest in the two Families. Some said that the elders had died first, and that the Mantis then worked its way through the clotted throng of merged and still-jubilant

Families, striking down humans as though it sensed their age. Moase, the aged woman who had the best mech-translating skills, had fallen.

The Mantis had seemed to skip over easy young targets, even if they were standing next to the newfallen. Killeen doubted that such shooting was possible in the swirl of suddenly frightened, scattering humanity. Still, it was easier to think of the children's survival as great luck than as another troubling feature of the Mantis.

They reached the huddled members of both Families. Quietly they sat, obeying an old rule that no one stood while rest was possible. Killeen felt his calf muscles stretch with the night's cold still in them.

Tutored by Nialdi, he had used pressure at skull and spine to temper the strain. But the old ways could not erase all the damage.

There was desultory talk between Ledroff and a member of the Rooks, but Killeen could not keep his attention from the cairn around whose base they had gathered. He had helped fetch and roll stones for it as halfnight gathered. The four-sided pyramid thrust up from the valley floor. Crude edges protruded. "Bad work," he muttered to himself.

"Naysay. Good," Shibo whispered in response.

The planes of the sides should have been flatter, and the edge-angles were off, but Killeen felt a warmth at hearing her words. He had gotten little praise lately. And he did feel some pride in having labored into the halfnight, just him and five others still strong enough. The Families had shared the carrying of the suredead, which exhausted many. Once Ledroff called a halt at this valley, some whined that it was too late, they were too tired to do the right thing. Killeen and Cermo and some Rooks had shaken their heads, silent in the face of such laxity, and had done what they knew to be correct.

The pyramid rested on the suredead, encasing them protectively. No ordinary passing mech would dismantle a human burial site. That rule had been handed down from centuries before. It was the last vestige of a time when a grudging equilibrium had held between the human Arcologies and the machines.

The dead would rest undisturbed. Killeen was tired and dragged in each breath as if it was a labor. But he was proud of having stuck to the old ways. A dim buried image came to him, of a far grander pyramid striking up from tawny sands, piercing a pale blue sky. It dwarfed the puny humans gazing up at it. Even the carved stone blocks that made it were taller than a man. He had seen it before, flitting before his eyes for an instant at earlier such burials, floating up unbidden from some deep Aspect. He did not know where the huge pyramid had stood, majestic in its silent and eternal rebuke to that which had struck down the humanity within it.

"Killeen?"

Ledroff's voice carried mild irritation. Killeen realized his name had been called before and he had not answered.

"Uh, yea?"

"The Mantis. How long you think before navvys reassemble it?"

"Never, I hope. Think we got it all."

"You yeasay, Shibo?" Ledroff asked.

She shook her head. "Knownot this mechtech."

"You can't say?" Ledroff looked annoyed that no one could give him clear answers.

"Didn't plug every 'ponent," Killeen said. "Not enough ammo."

A man named Fornax leaned forward. The Rook Cap'n had died yesterday and this man seemed to step naturally into the position. He was worn and wiry, with a drawn look to his face as though he had seen too much he didn't like and was going to see more. Long grooves ran from just below his eyes, creases like rivers which were fed by interlacing tributaries that spread across his cheeks. "This Mantis, figure it's just passing?"

Ledroff said, "Could be. We had a run-in with 'nother."

"Same Mantis," Killeen said.

Fornax scowled as if he didn't want to believe it. "Sure?"

"I took a leg strut from the first. This one had a gimped-up leg."

"Could be accident," Ledroff said.

"Damnsight strange, then," Killeen said dismissively.

Fornax said, "We never saw a Mantis. Heard 'bout somethin' like it, though, from my mother."

Shibo murmured, "Mantis kill Knight."

Fornax looked puzzled. "Yousay Stalkers, Lancers, Rattlers did it. They surrounded you Knights, yeasay?"

Shibo said impassively, "Mantis lead them. Mantis take us if escape."

Ledroff asked, "You mean Mantis led the Marauder group?"

Shibo nodded silently.

Killeen asked, "How'd you get away?"

"Crawl into rocks."

Killeen remembered her sleeping place. "When was this?"

She paused, consulting an Aspect. "Six years, 'bout."

He regarded her with respect. She had lived for years on her own. "Then the Knight Citadel fell 'bout same time's ours. We call it the Calamity."

Fornax nodded, his eyes hooded. "Ours, too. We held the Marauders two days. Then they broke our walls and drove us out."

Killeen said, "We lasted three. Some said they saw somethin' big, big as the Mantis, in the distance."

Fornax sighed. "Easy to mistake. Lots wild stories then. What'd Mantis be there for, anyway? Bunch of rods and pods. Don't look much like a fighter."

"Mantis quick," Shibo said.

Ledroff said, "I figure it got lucky, is all. Caught Fanny at a bad moment. Killeen got it with one shot, 'member."

Killeen said, "It was me was lucky, not Mantis."

Ledroff shrugged this off. "It jumped in right when we were distracted. Families meetin'."

Shibo shook her head again in a slow, sad way but again said nothing. Fornax was eyeing her closely, as though she were a rival. Killeen knew this could not be, though, for no matter how good Shibo of the now-gone Knights was, she could never be Cap'n of the Rooks. So Fornax must be learning things he had never heard, even though Shibo had been with the Rooks for quite a time.

This didn't surprise Killeen. She spoke little beyond the essential. Killeen had heard from Cermo that she had een living on her own, in the shadow of a mech factory, when the Rooks passed near. They accepted her, but the Knight ways were different. She ate and worked and marched and sexed her own way—in fact, was close with no Rook at all. Fornax felt that.

Killeen said, "Mantis has brains in all parts. So we plugged as much as we could."

Ledroff said, "I grant we've seen no such mech before. But we got it this time."

Shibo shook her head. "Mantis replace."

Fornax twisted his face into a look of dismissal. "With what? We left its parts on the ground!"

"Something could carry parts for it," Killeen said mildly. "Maybe even mechminds."

"Easier to send 'nother Mantis," Fornax countered.

Killeen answered, "Not if it's specially made."

"For what?" Fornax asked.

"Hunting us."

Fornax slapped his knees in derision. "*All* Marauders hunt us."

"Marauders do jobs, not just look for us," Killeen said. "If they see us, they track. Attack, if looks right. Not able to send illusions straight into us like Mantis, though."

Fornax sniffed and shrugged. "Lookyou, I know you downed the Mantis."

"Twice," Killeen said.

"Good. But no reason make big noise 'bout it."

Killeen knotted his fists and made himself say nothing. There was no room for dispute between Rook and Bishop.

"How you suppose it knew where so many of us were together?" Ledroff said, obviously breaking in to soothe matters over.

Shibo said, "Made."

"What?" Fornax asked.

She looked at him with eyes of pearly white against a skin long tanned into a deep though somehow translucent mahogany. "Made us meet."

"Our two Families?"

"Yeasay."

Fornax said loudly, "Nossir noway! We sighted a Baba Yagga two days back. Came this way, gettin' clear. Saw a

Rattler crossing on a far ridge, south. Just accident we come
down that valley, makin' distance from the Rattler before
we turned south again. Just—"

He saw the point then and stopped. There came a long
silence as Killeen felt the true enormity of what they faced.
The Mantis was using Rattlers and Baba Yaggas and all the
other Marauders. That undoubtedly included whatever had
cornered them back in the Trough, and surekilled Jake. All
to drive the Bishops toward the Rooks and in the moment
of their meeting harvest a field of death.

Jake was a minor loss, compared to the catastrophe
which had hardstruck them in the moment of their human
vulnerability. The joy of reuniting and rekindling the
human connections which were in the end what made them
human at all. That had been slamshut in a grotesque
instant. And now the survivors carried the inner festering
sore of that moment too well remembered, the acrid
welding of jubilation with terror—and that union, too,
would exact a price. Killeen felt without thinking through it
that the Mantis was far more understanding of humanity
than any mech had been. It knew how to wound them in
their selfhood, their abiding sense of community. And was
therefore far more dangerous than any crafty Lancer or
Barb.

TWO

The two Families decided that morning to continue with
separate Cap'ns. A single Cap'n would mean a single
Family. Losing a full Family from the Clan was intolerable.
Likewise, neither Family would accept its own formal end.

The talking took hours. Ledroff and Jocelyn negotiated
with the Rooks at a full Witnessing, since the Rooks had no
Cap'n. They observed all titles and rituals and other
proceedings, not hastening a single phrase or gesture. Each
step carried the same liturgical gravity and sober, attentive
detail as had been the tradition for centuries.

There was a quietly forlorn and obliging comfort in
this. Humans used the shaping and polishing of phrases as a

refuge from the raw rub of their lives. The telling of stories, the artful arch of talk—these made ornate and prettily baroque what otherwise and most logically would be usually a swift and simple business. This, too, gave them the momentary soft shelter of the vast human heritage, even though only half-remembered, fogged and blunted. They talked on, relishing.

In the Citadels such conversations had followed on a month's rapt preparatory gossip. Witnessings were once wreathed by ceremony in arched, chromed vaults. Now their high officers conferred as they squatted, scratchy and grimed, about the rude pyramid of the newdead. Once each Family had numbered thousands. In this tribal talk no one yielded even a phrase which admitted to their shrunken status.

The Rooks made Fornax their Cap'n. They would have integrated the Family Rook topo display into his sensorium, too, as was traditional. But the woman who knew how to do that was a wizened old techtype named Kuiper, and she had fallen the day before.

Fornax and Ledroff seemed not to get on well. They did agree that the Families should march. It was risky to remain anywhere near the Mantis carcass, even after its dismemberment. Passing Marauders could perhaps repair it. And there might be more than one Mantis.

Killeen felt a vague unease, for no one seemed to have grasped the essential difference between it and the other Marauders. The Mantis died but rose again. It seemed to have been designed for persistence, for unflagging and remorseless energy, and especially for tracking humans.

Only the narrow human sense of category had lumped it together with the Marauders, as though the Clans were unwilling to grant it in their language the status of a preserve beyond and above the well-known pillagers of human destiny. Though they knew of vast mech cities, of bewildering constructions and enterprises unfathomable, something in the human spirit drew back from assigning a name or emblem to the unreachable heights a Mantis might imply.

No one had ever seen anything like a Mantis scavenging or navvy-policing or hunting the assets of other mech cities. It was not from a class of laborers. Unlike Marauders, it did no apparent work. It had no known interest but human-hunting. Killeen's own father had sighted something resembling the Mantis a few years before and lived to report it. Clannish legend spoke of various seldom-seen mechs, striding down through centuries of obliterated foraging parties and terrifying moments when many-legged silhouettes scrambled across a distant horizon. These higher orders left broken lives and widestrewn suredeath, but even more tangibly now they bequeathed to the Families a tradition of inherited horror, both ghostly and undeniable, living in the dry sure images of Aspect memory as well as in rumored encounters which few humans ever survived.

It was impossible for Killeen to believe all this could be due to the Mantis.

Killeen's own father had carefully laid out for his son the whole litany of Marauder types, the slow, resonant precision of his voice bespeaking the high human price that learning each facet had cost—and, if forgotten even for a terrible moment, could cost again.

Killeen now knew each Marauder signature from experience in the open ground. But even more strongly he felt it in the remembered mournful way his father's voice had lowered as he gave over to his son the ancient folklore and skills. *Thing about aliens is, they're alien*, he had said innumerable times. With a gravelly chuckle he would add, *Plan on bein' surprised*.

The most terrible fact of all was that Marauders killed only as a side task. Even Lancers, the vicious, darting, smalleyed protectors of factories, would attack humans only at the factory site.

Only the Calamity contradicted this rule. Perhaps it was fitting that his father had fallen at the Citadel Bishop, for that had ended an era. Killeen had not seen his father's end, had caught only scattershot words over the comm while himself fleeing with Toby, and heard later the lists of those gone. So the details, perhaps best not known, had mingled with so many other questions, lingering in the twilight of all things unfathomable.

* * *

In the freshening air of halfmorning they harvested the property of the dead. Killeen found himself a bubble pack made of some shiny mechstuff he had never seen before. It saved him kilos of carrymass and caught snugly at waist and hips and shoulders. Each of the dead yielded up their compacted food and water flasks, by far the most useful of the mute legacy.

Killeen stood and chewed on a wad of tough gum that Old Robert had been carrying. He watched Cermo fit himself with a carbo-aluminum set of shank compressors, clasping the mechmetal so it snugged into his flared-out boot cuffs. Others wore makeshift hip shock absorbers and double-walled helmets, loading themselves up with equipment Killeen full well knew they would spend a week discarding as it proved heavy or vexing. Killeen preferred to carry food and fluids and forget the extras. Twice he had broken ribs in falls because he'd worn no chest protector.

While others hammered and fitted, Killeen rested, using only his web-jacket as a pillow, and hooked a derisive eyebrow at the softrolls some toted to sleep on. He had to stop Toby from trying to load on a cook-kit. It was a marvelous little thing, subtly shaped from flexmetal by some ancient hand. It would flare into life with bluehot flame. But it gave the boy too much packmass and Killeen had no idea how to find the fuel for it. He seldom ate cooked food anyway. Marauders could sniff the fumes halfway around Snowglade, he suspected.

The Families slowly pulled themselves together as morning stretched into noon. Ledroff and Fornax consulted their Aspects and argued over what route to take. Killeen stayed out of it. Jocelyn invariably backed Ledroff's ideas, and gave other small signs that her relationship with Killeen was now cool at best. Killeen shrugged this off, though it hurt a little.

The Families were listless, the emotional backwash of yesterday leaving them pensive and slow. He felt some of it himself. It mingled with his hangover, from a small transparent vial of aromatic fruit wine he had found on the body of Hedda, a woman of the Rooks. He had shared it out with three Rooks and Shibo. Even a cup of its amber silkiness held a vicious punch. He had not sipped much but still he was ashamed that he had fled into drink again. A thickening headache spread across his brow and burrowed into his eyes. That reminded him of his trouble seeing detail at long distances, so he went in search of Angelique.

She seemed to welcome his asking, and broke out her tools. Killeen had always rather liked the feel of being worked on as the camp commotion around him gradually quickened. He relaxed into the softness of humanity, the implicit reassurance of daily ritual.

He was sitting rock-still when he noticed the woman nearby. Angelique was tinkering with the farseer at the back of his neck. He couldn't turn his clamped head but he did shift his eyes a fraction. The woman was unnaturally still. He swiveled his eyes farther. Even this made Angelique grunt and hoarsely swear at him. She was the last Bishop who knew anything about farseers. She made a few adjustments in his neck, slapped the fleshmetal cover closed, and poked him sharply in the ribs with her fibertool. Killeen yelped.

Angelique said coolly, "Just checking your reflexes. Seem fine."

"Like hell."

"Next time sit still." Angelique grinned and walked away, her chromed leggings reflecting crisp Denix-light.

Killeen massaged his neck and tested his eyes by closeupping the woman nearby. She was a Rook, young and well muscled. Her black hair swirled up from her temples like an ebony firestorm, poking jagged teeth into the air. He zoomed in on her eyes and saw there blueblack threads entwining with crimson blood vessels. She sat stiffly, unmoving, head canted as if she were listening to someone unseen.

She was. Her lips moved rapidly, soundlessly, as she tried to give voice to the torrent of Aspect talk that raged through her.

Killeen had not seen anyone so possessed in a long time, not since the retreat from the unfolding disaster of Big Alice Springs. Drool formed on the woman's lips. Her left hand began to jump. In a moment a twitching around her right eye seemed to answer the hand.

Killeen sent a signal to Fornax. It was his job to take

care of his own. Toby came ambling over, his pack already mounted, and stared at the woman. "Jazz, a clowner," he said.

"Don't call them that," Killeen said, watching the woman carefully.

"She's really goin'."

"Be okay."

"Don' look it."

"Gotta expect some of this."

"*I* don't 'spect it."

"Aspects die if their hosts die, y'know. They got a righta be scared."

"What're they doin'?"

"If they get panicked, they start talking all at once." Killeen felt awkward apologizing for somebody else's Aspects.

Toby stared with the unashamed fascination of the young. "Can't she turn 'em off?"

"Not if they're all goin' at once."

"Why're her eyes rollin' up?"

White showing all around her irises. Lips pulled back in a rictus from yellowed teeth.

"Damn! Where's Fornax?"

Killeen touched the woman's face. It felt clammy, spongy.

"Lookit her hands." Toby didn't know to be worried.

Killeen glanced around, saw no Fornax, nothing but some Rooks looking their way. "They're taking big chunks of her sensorium. Living through it."

"They can see us?"

Killeen hesitated. He didn't want Toby to have to think about things like this, not added on to everything else that had happened. But the boy would wonder anyway, now that he'd seen. "Yeasay. When Aspects get like this, they drop the filters we have. They let everything flood in. Try grab all the world they can, while they can."

"Jazz . . ."

"But if they overdo it—"

The woman jumped to her feet. She began to dance frantically, kicking high with her boots, flailing her arms in impossible arcs. Her feet and hands were in the air at the same time, forming strange arches and rhythms. She crashed to the ground. Legs flailed and she kept dancing. She kicked wildly against the dirt and stones. By sheer effort she thrust herself upright again, legs still pumping wildly. Her whole body writhed in absurd fast-time, counterpointing every movement of hands or legs. Sweat jumped out all over her and yet her face remained impassive. She blinked incessantly, as though strobe-cutting her vision, and her eyes rolled farther into her head. Her mouth opened. A low, guttural song. The notes slid into a moan as she heat-danced faster, throwing up a cloud of dust.

Toby backed away, startled, his mouth turning down at the corners with dismay and fright. Killeen pushed him away farther and then leaped at the woman's back. She twisted, all the while keeping up the mad rapt dance. She flailed at him open-handed. Her right foot caught him in the knee with a back kick that was part of the frantic syncopation and he went sprawling. He looked around. Family were running this way, but he could not see Fornax. The woman got back to her feet from sheer force of her drumming heels. She began to leap higher and higher, using her boots to perform huge, exaggerated pirouettes. Abruptly a soprano shriek burst from her.

Killeen lunged at her again. This time he caught her as she prepared for another grand leap. He popped open a small capillary mound on her shoulder. With a wrench he rolled her back over his hip, thrusting his weight against her to stop her from moving.

The capillary socket was an ageold feature of every human. It had been designed directly into the human DNA to give ready access to the brain. Using it demanded precise tools. Opening it required delicate adjustments. It was the most exacting portal in the body.

Killeen stuck his finger in it.

She howled, flexed—and went limp.

Toby helped cradle her to the ground. Killeen clapped the capillary shut and was thumbing the tablock back in place when Fornax's voice boomed from above. "Don't open that. Don't you know—and that's Ann! One of ours!"

"Yeasay," Killeen said, getting to his feet. "I won't open"

"You—you've *already* popped it." Fornax looked ghast, his pale lips pulled back above his scraggly beard.

"No choice. Aspects were ridin' her."

"You could've—"

"Let her hurt herself, pull a muscle, pop a seam. ure."

Fornax bristled. "That is a Rook Family matter!"

Killeen saw Fornax was going to stand on principle and that moment took his measure of the man. "Yeasay, and I pologize."

"You put your *finger* . . ."

"Stops 'em, usually."

"You might've caused mental damage!" Fornax was still ngry, unable to let go of it right away even in the face of an pology. Even as his eyes still flashed their stern admoni- on, his mouth pursed in momentary inner reflection. illeen saw that the man let his emotions run on until his ead caught up, put a brake on things. Not a good way to be ap'n. At least Killeen knew that much.

"Her Aspects got so much spunk, let *them* fix her ental stuff," Killeen said.

"Well now, I—"

Toby burst in, "*You* weren't here. Had do somethin'!"

Killeen patted him on the shoulder, pleased and yet ot wanting Fornax to get the idea the boy was a nartmouth. "Rooksay wins here, Toby."

Toby persisted, "But it—"

A long, steaming moment passed between the two en.

"Thanks for your help," Fornax said gruffly, suddenly ware of others watching. "Both you," nodding at the boy.

Killeen touched his forehead in way of tribute. Fornax ad made a good, quick change, showing the sort of control eople expected of a Cap'n. He decided Fornax wasn't half- ad. The march to come would be a finer, truer test. Still, e could see that Ledroff and Fornax might weather and row into the kind of Cap'ns the Families so desperately eeded. Neither of them was worth Fanny's left thumb, but en, who was?

* * *

They marched hard for two days. On the open, sunwashed plain their only safety lay in fluidity. Ledroff an
Fornax kept the Families separated into two triangula
wedges with three fore-scouts, four flanking, and thre
trailers. Marauders had a history of attacking from the rea
flank, often using as approaching cover a ridgeline jus
crossed by the trailers.

They headed inward, toward the apparent center c
the Splash. They had only crude navigation and no on
knew how old this Splash was. Yet as they skip-walke
across sloped valleys the evidence gathered about them
Brambles gave way to thick-leaved bushes. Dry scru
slowly ebbed. Tufts of tan sprouted in the shadows
Streambeds yielded moist soil only a single spadeful down

Midafternoon of the second day, the Families wer
beginning subtly to intermingle. They traded encourage
ment and information about easier routes with the ease c
worn veterans. Killeen could feel a slow melding. Perhap
the genetic and historical basis for keeping Familie
separate would recede before the tide of necessity an
diminished numbers. But this was a detail, compared t
their seldom-spoken yet always-felt dilemma. They sough
refuge.

They were a people seasoned in the Citadels, in th
enveloping comforts of a fixed sanctuary. Only the daring
the brave and young, had gone forth from the Citadels t
capture and steal from the mechciv. Now all the Family ha
to live as nomads. Their only hostels were the Troughs and
the rare Casas. So they clung to the hope of some fina
resting site, some permanence in a reeling world.

Killeen ruminated on this vaguely, glad that they ha
Cap'ns to confront such issues. He felt Arthur's presence
simmering in the back of his mind, and the cool, ironi
voice arose:

You realize, don't you, that humanity started as
nomads?

"Back before the Citadels?"

Far before that, of course. Surely you remember
what I discussed before?

"Damnation, I can't recall everything! You'd rather talk
than *breathe*, way I see it."

I've told you, I don't have adequate maps of this
Splash. It is recent. But I *am* sorry about that
messy episode when you awoke two days ago.
We *are* worried; and I suppose it does come out
at the worst times for you, and in the worst way.

"Just keep your place. No jabber. I got be sharp."

Let me merely add that the nomad way of life is
genetically quite all right for us humans. Civilization is a relatively recent invention—

"Mechciv you mean?"

No, *our* civilization. Not simply the crude forms
we had in the Citadels. The *original* human
society. It was vast, glorious! They built the ships
which brought us here—a voyage of incomprehensible distance. They came to make contact with the voices they could hear over radio.
They—

"Whose?"
Arthur's voice begrudged the fact:

Well, apparently the transmissions were leakage
from a faction of mech civilization. But understand, it spoke in a difficult code, one we may
have misinterpreted. The original Captains were
coming to find what the message promised—a
library of all galactic knowledge. Think of it!—
the collected writings and pictures and songs,
who knows what wealth? The Captains' ships
could cruise just under the speed of light. Even

so, their voyage required over seventy thousand years. Such sacrifice—

"They came to learn from *mechs*?" To Killeen this was as incomprehensible as learning from a stone, or the air. Mechs simply *were*, a force of nature beyond communication.

Well, admittedly—

Shibo's high-pitched call came to him, —Duster!— from the other side of a narrow, stony valley. It jolted him from his running-reverie.

The Families instantly dropped to the ground and sought shelter. Over a far mesa drifted a four-winged thing that glinted like finespun copper in the Eater's slanting hotblue radiance. It had a light and lazy look, Killeen thought. He had not seen one for some time but this one did not have the determined straightline way to it.

Shibo's clipped voice showed she had made the same conclusion. —Duster empty. Looking.—

"Figure it's on its way back home? Surveying?" Killeen squinted at the slender sweptback body. No signs of the pale white dust that usually descended in a thin, precise stream.

—It saw.—

"Dunno if it pick us up. Pretty far away."

—Not dusting. Looking.—

The Families lay downdoggo for a long while as the craft swooped and glided in elegant curves. Killeen appreciated its movement, waiting silent and unthinking for it to go. They had all learned long ago to let mechs pass unopposed unless the odds were lopsided for them. Against Dusters there were never any advantages.

When the Duster dropped below the horizon they began a fast skip-walk in the opposite direction. Killeen had Toby come closer and watched the right near flank more often. The Marauders never worked with Dusters, as near as anyone could tell, but since the Mantis Killeen expected anything, everything.

So it was that he heard the sound of metallic agony

before the others. It wafted over his sensorium in a high, skimming note and then was gone. Killeen signaled to the rest and compiled a vector fix. It pointed to a nearby brush-choked arroyo.

Killeen slipped through wiry brambles and glimpsed the source of the thin, microwave scream. A Rattler, absorbed in its work.

The thing had seized a whole squad of alloy-navvys. The navvys were apparently trying to set up a processing plant next to a rich ore seam. The Rattler was devouring each, its belly already fired up. Killeen could hear the deep bass ground-shaking tremor as it melted them down into easily portable assets. A gut-roar came from the Rattler as it digested, its ceramo-ribs contracting with pops and groans as it forced navvys into its innards.

Nearby, two burning hulks still fumed. They were the manager mechs that had been watching over this work crew. With these eliminated, the navvys could only squeak calls to their distant city. This far into the Splash, the Rattler's own transport would be here to carry away the plunder before help arrived.

Killeen signaled the others to stay back.

Rattlers were not dangerous when working at their main tasks. Some Marauders were scavengers, like the Scrabblers or Snouts. They were fairly easy to avoid if you were quick and posted scouts. Others were agents in the incessant conflict between different mech cities. The Pickers and Rattlers and Stalkers had started to appear long before Killeen's father's time, seemingly in response to the inevitable scarcities of raw materials.

Rattlers were elongated, treacherous machines which seemed to coil and recoil as they moved. They searched out low-level mechs of other cities and dismantled them, breaking them down for spare parts or simple metals. Their jointed, slipsliding skins housed long tubular smelters and foundries.

Killeen had come upon one with his father, long ago. It had been trying to eat some minor mech. The Citadel had needed large-scale spare parts then, the kind that Marauders had in plenty. So their band had waited until the Rattler

was fully distended, lying like a gorged tube of scratched
aluminum, beginning to excrete ingots of ore.

They had descended at that vulnerable moment and
gutted it quick-clean, tearing away parts and frying its
mainmind. They also ambushed the Rattler's ore carriers,
when they dutifully arrived.

That had been one of the best times he had ever had
with his father. Just the two of them, prowling the flanks of
the scavenging band. Killeen had potted a Snout that
carried edible foods for its organic parts. They had both
stuffed themselves with the greasy goo.

They had been out six days in all, and returning on the
morning of the seventh they had learned that Killeen's
mother had died while they were gone. There was nothing
they could have done. She had caught one of the plagues
left over from the era when the mechs had tried to elimi-
nate humanity through bioengineered virulence. Plagues
seldom surfaced anymore, mostly because the biosphere
was too weak to support them long. But even the old epi-
demics, lying dormant in some ditch, could mutate and
infest again. Her death had brought Killeen and his father
closer in the narrowing years before the Calamity.

Staring at the gorging Rattler, Killeen felt the old
struggle within himself. His vision narrowed to a red-
rimmed halo around the booming, insufferably ugly thing.
The pipings of the Family dimmed, his sensorium world
fell away. Crisp lightning forked bluehot in his eyes. He
seemed pitched forward, balancing on the balls of his feet,
ready to rush in a satisfying pureblind rage, to bring
desolation and dismemberment to the self-absorbed and
smug-ugly Rattler.

Then he felt a hand on his arm and Shibo whispered,
"Still."

"I, I got—"

"Go."

"Kill 'em *all*, the damned—"

"Go now."

"I . . . I just . . ."

Her hand lay cool and strong on him. He felt the
tightness in him ebb. He sensed the others hanging back at

the mouth of the arroyo, felt their puzzlement at why he had ventured this far in.

"Needless. Rattler's carriers arrive soon."

"I . . ."

"Only way beat Marauders is *learn* them."

"But—"

"Not risk self. Remember Toby."

"I . . . yeasay. Yeasay."

They left the Marauder to its meal.

THREE

They moved swiftly, driven by the mere glancing encounter with the Duster and Rattler. The slowly thickening vegetation around them had seemed an unspoken promise of verdant peace. Only as they put distance behind them did this assurance return.

The Families whispered among themselves about the air's soft moisture, the pale emerald grass, the twisted brown vines and creepers which sprouted from crevices and small sheltered basins. To find a Rattler obliviously doing its job in this surrounding undercut their unvoiced dream. It propelled them faster toward the center of the Splash.

Killeen himself felt no such flight response. Marauders angered him without touching any longer the wellsprings of fear. To him they were a constant threat, hateful but natural.

Even in the first moment of glimpsing the Rattler he had thought it blandly evil, a scene without any possible protagonist. The navvys being eaten as they cried for their distant protector were no less an ancient enemy than the Rattler which digested them. And even as red rage had seized him and his memories had swelled, he had taken the time to notice that the Rattler's treads were snarled with brambles caught in the links. It was harder for mechs to move in the plant-clogged terrain here. Another small advantage. Another way that Splashes revived the once-green world.

Ledroff called for a song. Across the comm sensorium soared an ancient Family march, composed far in the past by some great groundstriding marshal. Killeen let the pounding spirit of the music come into him. Family song poured from his throat.

This was his favorite legacy, far better than the Aspects' whole gobbled lifetimes of streaming talk. He liked this form of the melodic art especially, the forward tilt to it, the wonderful, sweeping Moze Art. How many generations back in the Family had the composer lived? Perhaps the man was a great-grandfather. Killeen would like to be able to claim close kinship. Arthur tried to blurt out some ancient lore, but Killeen was too transfixed by the artful rhythms to pay attention.

As he loped to the song's surge and play he noted that the Family was moving faster. Ledroff had summoned up the firm rhythms to get them quickly away from the Rattler, damping fears. It had worked.

—Duster!— someone cried.

The music stopped abruptly.

Killeen was caught in midstride. He glided for a long instant, hit, and rolled into a narrow dry rivulet. He sniffed through the long wavelengths. "No mechsmell."

He located Toby and then listened to the Families seeking shelter. Rook mothers and fathers called, plaintive and hysterical, for their children. Panic edged the sensorium.

Shibo sent, —Naysay. Look.—

He closeupped the horizon and at first could not believe what he saw. Had Angelique fouled his farseer? These flying objects looked distant, but they smelled to be close by. . . .

Shibo sent a clear, calm, —Birds.—

Astonished, the Families got to their feet. They brushed off dirt and peered at the fluttering, living skyfog. Hundreds of specks darted and twittered above the bushes.

For a long moment no one said anything. Then a cheer rang through the comm. Some of the younger ones had never seen a thing aloft not made of metal. They had thought only mechs ruled the air, much as their emissions stained the dawn sky a milky gray.

Toby ran forward, shouting "Heyyea! Heyyea!" The tiny agents of organic life, instead of greeting him as a member of their kin, burst upward into a surprised, fleeing cloud. Toby blinked, startled.

Killeen laughed. "You'll have go easy with 'em."

Toby frowned. "Don't they *like* us?"

"Life's born scared."

"Scared even of life?"

" 'Specially."

"Mechs aren't."

"Mechs're 'fraida mechs. 'Member those navvys calling Mayday back there?"

Toby nodded decisively. "Mechs're 'fraid *us*, too."

Killeen gave his son a wan smile, knowing exactly why the boy wanted to assert himself with such a baldly false declaration. "Maybe," he answered mildly.

"Are." Toby fingered the burnished-steel disk pistol on his belt, unconsciously stroking this small emblem of power.

"Navvys and managers'll call Mayday when they see us, but that's 'cause they mistake us for enemy mechs."

Toby's mouth twisted into a look of derisive mirth. "Naysay!"

"Is."

"We're two-legged. Mechs're treaded."

"So?"

"Mechs see that."

"Our 'quipment's mechmetal. Navvys see that, is all."

"Nosay noway," Toby said firmly. To end this slight affront to his inner picture of human status, he booted off to his marching position. Killeen watched him go, a thin figure skip-walking with oblivious lithe grace over rumpled scrub and gully.

Toby needed to feel that humanity dealt at least on even terms with the mechs, that there was a scheme of loss and gain to their endless running. It was a way to accept and put behind him the slaughter of the day before. Killeen would not lie to him, but all the same he could avoid saying plainly what the boy was slowly seeing: that humans mattered so little even navvys were unprogrammed to react to them. Only Marauders carried orders regarding humans, and those were rules of simple extermination. Even the fearsome Mantis probably had no great status in mech culture.

Killeen himself needed to let the slaughter slip behind him. He could not simply spend long hours arranging his hair, staring pensively into space, as some like Jocelyn did—building arabesques that would dissolve the next time he put on his helmet. That never worked.

Killeen felt the shocked regret and sorrow as a heavy, black, blunt pressure inside, undefined and unreachable. He seldom talked of such dimly felt obstructions. There had been a time when Jocelyn had tried to get him to handle his feelings that way. It had only made him feel awkward and stupid, his tongue a dumb, leathery, betraying instrument.

He decided to work out his frustration as he had so many times before. He called to Ledroff, "I'll farflank left."

"Yeasay!" Ledroff answered with evident relief.

All morning the Cap'n had been the target of nags and whines. The slaughter's burden had mixed with sore feet and pulled muscles to brew a salty soup of discontent. Jocelyn had taken left flank all day and needed someone to spell her.

The land was smooth and young here, as though the blunt elements had smudged instead of cutting. The hills ran in jumbled groups where massive ridges slumped. Killeen ran in long lopes at the farthest extremity of the Families' sensorium. He saw from this distance that they were crossing regular undulations in the terrain. These rises and falls slightly curved away from the advancing human triangles. Killeen frowned at this puzzle.

A coy tickler came from Arthur:

Given that we are in a Splash, this is unsurprising.

Killeen sensed the Aspect's mild pique at not being directly consulted. Still, he was damned if he'd be coaxed into asking. He waited a moment and Arthur said nothing more. Killeen eased Bud's Face into full activity.

1. Splash makes shock waves.
2. Spread out from center.
3. Compress rock.
4. Leaves ridgelines.
5. Ridges curve around center.
6. Easy to see.

Before Killeen could respond Arthur spat acidly,

That is *one* hypothesis, yes. And only narrowly is it the most likely. I would venture that these ridgelines were formed by a reflected set of shock waves. Recall that this tundra had been laid sometime before by the Dusters. Under it lies the glacial ice of Snowglade, which the Dusters have isolated from the biosphere, thus making our environment so dry. The shock waves caused momentary melting of these ice beds. This forced upthrusts, forming the ridges. When—

1. Too complicated.
2. Just follow the curves.
3. Should get greener.

Killeen shoved Bud and Arthur back far enough that their continuing argument came to him only as a faint, querulous mutter. His boots propelled him over the next ridgeline, a feeling of freedom and quest welling in him. He saw that indeed the next rounded, lumpy hills were slightly greener. Enough of their talk had sunk in to prick his interest. The green was deepest near the hilltops, as though ice dwelled nearer the surface there. It would melt enough on a warm day to feed deep roots.

This was about as much as he could remember from his boyhood farming drudgery. At the Citadel he had preferred to rove and plunder, as had his father. Still, the art of watering crops with icemelt had stuck with him and now pricked his sense of approaching lush refuge.

He landed beside a gnarly ball of chaparral to deal with his toilet. This demanded some preparation. He had to

unslip his chest straps, his carrybelt, and his traveling
jockbrace. Adopting the position left one vulnerable, but
still he preferred solitude. The gratification of his daily
squatting came first from being alone and momentarily free
of Family. Second, there was the abstract satisfaction of
aiding green life through his unwanted excretions. Third,
in the desolation of Snowglade the act gave vent to his
sweaty self, his internal squeezings and bubblings, processes he no more thought about than he did his cyberrhythms
and circuit defenses and sensoria. In a hard world it was—
though he never would have admitted it—a simple,
eloquent pleasure.

He relaxed into elemental sensation, just as he eased
into the moist clasp of alcohol when he could. As he
squatted and relieved himself he was abruptly surprised to
see a small mouse venture from a tangle of crusty vines and
stare at him.

This was the first animal Killeen had seen in years. He
blinked, startled. The mouse peered up at the man-
mountain and squeaked. It seemed unafraid but in some
way puzzled.

"Know what I am?"

Moist eyes studied him warily.

"I'm like you! See?"

Tiny paws arched, ready to run.

"We both crap, even."

A nose twitched skeptically.

"See? I'm flesh too. Not a mech."

The small furry thing was fascinated with Killeen's size.
It sniffed audibly. They studied each other across an
unbridgeable chasm.

Finally he finished his toilet and stood up. "Heysay,
found a mouse," he sent on the general sensorium. This
provoked cries of delight. When Killeen booted off the
hillside and onward, the mouse was still gazing, tiny eyes
bright and clear.

That night they camped between two twisted hills.
Ledroff gave Killeen the midnight guard duty, though this
was the third night in a row he had stood it. Ledroff was

growing into the Cap'ncy, but leaned on Killeen a bit harder than on the others.

Shibo did part of the watch with him. She was firm about keeping talk to a minimum, so their sensoria could pick up the smallest signal. Killeen liked the simple feel of her company. The night was cloud-shrouded, but stars broke through in patches.

Her watch was next and they had to circle the camp once as he showed her the minor telltales he had spied in the shadowed plain. It was pleasant to walk beside her, even if they spent the time in nearly wordless, sensorium-linked communion, than to lie inert and resting in the camp, sleep shot through by conflicts.

"Quiet?"

"Plenty," he answered.

Her broad smile split the gloom, a white crescent. "Tired?"

"Naysay. Could kick down a mountain."

"Ummmm!" she murmured in mock admiration.

"Sleep good?"

"Hard ground."

"Ball up some them bushes, make a pad."

"Best pad human."

Her glittering eyes caught the dim Eater disk-radiance and he saw that she was jazzing him. "Man or woman?"

"Man best."

"Nope. Woman's best. Got more fat."

"Fat? Naysay."

"You got more'n me."

"No porker, me."

"Right kind pork. Just right."

"I lie not-flat under you."

This was not only the longest sentence he had ever heard from her, it was the most interesting. "Wouldn't 'spect you to lie flat."

"Good." Again the quick, white smile. He couldn't think of anything to say next. The ever-strobing sensorium subtly invaded them, made their worlds prickly-acute. But with him downtuned in the sexcen, the banter and wry, sideways glances finally sputtered off into the quilted halfnight, fruitless and without a sure vector. Killeen

regretted this and fumbled for a way to say it to her. But
then an animal bolted from scrub nearby and they had to
spend a while parallaxing it and being sure it was nothing
more. By that time the moment had trickled away and he
did not know how to bring them back to where they had
been. It seemed things were slipping away a lot like that
lately, that the world was hurrying by before he grasped it.

Skirting a cracked plain, Killeen heard a cool, dry
ratcheting.

"What's that?" He had been trying to coax a word or
two from Shibo. Now he stopped suddenly, head cocked.

"Singing," Shibo said.

"More Families?" Killeen asked hopefully. For years
the Bishops had thought themselves alone. Now he dared
imagine repeated miracles. Toby spent every free moment
with his new child-friends, and hungered for more.

"Strange."

"Not singing," Killeen said after a moment.
"Sorta . . ."

"No acoustics."

"Like a voice far off," Killeen said. "From a mouth
made of metal."

They scanned all directions, eyes running up and
down the spectrum, all sense amped to max. Nothing.

"I sense no mechs," Shibo confirmed.

"What's it saying?"

"Heard such once. Magnetic."

"Huh?" Killeen shifted to the ultraviolet and caught a
faint radiance.

He felt the hairs rise on the back of his neck.

Something hovered in the night.

But nothing made of matter.

He had been looking for approaching figures on the
hummocked ground and had not paid attention to the air
above. He saw above them playing tides of gauzy luminescence. Down from some lofty focus sprayed lines of tangled
bluewhite light. He amped his eyes still more, blessing
Angelique's expert craft.

The lines made an immense dim web. It spread
angularly across the sky, narrowing and converging toward
the south. Killeen sent a silent question to Arthur.

You're seeing the dipolar lines of Snowglade's magnetic field. It varies inversely as the cube of the distance from the southern pole—which lies below the horizon, beyond that butte. This local pattern, however, is some type of anomaly. I do not understand it, but I can speculate—

"Answer!" Shibo urged.

She heard something he did not. Killeen's caution made him hesitate. The thing might be an extrusion of the mechs, after all.

He listened hard. Once he'd shut off Arthur's small, warbling voice he could just barely pick up a strumming.

I stem and break and waver. Hear me out. Now!

Killeen shot a questioning glance at Shibo. Her smooth face was rapt.

"Where're you from?" Killeen asked on the sensorium. With effort he made his voice a blend of acoustics and electrospeech. He constricted his throat like a man trying to imitate a frog. The effect, transduced and filtered by buried chips, sent electromagnetic ringings into the fine, thin air.

There was a long moment of wind-stirred silence. Then,

The storms howl where I am. You are but vague whisperings. You talk so fast.

"I said, where're you from?"
Again the stretched moments.

I circle the Eater.

"So do we," Killeen said, exasperated.

Above he saw flickering orange gouts descending along the blue field lines. Arthur's voice squeaked in his mind, pointing out that these were particles infalling toward the pole, striking the atmosphere, making a gauzy aurora.

These tracers showed him the enormity of it. The auroral voice-thing had shaped the local field lines into a magnetic cone which spread down from a point far above. A tentlike web fanned evenly to all sides. Killeen saw he and Shibo were at the center of the circle it marked out. So it was no accident; the thing intended to speak specifically to them.

> I am slow. Stretched this far, I tire. I wanted to reach a being called Killeen.

Killeen blinked with such startlement that his eyes flipped into the gaudy infrared. "Wha—? That's me!"

In long seconds of silence he thought he heard several faint, timorous voices whistling down the field lines. Sliding forth from some immense, outlined presence.

> I have a message for you. Here.

Subtly the ringing tone shifted, as though reciting.

> Don't try to build a Citadel. Keep moving. Ask for the Argo.

"What? What's an Argo?"

> I am relaying this message. I do not understand its content.

"Where's it from?"

> It comes from further in. Toward the Eater.

"Who from?"

> I do not know what kind of thing sends it.

Shibo asked pointedly, "What're *you* then?"

> A knit of magnetic flux. A mere garment, some say, for plasma winds to wear. I swim in copper-hinged light, beside the mouth that knows no end. I

am trapped in many-poled field lines, wrapped
rubbery about the accreting disk of the Eater.

Killeen sputtered, puzzled, "How in hell did you *get*
here?"

I once was something else. I do not know what.
Perhaps an Aspect. Now I am a holy anointed
spinning toroid of plasma and field.

"Why?" Killeen asked.
Whisperings, drones.

Why but? What else is worth a glance? I tell
you, little Killeen: Not marble, not the gilded
monuments of princes, shall outlive me.

Fancy language lost him immediately. "Huh?"

Immortal, I am. They say.

"They?" Shibo asked.

The makers of this place, this soft castle that
flies on turbulent winds, above the glaring stretched disk of infalling, roiling hot.

To accompany this sharply spoken line, jade-cool
glories lit the elegantly curving field lines. Killeen wondered how far those energetic stabs of phosphorescence
had come. If the thing that spoke was at the Eater, which
loved in the far-off sky . . .
"You're *in* the Eater disk?"

My tangled feet are, aye. My head scrapes
against the stars.

They stood in stunned silence. "Were human?" Shibo
ventured at last. Along the wispy field-strands flowed
yellow, burnt-gold, orange, as though the being was
marshaling its resources, or riffling through vast dusty files
of magnetic memory.

> **Again, I do not know. I was some form of being, mortal, awash in entropy's swamp. Long ago. Something within me hails from long-gone fossil ages.**

Killeen struggled with conflicting impulses. There was something horrible about a thing so grotesquely big. But it spoke with a stringy tone that recalled cables under tension, a tight-wound humming. In some way it was human. And it had a message for him.

"What's an Argo?"

> **Let a moment pass in reclaiming a distant part of me . . . yes, here. Not exactly Argo, but Argos, yes. More than one Argo? My phase-memory replies to me that Argos was "an early rival of Sparta." There you have it.**

"What the hell's Sparta?"

> **A city.**

"Where?" Shibo asked.

The field lines rippled. Crimson flecks shot down them.

> **I have no data. Hopelessly old, this file. And this language you use! Hobbled, rude, a simpleton's dull way of herding meaning into linear, boxy cages.**

Shibo said, "Good enough for us."

> **No doubt. To give you your due, I remark that while scanning its vocabulary I do find there entries oddly artful, even obliging. Seersucker. Sibilant. Straitlaced. Such words! With grace, they hover on the edge of meaninglessness. Argos though is without grace or content. Well, enough. I only bring this message, as was my charge, and now depart.**

"Wait!" Killeen called.

Dappled glows retreated up the field lines in a gathering rush. As they dwindled, the customary dovetailing planetary magnetic fibers reappeared, intricately pointing toward the south pole.

They watched for a long time but the presence did not return. Killeen talked about it as they finished his round, with Shibo replying in her usual grudging monosyllables. The entire episode was incomprehensible. Easy enough to obey, at least. No one had hopes of a fresh Citadel. Keeping on the move was a necessity, not a choice.

"What in hell's an Argos?" Killeen demanded of Shibo, exasperated.

"Ask Aspect."

Arthur piped in immediately:

I suspect this is a transmission error. Argos was a city in classical Greece, on Earth. Its role in early intellectual—

Killeen cut off the Aspect's wearying ramble and strode along beside Shibo. Whatever the field-being had meant was of no matter now, for the message was plainly old and pointless. Killeen resolved to do as he usually did, and not trouble himself with the warehouse of dusty data and massing history that the Aspects were forever pressing upon him.

Many of his older Aspects gave less and less information as they aged. A kind of senility set in. The nattering insect voices could recall a party three centuries ago but were vague about mech insignias seen last week. And the fineries they recalled from the Arcologies—opulent, crystal ballrooms the size of hills, sideboards groaning with sweetmeats, gowns translucent yet crisply warm—filled Killeen with a resentful, shamed envy.

The oldest Aspects were the worst, yammering of impossible glories. Other Family members felt the same. Jocelyn could hardly bear to call up hers; they were unusually aged and sent her pictures of wealth she knew had to be faked.

Images of the magnetic being ricocheted in Killeen's

mind, mingling with faint Aspect talk. He shook his head to clear it.

Pay Aspects true attention and they would rob him of the grittiness of the world, its supple rub.

He left Shibo and made back toward camp, letting himself feel the slumbering wealth of the Splash. He never tired of it. *So green*, he thought. *So green, green, green.*

FOUR

They marched on amid a sense of greening and convergence. The undulating hills gave their pace a sensual rhythm. Small, squeaking things scampered from underfoot. Verdant wealth and sweet air lulled them. For a full day they saw no sign of mechlife. It was as though the dry, dead world the mechs had made of Snowglade had vanished. From long-slumbering depths seeped out old moist richness.

Ledroff and Fornax had fallen to disagreeing at each rest stop. They kept their steadily running dispute well within Clan bounds, yet could not repress their edgy irritation with each other. Even the pacing of their march was disputed, seemingly resolved, and disputed still again.

Ledroff urged caution. Fornax wanted to reach the center of the Splash quickly, holding that it would be rich and rife with natural foods. Fornax kept leading the Rooks out ahead of the agreed two-pronged formation. Ledroff swore at Fornax over the comm, and once slammed his own helmet to the ground in exasperation. Since helmets were the hardest piece of mancraft to make, and nobody had spares for most of the chips a full one required, this was an act both striking and impressively crazed.

They navigated by the sky. Both Families had long since lost their global survey gear. Denix gave them a sunset. Night was tempered by the Eater's wide-cut swath across the sky, making a wan, silvery twilight. Both Families stopped to rest then. This often seemed the only concrete point of agreement between them.

Killeen avoided this evening's dispute by going on

flank patrol. He took Toby with him. They walked in silence, letting their collective sensorium detect the latent caressing strum of hills and gnarled, stubby trees. It was harder here to catch the rippling tenor of distant mech movement, or sniff the oily tang of them. Life interfered. They picked up a scurrying, twittering symphony.

"Dad?" Toby's throat was raw from the day's hard skip-walking.

"Hear somethin'?"

"No, nothin' here. I was wonderin', though."

"'Bout what?"

"That woman couple days ago."

"The Aspect-crazed one."

"Yeasay."

Killeen had been expecting Toby to bring it up. "Most aren't nearly so bad."

"She be all right?"

"Prob'ly. Can walk now. Her Aspects're still a li'l scared. Want live some."

"Crazy dancin' the way she did? That's livin'?"

Toby stopped walking and turned toward his father. They stood lean and flat-muscled, shorn of padding and walkwear, stripped down to wrinkled jumpsuits. A wedge of the Eater's broad disk stuck above the horizon, spattering blue-tinged shadows on Toby's face and making it hard for Killeen to read. The boy's mouth was twisted to one side, as though containing words that tasted bad.

"She carries maybe dozen Aspects," Killeen said. "They all try to run things, they . . ." He breathed deeply, struggling to explain a sensation beyond words. Of yammering mouse-voices. Of tiny hands pressing. Itching against your inner eyeballs. "They coming at you so fast, you can't tell you-thinking from they-saying."

"Sounds . . . well . . ."

"Terrible."

Toby's mouth was still tight, the lips pulled around strangely. "Yeasay."

Killeen spread his hands in a gesture he hoped was casual. "Look, things're running pretty foul right now. Ever'body's jumpy. Aspects're people, 'member. Just kind of shrunk, is all."

"Will they be like that when they ride me?"

"Nobody said they'd ride you." Killeen spoke this halflie in hopes that it would deflect the building anger he sensed behind the misshapen mouth, but he saw that it was useless.

The words came out of the suddenly loosened lips, each one ejected like a spat tack. "Damn if they will!"

"Can't," Killeen said rapidly. "You're too young."

"I *won't*, I tell you."

"Nobody's talkin' about it, son," Killeen tried to reassure.

"Soon's we get situated, they'll start in. I'm of age, damn near."

"Not yet!" In Killeen's quick rejection he felt his own buried hope, his desire to turn back time and preserve in his boy some semblance of what his own life had once been.

"Soon."

"We got nobody can do it, anyway." The Bishop woman who could make the transfer of stored Aspects had fallen to the Mantis days before.

"Craftwoman over t'Rooks can," Toby said adamantly, and Killeen saw part of what had brought this on.

"Who?"

It all came tumbling out. "Name's Pamela, she worked on three Rooks while we were campin' back there, I saw her do it, just pops open the slot on their necks and they go numb and stiff and then the chip's in right and they get up and it's different, their eyes click all around like they never saw any ground or sky before, and they talk a funny flat way, too. Like they weren't the same people anymore even."

Toby's face now shaped into an eager, inquiring expression, as though he had let out a buried question. Killeen pulled off his fiberweb glove and grasped Toby's shoulder. "That happens every time. Aspects got be set right. Day or two, those Rooks'll be fine."

Toby's face cracked, his eyes watered. "They looked . . . looked . . ."

"I know. I know." For a long moment neither said anything, standing together on a worn slab of speckled brown rock, their faces half in chromatic shadow.

Killeen clasped his son tightly around the shoulders.

He sensed that most of their words were wasted, expressing unfinished emotions. Lots of things came out when they were supposedly discussing something else entirely. This time Killeen sensed that between them lurked sadness stemming from not just the last few days, but from years streaming backward, from the whole tortured flight down a corridor of ruin and destruction branching out from the Calamity. And of that there was nothing to say. Their lot was to endure and go on, and yet, in tribute to all that was finally human, to not forget, either.

He coughed, cleared his raspy throat. Before the moment could slide into awkward, spent lassitude, he said, "Aspects, they're our way of keepin' enough skills among us. Otherwise, we'd—"

"I *know* all that. But, I mean, I'm . . . I'm . . ."

Killeen embraced his son so the boy did not have to struggle to say more. They both knew what he felt and that there was nothing either of them could do about it. Toby was growing fast, even while on the run continually. Soon somebody would notice and the Cap'n would have to answer to the Family as a whole why Toby wasn't carrying an Aspect. There were many Aspects available, stored in chips that Ledroff toted on his right hip. Each could give the Family access to information or crafts that they might well need in a hurry sometime. And with the Rook woman available the insertion would be pretty easy.

Killeen wished he could tell Toby that he'd stop them, delay the mounting of an Aspect on the boy. But they both knew he would have to obey if the Cap'n decided.

"Look, I—"

"It's okay, Dad," Toby said, his watery voice muffled against the rough tightweave of Killeen's jumpsuit. "I know. I know."

Killeen sent Toby in after they completed the first wide circuit of the camp. The boy needed sleep, and Killeen needed to think.

To carry an Aspect was of help to the Family but it could hobble a boy, bombard him with brittle confusions, set his fresh ideas among mutiny voices. The Family was in its worse situation ever. They had lived all right for a few years after the Calamity, laying up in Casas and Troughs for long chains of comfortable days. Then there had been plenty of time to acquire an Aspect, to reconcile the tiny, disparate souls.

But now they lived on the ragged edge. There was no sure refuge. The Aspects sensed the growing desperation among them all, smelled it in the back corners of the mind. If Toby was mounted, and soon after they had to hard-march, or were attacked . . .

Making the next several circuits, Killeen several times shook his head furiously as though to clear it. Each time he had carefully thought through their situation, and had envisioned Toby's accepting an Aspect. He could not let that happen. Yet even stronger was the injunction to live by the stern rule of the Family. He saw that he would have to find a path between these two unmovable truths. There seemed no way to avoid the boy's fate.

They had been moving at a good pace the next day when Killeen made his discovery.

He came warily over a hill and saw a cracked valley where a broad slab of stone had resisted the Splash's upthrust. Small streams cut it.

He called to Jocelyn, "Easy passage to left. Open water! Bear hard by the saddleback when you cross." He headed fast downslope, across the dimpled valley and up a narrowing pass which promised a quick way through. He drank his fill in a stream. It was cold and sharp-flavored and stung his hands as he scooped it into his mouth. Then, as Family appeared over the ragged ridgeline behind him, he moved on.

It was halfway up the steeply rising slope that he saw the lonely rock slab, tilted over halfway to the ground. It had to be manmade. Mechs polished and laser-cut their rockwork. This was a rough speckled gray granite, seamed with alabaster, crossed by whispery signs. The worn edges and discolored grooves of the lettering spoke of age. Even the Citadel had not held rocks so ornately worked, so old.

He puzzled at it and at last heeded Arthur's insistence.

It's quite aged, I'll grant. Far older than I. Archaic. Not the sort of thing I would ever write, even though I was something of a scribe and bard in my first life.

"Read it."

Here, I'll have to give it the form and voice appropriate.

He,
on whose arm fame was inscribed, when, in battle in the vasty countries, he kneaded and turned back the first attack. With his breast he parted the tide of enemies—those hideous ones, mad-mechanical and unmerciful to the fallen.
He,
who crossed in warfare the seven kinds of living-dead. By his victory Snowglade did fall to Humankind.
He,
by the breezes of whose prowess the southern ocean is still perfumed.
He,
whose great zeal utterly consumed the machines by great glowing heat.
He: Like a burned-out fire in a great forest, even now leaves not his treasure, Snowglade.
He: Who led Humankind from the steel palaces aloft.
He: As if wearied, has quitted the obvious life. We give him now a bodily form in others, so that having won sole supreme sovereignty on this world, he may walk in.
Snowglade: Acquired by his arm.
He: Having the name of Chandra.
He: Who set forth Humanity in the names of the Pieces.
He: Who divided the ice among the Families.
He: Who strides among you as able forefather. He lies here as well.

By the time Arthur had finished the long, singsong chant, others of the Family had come to stand beside Killeen. He had opened Arthur to their sensoria. The low easy rhythms of it captured the Family. Even though they could not read the words inscribed deeply into the rock they had a sense of the weight of time that pressed against this message.

Mutely, one by one, they touched the slanted stone. In front of it was a slight square depression where Killeen suspected the man Chandra was buried.

He sighed and moved on up the hillside with Toby. They said nothing. Somehow the sentences from a time unimaginably distant seemed to weigh more heavily than the slaughter of yesterday. If Chandra had indeed come here long ago and driven back the mechs, he was a truly great figure.

Was Chandra an Aspect? Try as he might, Killeen could think of no Family member who carried an Aspect so named, or so powerful. But if Aspects of Chandra still lived, and Killeen could fit such an Aspect into himself, perhaps it would make him a better Family member, or better father. . . .

He was walking without truly seeing, which is why Toby glimpsed it first. "Dad. See there? Looks like a mech building."

In the sensorium no one had noticed it yet. They were talking of the Chandra slab. Voices slurred and nipped, the steady background roundtalk by which humanity sewed up the frame of their experience, smoothed the rub of their world.

He frowned again. They avoided mech places, and this odd thing ahead . . .

He saw abruptly that it was not one mechwork, but two.

One moved. A Rattler.

It came at them from right flank. The Rattler moved with a coiling and recoiling motion, treads grinding beneath. Killeen could hear its gray ceramo-ribs pop with exertion.

The Family was already running even as the Rattler's angle of attack fully registered. They could not make the canyon mouth beyond. There was precious little shelter in the dry streambeds nearby.

"Make right!" Ledroff called. The Family vectored immediately, seeing his intention. The mech building would provide some shelter.

They had only moments. Three Rook women used all their boot power to accelerate ahead, then turned to lay down retarding fire.

Killeen added to it without slowing, firing on an awkward tilt. No point in being accurate; their shots pocked and ricocheted but did not slow the smug-ugly and inexorable Rattler.

They would not all make it. "Toby! Faster!" he called, knowing it was useless and yet wanting to give vent to his knotting apprehension.

This was the Rattler they'd seen before, he was sure of it. It must have disgorged its half-finished meal to follow. Never before had a Rattler been so aggressive as to track them.

A figure ran slower though no less frantically than the others: Old Mary. She had not been feeling well these last few days. Already she had dropped behind. Killeen heard her labored panting turn to gasps.

He turned back. She came struggling up an incline and Killeen fired over her, directly into the bluehot mouth of the Rattler. The thing barely acknowledged the antennae blown off, the gouges in its obdurate face.

It caught Old Mary. Arms and the quick-opening mouth ingested her almost casually. It never slowed its oncoming momentum.

"Mary!" Killeen cried in rage and frustration. He knew the Rattler would only later discover she was not metal throughout, like a mechthing. Taste her, find her indigestible, spit her out.

Killeen had no time for remorse. He whirled and fled, realizing that he was now the most exposed. The Rattler undoubtedly saw them all as a covey of defenseless metal-sheeted beings and mistook them for free sources of cheap ore. Since they did not carry the eat-me-not codes of this Rattler's city, they were fair game.

Killeen gave himself over to the running. The Rattler came flexing and oozing over a weedy streambed.

A hollow *shuuuung* twisted the air by his head. It was a blaring noise-cast, blending infra-sonic rumbles at his feet with electromagnetic screeches, ascending to teeth-jarring frequencies.

The Rattler was trying to confuse him, scramble his sensors. He ducked his head reflexively, though it did no good, and made all his receptors go dead. Except for his fast-lurching vision he heard and felt nothing.

Toby stumbled ahead. Killeen grabbed him by shoulder and haunch and lifted him up a sandbank.

Another *shuuuung* echoed dimly in his sheathed mind. It was so powerful it caught Toby unaware. He crumpled. He bent, sucked in breath. With a rolling motion Killeen took Toby's weight across his back.

Close now, the Rattler sent a feverhot neural spark forking into Killeen's leg. The muscles jumped and howled and then went stonecold dead.

Killeen stumbled forward. The mech building ahead loomed. It was tall, imposing, far higher than the usual mechwork.

He wasn't going to make it.

He staggered. "Killeen!" someone called.

Sand slid beneath his boots. The sky reeled.

He fumbled for his weapon. The Rattler would be on him in a moment. If he could fire sure and quick and steady—

Then the world came rushing in. Sound blared. The Rattler's crunch and clank was hollow, diminishing.

Someone was pounding him on the back.

Toby's weight slipped off.

His sensorium flooded with scattershot pricklings, tripped open by some freeing signal.

Killeen turned to confront the Rattler. He saw only the rear of it as massive gray cylinders slid and worked. It was retreating.

Cermo-the-Slow was shouting, "—hadn't shut down your ears you'da heard it bellow. Right mad it was."

"Why? Why'd it stop?"

"That li'l thing there."

A small pyramid poked up through the sandstone shelf they stood on. Killeen had passed it without noticing.

He blinked at the finely machined thing. "How?"

"Dunno. Musta given the Rattler orders."

Killeen had heard of such things, but never seen one. The four-sided monument of chromed faces and ornate designs must have told the Rattler to come no closer.

Family shouted at him joyfully. Toby was fine. Shibo beamed. Considering their terror of only moments before, their glee was permissible, even after the loss of Old Mary.

Exhausted but exultant faces swam in his vision. They brought him up toward the large mech building. Friends brought him drink. Children clapped their hands in glee.

Mechs could not violate a command to leave a mechwork alone. Humans could. Thus they stepped with impunity into the grounds of the massive construction. The spacious plaza's flatness felt odd after broken ground.

Killeen frowned, puzzled. What was so different about this place?

Ordinarily he ignored whatever mechs built beyond what he could pillage. This thing, though, had saved his life.

It was broad and high. And impossibly shaped.

Atop a huge marble platform sat what Killeen at first thought must be an illusion. Only mechs made mirages; he was on guard. But when he kicked the thing, it gave back a reassuring solid thud.

It was massive, made of plates of ivory stone, yet it seemed to float in air. Pure curves met at enchanting though somehow inevitable angles. Walls of white plaques soared upward as though there were no gravity. Then they bulged outward in a dome that seemed to grow more light and gauzy as the rounded shape rose still more. Finally, high above the gathering Families, the stonework arced inward and came to an upthrusting that pinned the sky upon its dagger point.

The arabesques of gossamer-thin stone, shining white, did not interest Killeen so much as the evident design. He had never seen such craft.

Around him swirled celebration. Their deliverance without even a battle was a signal for exaltation. Cermo-the-Slow got into the strong, rough fruit brandy that served both as ritual fluid and as a valued currency among Families.

Ledroff and Fornax hesitated, then decided to let the festing go on. It was only midday, but the Families had been under strain. A wise Cap'n let vagrant energies dissipate.

Killeen watched them make this decision, heads bowed together. He didn't like it, but he went along.

Hoarse voices rose in song. Hands plucked at him. Two Rook women beckoned to him, their intentions clear. Their smooth skins, browned by the double suns, could not match the ghostly pale of the stones he crossed. The Rooks, despite all they had suffered, had not disconnected their sexcens. He murmured thanks, stroked their shiny hair, and moved on. Shibo was not nearby, he noted.

He explored, ignoring the ricocheting voices. At the borders of the vast square marble platform stood four delicate towers. Killeen walked between them, eyeing their solemn, silent upjut. They stood like sentinels at the monument's corners, guards against whatever rude forces the world could muster.

He saw that each tower leaned outward at a tiny angle. Something told him the reason. When the towers finally collapsed, they would fall outward. Their demise would not damage the huge, airy building at the center.

On the back of the last marble wall there was a single plate of solid black. It seemed like a dark eye that gazed out on a land inhospitable. Written above it in ebony script was *NW*.

As Killeen approached, it blinked. A ruby glaze momentarily fogged its surface and into his mind came a steady, chanting voice that spoke of glories gone and names resonantly odd.

Killeen felt the words as crystalline cold wedges of meaning, beyond mere talk. He gaped as he understood.

The thing was, incredibly, not mechmade.

It was instead of human times and 'facture.

Yet the mechs had left it untouched.

Killeen listened for a while, comprehending nothing beyond the singular fact of it: that men and women had once *made* things as fine and ordered as mechs. Far more beautiful than the Citadels. And had done it so well that even machines gave their work tribute and place.

Dazed, eyes opened but unseeing, he did not hear Cermo-the-Slow until a hand clapped on his shoulder.

"Come on! You get first hack."

"What . . . ?"

"Gone take one these down."

"One of—"

"Big crash time! Big! Cel'brate!"

Already some of the Family were scrawling marks at the base of one of the slender towers. Cermo-the-Slow tugged Killeen toward them. It was no longer interesting to pillage mech factories, but this strange place was different.

"You don't understand," Killeen said. "This isn't a mech building."

Cermo snickered. "Think's a hill? Huh?"

"Humans made it."

Cermo laughed.

"They did! There's a voice from over there—"

"Hearin' voices," Cermo called to the others. "Rattler musta addled him some." Raucous catcalls answered.

"*Humanity* built this. That's why it's so, so beautiful."

"Mechstuff, 's all." Cermo walked to the foot of the tower.

"No! Long time ago, somebody—men and women, *us*—did such work. Look, just *look* at it."

Cermo had the others with him, faces smirking and chuckling and preparing in their bleary way to do what men and women did whenever they found undefended mechwork.

"More damn foul mechstuff, 's what it is," Cermo said with a touch of irritation. "You don't want part of it, we'll take it all."

Two women laughed and handed Cermo a cutter-beam tube, one ripped from the Crafter so long ago. Cermo thumbed a button and a ready buzzing came from it.

A fevered mix of anguished rage propelled Killeen forward. Cermo half-turned to the tower and pointed the cutter-beam at one of the creamy stone plates. The crowd made a murmuring noise of anticipation, highpitched threads of glee racing through it.

Killeen hit him solidly in the back. Cermo lurched. His face smacked into the tower. Killeen caught him with a roundhouse kick in the ribs. The cutter clattered on marble.

"You—" Cermo blurted. Killeen kicked the buzzing cutter away.

Cermo feinted and hit Killeen squarely in the right eye.

Killeen staggered back, trying to focus.

Cermo ducked down and lumbered out. Killeen tripped him. The big man struck a broad stone plate and groaned.

Killeen looked for Ledroff or Fornax. They were far away and seemed unconcerned. He shouted to a sea of angry faces, "Leave it! It's ours. Human."

A woman called, "You protectin' mech garbage? I—"

"People 'way back did this. People different from us."

The woman bared her gray teeth. "Who says? This's mechwork!"

"Not going argue with you. Back off." Killeen stared at them, stony and redfaced, eyes wide.

Slitted eyes regarded him, assessing chances of taking him in a fight.

Hands grasped at air, eager for the weight of a weapon.

Wind whistled among the high bright towers.

And the moment passed. The crowd shuffled to the side, muttering darkly, eyes averted. They went to try to recapture their merriment.

Killeen helped Cermo sit up, brought him water. Cermo was a man of quick moods and the anger had passed. Killeen shared some brandy with him. They embraced. The matter was over, except for Cermo's sore ribs and Killeen's bruised eye.

Then he stood and watched thin cirrus skate across the sky, framed by the towers and the enchantment of the great curving dome.

Again he listened to the ancient hollow voice and its singsong chant. He paid little attention as Ledroff and then Fornax briefly spoke to him about the incident.

Toby peered at the towers for a while and Killeen told him it was a manwork. Toby wrinkled up his nose with blithe boyhood wonder and a few minutes later was playing again with the Rook children.

He told Shibo and she nodded but said nothing. Around them the momentum of celebration spent itself.

The Cap'ns decided to put distance between them and the Rattler. The Families, after all, had eaten, and could regain their earlier pace. To groans and complaint they ordered the Families back on the march.

Killeen shook his head and tapered the aged voice down to a dim dry warble. He, too, would like to rest here for a while. To grieve for Old Mary. To fest. To relive through story and celebration the humiliation of the Rattler.

Tugging on his pack, Killeen frowned. If mechs honored this human place, then humans should too. Of that he was sure.

"March!" Ledroff called. "Flanks out. Go!"

They left the flat plaza without looking back.

Arthur was excited but Killeen was in no mood to listen closely. The Aspect could not explain how this monument got here or why. Arthur knew of nothing like it in his own time. It seemed to have no connection with the slab of Chandra nearby. Killeen tuned down Arthur's puzzled excitement. Again he took flank left for the journey ahead.

Arthur kept repeating a name. He turned it over in his mind, trying to make sense of it. It was like no language he had ever known.

Finally he gave up. Lost in time, it meant nothing, though he did note that the slow and gravid sound, Taj Mahal, rode pleasingly on the lips.

FIVE

The next morning Killeen rose to news that buzzed through camp. On the night watch Shibo had spotted a navvy reconning them from a distant hill. She had shot at it but her bolt either missed or, ominously, was deflected.

Ledroff and Fornax decided to send a tracking team after the navvy. The two Cap'ns took the Families off at a diverging angle.

Six formed the party, all volunteers. Two were Bishop men still smoldering from the Mantis-brought deaths of relatives. Two were women from Family Rook, lean and angular. They wore their hair chopped short and curled in tight knots, forming a design and lettering from some ancient monumental symbol whose purpose no one remembered. They were outrunners, trained for hunting and led by their own character to the passion of pursuit. Shibo, though not an outrunner herself, was their friend and volunteered as well.

They laughed and joked with the two men and seemed to Killeen—who was the sixth—no different from other women he had known. Family Bishop had no women hunters, though Jocelyn was an outrunner of sorts. Killeen gathered from their talk that the Rooks had always kept scrupulously equal divisions of labor, so that men and women shared in cooking and hunting, defense and craft, even in carryweight and outrunning. The Rook women displayed through their graygreen tightweave great slabs of muscle in thigh and calf. Yet they carried themselves with a light and airy nonchalance.

Killeen found them all agreed: the special navvys could lead to the Mantis, and taking the Mantis by surprise was a lot better than the other way around.

So they set out on a long and wearisome day. Though centuries had shaped them for running, Killeen knew he had to pace himself. Age had begun to tug at him. Aches and familiar soreness in his knees and hips told him that he was pushing his endurance. Thin sensations came from embedded sensors, reporting micromolecular inventories. Killeen automatically took these into account without the faintest notion of their origin.

Shibo sent, —Toby safe.—

Killeen blinked. "I'm that obvious? But you're right—I don't like leaving him."

—Mantis goes for elders, seems like.—

"That's what I keep tellin' myself. Worth the risk, I figure, if we get the jump on the Mantis."

—Hope. We hope,— she said pensively.

They followed the navvy treads along an arroyo swampy from runoff. Streams broke freely from the loamy hills. The ice was melting underneath and seepage welled up in the low pockets, celebrated by flourishes of greenery.

They followed the treadmarks out onto a broad plain. Killeen got more and more exasperated as they searched the area. He knew the navvys' typical speed, their general ability to negotiate terrain. These tracks followed a clean, intelligent path between outcroppings of ice-worn stone and the boggy low washes where treads would foul and jam. This navvy was smarter than any he'd seen. As they covered the plain in lengthy, skimming, boot-boosted strides, the others noticed it too.

—Naysay,— one of the Rook women called over comm, —track stops here.—

—Wind erased,— Shibo sent.

The area was parched and took a print well. Where the firmly packed clay gave way to sand the treadmarks faded. Killeen sped over the tawny stretch. "Can't see where it came out," he said.

—Perimeter it!— the other Rook woman called. She was in charge and seemed to take as a personal affront any delay in finding their quarry.

They traced the outer boundary of the broad, shallow wash. Nowhere did a track emerge, yet in the wide area there was nothing substantial to hide a navvy.

—Section search!— the Rook woman called. They divided the oblong area into pieces and paced off a regular grid search, peering under every bush. Nothing.

The Eater and Denix were both low on the knobby horizon before she gave up. There was no sign of the navvy.

—I hate going back without even a sighting,— the woman said.

—No damn sense innit,— a Bishop man said in fatigued exasperation. —We'd've seen any transporter come, pick it up. No place navvy could go.—

Shibo said, —Air maybe.—

—Navvys that *fly*?— the second Rook woman snorted. —Never heard such.—

And a Bishop man added, —Navvys're too dumb. Always were, always will be.—

On the march back they had to scale truly mountainous terrain. It was the first time Killeen could remember going over high passes, for the Bishop tactic had been to keep to the valleys, avoiding conspicuous heights. The Rooks seemed more used to it, and their woman leader made a good case that they had to go over the saddlebacked peaks if they were to reach the Families by dusk.

On the long climb Killeen reflected on what the man had said. The Families had always carried in the backs of their minds that assertion, uninspected and capricious: *always were, always will be*.

Yet everything now pointed oppositely. It struck Killeen suddenly that they were always behind the zigs and zags of the mechciv. Humanity needed the traditions and rituals which held the Families together, and had once united the Clans. Yet change was their only true weapon now, not the puny and often ineffectual pistols and guns they carried. Or looted, rather—projectors plucked from the inert carcasses of Marauders, or lasers ripped from ore-seeking burrowers like the dumb Snouts. Weaponry adequate for the day but not for the slow steady passage of this unending war, a conflict desperate on one side and almost casual on the other.

He called Shibo on close-comm and asked what she thought. Her self-sufficient, enclosed distance had melted slightly, and Killeen had overcome some of his shyness. Even so, he was gratified when she immediately answered, —Must learn mechtech, yeasay.—

"Y'mean scavenge better?"

—No, *build*.— Her voice was flat, firm.

"From mech parts we could build mech weapons, yeasay, but—"

—Build *human* weapons. Not just copy mechs.—

"People *hate* mechs, Shibo. Don't want learn it. Can't, anyway."

He could hear her flinty *um-hummm* though she was some distance away. They had spread out to avoid ambush. The team was making quick time through a raw mountain pass. Snowglade was so young a world that the mountains had no topsoil at all. —Mechs deliberately make understanding hard.—

This startled Killeen. "You figure?"

—They defend their tech against other mech cities. What'll confuse them'll confuse us.—

"Sounds hopeless, then."

—Naysay. Human tech we could learn. Did learn, in the Arcologies.—

He didn't want to hear about how great things had been in the old days. To keep her talking, though, he said, "You mean that Taj Mahal thing we saw?"

—Yeasay.—

"If humans could do that once . . ."

—We could again,— she said simply.

"That weapon yours—how's it work?"

—I'll show you tonight.— She hefted the long, tubular gun. —I sized it out for human use.—

"Damnfine." Killeen was impressed.

They reached camp as the small sheltered fires started. There were burnable brambles in the sequestered notch Fornax had found for the Rooks, and over a nearby hill spread the Bishops. It would be demeaning to give up the dignity of separate and defensible campsites, no matter how diminished the resources of each Family. So each built the ordained three fires and covered them with a stretched-frame tent of tightweave. The flame was far too visible in the infrared, but the wide and steepled tent would disperse the image too broadly for a mech sensor to pick it out. Or so went the litany.

As he clumped heavily into camp, shrugging off his equipment, Killeen was acutely aware of the curiously comfortable way the Families bedded down among their

own softening assumptions. They used rules of thumb
inherited from grandfathers who had fallen in conflicts
which now, in the swift compression of their own legacy,
were but names: Skipjohn's Draw, Stonewall, Grammaw's,
Bowlesson's Surprise, The Three-Rattler One, Chancellors-
ville. Fine names, spoken of reverently around the fires.
Killeen wondered, though, if for each name they also
inherited in equal measure an unseen vulnerability. This
thought troubled him, for until now he too had felt without
thinking that the Family's survival lay in their traditions.

He ate with Toby and Jocelyn and Shibo. They all
scavenged for roots or berries that could mix agreeably with
the hardpack grub brought from the last Trough. Checked
for human biocompatibility, mashed and heated with
streamwater, the paste gave off a fructifying aroma. They
made short work of it.

Then the Family entered into that most pleasurable of
hours in their days, a time of relaxed muscles and the loggy
stuffed feel that casts an obliging film over the coming
sleep. The talk began then. It stirred around the three
encased fires like whorls of enchantment, taking them away
from their sore bodies and constant low apprehension. Two
Rook visitors described their flights and battles. Rook
women traded stories of mech giveaway smells and signs,
how to read their tracks for age and intent, how sometimes
they would lie craftily in wait near springs and ponds. First
Fornax led a mild ranking, then Ledroff.

They all savored the blending of Families, for it meant
the wash of new tales, jokes, stories. There was rumor of
romance, too, though this Ledroff cut short with a raised
eyebrow and bemused scowl. Better not bring this up.
Despite their adversity, the Rooks were not all downtuned
in the sexcen, and the Bishops could scarcely reply with
intimations of their own dehydrated lusts. This might
provoke a certain wan and wistful discontent.

Success has many voices but failure is mute. It would
have been good to have a tale to tell from the day's tracking
team. Killeen brooded over their losing the navvy's trail.
He took only nominal part in the singing after dinner, and
listened to only the first of the talk, before sneaking off.

Cermo saw him go and caught up, offering a flask of

coarse but powerful brandy. Killeen felt a quick, darting hunger for it, reached out—and drew back his hand. "Don't think so."

"Aw, c'mon. Hard day. Li'l alky'll set you right."

"Set me on my ass. Set me dumb. Get me started, I'll slurp up all you got."

"Not 'fore I do," Cermo said merrily, and Killeen could see the man was already far gone.

"Sorry, Cermo," he said gently.

He had to consciously make himself walk away from it. He could already taste the rough cut of the brandy, smell its thick vapor. But he knew what it would do and what he would keep on being if he took it.

Running away into the mind's own besotted refuges was too easy. He had been damned lucky so far. Nothing dangerous had happened when he had been drinking, or hung over, or tapped in to a stim circuit in a Trough.

But nobody's luck held forever.

He would have to keep his head clear if he was ever to learn. He made himself go over to where Shibo sat alone. Her high cheekbones caught the dim halflight, shrouding her eyes and making them unreadable, mysterious. As the last Knight, she would always be welcome around the campfires. But she seldom went, preferring to tinker with mech parts she carried in a black knapsack.

He spent an hour with her but it felt more like a day. He had not felt so daunted and humble since the days when he first went out with his father on simple scavenging raids.

Shibo had not merely mastered mechtech, she had made it comprehensible. She could recase her own ammo for her gun. She knew how to realign its bore. From mech scrap she had fashioned a self-loader that folded neatly into the gun stock. It fit snugly into her exskell, so to load while firing she had only to breathe. Killeen admired how deftly she had made her deficiency—the ever-moving exskell ribs—into an asset. Her rate of fire was higher than any Killeen had ever seen.

As she taught, she spoke more than she ever had. She had been fitted with the exskell as a girl. A craftswoman had made her exskell of foam polycarbon, worked from Snout debris. Killeen suspected that had kindled Shibo's ability to translate mech tangles into human terms. Perhaps this had saved her after the Knight Calamity.

As she taught him she showed no smugness, no preening pride, nothing but a penetrating attention to the job at hand. Many in the Families disliked mech artifacts and tolerated only those clearly shaped to human use. Leggings, calf-clasping shock absorbers, moly-vests—these Killeen was used to. He had to overcome his distaste as Shibo taught.

Then, slowly, he became intrigued. In her hands the alien objects took on a redeeming human dimension. Her quick, incisive thinking opened paths for him, banished mech mysteries. When she said, "Well, done. Sleep now, yeasay?" he was sorry the time was over.

Cermo snored as Killeen passed by him. The big man's mouth yawned slackly at the sky.

Killeen felt restless despite his fatigue, yet he did not want to join the figures around the campfires. Though he did not mind the stink he carried from days of hardmarching, he remembered his mother's old rule—bathe when you could, because no one knew how well Marauders could smell.

He found a small stream nearby that gushed out of a horn-shaped rock formation. The water numbed him immediately and then brought pain seeping into his feet. Still he stayed in for long, agonizing minutes, savoring the sparkling lap of more water than he had seen since the Trough.

After, he had to walk awhile to bring the circulation back into his legs and stop the quiet ache in them. That was why he was standing some distance from the fire tent and alone among the Bishops could see the Duster coming, though he was nearly naked, without equipment, and could do nothing about it.

The Duster was on top of them before Killeen, running among the bushes toward his weaponry, could do more than shout. Bishops came spilling from the ruby-walled fire tents. The Duster came in low from the north and was spewing a dark cloud behind it even as it breasted the horizon. It whirred and droned, approaching with stolid momentum. Killeen could not tell if it had made a particular target of them, for it did not appear to slow as it wept over the Rook and Bishop camps. The black fog billowed behind it and then fell with a graceful buoyancy, as though in no particular hurry to reach the ground and begin its work. Killeen saw the darkness advancing and swept up as much of his gear as he could. He took several steps, realized he would do better with his boots on, and so made himself methodically sit down and put on the boots despite the pandemonium which ricocheted through his sensorium from the outfanning Family.

When he stood up Toby was running toward him and the cloud was descending over the Family like a huge black hand. It came down in the Eater's blue-shot twilight, catching the last incoming horizontal yellow shafts of radiance from Denix, which cut across the descending swarm. For swarm it was now, not the simple layers of corrosive chemicals Killeen had experienced before and which had killed his grandmother. This was not alkaline dust but rather nuggets that seemed to writhe and murmur in the air. Toby reached Killeen and for once the father was glad to see that the ageold and sometimes even endearing sloppy habits of a boy were of use, for Toby's boots were still on and he had only half-shucked his marching gear.

Toby scooped up his mainbelt and shrugged on his harness, which carried some weaponry. Against chemicals this would have been utter useless deadweight, for the thing to do then was to run fleet and upwind. But they both agreed without wasting breath to speak that this settling threat was fresh. The things that came coasting from the sky hit the ground with rebounding skill. They were no bigger than three hands across. One rushed at Toby's leg, extruding blunt dowels. It was about to attack his boot when Toby blew it to pieces. But by then three more had landed around them and one more came down on Killeen's back.

It knocked him flat. A gust of horror shot through Killeen as he grabbed at the thing. He could feel the snub-ended arms press against his neck. A smell like sharp, corroded tin filled his nostrils. His hand slipped on slick cowling and something whirred at his neck. It brought a steel-cold pinprick that spread into a roaring, hot pain. He got a grip on the thing and wrenched hard and down. It

held on. He found a hold with his other hand and heaved a
it. Still the weight pressed down on him. He tried to ro
over but the machine somehow thrust against his roll an
held on.

He had not put on his gloves, and when his han
snatched at the two blunt prods against his neck his finger
touched something whitehot, unbearable. Tiny iceknive
scrabbled at his face. Going by feel, Killeen tried t
imagine what the thing was shaped like. He found th
underlip of it and yanked but it did not budge. He twiste
and got both hands under the lip and was about to jerk at i
when suddenly the weight was gone. He rolled over. Tob
had pried the thing off using a shovel. As Killeen got up
Toby smashed the shovel into the squat, square thing. I
buzzed and went dead.

Then they ran. The small machines were falling lik
slowmotion hail. Killeen remembered for an instant—i
the frozenframe way that the height of battle could bring—
romping beneath snow as a boy, and having it turn t
pebble-hard nuggets, sending him wailing back inside th
Citadel.

These midget mechs showed no preference for hu
mans. Those who landed on the Family tried to buzzsaw
bore their way in. Three people were hurt before other
could pry the machines off. But the other mechs turned t
the rocks and tundra, inspecting and burrowing in. Soo
fumes drifted from their labors, acrid foul clouds that di
more to drive the Bishops away than had the assault.

They regrouped, calling names until every Bishop wa
in formation. The machines blanketed the area and the
Family trotted to a nearby rutted rise before looking back
The voracious specks were uprooting and converting a
lengthy swath that stretched from the far hills. The corrido
had missed the Rooks entirely.

"Damned if I ever saw a Duster drop sucn," Killee
gasped.

"Looks like they're *eatin'* the rock." Toby pointed.

—Dusters tried to smother us, as I remember,—
Ledroff said moodily over comm. —Not this.—

"They fight tundra," Shibo said, her face withdrawn a
she studied the spreading mob of noisy machines. She

tood erect, composed, all equipment in place. Killeen
noticed, though, a scrape on her suit, as if something had
ried to hold on.

"How?" Toby asked.

"Grind down rock?" As Shibo shrugged, her exskell
whirred and flexed. "Seal in ice?" Another shrug.

Killeen nodded. "Tryin' repair the damage the Splash
lid. Stop the greenery."

Toby asked, disbelieving, "Weren't after us at all?"

Shibo grinned, shaking her head in a sad, slow way.
"We not important."

"I still don't understand how it works, these li'l bugs
ever'where," Toby persisted.

"Neither do we," Killeen said.

SIX

They had lost some gear to the gnawing machines. There
were two walking wounded.

A sour brown cloud billowed from the crawling
appetite that edged like a locust tide over the hill and began
to forage among the rocks of the narrow valley.

Family Bishop linked with Family Rook and they put
two ridgelines between themselves and the horde. They
settled again for the night and slept in edgy awareness of
the blank sky.

They rose and readied themselves in the first glimmerings of the dual sunrise. Denix and the Eater brimmed at
the horizon, with Denix showing its soft yellow.

As Killeen and Toby ate chaws for breakfast, Killeen
could see the swooping, obliterating clouds that necked
into the disk of the Eater. They filled a full quarter of the
sky, letting no stars shine through. He tried to think of
these shapes as outlines of three-dimensional forms but
could not figure why the clouds seemed to narrow down as
they neared the Eater disk. Arthur's prompting voice went
on about dustclouds shaped down into the thin disk by the
rubbing of tiny particles against one another, but Killeen
could follow little of what the Aspect said.

He tried, though, more than he had for many years
Shibo's simple but clever devices had rendered a fragmen
of the world comprehensible. He felt concretely a growin
conviction: to live, the Families had to imagine, to invent
to change.

Despite the unnerving Duster assault, he had slep
well. Around him, Bishops went about their breakfasts with
faces unlined by fear. He smiled at this.

Sorrow was the lot of humanity, Killeen knew tha
bone-deep. All the Aspects' bragging of past glory could no
hide that. The Family's songs and tales rang with woe—bu
equally with joy.

In ancient days, when the first mech intruders ha
attacked the crystal Arcologies, children had played in th
shattered ruins even as fresh bombs were on their way
Lovers found each other amid chaos and destruction, an
delighted in their discoveries. In besieged Citadels
doomed to fall, romantic ballads were sung in dim cabaret
and crowds laughed at the jokes of comedians. Ancien
scholars quietly labored to the day of their deaths on th
work to which they had devoted their lives. Soldiers an
scavengers of the Families had eaten and drunk with relish
mere hours before mustering forth on suicidal attacks. An
he and Veronica had celebrated the arrival of Toby as th
threat of Marauder assault had closed about the darkenin
Citadel. Humanity had a gift for finding the persisten
glimmer in a pervading night.

Ledroff's orders rang in the comm, —Form th
wedge!—

Killeen took a right-flank edge position. They headec
directly toward the apparent Splash center. Green in
creased through the morning and Killeen relaxed some
what. Last night's wildness and flight slipped away. Killeer
let Toby come up from the midranks and take a spot one
man inward from him, along the axis of the moving Family
arrow. The Rook arrowhead kept good pace a hill's-width
away to right.

They were moving uphill when two things happened
at once. Toby called, —Yeasay, I heard somethin',— in
evident reply to a hail from left flank.

Killeen asked, "What's that?"

—Some piping on the comm. Not from us,— Toby said.

"Rooks?"

—Naysay. Came and went. Not mech, though. Left flank is goin' out, have a look.—

At that instant Killeen opened his mouth to reply and he saw the navvy. It was nipping to his right down a draw, fast, headed for a saddleback indentation that would take it over the hill. It carried the telltale crosshatching.

Killeen did not think twice or even once. Losing the navvy before had chewed at him and now he took off at a quick pace, boots on full. His alerting yelp rang through the sensorium, less like the call of a man than the blurted cry of an animal in hot pursuit.

His boots dug into the gravel and loose soil as he plunged ahead, angling close to the ground in a running position, tilted forward and thrusting, momentum nearly parallel to the sloping ground. Dimly he sensed Toby churning uphill behind him, Shibo farther back. Even Cermo-the-Slow moved up from rear flank, which was contrary to standing orders. Cermo showed no slowness from hangover, and sent a hunter's whoop through the comm.

The navvy disappeared over the hillbrow. Killeen ran to cut it off, figuring that it would ease downslope to pick up speed and not simply wrap around the hill. Only when he crested the rise did he think that the navvy might have been with the Mantis, and when the idea struck him he let his momentum carry him down into a sheltering hillock of soft grass.

He closeupped the valley beyond. It was empty. He tried shifting through his filters and jerking his vision to bring out any projected mirages. Nothing. Just the figure of the navvy making good speed downhill, heading right.

That course would take it into the Rook pointwoman within minutes. Killeen checked the valley again. No distortion, not the slightest jigsaw-vision. No Mantis, as near as he could tell. Toby came pounding up and nearly fell over his father.

"Yeasay Isay. Let's skrag it!"

"Hold a minute." Killeen carefully studied the fleeing machine.

"Same one's yes'day?"

"Looks like."

"Let's *go*. They'll *be* here in minute."

Killeen could see the Family drawing up into fight-or-flight formation, blue pips in his right retina.

Toby cried, "The Rooks'll get it!"

"Let's try from here," Killeen said, unclipping his weapon. "Better shoot from shelter, just in—"

The navvy lurched sideways, bringing a jumble of boulders into Killeen's line of sight. "Damn!"

"C'mon, let's *do* it."

"Wait, I—" But Toby was up and skittering diagonally downhill, going for the maximum angle on the navvy. "Toby!" Killeen launched himself on the opposite tack, to be sure he had a crossfire position.

All this caution for a navvy would probably make him sheepish later. This might well be a Mantis navvy, but even so, navvys were dumb and vulnerable.

And Killeen wanted to have a close look at one, take it apart, get Shibo's opinion. They had to learn mechtech, and fast.

Still, Killeen was suddenly acutely aware that Toby would be exposed within seconds. Quickly he fired a burst at the place where the navvy, still out of sight, would probably be. He counted on the heavy rounds at least to confuse the machine.

His boots drummed along a gully, shortcutting through, and leaped some brambles on full power. He began panting heavily.

When he came into the clear he saw the navvy churning away from Toby's line of sight and into his. Its treads bit heavily, spitting gravel, and it buzzed swiftly away.

There would be a clear shot after all. The navvy didn't seem in all that much of a panic. Its brushed aluminum carapace stood out against the green valley beyond. The range was reasonable.

Killeen raised his weapon and heard a burst from Toby, who couldn't have a good angle yet and was wasting fire.

Rounds kicked up turf, far wide and high of the navvy. A second burst came closer but still high.

The navvy stopped and seemed to look around. Crosshatching was clear on its side panels.

Killeen shot it. He saw pieces of the cowling tumble away in the clear air.

The navvy made a quick motion and a dark spot came up the slope fast and low and hit him in the face.

It came in through his right eye. He toppled backward and felt a swift black storm squirt into him. A searching coldness spread through his forehead and left arm and hand.

Ice ricocheted blue in his eyes. Chrome-hard lightning stung in his left elbow.

Vision came back. Smells. A roaring.

He was rolling downhill. He tried to stop himself. Stones dug into his side and his left hand wouldn't move. He kicked at a boulder with his feet and that slowed him enough to fetch up against a bush.

He tasted warm blood. Somebody was shouting. Bitter cold seethed in his neck, down his chest. Shouting, loud and too fast to understand.

He rolled over. Heavy firing, quick hard slaps in the stillness.

He used his right arm to prop himself up. He had rolled a pretty fair distance and the navvy was on its side nearby. Its guts spilled out in a gray tangle.

He tried to lean on his left side and gasped as sharp yellow barbs thrust up into his shoulder. It felt as if something raw and rough was chewing on his left hand.

He managed to get out a strangled cry. Purple specks swam in the bleached air. Voices called incoherently.

Killeen looked around wildly and nearly lost his precarious balance on the hillside.

Shibo came over the horizon on a high leap. She landed with legs spread to pivot and fire in any direction, weapon at the ready.

Killeen called, "Toby . . . I . . ."

—Over there.— Shibo pointed.

Buzzing hot gnats circled his head, nipped at his eyes. He wrestled himself over onto his left side. The hill

veered, tilted, wavered in shifting greens and yellows.
Killeen blinked to clear his watery vision.

Toby was down. He sprawled on his back, eyes
fastened on the sky.

"Son!"

Toby's eyes moved. His hands scrabbled down toward
his twisted legs. Across the sea of Killeen's sensorium came
a weak, "Dad . . . I . . . can't move . . . my . . .
-legs."

"Lie . . . lie down," Killeen managed.

He opened his mouth to speak but nothing would
come out. The sky, he saw, was utterly clear and empty of
meaning. He had to get up.

Gasping, he pushed with his hands so he could sit up.
His right arm was rubbery and shot through with tingling.
His left arm was a hollow weightless vacancy.

He could not sit up. With a grunt he rolled partway
over so he could see most of the hillside. The navvy was not
moving. Shibo came down the hill, leaping among slate-
gray boulders. Cermo was behind her. They were all very
slow and shining in the bleached hard light that slanted
through the air.

And the buzzing gnats were biting his eyes now and
they would not go away.

SEVEN

Twilight came laced with high orange clouds.

Killeen felt as though he walked on similar high puffy
softness, for he could barely feel his lower legs. He had
been marching for some time, unmindful, knowing only
that he had to press forward into the neutral, dimming air.
He felt himself merge with the settling mind-mist that
swarmed about him, a fog through which he could see the
details of a long, downsloping valley slide past. The scenes
jogged and rocked so he knew he was walking through the
cool dissolving grayness.

Some had said he should be carried. A part of Killeen
had wanted to yeasay, to ease onto a stretcher. But he knew

the subtle balance of the Family. Toby had to be carried, since his legs were gone entirely. On even a moderate march the carriers would tire. Best not to double the cause of complaint by adding Killeen's heaviness to the Family burden. For the rule of the Family was plain: no permanently disabled were toted on the march. They were left—sadly, with proper ceremony—to whatever fate they could meet.

This time was different. Killeen knew this but could not immediately summon up how and why. He simply walked numbly through the pearly fog of his own diffused and quiet world.

Directly ahead of him Toby swayed in a shoulder-hinged carry between two men. The boy was sleeping. Even so Killeen could see Toby's eyes roll and jerk behind pale lids.

Killeen wondered if the boy felt anything below the hips at all. It had been hard to get him to talk as they lay together on the rounded hillside. The grass had been cushion enough, but Shibo and Cermo had brought sleep pads for them, a luxury neither had felt in years. They had lain there and Toby said little as the Family fretted and busied themselves around them.

Killeen had felt as though he were a boy himself. It had been like that long ago, lying in the fields near the Citadel, drowsy and speculative as he gazed into a sky that unfolded into infinite cobalt fineness. This hillside also gave itself to the sky as though he and his son were offered to it on an altar. Killeen had tried to focus himself then but faces and times had come flitting into his mind like birds: His father, leaning with casual grace on a mech strut at the end of a successful raid, grinning in a way Killeen found mysterious until he saw years later that it was triumph tempered by still-raw memories of many defeats. His mother, picking among mechwaste and coming up, prettily agog, with silvery cloth no one had seen before. All the pictures had flowed by as if behind thick glass. He had talked to Toby about them in the unthinking way a father feels that the merest detail of the past, shared, preserves that instant in the character and perspective of the son.

"Near now," Shibo said at his elbow. Killeen nodded. "Kingsmen come."

"Kings . . . ?"

The word triggered memory. The scattershot piping voices heard on the left flank had been hails from the Family King. While the right flank pursued the navvy, the left was held back by Ledroff's order to group defensively. So meeting the Kings had been delayed until the navvy was dead. The wonderful news from and of the Kings had come to Killeen as he lay sprawled, his sensorium a sheltering hazed cocoon.

And there ahead were the Kings.

Ledroff had sounded a full alarm. Outrunners watched all approaches. But this time there was no sign of the Mantis as the Families met.

The Bishops came down a dusty draw canyon and emerged onto a plain ripe with swelling green life.

A man led the small party which met them. He was tall, with thin, blackclad legs and gaunt arms, and his every gesture said he was Cap'n of Family King. His face gave him his name: Hatchet. The brow was wide and bare, beneath a fine red carpet of hair cropped to avoid the rub and snarl under a helmet. A blue tightweave rag circled above his ears. From a square forehead tapered an angular nose and slanting cheekbones. A narrow yet powerful mouth checked their descent. Below the full lips Hatchet's face came together in an extended sharp triangular wedge, bare of beard.

All this swam toward Killeen in layered air as Hatchet approached, the Kings' Cap'n radiating authority with every step. Around them the Families greeted one another. Ledroff escorted Hatchet and made introductions but it was not until Hatchet directly said to him, "Just the arm, is it?" that Killeen registered anything.

Killeen shook his head, not in rejection but to sense the vacancies in himself. He lifted his left arm a fraction with great effort. "That's . . . all," he said through lips that felt fat, swollen.

"This your son?"

When Killeen nodded Hatchet bent over and examined Toby's eyes, which still moved restlessly under the filmy lids. "Ummm. Might get some this back. Legs, is it?"

"Dunno for sure. He breathes fine."

Hatchet's hands moved expertly over Toby, pinching and tugging. "Moved his arms?"

"Some. Said he couldn't feel his legs. Then fell asleep."

Hatchet waved a hand without even looking up and the line resumed its march. "Could come back. I seen cases like this. Just luck the Marauder only got partway through his sensorium. Hadn't finished its work."

Hatchet's face scrutinized Killeen and something in the gaze blew away the last of the clammy fog that encased him. The stark world came rushing back and with it a surge of fury and despair, familiar because they had been there all the time, behind the mist. "It was a navvy!" Killeen blurted.

Hatchet frowned. "Navvys can't fight."

"A Mantis navvy."

Hatchet frowned. "Mantis? What's that?"

When Killeen described it haltingly, with thick lips, Hatchet said, "No Mantis 'round here I know of."

"Is now."

Around them had gathered oddments of the Families Rook and Bishop and King. Flanking guards covered the hills. The hundreds remained spread out, watching all approaches as they made their way steadily down the long grade to the plain.

Killeen's words had made the King party rustle with dispute and incredulity. He heard their objections through a thin, distorting haze.

Shibo came forward and added, "Navvy had midmind."

Hatchet turned to her. "A navvy with a big-size mind? You *sure*?"

Shibo never answered such questions. She simply stared directly at Hatchet and let her silence give assent.

More murmuring from the Kings. When they paused Killeen said, "The Mantis navvys put the Mantis back together again, I figure. Twice now it's done that."

Hatchet blinked and his air of authority lessened a fraction. "The Mantis mind's dispersed?"

Killeen was glad Hatchet had seen the answer right away. Ledroff still didn't believe it. A Cap'n who was smarter than the rest of the Family would be a relief. "First

time we brought down the Mantis it had a mainmind.
Second time it surekilled plenty Rooks and Bishops. Then
it had midminds."

Hatchet scowled. "Stowed in different parts?"

"Yeasay," Shibo said.

"What'd you do?"

"We blew all them."

"That shoulda killed it," Hatchet said.

"Didn't."

Killeen said, "This navvy's a new kind. Suckered us
in."

Hatchet and the other Kings glanced at one another,
liking none of this. "Mantis followed you?"

"S'pose so." Killeen noticed he was rocking slightly
from sudden giddy fatigue.

Ledroff said something Killeen couldn't follow and
Hatchet brushed the remark aside. "We're founding a new
Citadel here and I don't want attract Marauders. Certainly
not this Mantis thing."

Killeen blinked. Shibo asked, "Citadel?"

Hatchet's voice swelled. "Citadel King. We call it
Metropolis."

And there it was. Killeen had been concentrating on
walking and watching to see that Toby was all right. It had
taken all his effort to talk. Now he looked outward and saw
rising from the plain before them a cluster of brown mud
huts of one and two stories. Tall doorways. Open oblong
windows without glass.

"See the crops?" Hatchet and the Kings smiled with
the pride befitting the Family which had first restored a
Citadel. "We plant in patches. That way the mechs can't
pick up a pattern from their flyers."

Killeen nodded. The huts seemed fused in place
beneath the twilight stillness, like earth that had itself
climbed upward and made a blunt gesture at the emerging
stars. A distant warbling sound seemed to skate on the air.
Killeen recognized birdcalls, dozens of cheerful songs
floating out from the lush trees and high bushes. "The
Splash. This the center?"

"Yeasay," Hatchet said. "We build on top the icemoist-
ness, our true and rich and holy Snowglade. Bring back
those times."

A far cry, Killeen thought, from the battlements and bulwarks of Citadel Bishop. In those days humanity had expressed its assurance in eternal stone. Now they used mud that promised to dissolve if a hard rain lashed at it.

Arthur piped up:

Yet this is a more beguilingly human environment.

"Primitive," Killeen muttered so only Arthur could hear.

Note the umbrella-shaped trees. The little lawns before each rude hut. See there—a pond. Sizable, too. I'd wager that inside we will find carpets, which are essentially lawn analogs. Humans evolved in a mosaic environment where there were trees to scamper up for protection, open water, and broad grassland for foraging. This new Citadel King unconsciously resembles the ancient savanna. Hatchet has made a new kind of Citadel, deeply reflecting the way we evolved.

Killeen nodded, wondering how the Kings had managed all this. Hatchet spoke on, welcoming the Bishops and Rooks with simple, direct courtesy. There would be a full ceremony later, he assured them, as befitted such a portentous event.

Ledroff asked for the privilege of dakhala. This required a Family to give shelter to any of humanity which fled for their lives. Never had it applied to whole Families in flight, but Hatchet nodded warmly and formally agreed. This shoring up of human tradition was greeted with applause. Hatchet presented them with bowls of scented water.

Killeen felt the weight of Hatchet's words, the blunt, inexorable force of the man. Hatchet, builder of the new Citadel.

In Killeen's mind blossomed a hope that this man knew something he did not, had firm basis for the incredible hope

here expressed in rude mud. After all, a Citadel meant
there would be no question of abandoning Toby.

As they marched into the shouted greetings and
fervent cries of their reception, Killeen banished all doubt
and let himself be drawn into the wondrous quality of it. He
could scarcely walk from the heavy seeping tiredness but
he shrugged it aside, wanting above all else to believe.

A day later he did not. Clarity had returned as Killeen
lay sunstruck through the inert morning and afternoon. The
throbbing ache in his left side eased. He still could not lift
the arm more than a few fingers' width.

Hatchet and some of the other Kings said the navvy
must have depleted whole sections of his and Toby's
sensoria. Interrupted, the probing mechmind had departed, taking Killeen's left arm control centers and all
Toby's leg command and nerve integrations.

Other things were gone, too. Rummaging through the
perpetual tiny voices in the back of his mind, Killeen found
missing a Face, Rachel, and an Aspect, Txach. He had
never used them much but still the vacancy left a quiet,
hollow void.

It was twilight again when Killeen went out to walk
the random streets of Metropolis. Pathways deliberately
swerved and veered among the vegetation to avoid mech
analysis from the air. Huts were dispersed, to present no
easy target. The Family King wore headrags and paid less
attention to their hairshaping. They all seemed invested
with purpose, busily cultivating and crafting. There were
hundreds visible in the windy streets.

Like the Bishops and Rooks, they wore shirts and
leggings of scavenged tightweave. Theirs were far more
ornately marked, mutely advertising the leisure they had to
stitch elaborate King emblems, loops, and wide swirls.
Each Family member had a different design. Some proudly
wore patches signifying their familial tasks.

Killeen had hoped the walk would renew his belief in
Hatchet's dream. As he shuffled down dusty lanes he did
feel a kindling of mute wonder at a Family which had
escaped the worst depredations of the Marauders and could
even thrust up crude, thick-walled structures.

Frying fritata cakes layered the air with pungent promise. Walls wandered, crudely shaped and misaligned. Though fresh-made, he saw them as tired. There was none of the precision Killeen automatically expected of mech constructions. To him buildings were mechmade, of precisely laid-out sheetmetal and ceramic. The only counterexample in his experience was the Citadel where he grew up, which was a majestic conglomerated accumulation of centuries.

Citadel Bishop had had interlaced warrens of rock and mechmetal, shaped and counterpoised to accommodate stories and stories piled upon broad arches. By daylight, this new Citadel King was an insult to the memory.

Still, he reminded himself, this was at least a beginning. He had no place criticizing.

He knew he should be encouraged by the fervent activity and solid walls. But he could think only of Toby.

The boy could speak weakly now. He responded to Killeen's easy massaging everywhere but in the legs, which were immobile. More than the physical pain, which was tapering away, Toby felt the apprehension that came with any disabling injury in the Family.

He had to be convinced—not by Killeen's words, but by the solidity of the hut walls—that he was in a home, a fixed place. That the Family Bishop would not need to march away. That he would not be abandoned.

Killeen had spoken to him. Slowly the points had come through. These realized, Toby's face had collapsed into a smooth calm. He had plunged into sleep.

Killeen's fears were not so easily quieted. He made his way back to where he had heard Hatchet was negotiating with Ledroff and Fornax. He let himself through the crude fence surrounding Cap'n Hatchet's own large lean-to hut. The fencing strip was plain unfaceted mechmetal but the pickets were fashioned crudely of wood and had to be humanmade.

He fidgeted with the latch on the gate and only then missed the use of his left arm. He had been able to swing it while walking, a wooden weight that at least did not get in his way. Until now he had been able to regard his injury as a mere sickness. As he walked to the lean-to he realized that he would not be able to run or carry or fight as he had before. Which meant that he was married to this Metropolis in a way he had never thought.

Hatchet was ushering Fornax out as Killeen arrived. There had been a full day of back-and-forth negotiation, Killeen knew. Skills to trade. Aspect and Face chips with rare knowledge. Already the bargaining instincts emerged. He had heard the occasional shouting a full three huts away.

There was an ordained manner for the Families to interact, a liturgical line. The Bishops and Rooks would be guests in this rude Citadel. Offering of food and restplace had its ornate protocols. These took time, but more essential matters like survival and defense consumed far more. Once protocol was done, the three Cap'ns had at one another with sharp tongues. Both Fornax and Ledroff could only gape at what the Kings had accomplished. Every standing stick or clay wall was a reproach to the other Families. The dignity of the Bishops and Rooks demanded that they not show a bare hint of envy, though, so there had to be some blustering and even outright arguing. Killeen was glad to have missed all that.

He asked admittance of the young woman guard outside. To his surprise, he was let in immediately.

Hatchet sat him down, gave him a cup of dark, heady, minted tea. Killeen downed it automatically, asked for more. Hatchet nodded with satisfaction, took the brewing pot, and poured into a larger cup from the shelf behind him.

"You've got my habits," Hatchet said with gusto. "Like everything strong and in plenty. Right?"

"Um."

"Thought more 'bout that Mantis?"

"Some."

"Why you figure there were brains in that navvy?"

Killeen slurped tea and squinted. "Mantis must've done it."

"How you figure?"

"We killed all the midminds it had in its main body, back when it killed so many. We didn't guess it was using navvys with midminds, too."

Hatchet's eyes widened with surprise. "It does?"

"Sure. That navvy we rousted and got burned by—that was no accident."

Hatchet did not respond to this. Instead—and unlike either Fornax or Ledroff—he simply sat and thought for a while, feeling no need to keep their conversation going or pretend to have understood everything. Killeen liked that. Hatchet was large and sat in a brown cloth deck chair of distended and misshapen form which seemed to have molded itself to him. He rocked forward, putting his big wide hands on his knees, and said finally, thoughtfully, "It's changing itself. Adaptin'."

Killeen nodded. "Looks like."

"Not like the other Marauders."

"Double naysay that."

It was a relief to be able to blurt it out this way, his stored-up and undefined misgivings. Ever since Fanny had suredied Killeen had felt a gathering vague unease about the Mantis and what it meant. The thing was no legend now, but a very real, if unseen, force.

Hatchet slapped his hands together, the hard clay walls reflecting the sharp clap and concentrating it. Killeen had been so long in the open the sound came as a surprise, intense and startling. "Just like that, eh? It changes its pattern. When you and Family Rook met, it surekilled plenty you."

Killeen frowned. "Yeasay?"

"But now three Families meet and it does nothing."

So Hatchet had seen it. "That navvy means it's nearby."

Hatchet nodded. "It knows of Metropolis. If not before, it does now."

Killeen did not like this line of thought, but since he had been over it before he could scarcely refuse to follow the idea to its conclusion. "So why didn't it attack right away?"

Hatched mused, his big lower lip thrust out in a pensive unconcern for appearances. "It may not have known we were here. Wants to look us over a li'l first. Or maybe it's afraid of coming up against a defended position. We got plenty mech traps 'round here."

"Didn't seem scared last time," Killeen said dryly.

Hatchet's eyes narrowed. "You tryin' say something?"

"Naysay. Just that I can't fashion it hanging back."

"Other Marauders don't want come this way, why should it? We're smack in the middle of the Splash. Wetlands. Why, over south there's even marsh. Marauder treads'd sink up over the rims there."

"Could be."

"Why else'd they stay away?"

Hatchet was getting irritated now. Killeen tried to figure why. He knew something of clay and mud from watching his uncles make spot repairs at Citadel Bishop. This new Citadel was no more than a couple of years old, judging from the age of the plastering on the better walls. He guessed Hatchet was trying to make out to Ledroff and Fornax that he was the natural leader of all the reassembled Families, since after all Hatchet had made a working Citadel. And kept the Marauders at bay. Somehow Hatchet had equated in his own mind the solidity of these clay walls, and of his own tenuous metal and wood fence, with keeping Marauders out.

Killeen had a sharp reply to Hatchet's question ready on his tongue. But then he saw which way the talk would go and saw too that he could make a choice. He could push Hatchet further and then end up stomping out, or he could take a fresh angle.

He made a few remarks about how impressed he was with Metropolis and how everybody looked well fed. Then he said casually, to draw Hatchet out, "What you figure all this points at?"

Hatchet rubbed his long, pointed nose. "What you mean?"

"Been what—six years?—since the mechs hit all our Citadels."

"Seems like."

"Yeasay, seems like forever. All the time since, we been on the run. Couldn't stop more'n five, six days. No thinkin' time."

Hatchet shrugged. "So?"

"Ever figure that might be the idea?"

"Huh?"

"Could be they don't want us thinking. Learning from our Aspects. Why'd they destroy the Citadels, anyway? Just because we poached on their factories?"

"They hate us." Hatchet said this as if it were self-evident.

"Maybe. Anybody ever ask 'em?"

Into Hatchet's face came a guarded look. "Who could?"

Killeen was concentrating on his own thoughts but he noticed the small hesitation in Hatchet's hooded eyes. The man's sharp chin turned and caught the dying light of Denix's sunset through an open hole that served as window. Hatchet was hiding something.

"Kings used be good at mechtalk."

Hatchet's mouth narrowed. "Yeasay."

"Thought you might've picked up some information since your Calamity."

"We spent years runnin', same as you."

"You've sure done a lot better'n us," Killeen said, to take the edge away from the conversation. Better to back off and come at it from a different direction.

Hatchet relaxed a little but said nothing.

Killeen went on easily, "We had one trained translator. Mantis killed her."

"Uh-huh. We got one translator, a woman."

"She learn much?"

"Nothin' real useful."

"I see."

Hatchet said, "You Bishops got any Aspects can translate?"

"Read signs, things like that?"

"Anything you can. Always need skills."

"Well . . ." Killeen asked Arthur, then replied, "No Aspects, no. One my Faces can, though."

"Any good?"

"Some."

Hatchet looked interested behind his veiled eyes. "Good."

"That woman translator—"

"She's sick now."

Killeen wondered what Hatchet was still hiding. It might just be private King Family business. Probably better to skirt the issue.

Ideas brimmed in Killeen and he could not resist giving them voice. "Point is, why'd they attack the Citadels?"

Hatchet pursed his lips, the expression drawing his face even longer in the shadowed burnt-gold twilight. "Irritated, maybe."

"Why send the Mantis now? Why build a special Marauder?"

"Finish us off." Hatchet was distracted, bothered, and did not want to show it.

"Why take all that trouble? A whole new design. First it used mirages on us, really good ones. Looked absolutely real. I never saw a Marauder could do anything near so good before."

"So?"

"We killed what we thought was its mainmind. Great. *Then* we find it's dispersed its intelligence into midminds. So we kill those. Looks okay. Then yesterday we run into a navvy carrying a full mind—*and* weapons."

"Hey, easy," Hatchet said, sitting forward.

Killeen realized he had been shouting, his right fist balled tight. His left hung useless, limp. "Well, you see. They're putting a lot into the Mantis."

"Yeasay to that." Hatchet sucked on his teeth, gazing into the distance. "You people've suffered a lot. More'n us. Mind, we don't begrudge you space, even if you've drawn this Mantis."

"We're 'preciative," Killeen said. The unspoken truth was that Metropolis might not be able to resist the Mantis. Hatchet feared that.

Still, the Kings had a lot of confidence. Several had already come by his hut and regaled Killeen with stories of how they'd crushed Marauder attacks. But Hatchet could see the Mantis was different.

The coming of the other Families might not be simply the blessed reuniting of humanity. Equally, it could spell the end of Metropolis.

Had this realization been what Hatchet wanted to hide? No, there was something more. Hatchet had quickly passed over what their translator had found out.

There was no point in suggesting that they go out and track the Mantis. Hatchet would never rob Metropolis of its main force. What's more, Killeen realized, he himself was no advertisement for the wisdom of tracking the thing. His left arm hung as a limp rebuke at his side.

He said a few more things to make their gratefulness apparent, though he was sure Ledroff and Fornax had done the same. It never hurt to layer on the sweet manners between Families.

He added, though, "Point is, though, *why* are the mechs tryin' mash us down in the dust?"

Hatchet said again, "They hate us. Pureblood simple."

Killeen took a breath and said decisively, "Naysay."

"How come, then?"

"I think they're afraid of us. We scare 'em some way."

Hatchet laughed strangely. Then he stood, the signal that Killeen's time was up, that the Cap'n of the Kings had things to do.

EIGHT

Dad . . . ?"

Toby had been asleep for so long Killeen could no longer resist the urge to shake him gently, seeking reassurance that the boy had not slipped into some downwinding neural spiral.

"Yeasay, yeasay. I'm here. You're all right."

"I feel . . . funny."

"Any pain?"

"No, I . . . kinda . . . can't feel."

"Where?"

"Legs. Just the legs now."

"Guts okay?"

"Yeasay."

"Sure?"

Unexpectedly, Toby grinned. "Sure I'm sure. Put your hand down there, I'll pee into it."

"Think you can hit a pot?"

"It's either that or try for the window."

Killeen found it harder than he'd have guessed to get Toby sitting up on the raised pallet. Toby, too, seemed sobered by the effort. Shadows passed in his eyes and his throat contracted with some interior struggle. Then it was gone, leaving no sign in his smooth, papery skin. He peed boisterously into the clay pot, laughing.

"When'll my legs come back?" Toby asked when h
was lying back down.

"Rest a bit, we'll see."

Killeen had tried to keep his voice easy and cheerf
but Toby caught something in it. "How long?"

"They don't know. Never saw a case like this, where
Marauder was surekillin' and got interrupted."

"Marauder? Looked like navvy."

"Well . . ."

Toby's face clouded. "Reg'lar one?" To be brough
down by a mere navvy . . .

"Naysay. Was a Marauder disguised as a navvy. Mant
made it, I figure."

Toby brightened. "Least I wasn't got by some dam
navvy."

"Nasty one, yeasay."

"How's your arm?"

"Not good." No point in lying.

"Use it any?"

"Can't even wipe my ass."

"Since when didja?"

Killeen grinned, the lines splitting his sunburned fac
like trenches. "Look I don't snatch off one them legs an
close that mouth with it."

"Least it'd be something decent to eat."

Killeen fed him supper. He carried on conversation a
wan halfnight fell, shadowing the room. He made makin
his own tour of Metropolis seem more colorful than it real
had been. Toby was enthusiastic about getting out an
seeing it on his own. Killeen promised to take him ou
tomorrow. He would have to carry the boy in his arms o
else devise some wheelchair. He had to struggle to keep h
voice from giving away much of what he felt. Hatchet an
the others who knew about these things said there was n
way any of them could fix Toby's damage.

Even Angelique, when she had come to visit in th
day, had mournfully shaken her head. She knew how t
adjust eyes and mouth-taste. She could get into some othe
chips at the skull base. Whole body systems were beyon
her, though. No one had even a hint of how they worked o
where their neural junctions came into the spine. Toby ha

three tapjoints set into his spine, small pink hexagonal notches. The woman who installed them had died at the Citadel Bishop. Nobody among the Bishops or Rooks or Kings knew how to connect through the notches, or even if Toby's damage was repairable through them.

He was relieved when Toby drifted into sleep, just as Killeen had begun rummaging for interesting things to say. He went out of the small square building to get more water from the King wells and met Shibo on the path.

Her look framed her question. Killeen said, "Seems fine 'cept for the legs."

"Head?"

"Well, he talks okay. I'll take him out tomorrow, test his reflexes maybe."

She blinked slowly in the slanted, dry light. Her eyelids slid like gray ghosts and he had the feeling that he could see through them to the ivory masks of her eyes. "You?"

"What, this arm? 'S okay."

She kneaded it with both hands. "Feel?"

"No, nothing."

"Fix?"

He shook his head, still thinking about Toby. Nobody knew how to fix much of anything, it seemed. They began to walk together, directionless. It seemed profoundly odd to be moving down a path, amid forms shaped by human hands. The small, almost obsessively precise details of mechwork were missing. In their place were agreeable errors, lines askew, artless curves.

"Hatchet say?"

"Family King doesn't know if any other Families survived. We're the only ones who've found them. If the Splash attracts more . . ."

He let the thought trickle away. He could not think far ahead to distant, theoretical possibilities when Toby's face bobbed in his memory, pale but still cheerful.

In the boy's eyes had been a puzzlement with his own body that would quickly turn to futile anger and then despair. Killeen knew the cycle. He had seen it on the march with the injured.

"You talk Mantis with Hatchet?"

He was always surprised at how much she knew without his telling her. "Yeasay naysay," he quoted an old rhyme, "mansay noway."

"Mantis?"

"He's worried 'bout it, sure."

"Wonders if Metropolis safe."

"Yeasay. I do, too. Hatchet's . . . hiding something."

"What?"

"Dunno. Me, I wonder why Metropolis is here at all. How come the Mantis left it alone?"

"I checked defenses. They're good, but . . ." He could tell by her arched eyebrows that she didn't believe this explanation.

"Wish Fanny was here," he said wistfully. This was the first time he had said her name in a long while. The events since her suredeath had opened a chasm in all their lives. He wished she had left an Aspect he could carry.

"Fanny?"

"Oh, course. I forgot you never knew her."

"Your Cap'n?"

"Was. Best damn one ever. She'd go through this Hatchet like a hot knife through butter." He liked this old phrase, even though it reminded him that he hadn't seen butter since the Citadel.

Shibo said abruptly, "Hatchet not right."

"Huh? 'Bout what?"

She tapped her temple. "Not right this way."

This startled Killeen. "Why you say?"

"You hear his welcoming speech?"

"No, fell asleep. What'd he say?"

"Metropolis greatest city ever."

Killeen chuckled. "These mud huts?"

"Great 'cause can withstand Marauders."

Killeen's mouth turned down in puzzlement. "Not many Marauders come this far in the Splash. They catch on we're here, we'll see plenty them. Hatchet's been damn lucky so far."

"Yeasay. Then he talk about reuniting Families."

"Huh?"

"He wants be Cap'n."

"Cap'n *all* the Families?"

"Think so. Kings cheer him all the time."

Killeen shook his head. "This Hatchet, he's done a lot, I give him that. He can lead. Look how proud the Kings are. Not a wise Cap'n, though."

"Yeasay." Softly she added, "Fanny wise?"

He smiled. "She used to say, old people don't get wise, they just get careful." He paused. "Or was that my father said that?"

"Not always true, anyway."

"Yeasay. Fanny was wise, even though she'd rag you for sayin' it. Hatchet, he's not."

"Yeasay." Her face was somber as she regarded passing warm yellow rectangles that looked into the narrow huts. Family singing drifted outward on the soft breeze.

Metropolis used a line of sentries and outer defenses beyond the ring of nearby hills. They could sense any mech approach. That made possible this casual indifference to an exposed light. Killeen did not think it wise.

The sprawled town shimmered in its fragrant haze of campfire smoke. Moist air cloaked his face, its welcome weight filled his lungs. This was the tang of life, riding winds and burrowing in the rich loam. Once, Arthur had told him, all Snowglade had been this way.

He forced his thoughts back to practical things. "Why'd the mechs rebuild the Mantis each time? After the Calamity the Marauders could've hunted us down, if they wanted."

Shibo said, "Tried. Pick us off if they run across us."

"Yeasay, but they didn't *hunt* the way the Mantis does." Killeen balled his right fist. "They just let us go for years. Forgot us, 'cept for Marauders we'd run into by accident. That was bad enough. Now they've sent the Mantis. Why?"

Shibo smiled. "Don't frown. Makes you look old."

He noticed that she had completely redone her hair. It swooped upward from her broad crown in twisted braids flecked with silver. Then it fanned outward in a frozen black fountain. Her eyes glistened and her jumpsuit was clean and brushed.

Ready for romance, he thought. She gave him a slow, up-from-under look.

He wasn't in the mood.

He could not bring himself to tell her that he was certainly interested in an abstract kind of way, but lacked the motivation. When his Family laid down the law about sexcens, Killeen had not minded so much. He'd been sleeping with Jocelyn then, but the sweet memory of Veronica kept coming back to him. He was past that wonderful time of his youth when the simple and almost unexpected pleasure of the act was enough to hold him entranced. It had been clear that Jocelyn could never be what Veronica had been, and that had brought a bittersweet aftertaste to every touch and gesture.

He opened his mouth to skirt around the subject but nothing would come out. *Damn! Like I was a kid!* He cast about for something to say, mind spinning in vacuum, and ahead of them saw a tube set on a frame.

He knew full well what it was but managed gratefully to seize upon it with fake puzzlement. His delight, though, was real.

The Citadel had boasted one such, and he could not imagine how Family King had managed to save theirs. Maybe they had rescued it from their own Citadel ruins, years after their Calamity. That would fit Hatchet's style.

He peered through the ancient viewer. Clouds drifted away, revealing a shimmering band of starlight. He could see that the dense stream of stars lay beyond the nearby ruby lanes of dust.

Arthur said:

A welcome vision! I have not witnessed this for so very long. That is the Mandikini—an ancient Asian Indian word of fabled Earth. It denotes the plane of the galaxy, the so-called Milky Way. The Indian translates literally as "great sky river," since they believed—

"Come look," Killeen said to Shibo, cutting off Arthur.

Shibo had never seen an electrotelescope before. She dutifully looked through it, scanning the twilight sky, and then asked him about something in the finder screen.

Killeen peered at the small, crystalline object. A

memory from childhood rushed through him. "The Chandelier," he said. "There's one still left!"

"What is?"

"A city. Human city! Didn't Family Rook come from a Chandelier?"

She shook her head, puzzled. Killeen said, "We all did, long time back. Came down, settled Snowglade."

Arthur had reminded him of these forgotten tales only yesterday. Killeen had been letting the Aspect speak more often, trying to learn more mechtech. He had not told Shibo this, hoping to pick up a few craftsman tricks to impress her.

"Families built?"

From the inner whisper of Aspect Nialdi Killeen plucked a quick fact. He was glad to have some area where he could at least seem to know more than Shibo. "Families were formed when humanity came down from Chandeliers. 'Way long ago."

"One Chandelier?"

"Uh, no, three," he got from Nialdi.

"*We* made?"

Her incredulity echoed Killeen's unspoken feelings. It was flatly incredible that men had ever known how to shape things in the high blackness, or even to fly there. Even the strange white-stone monument they had found the day before seemed an impossible accomplishment.

Yet when he had first seen the Chandelier as a boy the world had seemed safe and humanity capable. Now he knew the truth.

Killeen sensed a seething unease in the back of his mind. He studied the Chandelier again, its glinting crystalline finery hanging dry and cool against a flat blackness. Scattershot emotions echoed through his sensorium. It was a lovely jewellike place among so much swimming nothing, so much an affirmation against the eternal denying blank.

But in him this provoked a sudden cry.

His Aspects sent smothered yelps of glee and pride and fervent desolated ache. They yearned outward from their recesses.

Bubbling voices washed over him. He gasped.

"You all right?"

Killeen realized his face must reflect some of the swarming frenzy that blew red and roiling within him. "Ah, yeasay. Just . . . let me look a . . . li'l longer. . . ."
Nialdi cried:

How lovely it is! Beauty! Humanmade!

Arthur shouted:

—If I had simply followed the advice of my good friends, in a timely manner, I would have gotten promoted enough. My turn would have come up. I certainly could have gained at least a *temporary* appointment to the Crewboard in the Drake Chandelier. And if I had—no matter how much you hoot, Nialdi, don't think I can't hear you, even if you do encode your insults!—I would have stayed in the Chandelier. And would *still* be there!

1. Mechs hit the Chandeliers too last I heard.
2. Even in my day nobody knew if they were working.
3. No signals from them.
4. Just hanging in the sky like Christmas tree ornaments.
5. You stayed there you'd likely be suredead.

You refer lightly to such great tragedy? When the devilworked hordes engulfed all that was left of life-giving reason and judgment in this foul abyss?

Really, Nialdi, you must stop giving us sermons. I don't care if you *are* an ordained philosopher. Can't you just gaze upon the Chandelier, man, and revel in it? The mechs haven't devoured it! Think what that might mean.

I sympathize with you, Arthur. No one wants more than I do the return of humanity—of all true living things!—to our original station. Yeasay verily!

1. **Then stop jawing so much.**
2. **Got to find a way out of here right now.**
3. **Stick to business.**

—So of course the Chandelier era saw a tragic end. We had assumed too much about machines, their rapacity. But that is *no* reason to indulge in your fevered nightmares about the mechs. We—

You deny that they chewed *most of our original ships? Killed most of our expedition?*

Naturally I—

—Then later returned, devoured our works again? Leaving—praise God!—this lone Chandelier. Merciful—

Stop this cheap religious hokum! You won't win me over with *that*. No one will be taken in by your—

1. **See Killeen!**
2. **I know we're overheated but look, it's bothering him.**
He reels! He's caught some of our feelings.

Your hothouse mind, that's what's done it. Your blind unreasoning hatred has—watch out!—

Killeen knew he was undergoing Aspect storm, but he could do little to stop it. He could not control his own body. It was like the woman days ago, her Aspects running hot and wild.

He felt silver teeth saw through his skull.

Rasping hornets filled the dusky air.

He fell on his leaden arm.

Snow pelted his nostrils.

Insects ate at his eyes.

NINE

The next morning there was what would have been in the old Citadel days a Confluence of Families. Today it was three lean, stringy-muscled men with straggly beards sitting in organiweave chairs inside a dull-orange mud hut.

Killeen heard of it from Shibo, who was taking care of him. It came as thickly spaced words, acoustic wedges, propagating solidly through silted silences.

He knew they were ruminating on matters he was in no mood to consider. Some thought they should integrate the Families in what was both the fresh new Citadel and also, for the more somber souls, humankind's final, tenuous redoubt. Others felt there was no real safety in numbers and they should burrow underground, or disperse into separate villages, or even go back on the march.

Killeen didn't care. His world had narrowed down to a simple set of intersecting forces, all hinged on definite objects.

Toby's legs.

Shibo's filmy eyes.

His own swaying cordwood left arm.

All solid and specific. He had to concentrate on them to bring back his full sensorium.

His Aspects had overloaded him. Now they cowered in the remote back shelves of his reverberating, honeycombed self.

He would heal, yes. A day, two.

One day passed without his much noticing it except as a bar of Denixlight that slid across the floor and up the far wall. He ate and seemed to sleep for a moment and then the solid yellow-white bar was back on the rough clay floor.

He sat and thought.

If the Marauders attacked Metropolis, Killeen would not be of much use in the defense. Even when he recovered, he would not be able to cradle a projector or gun accurately. And if Metropolis fell and there was another in the long series of humiliating retreats, the Family would leave Toby behind.

His sputtering Aspect voices called him, their thin whispers resounding when he gave them the least chance.

But they had little useful to say. He had to get his arm function back, they said. Forget Toby.

Killeen sat in the cramped soil-damp hut, watching Toby sleep. He knew that Fornax and Hatchet and Ledroff were talking only a short distance away about what were for him and Toby matters of life itself. Yet he did not stir.

Every parent, he realized, knows at some point that his own grip on the future is slippery and must eventually fail. That comes with the weathering of age. In a way children were life's answer to mortality. Their small but persistent presence was a constant reminder that you were no longer in the frontier generation. That history was preparing to move on beyond you. That for them to flower, their parents finally and justly had to wither and give ground.

This was natural and proper and came without discussion or even clear thought. Killeen felt it in the pressing quiet of the hut. The random sounds of Metropolis came through the window as from a distant and filmy place, the mumble of activity like a voice that could be heard but never understood. He watched his son and knew he had to do something, but the hinge that would set him in motion refused to budge. It would not deliver him into clear action. He felt this as a sullen knot in him.

He did not mind giving ground himself. His own life carried as little weight as his own frugal backpack. Years of death and steady retreat had not diminished his opinion of the valor and dignity of humanity, but it had impressed him with the random and uncaring way of things. That he could be obliterated by a casual blow from a passing machine which knew neither pain nor remorse—that was the central fact of the world. But that this world could now so easily annihilate his legacy, Toby—that was a truth he could not allow.

Killeen watched the slow, grave heave of his son's chest beneath rough tightweave blankets. A fly droned in through the sunstruck window. The tiny circling saw inspected the bare necessities of the hut and then lit on Toby's hand and wandered busily on it. Killeen let the fly go. It was alive and so carried its own rights. His father had taught him his burden and duty to all lifeforms, as their greatest representative. Humankind spoke for the kingdoms of doomed life. It could not transgress against forms lesser and unknowing. Killeen tolerated the fly until it started to crawl on Toby's face. Then he scooped it up and carried it to the window and set it upon a passing breeze.

The rise and fall of Toby's chest was itself a small, persistent miracle.

He thought of the mechs and the Citadel and his own mutinous arm as he watched the simple majesty of breathing. He knew he was thinking, but as a man who did not as a matter of habit make his conclusions achieve the solidity of words, he thought without the pressure of any result. There simply came a moment in the tranquil, hovering air when Killeen knew that he would sense what to do when the moment came. Then he watched his son awhile longer for the plain pleasure of it. The thought had struck him that this might well be the last time when he ever could.

At last Killeen got to his feet, feeling muscles stretch and complain in his legs. From his left arm he felt nothing and expected that he never would feel again. His head swam as Aspect voices rose with their gusty advice.

He squeezed shut his eyes and forced down the fibrous words. He could understand their worry about their own safety. Still, none of them had anything to say that he had not thought of before, and their incessant talk was a churning irritation worse than the fly.

He strode toward Hatchet's picket fence. His unsteady walk stirred dirt into the soft wind. He thought the fence looked even more ridiculous than before, a puny gesture against the silently implacable world. As he approached, the meeting inside broke up and the three Cap'ns came out. Each wore newly cleaned vest and pants and leggings of tightweave. Killeen dimly remembered that he should have cleaned his own, just as he should have tended to his hair. He ran fingers across his scalp and could tell that he sported not an artful cut or wave but a storm-racked sea of knots and spiky tufts.

Fornax saw him first and chuckled. "Better?"

"Yeasay."

Hatchet studied Killeen with slitted eyes. "Ledroff here says you're a fast man when you're not sick or drunk."

"So's he." This made everybody laugh but Ledroff.

"Said you got a Face we can use."

"What for?"

Ledroff grinned the small grin of someone divulging a secret and wanting to play it out for a while. "A li'l job. Translation."

"I don't—" Killeen stopped.

Ledroff grinned wider at Killeen's evident confusion. "Ever seen a Rennymech?"

Hatchet had told something important to the other Cap'ns. They'd all been planning together.

"Heard 'bout 'em." Killeen was cautious and kept his voice flat and neutral.

He had never seen a Renegade. They were mechs which had gotten into some kind of trouble with their own kind. Outcasts. Loners. They lived on the outskirts of mech civilization. There were few of them.

There had been sporadic cooperation between men and Renegades in the past. Contacts occurred by accident, when a Renegade was desperate. Negotiating was difficult because there was no shared language. Relations had seldom gone beyond simple trade. Most Renegades treated humanity as scum. They would deal with men and women only if in extreme need. But Renegades lived longer than men and so their contact with the Families spanned generations and became legend.

Bud, his Face, had translated when Family Bishop had dealings with two Renegade mechs. That had been long before Killeen was born. There had been a prearranged meeting signal. Both Renegades had vanished inexplicably.

In the space of a heartbeat Killeen summoned Bud and threw quick questions.

1. **Both the Bishop Rennies got caught by Marauders.**
2. **Died the suredeath I guess.**
3. **I knew some their mechspeak then.**
4. **Mostly tech stuff though.**
5. **I didn't understand whole lot mechtalk.**

Hatchet said, "We been using a Renny for two, three years now."

"*That's* how Family King built this city," Ledroff said.

Killeen nodded, even though he was still stunned. This was why the Kings were so sure they could burn uncovered fires at night, too. They had help from a mech itself. Some kind of deal that deflected Marauders from the center of the Splash. He asked, "What kind Renny?"

"A Crafter," Hatchet said.

"Trust it?"

"Have to."

"Why?"

"So can get any damn help at all, is why!"

"What kind help?"

"Information. Supplies, even."

"In return for what?"

Hatchet looked uneasy. "This one know who he *is*? Rest your people like this?" he asked Ledroff and Fornax.

"Killeen's a hardass," Ledroff said.

"Better humor him or he'll never go along with anything you say," Fornax added.

Hatchet nodded, looking sour. "We got do some jobs for the Renny Crafter."

"What kind?"

"Steal things, mostly."

"From where?"

"Mech storage tunnels."

Killeen didn't say anything. The look on his face was enough to make Hatchet explain, "Hey, look, we got ways. Tricks."

"You better," Ledroff said flatly. "You heard what we agreed. You better have *good* ways. Else I don't send any my people."

The three Cap'ns argued a little then, giving Killeen the chance to watch Hatchet's face. Their words volleyed across the space between them.

It seemed to him he could see all Hatchet's inner tightness wound down into the knot at the end of the sharp chin. The little knob of flesh there jittered, as though it weren't attached to the rest of the face at all and could express whatever it wanted. It was anxious, small, nervous, while the rest of Hatchet's face was shrewd and sure. The straggles of black hair on the wobbly knob seemed alive.

Hatchet was plainly the best leader of the three. Killeen was going to have to use him, without being too obvious about it. He had to take the role of a Bishop Family member with a legitimate problem. That would let him deflect Hatchet onto the other Cap'ns.

Killeen recalled Shibo's gesture, finger to temple. *Hatchet not right.*

Well, maybe Hatchet was a quirky but brilliant leader. The man was certainly clever. He controlled his face well, making it convey what he wanted without giving away what he really thought. He could produce a broad, friendly grin and then slowly cloud it as it dawned on him that his friend wanted something that Hatchet, for the best of reasons, could not give.

But the face wasn't perfect. Hatchet's inner tensions tapered into the waxy ball chin. A drop of sweat formed among the black fuzz and trickled to the underside. It hung there, jiggling as Hatchet's mouth worked, making hard, savvy points to the other Cap'ns. The fragile drop clung to the oily skin like a desperate man on a ledge. No one else seemed to notice this small drama. Killeen suppressed a smile. Cap'ns had a dignity and position that everyone wanted upheld. Maybe they didn't even see the drop.

Killeen waited until the Cap'ns had finished arguing and three or four other people had come and gone with minor bits of business. There were plenty of delicate issues having to do with matters between Families. As hosts of the only human settlement the Kings had the upper hand. But ancient human custom gave the other Families nominal equal status and that was what Killeen had to use.

At a lull he asked, "Can this Renny Crafter do medical repair work?"

Hatchet frowned. "I got it to fix something for the woman Roselyn last year. It knows some subsystems. But you're not—"

"Sure I am."

Hatchet looked at Killeen's arm and then at Ledroff. Best to let the Bishop Cap'n deal with this.

"No, Killeen, look," Ledroff said. "You got an arm out,

yeasay. But we can't be trying patch ever'body up. Go
along. Translate some. You can't carry goods, after all. Don't
'spect too much."

Killeen nodded. This showed that he acknowledged
his Cap'n but stopped short of active agreement. There was
something more here and he wanted to uncover it, use it.

In a level voice he asked Hatchet, "How come you
don't use your own translator?"

Hatchet's face closed more tightly, making shadows
cleave from his high cheekbones. "She's sick. You know
that."

"What from?"

"Aspect problems."

"Like what?"

"King Family business."

"Anything she got from the Renegade mech?"

Hatchet barked, "You forgetting I'm a *Cap'n*?"

Ledroff started to apologize for one of his Family
talking this way. Killeen cut him off with, "Don't want know
who it is, just what's wrong. I respect King Family
matters."

Fornax said, "Man's got a point."

"I don't have to answer questions 'bout Family."
Hatchet's lips compressed into thin bloodless lines. His face
became a mask of adamant withdrawal. But his ball chin let
a generous bead of sweat drop.

Fornax and Ledroff scowled. They looked at each
other. They were both less powerful than Hatchet but on
this point Killeen saw that they could hold firm.

"Want help on this job, you'd better," Ledroff said
ominously.

Hatchet didn't like this. He studied the two Cap'ns.
Keeping his face clear and sure, he said grudgingly, "She
had some kind overload. Not like yours, though. You look
okay. She just stares at the wall."

"What happened?" Killeen persisted.

"She was on the last contact we had with the Renny.
Came back with the others all right. Then she had an
Aspect storm and . . . stayed that way." He looked away.

The other two Cap'ns stirred. When things got worse

there was more Aspect trouble. Nobody knew what to do about it.

"I respect your problems," Killeen said seriously. "I share them. I'll go, of course."

"For your arm?" Ledroff asked. "I know you need it, sure. But chances are you won't get any help from a Renny. Just you do what you're told, right? Family can't let you go if Cap'n Hatchet here can't trust you. As Cap'n I—"

"Going for Toby," Killeen said. "*With* Toby."

He turned and moved off without waiting to hear what they would say.

There would be no more bargaining now. He had said his piece and it was time to stay silent. Let Hatchet consider. Let Fornax and Ledroff think a bit.

They would come around. Killeen had in his Face, Bud, the crucial thing Hatchet needed: translating ability.

His arm hung slack and dead while the right one took up the pace of his walking.

PART III

THE DREAMING VERTEBRATES

ONE

They had to walk a full day to make contact. Hatchet led their column out of Metropolis.

Hatchet had let no one witness his transmission to the Renegade mech. A Cap'n's private rooms were inviolate, by old Citadel tradition, and Hatchet made much of the things he had there. After he had spent fifteen minutes in the small, rock-lined hut he came out smiling. He had a look of pride and some relief and talked to several of his own Family about how hard it had been to arrange everything with the Renny mech, using a prearranged code.

The Renegade had no way to encode human speech, Hatchet said, and used a system of number-signs. Killeen's Bud Face reported that this was good. The Renegades Bud had worked with long ago had used a barebone number-code, too.

At close range, though, Renegades could speak to the Aspects in a human's head, relaying more complex sentences through the host-sensorium. Killeen had no experience with this and took it as more past lore, a tool, and did not waste time trying to figure what in the distant past would have yielded such a thing.

Hatchet loped steadily on the move and with surprising grace. He covered ground quickly and was impatient at

Killeen and Shibo, who were carrying Toby in a sling. Shibo had found a way to attach the sling to her exskell and this made the going easier. Hatchet took upon himself the job of patrolling, giving his energy over to long sweeps of both sides of the column.

There were ten in the party. The Cap'ns had agreed that sending members from each Family would help bond the Families together. Hatchet would lead, as he had in all King raids before. Three seasoned Kings came, and three Rooks.

Ledroff sent Cermo-the-Slow, because he was good at carrying loads. Killeen would have preferred Jocelyn. His old closeness with her was gone, but she was sharp and quick. Killeen refused to go unless Ledroff agreed to send Shibo. She had a quiet, sure way of dealing with mechs that he admired. Without his asking, she volunteered to help with Toby.

Ledroff did not like sending her, but Killeen dismissed any other possibility with a single shake of his head. Only later did he realize that Ledroff and Fornax might be quite pleased with an arrangement that took feisty Shibo and Killeen, plus the rival Cap'n Hatchet, on a dangerous raid.

None of the Bishops or Rooks had had dealings with a Renegade in this generation. They were edgy without wanting to seem so and that made the pace a little faster. Killeen and Shibo labored to keep up. They dug hard into the soft loam of the narrow valleys and panted heavily when Hatchet led them up into sloping, sandy arroyos to make shortcuts.

They all carried only lightweight arms. Hatchet wanted minimal marching mass, to give them speed. He argued that if they got into trouble it was far smarter to run than to fight, anyway.

Toby bore up well. He swung in the carrysling without a murmur, though occasional spasms flickered in his face. Killeen checked with him every few minutes and tried to carry on a conversation, but the boy was lethargic. He slept most of the time, which was just as well.

Hatchet was a good leader on the march, as Killeen had expected. The man knew how to keep spirits up. He even got them all into a mild, humorous ranking session.

This was hard to do on the move and doubly so among people who didn't know one another well. Hatchet made it a contest, bringing out the best, most pointed barbs of each Family.

About a fellow Kingsman Hatchet said, "He's such a tightass, needs a shoehorn just to fart," and that was the key remark that started them all to laugh and forget their apprehensions. Killeen remembered Fanny doing this, joshing each Family member in turn as they marched. It got so you waited with pleasure, hoping she'd lay into you next, because she had a limitless fund of barbed one-liners.

Hatchet was better than Ledroff or Fornax, but something about the man put Killeen off. Hatchet didn't have the rock-hard sense of honesty that Fanny had projected without trying.

The land they covered grew drier as they left the center of the Splash. As life ebbed Killeen grew more alert. Machines naturally shied away from moisture, but the factory they had breached before showed that the mech civilizations were encroaching into wetter zones.

"Don't fret," Hatchet said while they were taking a break to eat some light provisions. "The Renny told me there's no Marauders along this route."

"It can fix that for you?" Killeen was impressed but tried not to let his face show it.

"Sure." Hatchet's angular face had seemed more animated out here on the march, more in tune with the curious bobbing afterthought of a chin.

"How? Me, I never heard such."

"It can reprogram Marauders, I figure. Least the smaller ones."

"Must be pretty powerful Renegade."

"The best," Hatchet said with casual smugness.

"It operating alone?"

Hatchet blinked, as though this was a new idea. "Yeasay. I never saw it with another mech."

Killeen didn't think that meant much, since mechs communicated through their sensoria over huge distances. He let it pass. "How'd you make contact with it?"

"The way things was, it found us," he said. "We'd been

running over a year after the Calamity. It tracked us some way."

"Maybe has a tip into the whole Marauder comm net?" Killeen asked. Shibo sat silently studying Hatchet, her face giving nothing away.

"Not a steady one," Hatchet said. "Else we wouldn't get the occasional Marauder wanderin' into Metropolis."

Killeen frowned. He hadn't heard of this. "Any get away?"

"Not that we know. We peg 'em square."

"So the Marauder net still doesn't know Metropolis is there?"

"The Renny takes care that."

"Risky."

Hatchet's ball chin stuck out farther as the rest of his face hardened. "That's in our deal. The Renny's got some trick, can tap the mech geo-survey. He kinda paints over the picture for us. Makes Metropolis look like somethin' natural."

"Call it 'he,' do you?"

Hatchet blinked. "Well, Rennies're almost human, some ways."

Shibo said, "Not good, think that way."

"Listen, I got Metropolis built," Hatchet said sternly. "Kings're settled, eating good. Better'n wanderin' like you!"

Killeen nodded but he didn't set his uneasiness aside. Mechs were enemies, no way around that. Any thinking that forgot that fact was dangerous, foolish. Who knew what Renegades really wanted?

The afternoon was hard going because Hatchet insisted they reach the target point by Denixdown. They were marching directly into the hotpoint of the Eater and the seeing got worse. Toby did not wake from his long swaying sleep but he made small troubled sounds. Killeen could not tell if the anxious groans and sleep-clogged sighs were from true pain or were the escaped remnants of nightmares. Everyone had those; among adults it was often Aspects striving to live. Toby's face wound into wrenching lines, eyes sliding spasmodically under eyelids. Somehow his injuries had triggered growth. Toby's hair was shoulder-length and his fingernails jutted out, slim white spikes.

Shibo was tiring of the load, her exskell slowing. Killeen could feel a spreading ache in his shoulders where the slingstraps bit in. He put his mind to ignoring it by making everything else in the world hard and sharp and clear, so clear it pushed aside the pain. He managed to keep that until he saw the landing site. It was a broad plain, flat without having been scraped by mechs.

There was nothing on the plain. No mechwaste, even. They took shelter under an overhanging rock ledge so nothing could see them from the sky. Then they waited. Denix reddened as it sank and a chilled blue came into the rest of the sky from the Eater-glow brimming at the other horizon. Killeen liked to watch the play of light on the few high skittering gray clouds. He had not seen many clouds in these last years. Arthur told him unbidden that most lands were now dried so much they could not breathe moisture into the sky anymore. He guessed that was why there were some flat, silver-fringed slabs of haze back toward Metropolis, with its upwelling icemelt. He squinted, trying to find the Chandelier as the blue above hardened. Then the Duster came up on them.

Killeen froze. The Duster kept on a straight glide. Its underbelly was seamless and polished, reflecting the terrain below. It came down low as though it was searching the plain. No hatch opened to spew forth vermin. Killeen sat absolutely still until Hatchet clapped him on the shoulder and said loudly, "Easy. That's ours."

A Kingswoman was already swinging on her pack, grinning at the little scare they had caused the Rooks and Bishops. Killeen saw the rest look a bit sheepish but he felt nothing like that. Just because the Kings treated the Duster as a known thing, something they'd dealt with before, didn't mean he should.

He and Shibo brought up the rear. Toby was asleep again, his mouth open and face a strange white. Killeen could see the pulse beating firmly in the boy's neck, though, so let him sleep.

The Duster gave a thin, high shriek as they straggled out onto the plain. It did not use wheels but instead seemed to hold itself up with air alone in a way Killeen could not understand. Then, when it slowed, he saw four things like skids pop down. A thick plume of tan dust burst forth behind. It slewed and came toward them. He had to make himself keep walking. The Kings were nonchalant as the Duster came rumbling near.

They were making a show of having mastered a Renny, of knowing what to do. Killeen knew they thought it was dumb to bring Toby this way, that the Kings had already written off the boy. If they hadn't been able to extract much medical help from their Renny, certainly this bunch of vagrant and battered Bishops wasn't going to. But they needed a translator and would tolerate his dragging along a doomed boy if that was the price. Hatchet's face had said that the day before, but the civility between Families still meant something, so he had not spoken it.

The polished belly split. A ramp clunked into the dust. Hatchet led the others up it, the Rooks and Bishops coming last, their eyes showing white and jumpy.

Killeen had to make himself go up the ramp. The prickly smell of active mechworks alerted him, set his senses dancing.

They settled among large, blunt housings that jutted from the walls. Inside the Duster was gloomy, the grids of struts and snub-nosed machines a looming canopy. Luminosities stirred fitfully in the walls. The vagrant bands cast dull red wedges of light into the strained faces of those sitting. Killeen remained standing and alert. He felt the deck tremble. A sudden bump sent him glancing off a smooth aluminum housing and made the others laugh. It was the first human sound anyone had made inside the Duster. Everyone chuckled as Killeen felt ruefully for a seat, and then they settled into an apprehensive yet silent waiting. A strumming filled the walls and soothed them. Toby slept.

Killeen watched the dim, smoldering darkness. Dirt and mechmess inhabited the corners. Everything looked old, worn. He guessed that the Duster was not smart itself, was just a tool other mechs used. He remembered that Toby had called the small machines that fell from Dusters "sky-roaches," after an insect that had infested the Citadel.

He had no idea if they lived inside Dusters. If he came up on one of them in the ash-glow dimness, he would kill it without question, no matter how jaunty Hatchet was.

Killeen watched the timer tick in his left eye. He managed not to think about being in the air, of how far down they could fall. It was more than an hour before he felt them slow. The others stirred as the Duster nosed down. Landing jarred several from their seats.

The ramp sighed down onto pale yellow concrete. Black skid marks and cracks forked across the rectangle Killeen could see. Hatchet led them down. They emerged onto a vast field of speckled concrete that stretched to the horizon. Mech factories dotted the hills. The first thing Killeen did when he reached the ground was closeup the hills and check them. Navvys swarmed everywhere. Wedge-backed trucks ground loudly among sloping roads and curious tapered towers. No Marauders.

Shibo whispered something and Killeen turned. He went absolutely still. A Crafter stood beside the Duster. It was doing something to an electrosocket in the Duster's side. Giving it orders, Killeen guessed.

But the *size*. It was fully five times larger than any Crafter he had ever seen. The general outlines were still there, ornamented and elaborate. Grainy layers of added housings gave it a muscular presence. From pylons fore and aft hung burnished conical pods. Antennae turned nervously to regard the humans.

"Like no Crafter I ever saw," he whispered to Shibo.

"Modified," she answered softly. "They get free, change themselves."

The Renegade Crafter squatted on heavy treads which supported the weight of a swollen hull. Ceramic curves bristled with retrofitted capabilities. Snouts. Antennae. Tools. Grapplers. Sensors. Polybind extrusions. Ports. Distorted gunmetal-blue pouches like livid sores.

He stood motionless as his internal alarms jangled with nervous, skittering fear. The Crafter looked dangerous. His sensorium shrieked with warnings of the electromagnetic net the Crafter cast about it. Cloying fields wrapped like cobwebs around Killeen. Probing. Poking brassy filaments into his sensorium.

"Killeen!" Hatchet called. "Translate."

He had to force himself to stop staring at the Renegade.

He turned to Shibo. Her gaze said to him silently that she, too, was fighting an impulse to bolt.

They exchanged rickety smiles. Killeen let out a long breath, then unlocked his internal alarms. His sensorium subsided into muttering, worried notes.

He and Shibo lowered Toby carefully to the spattered concrete. "We're safe, standing here?" Killeen asked Hatchet.

"Safe as anythin' gets. The Renny's already sent out identifyin' codes, say we're a mech work team."

"But a mech could *see*—"

"Wouldn't bother. 'Round here, work area, they just go by the electromag-tag, the Renny told me."

"Still, should we—"

"Get goin'! Tell him 'bout that list things we want."

Killeen took hesitant steps toward the Crafter. It towered on its augmented treads. Wads of compacted mud and mechwaste were trapped in the lower grooves of it. In some places the metal was slick, polished, and fresh-turned. Back behind that Killeen could see a scabbed, pitted carapace—the original Crafter, which had mutinied against mech civilization to save itself.

Killeen called up Bud. The Face said:

1. **Ready to try.**
2. **Can't promise I'll get it all.**

Killeen studied the Crafter warily. A long moment passed. Without thinking he held his hands open in front of his chest. It would not help make contact but it did give him the feeling of being ready for whatever the Crafter might do. Abruptly Killeen remembered the mouse he had seen long days ago. It, too, had stared in fascination at a being huge and unknowable. It had put its paws up, as if to touch the untouchable. Killeen had been squatting to relieve himself. The mouse might not have understood even that much.

Killeen searched among the Crafter's many sensor probes. He could not tell which might be watching him.

"Trying to reach it?" he asked Bud. He had tapped Bud's dry presence fully into his sensorium. At this range the Crafter could easily pick that up from stray fringing fields.

Killeen sensed something gray and huge sliding into the cloudy verge of his sensorium. An angular weight.

1. Feel something.
2. Language is changed.
3. Lots of this I don't remember.
4. I'm trying to—

A spike of color exploded in his head. It swelled and faded within one heartbeat and left him.

1. It reads the list from you.
2. Approves.
3. Will get most of it today.

"When?" Killeen asked.
Another soundless splash of color. Then a raw scrape, like sand in his throat. He blinked.

1. While we do our work.
2. Wants us go with it.

"Where?"
This time the colors dispersed in waving ivory filaments.

1. Factory nearby.
2. We steal some things.

Hatchet asked, "What's he saying?"
"Wants we steal from one these factories."
Hatchet nodded. "We been here before."
Killeen slowly thought words without speaking. *I want*

medical help for my boy. He had to visualize each word separately to be sure Bud got it. The Face was good at picking up on speech, but faulty at internal work.

A pause. Then fine traceries of amber crackled in him.

1. **Boy has Aspects?**

What difference does that make? There was no point in telling it anything extra.

1. **Is good if not.**
2. **Boy is young human?**

"Of course," Killeen said irritably.

There was some translation difficulty between Bud and the mech. The Crafter had no word for "children."

Hurry up. The soundless, livid explosions in his mind burst against his eyelids.

1. **Boy not have even full human sensorium?**

"No, not yet, I—"

"What're you telling it?" Hatchet demanded.

"Leave me be, I'm—"

"Dammit, don't waste time on—"

"Back off!" Killeen pushed Hatchet away one-handed without turning his head.

Not yet. Look, a navvy caught him with some Marauder-class weapon. Got my left arm, too, see? Whole control complex is cut off. If—

1. **Boy is like animal then.**
2. **Crafter says is useful.**

We're not animals! You—

1. **No.**
2. **Says is *like* animal.**
3. **If boy without Aspect disks in head.**

I asked for help, I'll bargain for it, see? We steal for the Crafter, it fixes my boy.

"Killeen! What's—"

1. **Crafter says you not understand.**
2. **Boy is to help steal.**

Killeen forgot himself and spoke out loud. "The boy isn't part that!"

1. **Boy must steal.**

"Look, he's not part of the deal," Killeen said angrily. "We want—"

Hatchet shoved Killeen. "Dammit, what're you—"

Killeen batted at the man with one hand, still looking up at the Crafter. He wished he knew which sensor to address.

Hatchet punched Killeen in the gut. Killeen hooked his boot behind Hatchet's leading foot and yanked it off the concrete. Hatchet fell. Killeen kicked him in the side and backed away. "Shibo!"

She glided between them from nowhere, hands held out in what seemed a casual way. But her fingers were rigid, curved cutting edges. Her exskell hummed. It would be good armor in a hand-to-hand fight.

Hatchet sputtered, swore. Cermo-the-Slow edged closer, automatically moving to help his fellow Bishops.

Killeen watched Hatchet get up on hands and knees, his big eyes judging the situation. Striking a Cap'n was a major offense. Hatchet might call on the other Kings to rush both of them. Killeen could see Hatchet think this through, his wobbly chin tucking under, and decide against. Then the chin bobbed up as Hatchet reset his face to mask some of his anger. "You make the deal straight, hear?"

"I am. Crafter's got some fool idea."

"You listen him!" Hatchet got up, dusting his palms. He stayed in a crouch. Killeen saw that if Hatchet gave the sign the others would come at them.

"I will. But—"

"Listen good!"

"It's talking about using Toby. The boy's in no condition—"

"You listen."

"I won't—"

"The Renny knows lots more'n you." Hatchet frowned, thinking. His face went suddenly blank. "Ah, right."

Hatchet had somehow understood what the Crafter meant. Killeen wanted to ask but knew he could not trust the answer. The man's face was now impassive. His chin was underslung, as if to disown what the mild expression implied.

Killeen let his breath out slowly. Best to stall. If Hatchet found some way of going around Killeen, of getting what the Kings wanted without using a translator, all hope for Toby was lost. "Yeasay . . . yeasay."

"Damn right," Hatchet said severely. "Talk out loud, too. I want hear everything."

"Yeasay."

Hatchet nodded imperceptibly to the other Kings. They relaxed slightly.

1. **Wants you all come.**
2. **Show you what to take.**

"How long will it be?"

1. **No measure.**

Killeen whispered, "Crafter won't say." The longer they spent here, the greater the danger. Some Marauder would see them.

1. **Have to march some.**

"How far from here?"

1. **Can't understand its units.**
2. **Some other stuff, too.**

3.   I'm only getting about half what it puts out.
4.   Thinks boy important.
5.   It will give ride.

"Good, we'll ride. What're we getting in return?"

1.   Everything on list.
2.   But can get more.

"Why'll it give us more than we ask?"

1.   Has job for boy.

No, Killeen thought emphatically. *Tell it no.* Then he said, "We won't take unnecessary chances."

"Hey!" Hatchet said gruffly. "*I'*ll decide what's too much risk."

1.   You will like arrangement.
2.   Crafter must show you.
3.   Boy not hurt.
4.   He not vulnerable.

Killeen suppressed a burst of wild laughter. *Surrounded by mechs—talking with one!—and this puffed-up junkpile says Toby's not vulnerable.*

1.   Want I translate that?

No. Killeen got control of himself.

Hatchet was glowering at him. He fought down the urge to press the Crafter about Toby. "My leader says we can talk about it later."

1.   Crafter says good.

"That's more like it," Hatchet said. "Just tell him we'll do as much as he likes."

Killeen breathed out carefully, thinking. He had to get this right. *You can fix my boy?* "Show us what to do."

1. Crafter can take us to special place.
2. It can get tools to fix boy.
3. Your arm, too.

At what price?

1. We'll see.
2. Crafter says no more.

"Party!" Hatchet called briskly. "Mount the Renny. We'll be done real soon."

We have to know what the Crafter means.

1. You will.
2. Crafter show.
3. First must steal what it wants.

As they climbed up the steep sides of the imposing, burnished mech, Hatchet glowered at Killeen. "Strikin' a Cap'n, huh? I'll have your ass for this. Wait'll we get back Metropolis."

"*If* we get back," Killeen said sourly.

TWO

Killeen could not get used to the feel of riding atop the Crafter. The haulers he had ridden before had been slow, easy.

This Crafter rolled with a grating murmur and lurched heavily when it crossed an arroyo. The swaying nearly made him sick. He and Shibo kept Toby firmly pressed back into a cubbyhole where the rocking could not dislodge him. The boy's legs stuck out like cordwood, stiff and useless. Around them the human party covered very little of the Renegade's cylindrical bulk. They held on to the myriad pipes and masts and vent-valves in the Crafter's ceramic skin.

They crossed rough country because the Crafter carefully stayed away from mech roads. This was the most

built-up complex Killeen had ever seen, a web of pale slab
pathways and blank-faced, perfectly cubic buildings. Traffic
fled down narrow gleaming rails. On the steep hillsides
foundries rumbled. Through a gradually thickening activity
the Renegade moved with crafty purpose. Its antennae
cycled endlessly. Each time a mech came within view,
Killeen heard sputterings. The Renegade was sending
some IGNORE ME signal into each mechmind, making itself
invisible.

Killeen could not relax. His eyes leaped from each
approaching mech to the next.

"Ease off," Hatchet whispered to him. "Renny knows
how get us through."

Killeen studied a bulky mech, a kind he had never
seen, racing along the nearby railline. It accelerated so fast
it was a blur as it neared the far end of the worn valley.

He asked, "How many times you done this?"

"Must be thirty, forty."

"All like this?"

"Mostly. Ever' one's different some way."

"How?"

"New fact'ry. Different tricks gettin' in, too."

"You never gone back, hit the same place?"

"Naysay. Too chancy."

"You figure the Renny leaves some kinda mark? So
they'll be waiting if it went back?"

"Could be. Mostly I think he doesn't take chances. Not
when he can get the stuff he wants somewhere else."

"What kind stuff?"

"Parts, looks like."

"Replacement parts?"

"Prob'ly. Thing's trying stay alive."

"Ever get trouble? Mechs catch on?"

Hatchet's words came a little slower. "Don't know as I
could tell. Things happen pretty damn mechfast sometimes."

Killeen hadn't heard anyone say "mechfast" since the
Citadel. On the march there was no comparison between
human speed and the blinding quickness of the Marauders.

"Any people hurt?"

Hatchet didn't answer for a long moment. He clung to

a brown vent-valve beside Killeen's perch on a level housing. The Crafter was plunging down a rough grade. Tan mechwaste clogged the shallow gullies. Coiled blue-green packing material blew in a thin, chilly breeze. It was colder and drier here. Mech weather.

"Lost two," Hatchet said at last.

"How?"

"Family business," Hatchet said adamantly.

"My people at risk, makes it Bishop Family business."

Hatchet didn't like this. He couldn't find a way to argue around it, though. His mouth twisted to one side as if he was remembering something he didn't want to. "Sometimes there's mech guards. Twice they come up on us, right in the middle. We ran. They got somebody each time."

"How?"

Hatchet looked irritated. "Shot 'em, course."

"With what?"

"I wasn't takin' notes, see? Just tryin' keep my head from gettin' blowed off."

"Were they firing solid shot at you?"

Hatchet smiled icily. "Sorry I didn't snag one for you so's I could fish it out my pocket, show you."

"No, I mean, were they using guns like ours? Or e-beams? Cutters?"

Hatchet was irritated now. It wasn't like a moment before, when he had been trying to keep from telling Killeen something. Now he didn't see the point to the questions. "Couldn't tell."

"Did you recover the bodies?"

"Damn, we were *runnin'*."

"I know. Point is, I wonder if it was just mech guards you ran into, or something worse."

"What . . . Marauders?"

"Could be. You get a look at what was after you?"

"Naysay." Hatchet's pride had resisted telling much about their past failures. But now he saw a pattern to Killeen's interest and his voice lost its tight, suspicious edge. "Shot at us from 'way up in the girders."

Killeen nodded. Just the way something had fired on the Bishops back in the last Trough they'd rested in. So whatever had killed the two Kings were not ordinary mech guards. They had hunted the humans. Yet they were small enough to climb on narrow girders. Which meant there was a new kind of hunter mech.

"You see your people get hit?"

"Naysay. Saw 'em down. No tracer from 'em in the sensorium."

"Could be you're right," Killeen said in a conciliatory tone, but not so obviously that Hatchet would see that was what he was doing. "They were just dead."

"You mean, 'stead of . . ."

"Suredead."

"Not much difference, is there?" Hatchet said. A deepening in his voice suggested a layer of sorrow carried but not revealed. "Either way, we got no Aspect of 'em. They're gone."

Killeen could not stop himself from saying with a flinty look, "You figure having your mind ripped apart by a Marauder is same as just dying?"

Hatchet didn't reply immediately. Both fell silent as they looked out at a passing yard of grease-filmed, partly dismantled machines. Skeletal ranks stretched to the distant hills, a gray, damaged army momentarily halted in its conquest. Each body was missing a hull or treads or, most often, sensors. Their arrogant juts and angles had struck fear into Killeen more times than he could recall. Now they seemed vacant gestures, forlorn. He imagined the Crafter scavenged such yards for parts, picking over the rusting, unresisting dead.

Hatchet said finally, "Don't figure it either way. Some things a Cap'n shouldn't figure."

Killeen felt cowed by this remark, simple and without the edgy proud bluster Hatchet faced the world with most of the time. There was nothing to say in reply.

He swung away, holding to some gas lines with his good hand. Moving was harder than he had thought it would be. The right arm was tiring already. He found Shibo cradling Toby where most of the party rested on a broad, grainy manifold cover. The Crafter was running flat and fast now with just a drumming coming up through its body. The tremor brought soft curves of sleep to Toby's pale face.

Killeen squatted to speak and abruptly the Crafter

braked. They all pitched forward, clinging to whatever the
could. Toby came awake and automatically grasped at h
father as the two of them rolled forward, over a polyme
manifold hatch. They fell a meter. Killeen landed wit
jarring pain. But he had gotten under the boy so Tob
merely had the wind knocked from him. They lay togethe
panting.

"Pile off!" Hatchet called. "Inside! Quick now!"

They had stopped near a factory. Killeen and Shib
carried Toby down the side. Most of the party was alread
running the short distance to an open grate-door tha
clattered up as they approached. Killeen tried to survey th
area but Hatchet was yelling at them to hurry. The grate
door started chugging down like slow teeth even befor
they were through it.

"Renny, he don't like this part," Hatchet said. "Clos
doors fast. Goin' in and out's the most tricky, he says."

"For it, sure," Shibo said dryly.

Killeen carried Toby into the shelter of a cluster o
stacked polyplastic canisters. He did not like the wa
Hatchet kept calling the Crafter "he"—a symptom o
thinking of mechs as manlike, of imagining that you coul
deal with them in terms a human would accept. Killeen
father had said to him once, *Biggest fact about aliens i
they're alien*—which was one of the reasons Citadel Bishc
had made fewer contacts with Renegades than the King
had. Killeen reminded himself to not fall into Hatchet's wa
of thinking about the Crafter. That was why he asked for th
facts behind everything Hatchet said. Facts were more us
than opinions.

The party moved away from the lowering grate-doo
Feet scuttled down narrow crannies in the crowded ba
Killeen had bent over to put Toby on the floor when he fe
a powerful *jjjjjaaaattttttt* explode in his head. Faint cri
skittered in the humming silence that followed the soun
less knife-edge violence. "What was—"

Hatchet's voice came as a dry rasp. "Crafter. Mus
shot at a mech."

Shibo said, "Electromag kill."

Killeen got up unsteadily and saw the Crafter crow
ing the stilled grate-door. Its antennae and sensor-snou

were all trained into the factory. They fanned and fidgeted with quick energy.

Cermo-the-Slow called from farther in, "There's a mech here. Burned out!"

Hatchet got up from behind a large crate and went to see. "Crafter can pick off these li'l guard mechs. He's too fast for 'em."

Shibo said worriedly, "Didn't see even mech tracer."

Killeen shook his head, his ears still ringing. "Me either."

Toby looked unconcerned. He pointed at the Crafter, which now was backing away. "What'll it do while we're inside?"

Hatchet had ignored the boy so far. It startled Killeen when he answered Toby's question with an offhanded kindliness. "It'll lie doggo. Freeze its externals. Make like it's dead, just used for spare parts."

"Like that yard we saw? With all the old mechs?"

"Guess so. Only it'll hunker down in some shed, I seen it do that. Guess that's why it lets its carapace get so rundown-lookin'."

"Fools the other mechs?" Toby asked.

"That's my guess."

"Hey, let's go see what's in here."

"Now you be quiet, boy. Rest yourself."

Killeen watched the Crafter lumber away. He was eternally astonished at the resilience of the young, at how they could take the completely new and blindingly dangerous and simply live with it. He wondered how he had lost that unthinking certainty. Something had worn it away in abrasions so subtle that you never noticed the loss until it was far too late.

The scorched guard mech had an odd look to it. Shibo approached as Cermo-the-Slow was wrenching at one of the mech's side housings. It came away with a clatter. Inside were exposed joints and thick, leathery pads. An oily sheen coated them.

"This's cyborg," Cermo said. "Lubed up, too."

Shibo kicked one of the joints. It gave, flexed, and returned to its original alignment with a persistent fluidity. "Organic parts."

Hatchet seemed unsurprised. "Seen that a lot in fact'ries. Don't get many these in the field."

"Let's go," Killeen said.

Hatchet looked faintly amused. "In a big hurry, huh? Wait'll the two men up front figure the tracer."

The Crafter had transmitted to the lead man a flatmap of where they were to go in the factory. It was recognition-keyed so they got a telltale in their eyes when they were going the right way. A flatmap was language-independent. The Crafter used commandeered navvys to search and make the map; entering a storage zone was far too dangerous for a Renegade.

The party followed the two lead men through a high, arched bay that slumbered in soft orange-green gloom. No mechs moved among the catwalks and bar-rigged balconies that punctuated the immense rising curves of the walls.

"Not much going," Shibo said.

"Old fact'ry," Hatchet said. "The Renny sends us mostly places like this. Mechs use 'em for storage."

"Had a guard, though," Killeen observed.

"Just keep movin'," Hatchet called.

They slipped down dark corridors. Inky shadows stretched among old, abandoned manufacturing lines. Drums half-filled with sulfurous colloids leaked across broken decks. The two Kingsmen who led brought them deftly to a dank underground warren.

At the entrance a portal gaped, rimmed with detection gear. Killeen recognized some of the standard parts from mechs he had stripped. Their party stopped and each person slipped through the portal carefully, moving slowly. Hatchet explained to Shibo and Killeen that the detectors were set at mech levels. They sensed not simply metal, but the network of electronics that any mech carried. Humans had so relatively little of this that they seldom registered on such automatic watchdogs. This was their primary use to the Crafter.

In the tunnels beyond the portal their work began. Long racks of modular parts lined the intersecting tunnels. The lead man located the items the Crafter wanted. The party split into teams to carry out the heavy items. Killeen paired with Shibo after they put Toby in a spot near the portal, where he could watch them work, and, not coincidentally, where they could check on him frequently.

Killeen felt the presence of the mech factory as a cold pressure seeping into him. His apprehension had subsided but it sprang forth with every distant flicker of movement or unexpected sound. Twilight tunnels ricocheted the clatter of their labor, making odd, whining notes. Worse, a few small robo mechs worked in the tunnels. The first time Killeen came upon one he very nearly killed it.

Shibo caught his gun hand and whispered, "Doesn't see us!" She was right. Robos were low on image sorting and texture definition and too dumb to sound an alarm. They simply fetched and stored, on orders from some distant inventory link. Still, their rattling, spidery gait unnerved Killeen in the shadowy tunnels.

The Crafter wanted parts that ranged vastly in scale. Tiny embedded polytron boards. Greenish, marbled photonic slabs no bigger than a hand. Ribbon-ribbed condensers that took three men to carry.

Killeen and Shibo hauled the Crafter's replacement parts out on their backs, or sometimes between the two of them, carrying a short distance and then stopping to let arms and backs rest.

They worked through a time that was for both of them wearying labor threaded by quicksilver instants of fear. The dulling rhythm of hauling without any mechanical aid numbed them. There were no metal carts around to help, and in any case Hatchet ruled out using any. No one knew precisely what triggered the portal alarm, so anything beyond the minimum was a risk. It took several hours to produce the mound of replacement parts they gradually built up near the grate-door. The Crafter would reappear only when the job was done. That minimized its exposure.

Luckily, Toby had fallen asleep again. Killeen checked him on each circuit between the tunnels and the exit bay. He and Shibo at last took a quick break in the depths of the tunnels to eat some dried concentrate bars. Killeen's throat was raw from breathing the acrid fumes of the factory.

"You do this much?" Killeen wheezed as Hatchet passed them.

"Whenever the Renny wants." Hatchet's eyes narrowed. "Listen, we'll do it much as we can. Without the Renny's help, we'd be busting ass runnin' from Marauders."

Killeen nodded mutely, saving his breath, and that was when he saw the approaching mech. It was no robo or navvy. He could make out a carapace as long as a man, with a set of tools bunched in front like a tangle of briars. It was coming toward them down a distant lane between storage racks, either oblivious or not expecting anything unusual. "Hatchet!" Shibo whispered.

They all pulled weapons. Hatchet blinked, as though he had never seen anything like it. "Fan out," he whispered.

The mech came on. Killeen heard in his sensorium an abrupt series like quick, strangled coughs. A voice, but not a human one. It spoke again. Cut-short exclamations, rapid but unforced, natural but eerie. Not words, not more than quick bursts of air expelled through a narrow, hoarse throat—

Hatchet said wonderingly, "What the hell . . . ?"
Killeen's Arthur Aspect broke in:

Barking! That is the sound of a terrestrial dog barking. I haven't heard that call-code for so long. . . .

Into Killeen's eye leaped a picture of a furry, four-legged animal yelping and scampering over a green field, chasing a blue ball that hopped away downhill. Something in the sound that flooded his ears carried a meaning of salute, of an element he had always missed.

"That mech," he said. "It's calling us."

Their talk had attracted it. Shibo was already braced, tracking the quick form as it raced down the network of racked supplies, leading it slightly so she could fire instantly if needed. Killeen put his hand on her shoulder. "No. I think it's all right. There's something . . ."

The barking rose to a crescendo, then abruptly cut off.

A warm, mellow woman's voice said clearly, "Human-kind! I picked up your scent. It is the longlost!"

Hatchet called out, "Don't move."

"To hear the voice of man is to obey it," the mech

called from somewhere in the racks. "I used the correct call, did I not?"

"You did," Killeen answered, peering through the twilight glow of distant lamps. Its steel hide was pocked, seamed, pitted. The worn jacket was crisscrossed with melted lines, rivets, weldings long since ripped away, tap-in spots, and rough scars. At a prompting from Arthur, Killeen added, "Good dog."

"Ruff! Ruff! . . . I . . . well, I am not actually a *dog,* you know."

Shibo said wryly, "We guessed."

The womanly mech voice came from an aged acoustic speaker mounted directly between two optical sensors. These glittered, tracking Killeen intently as he approached. Shibo and Hatchet edged in at the flanks, still ready. Shibo looked distant for a moment, consulting her own Aspects. Killeen saw Cermo-the-Slow easing around behind the mech, grinning in anticipation of blowing it away. He raised a cautionary hand.

"Barking is simply an attention-getting device." The mech had a full-bodied, resonant voice now. Killeen wondered if dogs spoke.

Of course not! The dog was an animal which long ago came to think of humans as, well, as sort of gods. They herded other animals, guarded things— Ah! Now I see it! This is an original, humanmade machine. Or at least it contains elements of some device humans must have made.

Humans made mechs? Killeen wondered. The idea was as odd as the assertion that humans had made the Taj Mahal building they had seen.

Shibo said, "That you did."

"I was told to use that call-approach method. To differentiate myself from hostile mechs." The machine scuffed its treads enthusiastically against the rough cement floor. Its throaty alto vibrated with emotion. Unable to restrain itself any longer, it rumbled up to within arm's length of Killeen, crying, "It has been so long!"

Killeen was startled. "How . . . how long?"

"I don't know. My inboard time sequencing was reordered long ago by the mechmind in these factories. I hope you realize I *never* would have labored for these beings if I had been able to escape them. I was wholly loyal to human direction."

Hatchet approached and the machine caught sight of him. "Oh, another human! So *many* still alive. Ruff!" The voice attained a timbre of awe.

This machine is remarkably doglike. Listen to that devotion. There must have been dog memory passed down from the original expedition vaults themselves. That ancient trove . . .

Hatchet asked, "What you want?"

"I . . . I was only meaning to serve you, sir." A whimper filled each word with remorse.

"How?"

"I . . . You must understand, I have been a good servant. All this while. I kept my instructions buried, where the mechmind could not find them."

Hatchet's forehead wrinkled. "You work here?"

"Yessir! I am valued for my ability to haul and to repair and to find lost items of the general inventory." It scuffled around anxiously, as though it wanted to lick Hatchet's hand. "Also I—"

"Shut *up*," Hatchet said with evident satisfaction. "What can you do for us?"

"Well, I can do all the tasks I am routinely assigned, sir. But there is—there is—there is—"

It is hung up in a command loop. There must be some information it cannot reveal unless we give it the right association or code word.

"Shut up," Hatchet said firmly.

The mech's stuttering stopped. It began, "I am most sorry for that. Ruff! I seem to have—"

"Look," Killeen said, "you know this factory, right? Are there any mechs around that are dangerous for us?"

"I . . . Not in this part of my workworld, no."

"How near?"

"Five prantanouf."

"What?"

"A distance the mechs use. I . . . do not remember how to say it in this speak." The mech's womanly voice became distressed, whimpering, almost tear-filled. "I . . . I am sorry . . . I . . ."

"Never mind. Do they know we're here?"

The mech paused as though listening. "No. Sir."

"How'd you find us?"

"I have sensors which pick up the human effusions. Wondrous manscents. They are long buried by the sludge the mechmind has carbuncled onto me. Still, they alerted me to your presence."

Killeen wondered how such a humanmade machine could have survived so long among the alien mechs. Arthur put in sardonically:

Precisely because of its unthinking obedience. Uncomfortably, that is exactly what humans required of animals if they were to survive domestication. We were not morally superior ourselves, when we had the power . . .

Aspect Nialdi's stern voice immediately broke in:

That was the proper role *of animals. Partners and servants of humankind! You cannot compare—*

Killeen cut off a rising babble of Aspect voices within himself.

The mech paused, its opticals registering others of the party who approached as they heard the talk. "*Many* humans. You have lived after all!"

"You worked in Citadel?" Shibo asked.

"Yes yes, madam." The mech lowered its front section in a stiff parody of a bow. "I functioned first in the Chandelier."

Killeen blinked in astonishment. Arthur was babbling

in his mind, a thin excited voice which he batted away like a fly. "Tell us what you remember before you came here."

"I was a worker for the humans who built the first Arcologies. Then, later, Citadels. I designed and labored for the three Citadels Pawn."

"When did you run away to the mechs?" Hatchet demanded roughly, suspiciously.

"I did not run away!" The machine sounded insulted, like a woman whose honor has been slighted in a casual comment. "Some human machines did so, I know. I was not among them! I was taken."

"Co-opted?" Shibo asked.

"My circuits overriden. New imperatives written directly into my substrate."

Killeen said, "They took the Citadel?" and watched the machine carefully. He knew of no machines controlled by men, ever. Certainly Family Bishop had none at the time of the Calamity.

"Oh, no. No. In those ages the mechs were a small band. They avoided humanity's Citadels, their festivals for breeding, all. They captured me when I was . . . was . . . was . . . was . . ."

The mech's audio rasped as it went into a circular-command loop. Something it yearned to say was blocked by a deeper prohibition.

"Stop!" Killeen ordered. He was beginning to believe the machine. His Arthur Aspect piped in:

We termed them "manmechs," in my day. The Expedition had an entire complement of intelligent machines, after all, and kept them in good running order. Otherwise, how could the first generation have been kindled? Humanmade robots united the sperm and ova brought from Earth. They tended the young, grew the first food—

So they did! Doubly evil, then, the manmechs' own perverse and traitorous act, to form alliance with those who pillaged the Chandeliers and now hound us in every cranny. This is an enemy of all

*mankind, this thing that insults us with its bark
and woman's soft tones. Kill it! That is the only—*

The mech civilizations captured this manmech.
You cannot attribute evil to it if it had no choice!
The mechs transformed some of its functions,
but apparently never extracted its fundamental
human-command overrides.

Killeen asked, "How come they didn't just tear it up,
mine it for materials?"

*It knows us. They kept this foul betrayer because
it can deceive us yet again! That is why I
command you to destroy it. Now! Yet—*

Probably it satisfies some arcane function in
mech society. Or its survival from the early days
may be mere chance. I advise against any sudden action such as the frothing nonsense Nialdi
advances.

You risk all if you suffer the traitor to—

Killeen cut off the Nialdi Aspect. He had no time for
that now. Nialdi and Arthur kept sputtering and sparring
with each other. He let them run as tiny mouse-voices in
the back of his mind, to bleed off their tensions, but
otherwise ignored them.

The machine coughed, barked angrily three times, and
came back to normal. "I . . . am sorry. I cannot reveal
that information without a key word command."

"How'd the mechs get you?" Hatchet asked.

"There was nothing I could do. I went with the mech
civilization and lost my place at the foot of beloved
humanity." These words were darkly plaintive, half from
broken memories and half a plea for understanding.

The cluster of humans looked at one another, confused. "You figure it tells true?" Cermo-the-Slow asked
Hatchet.

"Could be."

"Damn strange, you ask me," Cermo said flatly, shaking his head.

"Mechs've never tried this before," Shibo said. "Not like a mech trick, this. I trust it."

Killeen said, "Yeasay. Mechs just try kill us, not confuse us."

The Kings and Rooks spoke, guardedly agreeing. The ancient manmech's acoustic sensors swiveled eagerly toward each speaker in turn, small polymer cups tilting around its oblong body.

Hatchet's yellow upper teeth chewed at his lip, his triangular face for once giving away his uncertainty. He reached up and unconsciously fingered his knobby chin, squeezing it slightly, as if to press firmness into the rest of his face. "Okay. So what? We're 'bout done here. Let's go."

The machine barked nervously, a high animated yelp. Then the womanly voice murmured, "But no! You cannot leave me here, sir. I am yours. Humanity's."

Hatchet looked uncomfortable. "Say now, I . . ."

"But you must." The woman's voice gained an edge of seductive softness. "I have been loyal to you these long times. And I must deliver my message to the Citadel Pawn."

"Citadel Pawn's destroyed," Killeen said. "We are all the Citadel Families that remain."

"No! Gone? But then well I . . . well I . . . well I . . ."

"Shut up!" Hatchet said irritably. "Come on, let's get movin'." He walked away.

"No, I must follow. You are my—"

"Yeasay, follow," Shibo said gently. "But *quiet*."

There were only a few more items on the Crafter's list. The party carried these out to the grate-door. The Crafter was approaching as they shouldered the last pieces onto the pile. Suddenly the grate-door began rising.

"Get to it!" Hatchet called.

At his signal the team began to quickly carry the items out and load them into a side pouch which the Crafter popped open. Killeen and Shibo and Cermo joined in the hurried scramble. Only moments before they had been joking at the curious machine. Now there was a taut

watchfulness as they finished the job, fully exposed to the
slanting pale light of Denixrise.

Killeen and Shibo carried Toby out as the last pieces
went into the pouch. They got him safely onto a ledge
halfway up the Crafter body. They were all getting tired and
it was hard to get Toby up the incline. Bud broke into
Killeen's attention:

1. **Crafter says climb up.**
2. **We go to another factory.**

Killeen relayed this blank-faced to Hatchet, who
asked, "How come?"

"The Crafter says he has something for us." This was a
flat lie, since Bud said:

1. **Crafter wants Toby's help.**

Impossible, Killeen thought.

1. **You will see, Crafter says.**

Killeen said, "Can the Crafter release this manmech?
Says it can't leave this factory 'plex."

Bud said nothing for a long moment. Then:

1. **Crafter has freed manmech.**
2. **Favor to you.**
3. **It says, remember, it wants Toby's help.**

"We'll see," Killeen said guardedly.

The manmech began to crawl up a side ramp of the
Crafter. Bud said hurriedly:

1. **Crafter won't carry manmech.**

"Why not?"

1. **Manmech is now free mech.**
2. **Can trigger detectors.**
3. **Make it stay off.**

"I want it with us."

1. Crafter will kill then.

"No, just a—"
Killeen heard the Crafter transmit a seething burst of static, which sent the manmech reeling.

1. That was warning.

The manmech cried, "Humans! Do not leave me!"
Tight-lipped, Killeen called, "No choice. You're free now. Good luck!"
As they lumbered away from the cubic factory the grate-door came ratcheting down. Looking back at it, Killeen felt a washed-out sense of relief. They had come through the dark tunnels and survived.
He was saddened to see the dog-woman manmech come clattering after them. He would've liked to ask that strange combination about its ancient life. A living entity was far more gripping than the dessicated little lectures the Aspects gave him. He was trying to learn more from his Aspects, but they lacked the manmech's poignant, humble truth.
He shook his head. His father had told him once that the smartest people were those who, once they saw they had no choices left, forgot the matter. He had never mastered that art. He shut off his comm, so he would not have to hear the manmech's fading, plaintive yelps and forlorn baying.
The Crafter accelerated away. Its antennae swerved and buzzed with anxious energy.
He lay back to rest. Toby moaned nearby. The boy's nerve-weave was beginning to fray and fret. Killeen levered his bad arm under his son's neck to provide some pillow. He closed his eyes. Sleep crowded in on him. He set himself against it. He had to think. To prepare for the real reason he had come here.

THREE

At first he thought it was a mountain. Then he saw its myriad worked edges and the smooth oblique inclines. It was a complex so large it seemed to be the landscape, dwarfing hills nearby.

The Renegade Crafter drove toward the towering network at top speed. They crossed an open plain that was seamless and hard. Other mechs shot along cross-paths. The silence was eerie. Some mechs swelled, humming, and then shrunk without seeming to be moving at all. Killeen could not follow the fast, undaunted traffic. It was like the swarms of birds he had seen around the Metropolis, but each moving in unalterable straight lines.

The Crafter did not slow at all. Its antennae sent pops and buzzes in all directions. A wedge-backed hauler bore down on them. It passed so close Killeen could see parts-index markings on its hull tabs. The backwash slapped them a hard *crack!* A black circle opened at the base of the mountain. Killeen glanced upward and saw ornate slate walls. An orange detonation unfurled halfway up the mountain face. Before he could see what caused it the tunnel swallowed them.

Even then the Renegade did not slow. They hurtled through unremitting black. A warm wind brushed them.

Killeen lay still, feeling the hum of the Crafter's momentum, waiting. He listened to Hatchet talking to some of the others on a hush-circuit. Hatchet gave orders for when they stopped, his muted mutter laced with anxiety. Everything depended on surprise.

They slowed.

Coasted in complete dark.

Slammed to a halt.

The team clambered down. Killeen didn't move but he felt Shibo nearby.

Abruptly, red light flooded them from above. They were in a huge vault. Blocky containers nearly filled the volume, stacked in an elaborate rising weave of interlocking helices. Killeen could see no mechs.

He and Shibo carried Toby off the Crafter. He could not see how the team neutralized two small mechs but he heard the quick scratching electromagnetic fight.

"Hustle!" Hatchet called to them. They scattered among oblong canisters. Something like glass snapped under Killeen's boots. Toby grunted and stifled a groan. Killeen did not look back to see what the Renegade was doing.

They reached a small knothole hatch. Already most of the team was through it. A fried mech stood smoldering nearby. Killeen carried Toby through on the carrysling with Shibo ahead, her pistol out.

Beyond was a simple square zone. Bluewhite mechs sped across it. They paid no attention to the small human band that emerged from a sheer, unmarked wall. More storage facilities, Killeen guessed. A distant booming came down from the ceiling.

—Tough part comin' up,— Hatchet sent.

The team ran toward a small arch. Plainly it was an entrance gate. Elaborate signifier emblems studded both sides. Killeen knew some recognition-code inputs from the days when he had scavenged with his father. He peered at the polished polycopper casings with embedded, snaking lines. These engraved silvery circuits were new to him.

Hatchet punched some instructions into the signifier circuits. There were hexagonal insert points embossed on the ceramo-metal wall. Killeen had never seen anyone make use of them.

Hatchet did not even pause. He pulled small cylinders from his flap pockets and stuck them slowly into the holes. He turned each one until it clicked. Through his efficiency, nervousness glittered, like sky seen through speckled clouds. The team watched him with drawn faces.

The portal's square polymer gate slid aside. No one made a move through the arch.

"This's far as it goes," Hatchet said, standing back. "Now . . ."

Silence. Edgy glances. Killeen suddenly knew that this was where the Kings had suffered their two deaths.

Hatchet said, "We need the boy."

"How?" Killeen said, his throat narrow and dry.

"He's got to crawl through that. Then null out the circuits on the other side."

"He can't. No legs, remember?"

"That's the trick," Hatchet said. "He's the only one can do it."

"Have somebody else crawl."

"You don't get it. Your boy, he's got no Aspects. So he's missing lots circuitry, the inset boards, all that. This gate senses that stuff."

"This is what the Crafter meant?" Killeen asked, stalling.

"Sure. He saw it right away." Hatchet's eyes danced, alight with possibility. "We've never been able to get through here. The 'quipment to fix up Toby, it's beyond this gate. The kid, he's got less circuitry. The mechs've set this gate so it'll catch even humans. We got practically no insets, compared with a mech—but this gate sees just a scrap."

"It killed your people."

"Yeasay. See, it's not just that your boy's got no Aspects," Hatchet said. Now his face was concerned, reasonable. He spread both hands in a can't-you-see? gesture. "The Renny, he figures with your boy's legs out, there's even less nerve-linked stuff for the gate pickups."

"You . . ." Killeen eyed the rest of the team. He would dearly love to ruin Hatchet right here, kick his balls to sour mush. But that wouldn't save Toby.

Sly and chilly the words came from the Cap'n of the Kings. "Want me to make it an order?"

"You don't know it'll work."

"Renny figures it will. That's why it asked about the boy back at the landing strip, right?"

Killeen nodded.

"Crafter's not risking *its* precious circuits," Shibo said dryly. But she saw the situation. She would back up Killeen but the decision was his. In the end nobody can carry another's weight.

Killeen saw that Hatchet had deliberately not told him any of this until now, when there was no time left to dispute it. "Even if the Crafter's right, Toby can't get through there."

Shibo started to agree. Hatchet held up his hand, his mouth set firmly. "Got arms, right? He can pull himself through."

Killeen stood rigid, unable to think of anything. He had to ward this off. But he had no time to develop reasoning, no argument against a Cap'n who had steered this whole raid toward this moment.

Killeen reminded himself that Hatchet had been on many raids, knew things, had done things for the Crafter. Called the Renegade "he," like it was human.

Ever since Hatchet had heard Killeen arguing with the Crafter out loud, he had understood. And not told anyone else. Because it solved some problem Hatchet had. Because it opened some possibility. . . .

"What's in there?" Killeen demanded.

"Bioparts. Fact'ry, supplies, storage, ever'thing."

"The Crafter needs 'em?"

"Yeah. He'll give us a lot, we bring out what he needs."

"That's worth so much?"

Hatchet said confidently, "With the right parts, right 'quipment, yeasay. See, the Renny can get metal parts pretty easy. Biostuff's harder. Mechs can't 'facture bioparts so easy. So they guard it."

Arthur's tinny voice darted in Killeen's mind:

I believe the mechs guard bioparts inventories precisely in order to thwart Renegades. Bioparts require more delicate manufacture. To suppress unauthorized use, biofactories are protected by such sensitive traps as this gate.

1. Crafter say is big complex.
2. We can get help here.

Killeen sensed a faint, strobing contact between his Aspect and the Crafter. Good. They needed a guide and—

Hatchet said warmly, "C'mon, Killeen. The Renny can fix up things. Your arm. Toby's legs. What other choice you got?"

Killeen stood for a long moment, not wanting to let the moment pass, trying to see a way clear. If he held on to the fractional seconds they could never add up to the awful moment when his son would have to—

"Dad?"

Killeen looked blankly down at Toby lying a short distance away. The carrysling folded around him, a tight-weave blanket above the pale, wan face.

"Dad, I might's well do it. I'm no use this way."

Written on Toby's face was stubborn endurance and a thin despair his father had never seen. Killeen felt a coldness in his stomach. In the space of a heartbeat Killeen abruptly saw his son as another person, not as a principle or a legacy but as a separate intelligence, now able to plot his own path. Toby had in his own way made the sign that signified his mastery of his destiny. Now the covenants of the Family Bishop released Killeen from his persistent role. Killeen saw that he could gladly grasp at this. But he could not bring himself to do it.

Shibo said quietly, "Toby right."

The team saw the moment for what it was, the crucial fulcrum that always must finally pivot a child's world into something larger. The change could come in sanctified ritual or on the field of battle, but once it had come, the turning instant between father and son could never reverse.

Killeen nodded. Toby had the right to risk. The right to die, if he chose.

They pushed the boy as close as they could. The matrix of gate sensors was a woven strip of polyrich sheen that wrapped completely around the inside gate frame.

It buzzed when Toby's hand reached across the threshold.

"Go on!" Hatchet urged.

"Don't bother him," Killeen spat out fiercely. "Let him feel his way."

"Gate won't wait long," Hatchet said. "Hurry, boy."

Toby reached another hand forward. His errant fingernails were long and pale. His legs trailed behind him, limp and useless. Under his green tightweave jumper the legs already looking shrunken and pulpy, as though from long years of neglect. Toby got a good grip on the gate frame. Grunting, he pulled himself forward.

"How long's he got?" Shibo asked.

"Well . . ." Hatchet licked his lips. "Early days, we had a girl. Hurt pretty bad. She tried to crawl through."

"Yeasay?" Killeen demanded.

"She . . . I didn't time it but . . . she was most the way through. . . ."

"Damn you! How long?"

"She . . . she got further than this. But it was longer. I—"

Killeen shouted at Toby, "Pull!"

Sweat broke out on the boy's chalky face. A quiet descended. Killeen could hear others draw in a breath and hold it.

Toby's fingers felt ahead and found a thin crack in the warped flooring. It was a polybind tile whose edge had curled up at a small angle. It provided enough of a lip for Toby's fingernails to pry at it. The lip curved slightly. Toby got all his fingers on the edge and pulled. He came forward minutely. This brought him into reach of another tile. He got three fingers over the lip of it and grunted.

Killeen could not see that the boy moved at all. The hard black frame of the gate seemed to swell in his vision until it filled his sight. Toby was halfway across it.

The boy slid with infinitesimal scraping slowness. Killeen leaned as near as he could without intersecting the gate fields. The background whisper of mech traffic seemed to fall away.

Toby inched forward. His legs dragged with a soft rasp.

The gate abruptly clicked. A faint whine started.

"What's that?" Killeen blurted.

Hatchet said, "Dunno. Time before, I don't remember—"

"Get him back!" one of the team called. Killeen did not know who it was or why they said it but the voice shook him. He took a step, hand stretched toward Toby's feet. Maybe Killeen could yank him back in one quick movement, before the gate sensed the approach of the inset circuitry in his head.

Fast. One quick movement.

He stepped again. Reached down to grab Toby's ankles—

Shibo struck him hard on the shoulder. Off balance, he fell sideways.

The gate whined louder.

"Damn!" Killeen scrambled back to his feet.

"Dad! Leave off!" Toby called.

"But—"

"I'll . . . do . . . it. . . ."

The boy dragged himself on again, clutching some fragmentary edge so thin Killeen could not see it.

Toby's face was pressed into the slick surface so that he could reach as far ahead as possible. But that meant he could not see.

The gate clicked.

Toby's face was filmed with sweat and dirt. Beneath that the skin was deathly pale with exertion. His hands grasped ahead and found nothing. The smooth flooring gave him no purchase.

"Lookleft," Shibo called softly. "Bump."

Toby ran his left hand along and found a ripple in the polished floor. He dragged himself a hand's length.

"Ahead now," Killeen said. "Looks like a ridge."

Fingers caught on the lip of some buried cable cover. Toby stretched. This time he got four fingers of each hand barely over the edge. Only the tips caught. The boy gasped and then held his breath. His forearm muscles clenched.

In the silence Killeen heard small popping noises. He looked around. The team was absolutely still. It took him a moment to realize that the sounds came from Toby.

Each was distinct and clear. An instant passed before he realized what the sound was. Toby's fingernails were snapping off.

The boy bit his lip. Blood trickled down his chin.

He expelled a breath like a cough. Somehow his fingers caught the lip right. He dragged forward.

A hand's length. Two. Three. His fingers scrabbled out ahead.

The gate whine stopped. An absolute silence descended.

Toby got up on his elbows. Grunted. Turned. Dug his elbows against the thin edge of tile that had brought him this far. Heaved. Wrenched himself sideways and—impossibly—*rolled* . . . forward . . . legs flapping over each other, carried by the hips . . . across the gate threshold.

The gate gave three clear, sharp notes.

"That's the okay," Hatchet said. His voice was tight and high. "See? Damn well *knew* it'd work. Just you flip those switches there, Toby."

Hatchet was still grinning, hands on hips, when Killeen clipped him hard on the point of his chin. Hatchet went down with a look of sudden, aggrieved puzzlement on his face.

It was a dank, foul-smelling place.

Crannies vented acrid clouds into a warm, moist atmosphere. Vats bubbled. Colloids flowed through transparent pipes that ascended high into a concealing murk.

Killeen could not see the ceiling. The roiling clouds up there sometimes parted to show darker layers above. Flying mechs darted into the vapor on odd, looping trajectories.

1. **Go to left.**
2. **Crafter wants in.**

The sliding gray intelligence that Killeen felt nibbling at the edge of his sensorium now quickened its rhythms. The Crafter was coming; he could feel it.

The team moved fast along a narrow hallway. Killeen and Shibo had to labor to keep up, with Toby swaying in the carrysling between them. Killeen's shoulders ached with a pain that came almost like spreading warmth. They passed between two colossal holding vats. Amber mist wafted into the air far above them.

They reached another archway. This was triple the size of the one Toby had negotiated. Hatchet seemed to know this type. He plunged two cylinder keys into an inset lock. The iron-blue web-metal gate slid open. The Crafter was not in the open space beyond.

Shibo asked, "Crafter here?"

Killeen's teeth worked at his lip. "Its directions said so. omethin' in here it wants. It don't give a ratsrear 'bout us ut it damn well better—"

The Crafter abruptly shot into view. It moved so uickly Killeen saw it only as a suddenly expanding wedge f high-gloss metal. It bolted through the gate, ratcheting oudly. Its treads crunched to a stop near the team.

Bud translated:

1. Get on.
2. Need speed.

Killeen signaled to Hatchet, who nodded. Silently the umans swarmed up the Crafter's side. Killeen held Toby n a mudguard over the treads. They barely got on before he Crafter started off at high speed. The Renegade passed ome mechs which gave no sign of noticing, just kept up heir eight-armed labors.

They accelerated. Smears of light and shadow passed. he Crafter surged through narrow alleyways, its treads lattering. The humans held on against sudden lurches and ssaulting chords of vibration.

Killeen tried to place Toby higher but it was impossi-le. Sometimes the mudguard would shriek, scraping a orner as they rounded it. The second time this happened, alf of Toby's tightweave blanket ripped away.

"Slow!" Killeen called. "We'll—"

The Crafter slammed to a stop. Killeen bundled Toby nto what was left of the tightweave. He saw that the Crafter had stopped not for them but because this was a ew manufacturing complex. Towers of sullen amber glass ose and twisted with byzantine grace. Fluids percolated in ome, rushed like mountain streams in others. The ceiling ooded them with a harsh, ultraviolet glare. Killeen looked t his hand and could see black veins beneath the skin.

1. Supplies this way.
2. Come.

The Crafter led them.

The mech could barely squeeze through a narrow gap

between two translucent, inverted cones which bubbled
with noxious currents. Harsh brown layers of gas drifted
silently overhead. Heavy air clasped at them, working
moist cool fingers into their sinuses.

They came into a gallery of identical pods. Green
polyalum casings rose in identical stacks into the vapor sky
above. Pipes led everywhere.

"Hold," Hatchet whispered. He gestured. A mech was
working at the far end of the complex. It could not see the
thin line of humans from this angle. The Crafter faded back
behind a boxy housing.

1. **That's smart mech.**
2. **Multiple processor, class 3.**
3. **Best it not sense us.**

"Can't the Crafter shut it down?" Killeen asked.

1. **Others notice it gone.**
2. **Crafter is afraid here.**
3. **Must be quick.**

Killeen relayed the message to Hatchet and then
soundlessly asked, *What's it doing to fix Toby?*

1. **We go to special place.**
2. **Crafter knows repairs done there.**

It better not be trying some trick, Killeen thought
precisely. A veiled threat, though he doubted any of them
could harm the Renegade.

1. **It says is honest.**
2. **Must hurry though.**

Hatchet conferred with his people. The Kingsmen
nodded, whispering. Cermo said the mech looked almost
done with its job; it was cleaning up, putting tools away.

"Too chancy to try a lateral maneuver," Hatchet said.
Everyone agreed. Nobody knew the way.

They waited for the mech to move off. Killeen and

Shibo put Toby down beside one of the pods. Killeen's nerves had been leaping as they turned every fresh corner. His sensorium rippled with pungent hints. A leap dripped somewhere, amplified by the polished reflecting surfaces. Obscure rumblings spoke of fluid movements beneath their boots. Steam whistled from a vat.

Killeen leaned against a polished bronze pod. This bewildering complex was far larger than anything his father had ever described. The Bishops had nibbled at the mere outlying fringe of something they could not understand. Here everything depended on stealth alone. There would be no hope of fighting or escaping, if they were caught. He wondered idly if any humans had found a way to live in such a labyrinth. Rats in the walls. Pests.

He felt a click in the machinery behind him and turned to see. A window in the pod had phased into transparency. Beyond was a mass of something moving in pale blue light. He frowned, puzzled. Levers and pivots worked with patient energy beneath a glistening wet film. But there was something about the angle, the bulky pivot collars. . . .

Legs. Human legs.

They were all pumping. Steady. Relentless.

The pivots were sockets. Ample hip joints were mounted to a shaft in the back wall. Thighs picked up the stroke of this steel shaft.

Farther down, the turning joints were human knees. Green kneecaps flexed as the thigh muscles worked beneath pale yellow, transparent skin. The legs pumped down through stringy shanks. But the calf sinews did not taper into tendons that attached to ankles. Instead, at each completion of its pump, a leg bunched and drove hard against something coarse and leathery.

He could see seven legs bunching and stroking, each at a different phase of the cycle. They delivered thrust to the complicated brown nexus where the foot should be, a power train that converted flywheel energy into a complex series of modulated crankshaft motions.

Pump. Stroke.

Flex. Turn. Kick.

A slick sheen kept the parchment-yellow skin moist. He turned away, breathing hard.

He had the impression that the arms and legs were growing, bulking out the muscles. But for what?

He deliberately made himself not think of what he saw. There was no room in his mind for anything but essentials.

His sensorium gave back a numbed hollow shock. At the base of his spine he felt a brimming warmth that was a temptation. The sensorium itself could move to protect itself. With stealthy fingers it reflexively tried to soothe the images in his mind.

A tempting oblivion. To let a blank indifference ease an icy slab between him and the remorselessly pumping legs.

No.

He wrenched away and crossed the narrow sheetmetal walkway. He must know more.

His fingers found a pressure release and here too a window fluxed.

Legs labored in a moist blue realm. At the far end of the pod the legs were shorter, as though they had not fully grown yet.

He quietly moved away from the others. A feeder line dripped out into the decking. He knelt and smelled a sweet aroma. Food.

He fluxed another window. Here more veined legs worked and he could see another production line above.

Arms. Bulging human arms worked against an intricate set of pressers and cam gears.

Feeder lines laced them. Wires hooked into the leathery biceps and wrists. As he numbly watched, one arm shifted to bring its rhythms to bear on a different set of pressers, and lunged more furiously for a short moment. Then it swiveled with quick grace and returned to its earlier job.

Six sets of arms labored beneath pale, sickly light.

Biceps tapered into massive deltoids. These anchored at double-ball-jointed shoulders set into the back wall.

There were no hands. The motive energy did not require such deft dexterity. Momentum flowed with jerky purpose into the ratcheting network below.

"Ho! It's leavin'," Hatchet called.

Killeen stood slowly, dazed. He got control of himself. Walking back to the team, he was grateful for the abrupt interruption. Splinters of pain shot through his back, reminders of the labor of carrying Toby. He only vaguely noticed this. He made no sign to Shibo. He just bent and picked up the end of Toby's sling.

Ahead, the Crafter lumbered off. The team marched on.

FOUR

The Crafter found its goal quickly in the cool silences of the colossal complex. A bin of separate compartments dominated the far wall of the towering room. Vapor poured from the faces of the enameled hatches. A tide of pearly fog descended on them from the wall as they approached.

Mist fell like a slowmotion ivory waterfall, chilling Killeen and setting Toby's teeth to chattering. The boy was tired from his struggle. He had a hacking cough. A gray pallor had crept into him. Killeen's good arm now throbbed in steady protest. He was grateful for the chance to put Toby down at the foot of the high, endlessly featured wall. Regularly spaced vault hatches stretched away, up into the swirling cloud layer high above. He wondered how even a mech could get up such a sheer face to open the high compartments.

1. Use grappler mechs.
2. Climb like spiders.
3. We don't need grapplers though.
4. Parts Crafter wants are low on wall.

Killeen relayed this to Hatchet, as he had been doing throughout the march. Hatchet listened, nodded. The entire team was edgy, eyes leaping at any sudden sound. The least surprise made hands grasp for weapons.

Killeen shared their jittery alertness despite his fatigue. To come here at all meant placing your trust in the Crafter. It knew mech ways. But it was a criminal among mechs and could not save them if things went seriously wrong.

Hatchet began organizing the work. Killeen relayed the Crafter's orders automatically. Bud's small laconic voice was a silvery tenor note in his mind among a rich burgundy surge of emotion. He was a mote tossed by deep loathings and fears that seethed within him but could not find a voice. He spoke woodenly. Hatchet nodded, seemed even pleased at Killeen's robotlike reciting of Bud's messages.

Killeen felt cold strike into his chest from the chilly refrigerated wall, like a long-fingered hand jutting from the enameled vaults and piercing his heart. He worked stiffly, trying to isolate his mind, to stop its endless spinning in a black abyss. He found himself gazing at his own legs as they moved, looking in absolute amazement at how easily they functioned, thinking of himself as a machine which did not know it was a machine.

He shook his head but nothing would clear it.

"Pop that first one. See? Yeasay, that one!" Hatchet was calling orders to Cermo-the-Slow.

The men pulled forth the Crafter replacement bio-parts. Each vault held organic segments in chilly isolation, fully grown. Killeen called out Bud's directions, his voice flat and dry. He caught Toby looking at him strangely but gave it no mind.

The vaults were the right height to allow men to slide the packaged units out and hand them down into an open hatch in the Crafter's upper cowling. Some parts required delicate handling. There were great disks of chunky, fibrous stuff like huge kidneys.

Many-elbowed articulating units like coiled bronze wire that could dance and weave, snakelike.

Small, intricate pumps that were clearly made from hearts.

Each had its attached tubes and monitoring wire couplers.

Each pulsed with muted energy.

Killeen tried not to look at most of the things the men took from the vaults. But he was standing halfway up the Crafter when Cermo-the-Slow jerked away from a vault he had just opened and cried, "Nossir noway! This's human!"

It was one of the legs.

Feeder tubes forced sluggish fluid through fat blue

veins. It was bigger than the ones Killeen had seen. The leg bulged with muscles and thick tendons. It wore collars of carefully shaped cartilage at each end, where the hip and foot should be.

Cermo dropped the leg. He backed away, eyes wide.

One of the leg's feeder tubes popped free. Its collar of gristle spasmed.

Hatchet came rushing over, yelling, "Pick it up! Don't let it lock up on you, it'll go bad."

Cermo stood stock-still. Hatchet fumed in exasperation and snatched up the leg himself. He plugged the feeder line back in. A tiny digital window in the cartilage flashed five meaningless symbols. Hatchet ignored this and shoved the leg into the top hatch. Some minor mechs inside the Renegade were taking the cargo from the men.

1. **Crafter wants you to know.**
2. **It must use human parts, yes.**
3. **Sometimes better than metal parts.**
4. **These legs can regrow selves.**
5. **Easy to reproduce.**
6. **Mechs need.**
7. **Efficient to use.**

Killeen smiled grimly. Was the Crafter apologizing? "So we're a resource? Why they kill us, then?"

1. **Crafter says humans also damage mech factories.**
2. **Mechs have to control humans.**
3. **Use them in factories though.**
4. **Cartilage good for shock absorber.**
5. **Not all of human used.**

"So I saw."

Hatchet stood with hands on hips, watching the last of the Crafter bioparts come out of the vaults. He licked his lips. "Best damn haul ever. Renny's gonna owe us a lot."

Killeen said, "You knew they use human parts?"

Hatchet's eyes slid toward him, then away, decided to

be offhand. "Sure. I was the one met this Crafter, set up the first trade. It was me took the risk."

"By yourself?"

"Damnsight right. We were down, had nothin'. I saw this Crafter limpin', treads all wore out. Figured I could take it. Only it didn't fight. Made some pictures in my head. I had my translator along, she explained the pictures. That's how I saw it was a Renny. Made my first deal." Hatchet said this flatly and factually, the way a man does so he can't be accused of bragging.

"You got it bioparts?"

"Yeah. Was easier then. Mechs've got smart since."

"You saw things like that leg?"

Hatchet pursed his lips and shot Killeen an assessing look. "Yeasay. Gotta understand, mechs have their own way. It just figures." Hatchet said this like a man explaining his religion, as if it were simply common sense. "We do what we gotta. Help our Families. Can't change the mechs." Hatchet smiled tightly at the very idea.

"Just you be sure this Crafter delivers."

"My Family's been dealin' with Rennies lot longer'n any Bishop ever did," Hatchet said mildly. He was right, Killeen knew. His father had told him once that the Kings had a dozen or more Rennies. They specialized in it, the way Bishops knew scavenging better than anybody, and Pawns could grow food better. It was a tradition that came down from the earliest times.

Still, the Kings needed his Face's translating ability. He could see that this galled Hatchet. They'd lost their translators on these raids, in ways Hatchet didn't want to discuss. All this made Killeen doubly wary of the King Cap'n.

He went over to see if Toby was all right. Shibo was helping hand down the last bioparts. The team stayed atop the Crafter.

1. Get on.
2. Crafter take us.

"Where?"

1. Fix you.
2. Then must go. Hurry.
3. Overseer is in complex.

"What's the Overseer?"

1. Image not clear.
2. Is small mech.
3. But many parts.
4. Very smart mech I think.

They mounted and rode. There were few mechs
working the huge bay. The Crafter froze them with staccato
microwave bursts. Killeen's eyes swept each lane as they
passed.

Hatchet was jubilant in a subdued way. He moved
among the team, reassuring, complimenting them on their
fast work. The Crafter hummed down corridors nearly too
narrow for it. Its treads clanked and at this lower speed
Killeen could hear it squeak and grind and whir. He knew
the sound of parts worn nearly to the breaking point. When
Hatchet passed by, using the pipes for handholds, Killeen
asked him how old the Crafter was.

"Plenty," Hatchet said. "It's been runnin' for its life for
long time, I figure."

"How you tell?"

"It's made from old stuff. Designs I never saw before.
My translator said the mechciv changes parts deliberate
like that. So's they cut off the Rennies."

"Make 'em come in like this one? Looking for replace-
ments?"

Hatchet shrugged. "Sure. More likely a Renny just
craps out. When I was a boy I saw some Rennies broke
down. Out in middle nowhere, busted. Marauder comes
by, catches it easy."

Killeen cradled Toby in his arms against the swerving
of the Crafter. "How'd this Crafter become a Renegade?"

"Dunno. Didn't answer the call-in, I guess."

"Call-in?"

"When mechs get wore out, comes a call-in. They
report, get dismantled."

Killeen frowned. "Even the smart ones?"

"'Specially them. Smarter mechs get replaced faster. I think that's 'cause the mechciv keeps redesignin', makin' them even smarter. Always changin'."

"Mechciv kills 'em?"

"Seems like. Enough reason not answer the call-in, huh? Rennies just want stay alive. Same's you 'n' me."

Hatchet's eyes bulged with an excited acuity which his stiffly held face sought to belie and disguise. Killeen saw the inner drive that this man had used, harnessing the Renny-craft heritage of his Family to save them from the wilderness-wandering all the other Families had suffered after the Calamity. He had been fearless, and had wrested from the Renegades a fragile Metropolis—all based on trust of mankind's deadliest enemies. And no one knew better than Hatchet how precarious Metropolis was. Every obligation Hatchet could use to ensure some added scrap of protection, even from Renegades who could themselves be snuffed out—every fractional help was worth risk. Killeen respected what Hatchet had done. But something in him curled a lip at the price.

The Crafter clattered, slowed.

1. **Repair station.**
2. **Crafter try find right circuits.**

The team dismounted before a glassy wall of complex machinery. Fluids bubbled in translucent lattices that wove among gnarled metallic work stations. The Crafter extended tiny six-fingered hands at the ends of tripod chromed arms. They found twin-barreled interlocks and inserted steel dowels. Its long workarms spun. Ceramic ears mounted on carbo-sleeves listened intently. After some minutes three sharp clicks echoed in the stillness. The work station brimmed with neon life.

1. **Boy goes first.**
2. **Put legs in receiver.**
3. **Hurry.**

Shibo and Killeen carefully worked Toby's legs into a soft-ply receptacle at the base of the station. It went slowly. The boy was wide awake now. His lassitude dispersed as the station began purring and muttering.

"I can feel something," Toby said.

"In your legs?" Killeen asked, holding the boy's shoulders off the green tile floor.

"Can't tell. Kinda fuzzy . . . like all over . . ." Toby's eyelids fluttered. "Ahhh . . ."

1. **Hold steady.**
2. **Crafter searches for code.**
3. **Has to silence station alarm.**

"Hold still, son."

Hatchet called from behind Killeen, "Crafter say how long it'll take?"

"No," Killeen said warningly. If Hatchet pressured him . . .

Toby jerked. "It . . . *hurts* . . ."

1. **Locked in circuit.**
2. **Searching for encoded flaw.**

Toby trembled. "I . . . I can't . . . *feel* anything anymore. My guts, it's creeping up my guts. . . ."

1. **Must check his service systems first.**

"All goin' *cold*." Toby began gasping. "Dad—I—gettin' higher up—I—arms—so *cold*—I'm scared—I—"

Killeen tightened his grip with his good arm around Toby. He tried to keep the boy from wrenching away from the effects of the station. The boy's hands curled, losing their tension. Killeen watched color drain from fingertips which were red-raw, the nails split.

Behind him Hatchet said, "What's wrong? Listen, this don't work, that's it. Got that? 'Cause time's runnin' and—"

"Shut up!" Shibo spat at him. She held Toby's legs.

Killeen ignored them. He tried to get more information from Bud but his Face would not answer.

Toby went slack. His eyes rolled up, showing pure white.

"Damn!" Killeen whispered to himself. He massaged the boy's skin. It was ghostly pale.

1. **Subsystems are reactivated.**
2. **Correcting.**
3. **Hold still.**

Toby let out a sudden explosive breath. His eyes shot from side to side. His arms twitched and the hands danced frantically. Toby's entire body seemed to jerk like a doll being animated by something within.

A relay popped loudly in the station panel.

"My . . . my . . ." Toby blinked. "My feet hurt."

Wonderingly, in the sudden quiet, Killeen and Shibo looked at each other.

They pulled him carefully from the receiving sleeve. Toby could move his legs but the muscles were stiff and sore. Killeen and Shibo started to help him toward the Crafter. Hatchet clapped Killeen on his bad shoulder and spun him around. "You want fixin', get back there."

Killeen levered his dead arm into the receiver. The soft-ply would take the arm only at a steady, slow insertion rate. He could feel faint throbs and hot flickers of sensation as something probed it.

The team watched in all directions, their feet scuffing nervously, weapons drawn. Fluids burbled in the elaborate frosty glassware that towered over them all. An orange vapor suddenly vented above, hissing down among the team. They fled from it with racking coughs.

Hatchet watched this and turned to Killeen, who knelt before the receiver, arm now up to the elbow. "Workin'?"

"Can't tell."

Around his shoulders ran hot, quick jolts. It was like having pins thrust into him so quickly they were gone before his nerves could react.

1. **Found code.**
2. **Crafter goes fast.**
3. **Says it smells Overseer.**

"Feel anything?" Hatchet asked.

"Yeasay." Soundless deep bass tremors echoed in his arm.

"Damn, I wish we'd—"

"Ah!"

The receiving sleeve released him. Killeen yanked his arm free. It ached but the fingers moved. His skin was puckered, hairless, clammy.

"Damnfine!" Hatchet waved to the team. "Let's go. Headin' home!"

Killeen stumbled toward the Crafter. His gait was off balance and he realized how much he had been compensating for the dead arm. He reached the mudguard and pulled himself up, sprawling on it clumsily with boyish elation. The Crafter churned backward, freeing itself of the station. Then the Renegade rumbled away, picking up speed. Killeen had to snatch for a venting tube to stay on the carapace.

Small buildings flashed by. These were set into the slanted decks and ramps of a colossal room. The floor was a labyrinth of odd, angular buildings. Conduits connected everywhere. Except for an occasional stain there was no sign of mess or sloppiness. Oddly turned-out mechs worked on some of the high ramps. They did not move when the Crafter shot by them.

Killeen clung to a pipe and hugged Toby. The tingling in his arm seemed to sweep into all parts of his body as his systems reintegrated. Images washed through his sensorium. Data had been stored in his arm, digital splashes which jittered and poked in his eyes. He saw sprockets coupling to oily drivechains. Heard long-dead Veronica's tinkling laughter. Tasted his mother's cooking.

Sensations released him into a kind of strength. Impulsively he kissed Shibo. She responded. Killeen laughed, enjoying the taste of pungent air sucking in and out of his lungs, every scent amplified in the backwash of the onrushing Crafter.

The whole team was talking, merry whispers sounding over the sensorium net. The Crafter slowed at a corner and Killeen glanced up. A large transparent panel was lit from within by pale green light. Inside Killeen could see something working. Gargantuan legs and arms. And connecting them were bodies. Racks of ribs labored like huge bellows. Bruised pouches hung on the bellies, like bags of entrails. Waxy skins stretched and thrust and wrinkled and stretched again.

He turned away.

The Crafter reached a broad plaza. Navvys crisscrossed it. A few larger mechs scuttled on darting missions. The Crafter speeded up. The humans held on as the Crafter veered to miss navvys, never slowing. The wind furled their hair and stilled their voices.

Killeen could feel a wordless excitement building in the sensorium net. The distance to home is the sweetest, yet the longest, as the mind leaps ahead.

They had gone halfway across the plaza. The Crafter went even faster, as if it sensed something.

A faint *whoooong* vibrated with reedy insistence through the sensorium.

Killeen turned. He could see nothing on this side of the Crafter that could have made the sound. There were no mechs bigger than a navvy within sight.

—See anything?— Hatchet sent.

"Naysay." Killeen pulled Toby closer.

Shibo's slitted eyes studied the high buildings. The plaza was so wide that the distance washed out the detail of the bioparts complex they were leaving behind.

—Keep your . . .—

—What's that?— Cermo called. He was on the other side of the Crafter and Killeen could not make out anything.

Something went by—*tsssssip!*—overhead.

"Get over on this side," Killeen called. "Whatever it is, the Crafter can give some shielding."

—Right, let's *move*,— Hatchet sent.

Shibo brought her weapon up. The Crafter plunged ahead. Its treads whined with exertion. Killeen thought he could hear them grinding against each other. If the treads froze up out here—

Whuuuung. Louder now. The pulse frenzied the air around them.

Hatchet sent, —Watch out!—

—No!—

—It got Velez!—

—Get over here! Over the top! The top! Scramble!—

—What *is* it?—

—Just go!—

—Don't look at it. That'll open your 'ceptors, it'll—
Whuuuuuung.

—Ah! Ah! My leg!—

—I'm blind! Gimme hand! Blind!—

—What *is* it?—

Killeen did not need to look. He knew the sound of the
Mantis.

FIVE

The Crafter swerved. Its engines rose to a clanking, roaring
din. Treads howled over the slick plaza tiles. Killeen could
hear or taste nothing through his sensorium but the snap
and sputter of electromagnetic warfare as the Mantis and
Crafter dueled.

The team clambered over the crest of the Crafter,
dragging the two Kingsmen who had been hit. Killeen
looked into the white-eyed, startled faces. "Dead," Hatchet
said.

"Suredead," Killeen added.

The Mantis had extracted their memories, hopes,
fears. It now knew of Metropolis, then.

And it had their Aspects as well. An immense corridor
of human time collapsed now into vacancy.

The Crafter seemed immune to the hollow *who-
ooooom* bursts that drove livid tunnels through Killeen's
sensorium. It hammered across the plaza.

They clung to its side like fluttering kites. Their
leggings and pelvic cradles rang against the humming hull.

"Toby!" Killeen grabbed just as the boy slipped.

He got a hold on Toby's right arm, hauled upward—
and lost the grip. The boy fell a meter and snagged on an
outjutting pipe fitting. Toby wrenched around, his hands

scrabbling for a hold. Killeen hung from a ledge and scissored his legs, stretching.

Toby reached up but lost his precarious hold. His right hand caught Killeen's legs, gripping the niche where Killeen's shock absorbers met the laminated boot guard. Toby whirled, spinning barely above tiles that flashed by below. Killeen swung him over to a vent collar and he grabbed it.

Then the Crafter skidded.

Killeen thought they were going to go over, roll with the Crafter on top. He sought a solid lip to brace his legs against. Before he could leap free the Crafter caught itself. It slid shrieking to a stop beside a monolithic slate wall.

"Off!" Hatchet cried. "Somethin's after the Renny!"

Killeen called, "And us. It's the Mantis."

Stunned silence. For the first time Killeen saw an uncomplicated, true expression in Hatchet's eyes—simple fear. "Damnall!"

Shibo called, "We got no big weapons."

"Hey! Can't leave the Crafter!" Hatchet shouted as some of the team jumped to the plaza floor. "Hafta protect it."

Killeen said, "Naysay. Shibo's right. Our e-beams and cutters no use against Mantis."

"If the Crafter disables it—"

"We'll be better off spot if we can maneuver," Killeen said.

Cermo called, "Yeasay, go! Use Crafter for cover."

Hatchet hesitated, eyes darting to the crest of the Crafter, where the suredead hung among struts. Killeen thought the man was considering carrying them away. Kingsmen made a solemn point of never leaving dead behind.

But no—Hatchet was watching for a sign from the Crafter. None came. The mech was busy filling the air with echoing booms.

Hatchet grimaced and nodded. He led the team directly away from the motionless Crafter. They left the two suredead without speaking of it. Another Kingsman stumbled away with no control of his arms. He staggered grimly, eyes fixed.

Killeen made sure Toby could move well. They headed for an alleyway in the slate wall.

The Crafter's antennae swiveled, sending sharp slaps through his sensorium.

Shibo called, "EM only."

Killeen saw her point. He had heard only electromagnetic cracklings. Humans might not be vulnerable to the EM assault now raging. The Mantis was using no guns against the Crafter, though that would be the easiest way to immobilize it.

Hatchet panted as he trotted toward the alley, "Cermo, you go left."

There was a loading dock for mechs left of the alley, covered with a jumble of yellow fan-shaped devices as big as a man. "Try hit the Mantis," Hatchet ordered. He sent a Kingsman to a different angle from the right.

Cermo started firing rounds at once. Killeen ducked down the alley and kept going. He dodged around large steel conduit housings, waving to Toby to follow.

"Where you goin'?" Hatchet cried.

"Mantis can't get back in here," Killeen answered. "Too tight for it." He did not slow.

"We got to help the Renny!"

Shibo called dryly, "Mice don't help mountains."

"Get your ass back here!"

Cermo said coolly, "Mantis comin'."

The rest of the team glanced at one another. They had been readying their weapons. The Crafter had not moved since they jumped off. It blocked their view of the plaza.

Now they heard through their sensoria regular thuds, like logs rolling over rocks. As though a giant were walking across the plaza. They started edging away from the mouth of the alley.

Hatchet shouted, "Lay down some fire!"

"Dumb," Shibo said.

Cermo came pounding over, yelling that the Mantis had disabled the Crafter's treads.

Hatchet looked wildly at the Crafter, then back at the beckoning alleyway.

"Renny knows the way out," he said desperately. "Back to Metropolis."

The team saw his confusion and took the opportunity to fall back a few paces. The thudding noise got louder. Killeen had never heard the Mantis make such a sound. Hatchet hesitated, then spat and backed down the alley. He stopped beside Killeen. "If you hadn't—"

"Look." Killeen pointed.

The Mantis reared into view over the riveted crest of the Crafter. Its antennae swept all angles methodically. Killeen whispered, "Shut down your systems. Quick!"

His sensorium dwindled, a multicolored fluid sucked down a black drain.

The Mantis was a spindly network of moving rods. Like carbosteel bones, they jointed at gleaming chrome sockets. Thin cables gave it jerky, oddly swift agility. This time it struck Killeen as more like a framework for a building, a mobile lattice, than an integrated mech.

Its antennae swept past them without pausing. Did that mean it had not seen them?

The Crafter still offered some combat. Killeen saw a small armament poke from a turret and fire at the Mantis. An instant later it dissolved in orange sparks.

"Move," Killeen whispered to Toby. They slipped around a bulky cylindrical array of valves and wheels, out of direct sight from the alley.

The Mantis reached the Crafter. It towered over the crescent back and seemed to be working at the Crafter's side.

The team edged back, following Killeen. Hatchet saw that he could not stop them without either making a lot of noise or making a fool of himself. He trotted after them.

Down a narrowing cleft between throbbing factories they ran. Muffled explosions followed them. Killeen thought it was the Crafter dying. He looked back and saw a small missile shoot down the alley they had just left. It was gone in an instant. Then it returned and hovered like a gleaming steel hummingbird at the intersection. Killeen felt a faint *ping* as it recognized them. The missile surged forward. Killeen had time to bring up his weapon. The missile vanished in a ball of white smoke and thunder slapped him in the face. The missile had detonated long before its fragments could have reached them. Killeen wasted no time wondering why. He ducked down a side passage, following the others, and gave himself over to running.

Nothing pursued them. They retreated through a crowded factory complex ripe with acrid flavors. Mechs worked the catwalks and corridors, giving the fleeing human figures no notice. Whatever the Mantis's powers, it evidently could not put all local mechs on alert. Or else did not feel it needed to.

Hatchet tried to slow them, make a stand to see if the Crafter had escaped. No one paid him any attention. They ran on. A desperate fever gripped them. Killeen saw in an abstract way how Hatchet felt, but his instincts told him otherwise.

He remembered his father chuckling once and saying dryly, "Brave man fights, smart man runs." Hatchet had not been on the march for years. Holed up in Metropolis, the Cap'n had lost his edge.

After passing through three factories they reached the wall of the entire zone. It was ribbed and veined with intricately intersecting pipes. The wall thrummed with fluid gurgles. Cermo-the-Slow had belied his name and gotten there first. He found a hatch which had a manual override. Evidently maintenance mechs used it to get at the pipe complex innards. The passage was tight. They had to worm their way through one at a time.

Without much discussion the team left the huge zone with its vast plaza. They had not revived their sensoria and had no idea how close the Mantis might be. Killeen sent Toby ahead with Shibo and stood rear guard beside Hatchet, looking back for a moment. "Damn close," he said.

"Don't matter much." Hatchet spat, puffing. "We're dead anyway."

"Rather be dead than suredead."

"Shit." Hatchet spat again. "Dead's dead."

Killeen felt a cool rage rattling in his chest. But all he said was, "You keep nothing from them, you're just like them."

"Crafter felt the same way," Hatchet said sourly. "Funny, a mech bein' just as crazy as you."

Killeen blinked. "Crafter wouldn't go suredead? But they're its own kind."

"Years back, when I was first talkin' with it, through the translator, it said it was a Renny 'cause it wouldn't give up its *self*."

"Ever ask it what the ordinary mechs think?"

Hatchet shrugged. "Near as I can tell, they don't."

Killeen's gaze swept the rectangular corridors that led away among ranks of noisily working cam-drive machines. A mech appeared but didn't look at the two men. "What you mean?"

"My father told me once. Mechs wear out, they're ordered in. Don't think 'bout it at all. Got a override command built in 'em. Get stripped for metals, raw parts."

"Same as they strip us down," Killeen said. "Suredeath."

"Get on in. I'll cover." It was Hatchet's right as Cap'n to be the last out, traditionally the most dangerous position. Killeen wriggled his way through the hatch. He had to work through tight intersections in complete darkness. Pipes poked his ribs, tried to trip him. The thought came that if the mechs wanted to take them one at a time this would be an effective trap. But then he saw a light ahead. A pipe caught his shock-absorber sleeve as he stumbled out into a ghostly ruby glow.

He was in a long slab of a room. From its low ceiling hung oddly shaped bundles suspended by translucent threads. The walls and floor emitted smoldering dim light.

The team had stopped, staring. Killeen, too, tried to see more detail. Hatchet emerged behind Killeen, took one long survey of the apparently limitless room, and whispered, "Get some cover. Quick!"

Killeen followed Toby, who was recovering his speed. They stopped beside a large lumpy thing that revolved slowly in inky shadows. Its lower edge hung near Killeen's head. He let his eyes 'scope out to detect any movement in the vast, stretching room. Even at max amp he could see no motion other than the achingly slow turning of the things suspended from the ceiling. Nothing touched the floor. A silky silence floated on chilled, antiseptic air.

This place had a feel of obsessive exactness, the clean spaces and rigid perspectives making a frame for the oblong, misshapen masses that spun silently. But as Killeen stepped toward the nearest mass he caught a sharp scent that tainted his lungs with memories of wood rot and mold. He remembered crawling in a basement of the Citadel, a boy exploring the damp recesses in search of treasure and mystery. Thick smells had assaulted him, moist soil and rancid clothing, crusted old boxes and half-filled jars of moldy sluggish liquids.

The faint, hellish light seemed to brighten. He held his breath.

He was watching something like a large mass of tightly wound conduits. That was his first perception, and as his eyes adjusted further he could see their rubbery, elastic sheaths. An oily sheen lubricated their gray, mottled surfaces. They moved. Slid and groped persistently, blindly. A machine. Bent on some purpose he could not imagine, not made of metal, veined and turgid, yes. But it had that strange machinelike, nonliving way of motion. It did not occur to him that this could be anything else. The coiled tubes were waxy in the dim buttery glow. Jelly lubricated their movements. Their slippery heave and slide had the momentum of programmed purpose. Thicker tubes wound among the slim ones. Accordion-pleated extrusions branched off to other joinings. With gravid slowness, oval fissures opened in the large tube nearest to Killeen, breaking the oily glaze. It was swelling. It sighed faintly and a fine blue mist rose from it. He caught the sweet sewer smell he remembered from the drop tower in the Citadel, a heavy lush hint of what would assault the nose if you ever leaned over the long drop and caught the flavored breeze.

His eyes moved beyond, trying to grasp overall movement.

The tubes pulsed. Here and there a spot on a slippery conduit showed pale porosity. As Killeen and Toby watched, a fissure broke open. It worked wider. Killeen saw that the tubes were hollow, flexing coils. The nearest made a wet, sucking noise. It writhed from the snakelike embrace of another and coiled away. Rings rippled in its skin.

Killeen sensed coiling momentum gather through the entire mass before him. Another tube broke free. It had a slick globular head which he saw only for a moment because it buried itself in a new, still-widening fissure nearby.

A furious clenching began in the surrounding mass. Killeen had the impression of a muscular gathering. Currents of moist, sour air brushed him. He heard faint smacks and slides. Then a soft, quickening, wheezing undertone. Like the breathing of a giant.

More fissures puckered in the walls of nearby tubes. They grew, their oval mouths ridged by ropy pink cords. They yawned, red-rimmed and slick, pocked. More wrinkled tubes wrenched free of the mass and waved in the thick air. Their blunt heads swelled. They sought and quickly found fissures that seemed to break and grow in answer to the freed tubes. The heads wormed among the working mass and plunged into the yawning fissures. A long shuddering accompanied each entry. The writhing pink mass shivered unspeakably. Killeen saw almost against his will that each was a coupling, male and female organs that formed of the gelatinous mass and met in a grotesque slithering, each calling up the other from the unshaped ooze that palped and stroked itself in jellied, blunt frenzy.

Killeen grasped Toby's arms and pulled him away. "Get . . . get back."

"What *is* it?" Toby's voice rasped.

"Something . . . awful."

As they backed away he could see round, leathery bulges hanging from some of the tubes. Balls. Balls conjuring some foul semen.

The engorged fissures were growing hair. Matted black wire sprouted along the tubes as he watched.

The waxy light around them quickly faded. Toby asked more questions for which Killeen had no answers and he shushed the boy. He took two steps forward. The light brightened. Did the restless slithering of the suspended mass quicken? He moved away. Yes, the diffuse glow ebbed. The mindless motion slowed.

"It's made to . . . operate . . . when somebody's near."

"Thought it was a machine," Toby said matter-of-factly.

"So did I . . . not sure now."

The others stared at other nearby shapes, frowning. Only a moment had passed but to Killeen it seemed a yawning, stretched time. Hatchet called shakily, "Form up! We got to move."

They obeyed mutely. Long lanes of the suspended masses stretched away. As they approached, each mass in turn stirred in sullen, waxing light. They soon learned to move quickly past.

Cool quiet enveloped them. Mist rose from the hanging masses, layering the air with acrid traceries. Their steps rang hollowly.

They knew they had no plan, that Hatchet was leading them without a clear goal. But it was better to go on than to endure the strangeness here, and the enveloping sense of awful forces moving with purposes beyond human understanding.

They walked quickly. Pools of brimming glow dogged them as the masses began their performances, then ebbed. The sensation of being followed, if only by automatic mechanisms, hastened their steps.

Ahead a dark blankness grew. It was a grainy wall of black mesh.

Hatchet dispatched Cermo to the right and the wounded Kingsman to the left to find a way through. The Kingsman was back within moments, gesturing silently. No one spoke. Hatchet revived their sensoria long enough to cast tentatively along the wall. Nothing showed. He sent a darting yellow call-back to Cermo, then let the web of sensoria dwindle to a pale nothingness.

The Kingsman had found a hexagonal hatch. Rails led to it from far down the lines of sculptures. Hatchet thought some kind of service mech probably ran along the rails. He used one of the key cylinders the Crafter had given him. The indented plate accepted it and clicked three times. The hatch slid aside.

Shibo went first this time. Killeen helped the Kingsman who had lost control of his arms. They all had to bend down for the short, wide little passageway beyond.

Shibo cautiously worked her way forward. People bumped one another in the dark. Killeen's back began to ache. He tried not to think at all about their chances. To think was to despair and that meant you stopped. Once you did that you were only waiting for the end. He had learned that in long years on the march, had seen good men and women cut down by the despair that reached into them like a claw of ice and seized their hearts.

Fatigue tugged at them all.

No one talked. Killeen's world had narrowed to the close darkness and the feel of his hand on Toby's shoulder.

Abruptly light forked into his eyes, bringing searing brilliance. A panel had opened automatically ahead.

"Looks clear!" Shibo called.

They stumbled out into a vault so large Killeen could not see either the walls or the ceiling. Buildings dwindled away in the distance. Complex machinery festooned each surface of the humming factories. Mechs zoomed high in the air below a canopy of gray fog. Amber blades of luminescence shot through rising bubbles of greenish vapor.

They blinked. Eyes darted nervously. The air smelled of harsh acid.

"Heysay," Hatchet called. "Let's go."

Cermo wheezed. "Where?"

"Out. Gotta find our way out."

Cermo said slowly, "Great. Which way?"

"We search till we find, is all," Hatchet said adamantly.

A Kingsman asked, "Think maybe we try find the Renny?"

"Renny's gone," Killeen said. "Mantis eats mechs like that for breakfast."

Hatchet's eyes narrowed, sharpening the V of his face. "You got better idea?"

Killeen shook his head wearily.

They started toward the far wall even though they couldn't see it. Hatchet said he had a good sense of direction and that this was the way toward the surface of the mountain-building that enclosed them.

They walked for an hour before the Mantis found them.

SIX

He stood in a warm valley between hills of bright green. Beneath his feet was a spongy brown mat. It stretched away about as far as he could throw a stone—but for the first time in his life, he saw no stones within reach.

The brown mat's ragged margin gave way to the hill's slick green, glinting in the sunlight. He peered upward but ivory clouds hid all hints of Denix or the Eater. Somehow the radiance still slanted down strongly.

He felt the fibrous carpet. It gave a soft resistance, suggesting something solid beneath. He wondered what the green slick stuff was. Grass? And another question. He groped for it. Something . . .

Toby. He whirled, looking in all directions.

Nothing. He was alone in a rolling landscape. A moment before he had been with Toby, he remembered, and now there was only the rough brown like tightweave beneath his feet and . . .

The hills moved.

The one ahead of him was shrinking. Ponderously, with a slight murmur. He turned to see the rise behind him swelling, its green luster catching glints from the skyglow.

He felt a surge. A faint rippling tremor came up through his feet. He was moving backward . . . up the slick mound. The brown mat slid upward, pressing him slightly farther into the soft resistance. He felt himself slowly rise up the green hill as behind him a polished green valley opened.

Somehow he was riding on something which could climb the smooth green hills. Steadily the brown weave beneath his feet made its way up toward a rounded peak.

Killeen took a step. The spongy mat cushioned him. He started walking uphill toward the edge of it. In the several moments this took he saw the hillcrest draw near and took advantage of the added height to look in all directions. There were other green hills, arranged in long

251

ridgelines. But no other mats, no feature to give perspective.

He reached the edge just before the mat topped the hill. Seen up close, the green was mottled and flecked with white and yellow motes. He reached down to touch the glassy surface rushing under the mat.

He had never seen moisture as more than the tinkling brooks which broke free of a rocky clasp. In the Citadel he had enjoyed three full baths, aromatic occasions surrounded by ritual. He had had one at his Outcoming, one after his first hunt with his father, and one more with Veronica the night of their marriage. There should have been another bath, shared with Veronica, at Toby's birth. But there had not been enough water then and they had put it off. The drought never lifted. Snowglade's slow parching deepened.

His heart gave three slow, solid thumps before Killeen could fathom what he saw.

The rushing polished green splashed over his hand. Water. He put his hand in again, unable to believe in so much water. White froth churned over his fingers. He blinked in amazement and threw some into his face. It was warm and tasted of a spice, salt.

As he looked up, the mat reached the top of the hill. He could see a long way now, over a landscape of endless green slopes and foamy crests.

Without slowing, his mat slipped over the edge and began to descend.

He could get some idea of his speed by watching the scummy streaks of white that streamed toward him and then slid under the mat. He turned and watched the far edge of his mat come over the crest of the hill. The long white streamers reappeared from beneath the brown carpet and fled over the mound.

Automatically he got down on his knees and pushed his face into the translucent water. He drank. The salt did not bother him. He had long gotten used to drinking water of all flavors and purity. You stored it up when you could. He drank steadily, working at it until he felt his belly fill. Then he sat back—and saw the water looming over him like a wall, about to topple.

But it did not. He felt a tremor through his knees as the green water hill rose still higher, towering against a soft ivory sky. But it did not fall.

He felt a downward surge and then his mat began to climb the green rise. Only then did he glimpse what must be happening. He was in the grip of water so huge and momentous that it made waves. His brown carpet was riding the waves in this immense water. He was on a . . .

An island. Yes. Or perhaps a raft. Yes, a raft.

This came from Arthur. Killeen eagerly asked more but the Aspect would not answer.

He stood, marveling. The hilltops were an emerald green, while the valleys shimmered with a deeper, glassy color. As he passed over the crest he saw a few spots break into white foam, then fade.

Except for the slow surge that came up through his feet, Killeen could not tell he was moving. He seemed to glide up one hillside and then down it to another, identical, hill.

So much water. A world of water, where even the spongy solidness of his mat was unusual. At the next hilltop he peered carefully all around and could see no other brown stain upon the endless rolling green mounds. The giant waves marched on to the far, misty horizon. A whole seething world of water.

The Mantis. The thought came to him suddenly with a sense of absolute conviction.

This was a fraction of the Mantis sensorium. Or the way it saw the world.

There was no place on Snowglade where so much water lay open. So the mat beneath him could not be there. It was an illusion, just like the false images he had seen before from the Mantis. Far more convincing, enveloping, *real*.

But what was this illusion for?

He remembered running from the Mantis, fevered and hopeless, Toby beside him.

Now he was alone on a brown raft. Adrift.

Wearing nothing, his suit and leggings and helme
gone.

He called up each of his Aspects and Faces, even thos
he had not used for years. None answered.

His sensorium gave back only a hollow, dronin
grayness.

He walked all the way around the outer edge. Ther
was nothing more to see, simply the same layered mes
everywhere. He stopped for a moment to drink agair
enjoying the sensation of burying his face in water whic
sloped up and was higher than the land. The slap an
gurgle of the small waves his hands made was to him
sound of uncountable wealth, a fluid richness without enc

When he got up there was a speck on the horizon. H
watched it grow, banking up and down the gravid wave:
approaching on a zigzag path.

It was another island. Larger, ridged.

Instead of a featureless plain, bristly vegetation cov
ered most of it.

Something moved there.

Killeen squinted as the long green undulation
brought it closer. There were dense, knotted bushe
growing atop a white ground cover. The other island ha
knobby small rises and hollows, unlike his. As it grew, hi
eyes searched for some human figure among the gnarle
growth but saw nothing.

Branches swayed with the swell of the huge wave:
Was that the movement he had seen?

The larger island seemed to slide effortlessly over th
crests of the green hills and Killeen had to remind himse
that the islands were not moving themselves, but followe
the contours of the waves. All his experience was no guid
here.

As the island neared he suddenly saw that it was no
heading directly for his. Instead it would pass som
distance away and even seemed to be gaining speed. H
tried to remind himself that this place was a sensorium, an
his instincts didn't apply. But he somehow knew the othe
island was important.

He stepped into the warm water at the mat's edge. H

had no idea how to move through water, or even if there was a way to do it. Then he saw something moving in the brambles of the approaching island. A human figure. It took no notice of him but kept walking into the vegetation. He could not tell who it was.

He stroked tentatively at the water and took a step. Abruptly he sank to his waist. This sent a shrill alarm through him, a sensation he could not have imagined: fear of *water*, the provider of life.

> Lie down in it. Then pull water toward you with your hands and kick with your legs. Hold your breath when your head is under water.

The quick darting information from Arthur broke his hesitation. He pushed away from his island and thrashed at the warm currents that brushed him. His legs churned. Water rushed up his nose. Briny pricklings invaded his sinuses and he sputtered.

But he moved. He got a dog-paddle rhythm going and managed to keep his head fixed toward where the other island would pass. He gave himself over to the rhythmic surgings, swooping water behind him like a kind of thick, warm air. Coughing, rolling in the swell, he made progress.

The other island-raft came at him achingly slowly. He felt no fatigue but his arms began to sing with the strain. Then a chance wave caught him and plunged him downslope at the island. Foam curled around him. He banked into the wave and felt it seem to bunch and thrust behind him. Startled, he cut a swath down the shimmering wall of green. And tumbled onto the mat below, gasping.

His head rang from banging into the ground. He got up and walked unsteadily toward the dense, clotted growth nearby. It looked impenetrable. He skirted around it toward one of the white open spaces. There was no sign of the human figure. This island was much bigger than his. Stubby trees dotted the high ground. There were other things farther back in the vegetation which he could not make out so he started up the incline of white—

And backed away, trembling.

The white ground cover was a jumble of bones.

The edge of it was made of small, slender fragments. Fingers. Hands. Toes.

Farther in were broken ribs. Forearms. A garden of smashed pelvises.

At the top of the small knoll were thighs. Intact barrel rib cages. Thick arms. Bleached skulls with their perpetual grins and gaping eyesockets.

The boneyard spread over hummocks and rises. It stopped at the undergrowth but reappeared halfway up a nearby knoll.

Killeen blinked, his fear pressing up into his throat. He tentatively angled toward an opening in the bushes. Their slender branches whispered as the sea swell deepened. Then he heard the other sound.

Steps. Slow, crunching steps. Dull thuds punctuated by sharp cracks and pops.

Something coming. He backed away, not knowing where the sounds came from. His eyes swept the horizon but he could not find his own island anymore in the green vastness.

He looked back at the low sloping hillside just as a chromed sphere appeared over the crest. It came into view on a lattice of working rods and cables, legs clambering and jerking, many-toed feet coming down with a curious delicacy. Where it stepped bones broke.

In a last despairing release Killeen stooped, found a knobby, bleached joint. He threw it straight at the topmost sphere of the Mantis. It bounced off with a sharp clang.

Killeen felt his Aspects buzz to fresh life.

1. **Wants to talk.**
2. **No harm.**

The machine is an anthology intelligence. It suppressed us in order to let you get your bearings. It can speak better through us than directly with you.

"Why?" Killeen's voice rasped with rage.

Obviously, we are far more like it. As stored intelligences we Aspects can, through our digitized manifolds, better perceive the coded holographic speech of a machine. The Mantis has been teaching us how to do this these last few hours. I—

"Hours?"
The Mantis came steadily nearer on thrusting, jerky legs.

You are in fact unconscious. This is a medium of communication for the Mantis. It incorporates us all into its . . . well, *sensorium* is too narrow a word. It has ranges and capabilities I cannot fathom. In a certain view, this place is a combined Fourier transform of both our minds and that of the Mantis. It is easier to engage such different intelligences in Fourier-space, where waves are reduced to momenta and a localized entity (such as yourself) is represented as a spreading packet of such momenta in the flat space-time of the Mantis. An interesting—

"You understand it?"

Not fully, no. Employing the help of this suitably tapered Fourier-space modeling, it still has difficulty communicating with even me, an Aspect. The Faces, of course, can barely fathom it. We are attempting—

"What's it want?"
The Mantis stopped and settled down on the sloping ground. Killeen had to consciously stop his hands from clenching. His feet wanted to turn and run. He stood his ground.

1. Human things, it says.
2. Has already much.
3. Wants to help humans live forever.

Killeen spoke with razor-thin control. "That's why it's been hounding us? Killing us?"

1. I report its true meaning here.
2. You would die anyway, it says.
3. It wants to help.

"Leave us alone!" Killeen exploded, his fists tight and shaking at his side.

1. Cannot.
2. The mechmind will find you.
3. Only the Mantis can save.
4. Even a scrap is better than nothing left.

"We're not a goddamn scrap! We're *people*. All that's left after you brought on the Calamity and, and—"

Killeen made himself stop. He had to keep control. There was probably no way out of this place, no hope of survival. But as long as he didn't *know* that, as long as Toby or Shibo or any of the rest might still be alive, he had to keep going. Keep control.

The Mantis knew that humans were congregating in Metropolis. It did not wish to disturb us. The Renegade Crafter was bound to make a mistake sometime and that would bring down the full force of the Marauders on the Metropolis. Surely, the Mantis says, we knew that.

"Knew we'd fight someday, sure. Give us time, we'd do damn well against the Marauders." Killeen put his hands on his hips to show he wasn't thinking of running anymore. Even if this was some kind of mathematical space—whatever that meant—he knew the Mantis would understand the signal.

When Arthur spoke the Mantis's reply there was a decided edge to it:

Such bravado is amusing, and perhaps ordained
in you, but unwise. Only because the Crafter
concealed your location did Metropolis survive
this long. And the Mantis helped with that, as
well.

"What? The Mantis . . . ?"

1. **It helped Crafter.**
2. **Crafter didn't know though.**

"But the Mantis killed the Crafter!"

1. **Mantis seized Crafter.**
2. **Crafter not dead.**

"I don't understand, Hatchet said—"

1. **Mantis kept Marauders away.**

"But Hatchet told me himself, couple Marauders
found Metropolis. The Kings blew 'em away, clean-easy."

1. **A few, yes.**
2. **Were necessary.**
3. **Otherwise Kings get suspicious.**

"Suspicious? Of what?"

The fact that their Metropolis was an enclave
supported by the Mantis. A spot where humans
could congregate and merge. The Mantis herded
the Bishops and Rooks toward Metropolis with
that in mind.

Killeen grimaced. "*Herded* us? It killed us! Suredead!"

The wording in human speech is difficult here.
The Mantis does not regard what it did at the
ambushes as killing. The word it wishes to
choose is, well, *harvesting*.

Something in the way this was said, calm and flat in the tiny voice of Arthur, made a cool fear come into Killeen.

"Surekilling . . . not giving us a chance to even preserve an Aspect . . ."

1. Aspects very limited.
2. Only get a little of us.
3. I was complex man once.
4. Now am tiny thing.
5. Senses dull or gone.
6. Never again feel it *all*.

Alas, my stunted friend is correct. You surely did not think this trimmed existence of ours was enough, did you? We are small dolls, compared to the men and women we once were. Do you blame us for rattling the bars of our cages now and then? Even the maddened among us feels our truncated state, wants—

Call me insane? I be the only who won't kneel to this devil-machine before you! I will not *yield—*

In a flash Killeen felt something huge and dark settle in his mind, snuffing out Nialdi's shrill cries.

"Wait! You can't destroy an Aspect just 'cause . . ." His voice trailed away as he felt the absurdity of this. He was embedded in the Mantis's mathematical spaces. Whatever he felt as real were mere phantoms. His protests were like the tiny squeakings of a mouse caught in a cat's paw.

He remembered again the mouse he had seen so long ago, the bright and eager eyes staring fixedly up at him. It had had its desires, too, its dim plans. Its dignity.

Killeen's mind spun in dry vacancy, swept by clashing winds of cold despair and brimming hot anger.

1. Wonder what is like?
2. To be harvested.

Sadly, we Aspects shall never know. We would doubtless drift away, needless extras, while the actual person was preserved. But the Mantis wishes to show you what its "harvesting" means. Perhaps only by exhibit can we learn.

Killeen curled his lip in chilly contempt. "Exhibit? I saw a lot back there. Those legs pumping. That awful sex-thing—remember?"

The Mantis stirred. Its dozen separate chromed spheres shifted on the carbo-rod lattice, crisp and metallic.

That was not finished work. It is part of a larger project.

"I could damn sure see what kinda—"

You—and we—did not understand. The parts of that "sex-thing" were mixed organic and machine. Made for a purpose. Somewhat experimental, yes. As were the other constructions displayed in that room. But what the thing became depended upon who viewed it.

"What you mean? It was grotesque, ugly—"

Such constructions assume forms expressing the subconscious of whatever approaches it. The work was intended as a kind of psychodynamic analyzer for mechs. It can display the conflicts and programming malfunctions attendant upon any advanced machine intelligence. What it picked up from you—from us—was a constellation of submerged feelings and needs. Admittedly, the depiction was direct and graphic, but the Mantis says that only through such explicit schemes can mechminds be cleansed, repaired, realigned.

Killeen paled.

The Mantis inquires whether you knew that the
shutting down of your sexcen would result in the
accumulation of these elements elsewhere in
your self. Indeed, it understands the practical
efficiency of this for the short term, but as a long-
term strategy this seems beset with complex—

"You shut up! Shut up!"

Killeen heard himself shout as if from a great distance.
It was as though he could feel himself being two different
people. One was furious at any revelation, while the other
yearned to escape from a sticky, clouded net. There was
something terribly wrong inside him, something he only
vaguely glimpsed. Threads of deep anger and longing shot
through him. How could he maintain the fragile reeds of
dignity and self against the Mantis when it could penetrate
to the quick of him?

He began shaking. The Mantis extended a long,
slender arm. The nub of it articulated into a spindly parody
of a five-fingered hand. With it the Mantis waved toward
the bushes. Then it pointed.

You—and we—can understand the fate of the
surekilled best by example. The Mantis wishes
you to see.

"See what?"

1. Go.
2. What else can do?

Killeen nodded grimly. There was no choice in any of
this.

He strode on wooden legs into the bushes. Most of the
vegetation repeated the same hues of brown and singed
graygreen. The clumped growths were curiously knotted,
as though made by someone who understood the principle
of plants but lacked the feel of how lightly leaves clung to
branches, of the roughness of bark, of the dense diversity of
life. These were bunched and gnarled things, subtly wrong.

He picked his way among them. Some had thorns and

nicked him as he passed. Rarefied mathematical space or
not, things still hurt here. The slow swell of the green
ocean made the vegetation sway like the lazy breathing of a
sleeping thing.

He could see nothing but these twisted brown plants.
He went farther, glad to be moving and not standing before
the Mantis. Then he rounded a particularly tall and thick-
grown plant and saw a human. Or at least it was like a
human.

It stood as though watching something in the distance,
its face turned away. The body was spindly, shanks lean and
mottled. Killeen had the perception of seeing through the
chalk-white skin, into the thick white fibers that bound up
muscle and gristle. Yellow tendons stretched, thongs
threading between bones. He blinked and the skin was
again an opaque, dead white.

It was a woman. Yet it was not fully human.

There were deep fissures beneath the one breast he
could see. From them whistled long, deep breaths.

It sensed him. Began to turn. The head swiveled with
jerky movements, ratcheting around. Circles of gauzy red
enveloped the breasts. The inky patch between the legs
seemed to buzz and stir with dark life of its own.

Ribs jutted out starkly. Below them were patches of
translucent skin. These pale spots gave glimpses through to
the body within, where blue, pulsing organs swam.

A woman. Yet a rose burst from her mouth, a beautiful
flare of delicate red suspended at the end of a long, thorned
green stem. The flower grew *from* her, stretching the skin
tight about its thorny base.

The rose stem issued from a shallow, toothless mouth
. . . that somehow aped a jagged smile.

There was no nose.

The chin was the same sharp angle he remembered.
The eyes told him everything.

He whispered in shock and without hope,
"Fanny . . ."

Arthur paused for a moment before he said:

When the Mantis surekills, it extracts the essence of the person to create varied forms. Not

simple replications, but . . . differences. This is
how humanity can live. In the hands of something far greater than themselves. As an expression of humanity and of their own selves. The
Mantis, you see, is an artist.

SEVEN

The Fanny-thing stood watching him. He heard the
working of metal and saw the Mantis clambering over the
tufted brush, coming into view.

The Fanny-thing could not speak. The rose wagged as
it moved its head, tilting its bright eyes in unspoken
question.

The skin—*her* skin, Killeen thought, but pushed this
thought away—was wrinkled and browned. The planes of
her face still held an element of her wry wisdom. And the
eyes—quick and sparkling, taking in everything with
evident intelligence.

But she could not speak. The rose silenced her.

Killeen felt his Arthur Aspect struggling with the input
from the Mantis. Somehow the Mantis heightened the
cool, reflective Arthur voice while overriding it, forcing it
to give directly the Mantis's message. Arthur laced in and
out of the flowing mind-surge, reducing it to words Killeen
could follow.

You must understand, this is an artform that the
Mantis is pursuing with profound results. There
is much excitement in the reaches of the mech
community, the Mantis says, for such combina-
tions of plant and, ah, fleshy life.

Killeen said nothing. Prickly waves swept over his skin
like brushfires. He watched the Fanny-thing, judging the
distance to it.

The Mantis believes that with such expressions it
can bridge the gap between mech forms and the
dwindling, purely organic life—of which we
humans are self-aware remnants. It wishes to
embody our traits, our inner landscapes. This
creation, for example, contrasts the poignancy
of the simple rose and its silencing of the
jangling mind—a poetic concept, here integrated specifically. What is more, the impact on
the mind of the woman-plant is, apparently,
satisfying to some aspects of the mech sensibility.

Killeen took a step toward the Fanny-thing, his face
full of wonderment and curiosity. He noticed that her hands
ended not in fingers but in small bursting pink rosebuds.

Understand, this is merely one of the uses to
which human minds and forms can be put. The
gallery we saw earlier was another—complex
artforms mingling organic and inorganic themes.
They reflect the inner thoughts of whoever views
them—interactive, trans-species art.

"So this isn't a factory. We were raiding an art
gallery. . . ."
Killeen looked carefully at the Mantis as it stopped,
towering over the brambles. Its focused cones watched
him.
The Fanny-thing slowly reached out one bud-tipped
hand toward Killeen. Its eyes shone. The hand beckoned.

The Mantis knows that humans do not com-
prehend the intention of the mech civilizations
regarding them. Humans are interesting precisely because they embody the highest form of the
mortal realm. They know they will end. Mechs
do not end. When mechs are harvested—as the
Crafter was—some fraction of themselves is
saved. This is incorporated into later mech

forms. No such avenue ever existed for humans, beyond the illusions of religion. That is, until the crude and stunted forms of Aspects and Faces emerged. But we Aspects are shrunken, hollow echoes of our former selves.

Killeen watched the Fanny-thing take a tentative step toward him. It moved stiffly, its muscles bulging and sliding but giving little net motion. The web of muscles and bones seemed to be working against itself, as though parts of the body resisted the will of the rest.

The tragedy of human life is this eternal death you face. Here, the Manis says, it solves this problem for us. To surekill a human is to bestow eternal life. The highest moral act. To harvest is to sow. To preserve. And that, too, is the role of the Mantis. Artist and conservator of the vanishing organic forms.

On the matted ground lay decaying gray branches from the bushes, gritty sand, even oblong speckled rocks. The details were quite realistic. Killeen carefully studied the ground between himself and the Fanny-thing. The Mantis was too far away to reach them quickly.

The most grave limitation of organics is their inability to reprogram themselves at will. Knowing that their behavior could be more efficient or productive, they nonetheless are driven by blunt chemical urges and ingrained instructions. The Mantis understands that evolution selected for many of these through Darwinian pressures, and appreciates the role organics thus play in expressing the fundamental underlying laws of the universe. Still, the flaw of organic forms is their locking of their behavior instructions into hardware, when it should properly be in software. Instincts easily date in a mere few thousands of years. The Mantis—

"Look, what's this . . . this thing *for*?"

The Fanny-creature took a trembling step. Muscles worked beneath mottled skin. Its arms clenched as though it wanted to use the budded hands and could not.

It was remarkable how removing the mouth made a face unreadable.

Still, there are portions of the human sense-world which the mechs cannot penetrate. Some mechs feel this is related to the overly hardwired feature of humans. Others like the Mantis feel this apparent difficulty is in fact rich ground for experiment and art. That is one reason to create sculptures such as the one you saw before, and the one standing here now.

"This isn't a goddamn sculpture! This is *Fanny*."

A Fanny whose skin worked with fevered twitches and trembles. As if deep pressures fought within.

It houses a great deal of the original Fanny. Surely you recognize the features, the body movements?

"That's not . . . She . . . she was . . ."

The Mantis wishes to know what you think the real Fanny was. This is a crucial point. The mech artists—of which the Mantis is supreme—sense something missing in these constructions.

"Fanny's *dead*. This is a, a recording."

But it feels itself to be Fanny. When the Mantis attacked, it was careful to pinpoint each feature of her. It devoted its entire recording and perceiving network to extracting Fanny's nature. That was the principal reason why you were able to wound the Mantis so easily. It was absorbed in its task.

"Figured we'd killed the damned thing," Killeen said bitterly. He watched the Fanny-thing struggle to take another conflicted step. He could not take his eyes from it.

It is impossible to destroy an anthology intelligence, even using the methods of piecemeal destruction you devised later. The true seat of intelligence is spread holistically among outlying mechs, beyond your range.

"Y'mean like that navvy that zapped Toby and me?"

Yes, that was a fragment of the Mantis. It wanted to extract you and Toby entirely, but had not enough time. Indeed, that connection is why the Mantis now hopes communication with you will prove easier than with the other humans. The Mantis apologizes for any pain and inconvenience this caused you. It dislikes—indeed, finds immoral—the creation of internal conflicts within beings.

"What's *that* mean?"
Killeen hoped he could keep the Mantis preoccupied with the task of funneling its communication through the narrow neck of Arthur's abilities. That would distract it from what Killeen was thinking. Maybe.

Mechs do not perceive pain as such. The nearest they come to it is a perception of irreducible contradiction in internal states. This it wishes to spare you.

"Mighty nice of it." Killeen asked sarcastically, "Is that thing over there feeling 'contradictions'?"

Apparently. It wishes to unite with you in some way and yet other essences impede this.

He took a short step toward the Fanny-creature. Its rose wagged in the air. Muscles jumped in its forearms. The eyes crinkled. With pain?

The Mantis hopes you understand that such a program of preserving a kernel of us—however ungrateful we may be—is carried out for the highest of motives. Art is a primary activity among mech society—though, to be sure, it is an art far different from human attempts. Mechs can construct artful superstructures made of their own programming, for example. But it is in the experimental working of such elements as humans and other races that the freest and greatest work comes. They—

"You mean like those legs and arms I saw back there? Growing 'em in farms?"
He edged closer to the Fanny-thing.

Those are useful in bioparts, yes. But the finest specimens of body parts are kept for artworks. Those you saw were being grown for a drama the Mantis wishes to present. An entire staged reenactment of a human battle against early mechs, perhaps.

A humming. Killeen was distracted by it as he took another step. Then he saw it was coming from the gouged nostrils under each breast of the thing. Slow, agonizing *mmmmmms* interspersed with *uhhh-hummms*. It seemed to be trying to say something.
Another step.
The Aspect's voice went on, coolly unconcerned:

The area which the Mantis wishes your help with falls precisely in the zone which the mechs have not been able to penetrate. The most intense human interactions seem to lie beyond their reach. The Mantis attempted to correct this by preferentially recording the oldest humans—

"That's why it took Fanny?"
A halfstep slid his foot under a triangular rock as big as his hand.

The thing hummed louder, its rhythm laced with anxiety.

The eyes beseeched him.

Yes. This matter has been a vexing problem for it, ever since the inception of its career.

"What . . . ?" Killeen had a sudden suspicion.

The Mantis began its artistic program with what the Families call the Calamity. Understand, the mech cities would eventually have destroyed the Citadels in any case, as part of their pest-elimination procedures. The Mantis supervised operations so that it could harvest a maximum number of humans, allowing few to die unrecorded. The Mantis preferentially harvested the older, riper humans. Just as it did, you'll remember, at the meeting of Rooks and Bishops. But some elements do not accumulate better in the old. Evidently, several categories of human life remain only as dim echoes in the memory. Thus the Mantis wishes to—

He saw his chance and took it. With one motion he flipped the flat rock into the air and caught it with his right hand.

Two steps forward.

The eyes of the Fanny-thing widened but it stood its ground.

He brought the stone point down heavily. It split the skull with a loud crack.

Killeen backed away from the falling form. As it crashed to the sandy mat the Mantis clanked forward, far too late.

Then it stopped. Killeen looked up at the impassive lenses and antennae and thought carefully, *It wanted to die. It needed death.*

The Mantis did not move.

Arthur said nothing.

Movement. Killeen turned.

Toby came running from behind the bristly bushes.
"Dad!"

"Run!" was all Killeen could think to say.

Toby reached out toward his father. His foot caught on
a root.

He crashed facedown. A fine net of cracks spread
across Toby's back. Killeen heard tiny, brittle popping
noises.

The cracks broadened to black lines, racing zigzag all
over the boy.

Before Killeen could move, his son broke crackling
into fragments, shattered like glass.

EIGHT

He blinked and was awake. His hands and feet were cold.
Grimy polymer flooring pressed against his cheek.

Killeen rolled over, his mind a jumble of disconnected
thoughts. He had been reaching for Toby—

Toby.

But he had been embedded in the sensorium of the
Mantis, he reminded himself. The sensations had been
absolutely real, gritty, full-bodied. Far deeper than the
dispassionate electrical imagery of the human sensorium.

Illusion. All illusion.

Now he was back in the world of stunted, normal
human perceptions. Staring upward into harsh lamps that
beamed streaming blue light down from an impossibly high
ceiling. Breathing not the moist clasp of the Mantis
sensorium, but a dry air tainted by acrid flavors.

He sat up. He was wearing his coveralls, just as he had
been when the Mantis came upon them. He patted his
pockets automatically. Everything was there.

Around him Hatchet and Toby and the rest of the party
were slowly reviving, shaking their heads, blinking, recovering.

Toby. Killeen got to his feet and unsteadily walked to
where his son sat. Toby, head hung between his knees,
gasping for breath.

"You okay?"

"I . . . think so. That place . . ."

"The islands? That ocean, with—"

"Naysay. I was in some sorta cave. Things crawling the walls. Real spooky . . ." Toby's head snapped up, alert. "Not that I was scared."

Killeen grinned. "Suresay, yeasay. Just a little show from the Mantis, it was." He didn't feel that way, his heart still raced, but there was no point in letting it roust them.

"It asked me lotsa questions. I didn't understand 'em."

"Forget all that."

Toby stood up. "Let's get outta here."

Hatchet came over, looking disoriented. "Whatever that was, I think we—"

The scissoring sound made them all stop and turn. The Mantis appeared from around a nearby corner. Killeen watched it now without real fear. They were utterly in its control and he knew enough to simply bide his time.

The Mantis approached slowly, high and angular, tiptoeing through a series of sculptures. The nearest work was an immense human hand, cupped upward to hold Shibo. She climbed out of it, holding on to a huge lacquered fingernail and swinging down.

1. Was easier with you all in my world.
2. But you truer to selves in real-form.

From the reactions of the others Killeen could see that they, too, heard this in their sensoria. The Mantis had now learned how to penetrate the human net fully.

"Let's go!" Cermo-the-Slow cried with bitter anguish.

Killeen wondered what Cermo had seen in his own private visit within the Mantis's interior labyrinth. Each journey had been shaped for the individual, he guessed. The Mantis had certainly known how to trigger Killeen's deepest emotions. For what dark purpose?

1. I have not finished.
2. Each must yield more.
3. I seek your inner senses.
4. Intensity is the prime element missing in my collection.

Around the humans dark sculptures began to stir with gravid life. Near Killeen a great eye opened, its lash like a huge fan. Yellow veins traced intricate patterns in the bluewhite iris. Tear ducts exuded globes of shimmering gray fluid.

It was as though the complex of human organs, here rendered separately grotesque, was responding to some summons. The monstrous eye batted its lash with a whispery, whipping quickness. The pupil contracted and expanded like a pulsing, spherical heart.

The Mantis had atomized human experience and now wished to integrate it, through them.

And when it was done with them . . .

Killeen grabbed Toby's arm. "Come on."

They started away, threading among the huge working things. Killeen deliberately did not look at them. The high ceiling lamps gave little illumination here. The sluggishly moving parts were veiled in twilight, giving off rank odors that cut the air.

1. Questions remain.
2. I ask for help.
3. In return comes freedom.

"How can we believe that?" Killeen asked.

They did not slow. He glanced back and saw the others were stilled, heads turned as though listening. The arms of the Kingsman that were paralyzed back on the Crafter had regained their function. He lifted them trembling to his face. For each in the party there was some special, unguessable message.

1. The trust between intelligent beings.
2. This is all you have.
3. Or I.

Killeen shrugged this off and kept moving. Then, ahead, something stepped from the veiled shadow. It had been lurking there.

He had thought that the things he had seen on the

glassy green sea were illusion. Now he wished they had been. The reality was worse.

The Fanny-thing stretched, muscles stringy and trembling. Its eyes flashed, liquid-quick. Circles of flaking corruption rimmed the stem where a mouth should be. Mucus clogged its sighing breath-hole beneath each shriveled breast.

"So you did make it," Killeen said with quiet despair.

Actuality holds elements not found in any synthetic construct.

"This . . . No . . ."
Toby stepped backward, mouth an incredulous O.

Some categories of human experience are apparently not memory-stored in sufficient detail for myself to harvest. Thus I require that you mate. Your close connection with this female human promises to bring a high response function.

Killeen froze. "You don't—you can't—"

Your reaction in the trial was most surprising. Gratifyingly so.

"Trial?" Then the entire illusion of ocean and islands and Fanny had been a preparation for . . . this.

Many aspects of human response remain to be analyzed and expressed artistically. However, it has been my impression that the emotions of fear and lust parallel each other. Often fear induces lust shortly afterward. This can be understood as an evolutionary trigger function. Fear reminds you of your mortality, so in answer, lust ensures some fragmentary sense of immortality—though a pale shadow of the true lastingness to be found in our recording of your selves, of course. It is this dimension of fear/lust that I wish to study now.

Killeen got a steely grip on himself. The Fanny-thing shambled forward in its agonized way.

He had killed a sensorium-construct of this thing. In some sort of reply the Mantis had shattered the sensorium-image of Toby. Was that a threat?

Killeen gritted his teeth. It was impossible to guess intentions. The Mantis had used the incident simply as information, one more icily abstracted data point. That was what they were to it. Masses of numbers and geometries, curved by the fragmented events that humans called lives, and that this Mantis viewed as mere interesting trajectories.

"You can't understand how wrong you are," Killeen said defiantly.

Toby's voice came to him, a wavering note of disbelieving horror, "Dad . . . Dad . . . it's not really . . . *her* . . . is it?"

"Not really."

1. **You refuse then?**
2. **I can make you.**
3. **I wish only data.**

As the shambling thing came nearer in the quilted shadows Killeen saw that it was a decayed construct. Instead of Fanny's sun-browned and wind-roughed skin, it had a mottled, purplish hide. Scabrous fungus ran from the great yawning nostrils below the breasts, a green scum that flowed down its left side to the heavy-socketed hip. The buds of each hand ended not in flesh but in a running shiny brown pustulance.

"It's sick."

Now the Mantis spoke directly, using Arthur's voice:

Constructing the entire organism from purely mental information is difficult. Combining it with other lifeforms is the very height of the artistic frontier. Admittedly I may have made errors, unaccountable errors, in some details.

"Mighty big of you, admittin' it."

Some are stylistic choices, as well. But I believe
you will find the production is quite fully human.
I ask of you a mere few moments of coupling, to
see if the powerful emotions engendered—

"No!"

Toby pulled at Killeen, speechless and terrified. The
two backed away as the Fanny-thing advanced.

The eyes of the thing seemed to plead, to beckon.
Killeen felt an ache rise from his diaphragm into his
clenched chest.

Then Hatchet said at his elbow, "Listen, man, you
gotta!"

Killeen turned, confused. "What . . . you don't . . ."

Hatchet had come out of the shadows as if called. He
gestured at the approaching figure. "You don't, we can't cut
any kind deal."

Hatchet's voice was bland and factual. His eyes,
though, burned with a fevered intensity.

"What did *you* do for it?" Toby demanded.

Hatchet curled his lip. "You never mind, boy. It asked
me, I did. Took only a minute. Now I heard it ask you for a
li'l somethin', and you sayin' no. So I come over. Seems
you're havin' trouble."

Killeen saw suddenly that the man believed totally
what he was saying. Killeen would never know what had
happened to Hatchet on his own time in the Mantis
sensorium, what deep demons had slipped their leash. But
he could see the effects in Hatchet's dancing eyes. The
man's entire face was open now, all calculation gone.
Hatchet could no longer conceal the manic expressions that
raced across his face, twisting his red mouth, making his
chin into a tight ball of hard muscle.

"Get away, Hatchet," Killeen said quietly.

"Listen, you gotta." Hatchet put his hand on Killeen's
shoulder in a warm gesture, showing that he had completely misread Killeen's mood. A jagged smile lurched across
his lips.

"That thing isn't human, Hatchet."

"Not all human, no," the man said, his voice chillingly
reasonable.

"You *can't*."

"Look, Crafter's dead. Only way we can protect Metropolis is stay in good with this Mantis."

"*No*," Toby whispered.

The Fanny-thing stopped, its glittering eyes watching them in the quilted glow. The rose bloomed garishly from the furrowed bones of its face. Its breasts were wrinkled and rosy-nippled. Beneath them a shallow breath whistled, giving a strange sour scent.

"C'mon. Just slip the old rod to it."

Killeen stepped back from Hatchet, his throat clenched tight, unable to speak.

"Dammit! Won't take a minute. What is she, an old woman, right? Made up somehow."

Killeen could tell that in Hatchet's mind he was patiently explaining the simple facts of the matter, showing how this hideous reeking thing was really only a momentary obstruction on the way to ensuring that Hatchet's lifework, his Metropolis, could carry on. Nothing else mattered in Hatchet's world and nothing ever would. Nothing personal or even human could stand against Hatchet's plan and destiny.

"An old woman with a flower. Only lookit the tits on 'er. Wouldn't mind eatin' some that fruit, right?"

The forced jollity brought a fine film of sweat to Hatchet's face and Killeen could see the idea bloom there, see it ricochet in the hot eyes.

Hatchet's head swiveled, listening. Waves of strain swept his face. Then he nodded. "Yeasay. Nice ripe fruit."

Hatchet turned and walked toward the wavering figure. Its quick wet eyes studied his approach. "Job calls for a *man*." Hatchet's voice was hollow, as though coming from far away in cloudy madness.

He reached the Fanny-thing. Dropped his pants. "Takes a man t'do it."

Killeen could not make himself move. He had killed the Fanny-thing in the Mantis's sensorium. Done it without thinking. The Mantis had watched him build up to it, talking to him all the time. And then had shattered his son before his eyes.

All, Killeen saw, in preparation for this.

He clutched at Toby, pulled his son to his side. Neither could say anything. They watched as the Fanny-thing stood slowly on one foot. It hooked the other around Hatchet's waist. Hatchet was stiff, ready. His eyes stared off into dreamy space while his hands were already braced on the Fanny-thing's shoulders. She lifted her free leg still farther to rest it on his jutting hip bone. As she moved Killeen could see that between her legs was something that rustled and trembled eagerly. At the middle of the shadowed cleft two furrows opened. The ridges pulsed, closed, pulsed. The narrow slitted mouth had whiskers that moved languidly in the still air.

The Fanny-thing's eyes rolled. Its rose bulged and reddened.

Hatchet's knees bent as he sought the angle. The creature cupped him with its blunt, budded hands.

All in absolute silence and darkness.

"Ahhhhh . . ." Hatchet sighed as he entered it.

Killeen shot them both. He used his small pellet gun. The charges struck each in the side of the head and ended it instantly.

He lowered the gun and gripped Toby tightly by the shoulders. If the Mantis sought retribution this time it would have to come at them and they would have some infinitesimal chance. Only a moment.

He looked at Toby and they both nodded, silently.

Bodies cooled in the soft gloom and the two humans waited.

But the Mantis did not come.

NINE

They made their slow recessional through a land cut and grooved. For some unknown purpose mechs had furrowed and shaped the rough hillsides into tight, angular sheets and oblique ramps. Huge cartouches marked laminated, swooping metallic planes. Clouds of pale, shimmering gray dust gathered in the air above gleaming mechworks. The Crafter had to twist and work its way through the labyrinth.

"I didn't know what it meant," Killeen said to Shibo abruptly, as though he were taking up a conversation where they had left off. But they had not spoken together since they were inside the mechplex.

"Can't know," Shibo said.

"For a while you think you do," he said. "It was showing us things, I know that. Things it thought would mean something, something human. I didn't care about that so much."

Shibo nodded. She had had a different experience inside the Mantis thought-space, he knew. They all had.

"Part of me was sitting back from it. I thought I could keep it that way. Just watching. The place was real and then it wasn't and then it was again."

She nodded again.

"I think it was proud. Proud what it had done. Art, it said. I kept it that way in my head for a while and then I couldn't."

Shibo watched him with flat, expectant eyes. "You killed what it showed."

"I didn't think."

"Didn't need thinking." She watched the slick surfaces go by.

"So when I saw the thing like Fanny for the second time there was a while when I didn't think it was real either."

She nodded.

"Then Hatchet was with it. I would have killed it a second time anyway I guess. Even without Hatchet," Killeen said distantly.

"It was not-us."

"No. Not-us."

"Mantis had it all wrong."

"Howsay?" she asked.

"It can't tell kinds love apart."

"Hard for us sometimes too."

Killeen's jaw muscles bunched and relaxed, bunched and relaxed. "When Hatchet went with it he joined it. Not-us."

"All gone now," Shibo said. "Forget."

"There might have been more to it than that. I didn't

know. Hatchet might have done that before. Maybe you make yourself do it the first time and then later it gets easier and finally you don't mind. Don't even think about it. Hatchet maybe did it before. I didn't think about that."

"Could ask the other Kings." She looked at him calmly, just letting the idea hang there.

He thought for a long time. Then he shook his head slowly, as though dazed. "No."

They watched the strange hills. In some places you could see down through into deep caverns. Translucent layers showed blurs of darting mech motions.

"No," he said again. "Can't ask a Family 'bout something that bad."

They rode for a long time without anyone in the party talking. Of them all only Killeen had killed but no one had said anything about it.

The Crafter was subtly different now. It moved less certainly, slower, with a murmuring drone.

Killeen sighed, stood, stretched. He searched for something to say.

"Guess when the Mantis 'harvested' the Crafter, that took the life out," Killeen said to Shibo.

They rode on a cleft in the Crafter's side. Toby swung from some piping below, climbing among them for the sheer sport of it. He seemed unfazed by all that had happened inside the mountain-sized building. It had only been a few hours and the adults were still dazed and silent, clinging to the Crafter's side and watching with absent stares as the landscape rumbled by.

"Mantis said needed Crafter harvested," Shibo answered.

Killeen nodded. The Mantis had penetrated each human's sensorium, deciphered ways of talking to each of them separately. This had dawned on him as he staggered away from where he had killed Hatchet and the Fanny-thing. Apparently each human had undergone some encounter with the Mantis. Each had been shocked into pensive silence.

They left the strange place of carved, laminated land and surged across a flat tan plain. Mechs buzzed and flew everywhere. Killeen felt himself getting edgy again, his

eyes shifting at each passing mech, hands aching to reach
for a weapon.

Arthur's cool voice came laden with the brittleness it
had when in the possession of the Mantis:

No need for alarm. I have cleared the way.

The tones were distant, scrupulous. Arthur was crammed
into a small compartment by an intruding personality of far
greater heft and power.

The Mantis had made no mention of the killing. It had
brought the Crafter with it and directed the humans to
board, like any ordinary mech quickly cleaning up debris
after a job was done.

Now the Mantis escorted them back toward Metropolis. Its presence was pervasive. Dry and distant, it answered questions and gave orders.

From what the Mantis had implied, Killeen now saw
how deeply they had been drawn in. The Crafter had all
along been operating, without knowing it, under a safe
umbrella cast by the Mantis. That was why the Crafter had
been able to lead Hatchet into so many mech factories
without getting caught.

The mech civilization was complicated. Separate fief-
doms regulated defense of the factories, so the Mantis
could not ensure complete safety. Two humans had been
lost to a new type of guard, developed by the factories to
defend against just such Renegades as the Crafter.

A similar, adapted mech had attacked the Bishops in
the Trough that night after Fanny died. The Mantis could
not completely control the Marauders, could not stop the
hunting of humans. On occasion it had to surekill humans
itself, or else arouse suspicion.

Still, it had managed to conceal the Metropolis; the
Crafter had spoken true about that. But the Crafter had
never known that itself was a tool of another presence.

Now that strange intelligence carried the human party
back to their enclave, a scruffy village that dared to call
itself Metropolis. And Killeen had a good idea of how the
Mantis would treat them henceforth: as pets. Clients. Raw
material for its art.

"We're going back on that Duster?" Killeen asked. He addressed the Mantis directly. The reply came in Arthur's voice, but the Aspect was only a narrow funnel through which a far greater bulk forced and compressed itself. Killeen could sense Arthur struggling to translate. Often Arthur would simply blurt Unintelligible and skip on to what he could render into human terms.

Yes. I can use the traitor Crafter to transport you, but it must return for demolishment soon. (Unintelligible.) I could not disguise its penetration of the biological warren. Thus it must be sacrificed, broken to its constituent parts.

"Gone tear it down?"

A traitor must be rendered to infinitesimal oblivion. There is always the possibility that it has in some limited fashion made of itself an anthology mind, like me. If so, all portions of it must be consumed and obliterated. The price for insurrection is true death.

"It worked with you. You can't save it?"
The answer came rimmed with iceblue calm:

It was a lesser mind.

"So're we."

Just so. Still, you do not betray your kind.

"Crafter was just stayin' alive."

It did so in a manner against our precepts. That is the crucial distinction. (Unintelligible.) I discovered the Crafter some time ago and did not report it because I knew I could use it for higher purposes. That is the only moral reason to suffer such an aberrant mind. It wished to retain all its memories, personality, everything. That is not possible when an individual mind is subsumed into the mechmind. (Unintelligible.) A portion of the individual experience propagates, yes. A sense of selfness, yes. But not the whole. That would require storage space and complication without end.

He closeupped the horizon and saw a fast transport platform. There rode the Mantis.

It had tracked them this way ever since leaving the biological factories, keeping within transmission sight but at a remove. Killeen had the uneasy suspicion that the Mantis was covering its ass in some way. If they were intercepted by some higher-order mechs, the Mantis could get away, pretend innocence.

Killeen felt himself relax, the tightness in his muscles draining. Something in him made him say with a jaunty lilt he did not feel, "No mech heaven, huh?"

You attempt to make trivial that which is exalted. To be recycled into the hosting mind, and then propagated outward again in a specific mind and place—that is the most any consciousness could hope for, surely.

"Is it all *you* want?" Shibo asked.

Killeen blinked; he had imagined his conversation was private. Slowly, without making any sign, the Mantis was invading and integrating the responses of the humans.

I am of a different order. An anthology intelligence cannot be fully killed, since it is arrayed over the entire surface of this world. (Unintelligible.) Even a maximal thermonuclear blast could end only my elements on the illuminated face. My sense of self is kept by the phase-locked coherence of each locale, much as a net of antennae spread over an area can see as though it were one eye of that size. Yet it is not an eye at all. In a similar way, I am not *a* mind but *the* mind.

Killeen grinned. "You didn't look so hot when Shibo 'n' me, we blew you all to shot an' scatteration. 'Member? Back when the Rooks 'n' Bishops met?"

He was reasonably sure the Mantis would not let any of them live long, but a manic urge in him made him poke at the distant mech with gleeful malice.

I was prepared for that. I had recorded many of you and needed time to sort, to digest. So I transported all self-sense out of those parts, to another locale. In your terminology, you destroyed hardware, not software.

"Slowed you some, dinnit?" Shibo asked. Her lean face split with a sardonic smile. She had caught Killeen's mood. They were all released from a dark compression. No matter what their fate, they would not be daunted.

True. Anthology minds pay such a price. We are accustomed to being unlocalized, however. That was why I could not fathom, at first, your feelings about my sculptures. I—indeed, all mechs—am used to being broken into parts, repaired, and reassembled. That is the natural way. I did not understand that for you mortal, organic intelligences, the iconography of the human body, rendered into parts, would be repulsive.

"Those *things* we ran into?" Killeen remembered the disembodied legs and arms, the hideous sculpture of human genitalia remorselessly working—

Indeed. I see the distinction now, one of those points which seems obvious only in retrospect. The sole time you see the inner workings of each other is when one is ill, malfunctioning, and must be opened. Or, of course, during decay. In either case the subject person is in pain, unconscious, or dead. Such occasions cast into the human mind sets of associations freighted with strong emotions. Negative ones, purely. None of us has realized this before. It is a profound discovery. (Unintelligible.) This is one of those valuable aspects which art can capture, giving us an enduring picture of the organic world.

"Don't count on it," Shibo said dryly. Killeen grinned.

What do you mean? I cannot read your—

Killeen said, "Those 'sculptures' of yours? *That* isn't humanity. It's a horror show. A bunch of freaks. You don't know shit about humanity."

Excretion, we know. Ingestion, we know. And all that lies between.

Killeen was startled when everyone in the party laughed, the sound rolling off the steely carapace of the lumbering Crafter. He was further delighted when the Mantis sent clipped, interrogating signals shooting like crimson streamers through their sensoria.

I see. You make those sounds. This appears to be a characteristic feature of your entire phylum.

Toby asked, "Fie what? That some name you got for us?"

You are the dreaming vertebrates. A curious subphylum, to be precise. And of course now quite rare. Some of my portions, which are themselves old almost beyond measure, can remember when there were many such as you.

Killeen glanced at Shibo.

You characteristically make this convulsive sound. Your programming manifests itself in this odd way.

"That's laughing," Shibo said.

A kind of . . . spice?

Killeen chuckled. He knew immediately that the
Mantis could not extract what it meant to laugh at the
world. "Well, maybe."

Shibo asked, "Is your palate so flat?"

I see that it might be. Each of you makes the
sound differently, in ways not fully explained by
the differences in genetic construction of throats
and acoustic strings. I cannot predict or even
easily recognize the pattern. Perhaps this is
significant.

Shibo said, "You're not getting it."

Getting what?

"Whole *point*. You laugh, you're . . . you're . . ."
She stopped, stumped.

When you make that curious sound, a brief
illumination shoots through you. It is a sensation
I recognize, at least in part. Something beyond
the press of time. It is as though you lived as we
do, for that quick stuttering verbal exclamation,
that flash. For that space you are immortal.

Killeen laughed.

TEN

They worked their way down through rutted valleys
swarming with machines. The Mantis conducted them
through a dense mechplex without seeming effort. It had
the power to redirect the rushing traffic, deflecting in-
quiries.

Then they broke into open country. It was barren, as the mechs liked it. Everywhere Killeen saw signs of the eroding biosphere. Gray weeds clung to mottled hills. Once he sighted a mountainside being gnawed away by a horde of the midget mechs who had dropped on them from a Duster, long ago.

Killeen felt at peace with himself. No regrets about the killing of Hatchet plagued him and he did not wonder at that fact. It had been natural, a final drawing of the line between what was human and what was not. If the Mantis later killed him for it, there was little Killeen could do to alter that outcome. Even this prospect did not trouble him. He talked to the others, letting in the soft balm of human voices.

He began to recognize terrain. The landing field for the Duster was beyond the next ridgeline.

Denix was setting at their backs. The Eater furled its own radiance beyond the rolling hills. Wavering in the high air ahead were fibers of orange luminescence. Directly before them fresh traceries frenzied the air. Killeen puzzled, and then remembered.

"Look!" he called to Toby and Shibo.

The Mantis, riding its crescent-shaped platform on a nearby hill, had seen the disturbance, too. Killeen could feel its pale swift intricacy in his sensorium, focusing forward, eyeing the descending lights.

He made his voice blend both acoustics and electrotalk. Transduced by buried chips, his words sprang forth as croaked stabs at the air. "You! The one from the Eater!"

The air wrinkled. Clouds made spindly, spinning feelers.

Wind-whisperings nearly covered the faint sound when it came.

Summer lashings veil me. I can barely hear your effusions. Speak louder!

"How's this?" Killeen gave all his voice to it, sending each word forth as a coarse, clipped wedge of electrosound.

Better. That is Killeen, no? I have sought you.

The Mantis said:

What manner of—ah!

Killeen was startled by the Mantis's abrupt shutdown of transmission. It had fled.

"Sought me for what?"

The Crafter itself stopped, its engines spun down to silence. The humans still clung to it, watching the sky develop a web of shooting colors. Faint whistlings shot downward. Sparks marked the magnetic field lines. The threads twisted and focused, bending down through the deepening cobalt vault of sky.

Killeen could see the entire geomagnetic bubble that shrouded Snowglade. It hung like a jeweled spiderweb and the stars seemed motes trapped in it. Then it began to deform. Speckled strands crunched together, as though a giant hand were wadding pliant paper. Where the fields necked together, sapphire-smooth glories flickered.

Columns of dim radiance blew in from the depths of the gathering night sky. They forced the field lines closer still, making a magnetic bottleneck. There, the rolling, deep voice became stronger. It was as though the words came to him as spoken straight out of a spot among the stars.

I have searched long and wary for you.

Killeen shouted, his throat already getting hoarse, "Why?"

You truly are the locus termed Killeen? I must be sure.

"Read me," he said. Killeen was curious if it could detect the lingering sour flavor of the Mantis in Killeen's sensorium.

Ah—it is you. But something is changed.

"Yeasay, there's—"

Humble greetings to the minister of magnitudes!

The jittery salute came so quickly Killeen could scarcely read it. The Mantis's tone was different from anything he had ever heard.

I sense a machine mode?

Yes, and amply honored to receive you. I hope this does not bode for an early intersection of our world with the massless ones? That would, of course, be a summation and an honor as well. (Unintelligible.) With great respect, I believe we in the machine mode are not prepared for such an august presence to—

No no, nothing like that. When the time for intersection and ascension comes, you shall be well advised. These matters are dealt with at higher levels, I presume you know?

Yes, of course! I did not venture to intrude upon the progressions and convergences of—

Then please us with your absence.

Oh! Yes!

Killeen felt the Mantis shrink into a fat knot of black confusion. It withdrew, cowed.

The amber-fluted voice rang down powerfully from a shadowed sky:

The motive entity which bade me deliver the earlier message—that inductance again wishes to speak to you.

Killeen blinked. "What . . ."

> It cannot speak directly, but must drive its meaning through electroflux and arching currents. It lives far further into the Eater than do I.

"Where? Who?" How could anyone know *him*?

> It dwells inside the time-confused sphere of the Eater itself. It has plunged beyond the accretion disk, lower still than where my own feet are anchored by thick traps of raging plasma. This entity has plucked magnetic fields and sent outward from its dark realm a message. And it compels me to bring it forth to you, along the stretched and rubbery magnetic ropes which are my body and soul.

The humans around him all stared upward, mouths gaping. Killeen had lost his awe and was now frightened. If the energies which could crush the geomagnetic fields so casually should err, and sputter downward into lightning, they all would flare and crisp in an instant. And that was not unreasonable, since the being above was so clearly mad. . . .

> The message is garbled. Strange storms of space and time blow in the Eater, tumbling words, muting all but a few. Still, I am enjoined by great and sufficient powers to relay what I can. The first portion of the message is this: *Ask for the Argo. Remember. Ask for the Argo.*

Killeen frowned. Again the meaningless word. "Argo . . ."

> I know no more than ever what this word means. The second portion . . . portion . . .

"It fades," Shibo whispered.

> But wait. This machine near you—I sense it struggling. It resists my presence.

Killeen shouted. "The second part! Tell me—"

No. I weaken momentarily . . . but I shall force this . . . this irritating machine . . . to speak . . . truthfully. . . .

Killeen looked far up into the shadowy sky. The intricate tapestry of magnetic field lines dimmed. Its constrictions loosened. "Wait!" he cried. "The message's second part!"

From the flexing field lines came only silence. Killeen frowned and amped his sensors to max. Did he hear faint words?

Into his sensorium coiled a dark presence. It was the Mantis returning, made bold again.

I have never witnessed such an order of being before. They visit these realms seldom, preferring the energetic storms at the Eater's margin.

Even through the filter of Arthur's cool tones, Killeen could sense the Mantis's awe.

"What *is* it?" someone of the party asked. Killeen searched the twisting folds of magnetic force that slid like ivory muscles through the sky.

A magnetic mind. A personality of dimensions unknown in material beings. It lives in the complex warpage of magnetic stresses, with its information content stored in waves which suffer no damping. In this way it is another facet of immortality . . . a higher one than we achieve here. Such spirits are anchored in the disk of bluehot matter which orbits the Eater. (Unintelligible.) The accreting disk provides a base for many such minds, while their true selves extend out into the gaseous clouds and stars circling the center. I am honored to have seen one. It is a high aim of our culture to entertain such a presence. Some say these minds were once embodied in such as we.

Killeen still watched the dark movements above, but something made him say sarcastically, "So you mechs've got a God?"

Magnetic minds are not the highest phase. There is something greater.

Shibo asked, "This Argo—you understand what the manmech means?"

I . . . the magnetic being . . . forces me to tell you. I can sense it, feel its pressure. It compels . . . In the last few seconds I have interrogated history compilations from all around Snowglade. There are vague traces of such a thing, something named Argo, perhaps several.

Killeen said, "I remember something about Argo being like some other city, Sparta. Help us find it."

This is impossible. The magnetic mind compels me to speak truly, but do not think it can dictate actions contrary to my interest. It is weak this moment . . . I can feel it. . . .

"Speak, damn you!" Killeen shouted angrily.

At best I can hope that no other mech intercepted this transmission from the magnetic mind. If so, perhaps I can conceal the information for a time. You must understand that I am your ally. (Unintelligible.) I wish to preserve the best of humanity, down into the eras to come when you will be extinct. Still, I cannot allow humanity to escape into the realm beyond Snowglade.

"Why not?" Shibo demanded.

You could upset workings which we have had in motion for millennia.

"How?" someone asked.

Killeen could feel the constricted agony of the Mantis. The magnetic mind, unseen, was still making the Mantis speak truly. There was a quality to it of a higher authority forcing a distant underling to kowtow.

There are other . . . organic beings. Some have . . . invaded . . . the zone near the Eater. We do not wish to provoke . . . alliances . . . among the lower lifeforms.

This stirred the party.

Killeen frowned. So there *was* some way the mechs felt threatened by the very existence of humans. He had guessed that before. Unbidden, the Mantis answered his thoughts:

The drive to exterminate you comes from higher up in our society. Though we have diverse, competing parts to our civilization on Snowglade some directives unite us. One is to *never* allow the organic beings to link up. They are unimpressive overall, but together can be a nuisance.

Killeen smiled but kept his thoughts to himself.

Around him people spoke excitedly. *Other life!* Intelligent, alien, but at least living. Maybe even other humans, around other stars. It was an intoxicating notion.

And it had all been triggered by the whispering intelligence that steepled filmy fields in the air, warping vast energies as casually as a man brushes aside a curtain.

He gathered himself, amped his systems, and bellowed, "I'm still here! Killeen! *Give me my message!*"

A drifting radiance stretched across the silent sky. Shibo touched his arm. He shook her off.

The mighty will not come to such demands. You
show arrogance unseemly in one so low. Get—

"Quiet!"
To Killeen's surprise, the Mantis presence shrank away,
as if afraid.
Murmurings.
Vague shimmering fluxes tightened. Ruby fingers
poked toward them.
Then the voice boomed forth again.

**I hear. A passing comet perturbed my raiments.
I have evaporated it and can reach up to you again
with my full presence. I did enjoy forcing that
presumptuous machine to treat you fairly. Seldom
do I have such innocent amusement. I hope a
breath of truth will be useful to you. Alas, when I
depart, it will return to its habits. Beware of it.**

"The second part!" he demanded.

**Oh, yes. It is ambiguous. I do not understand
how this can be true. The message comes from a
solid craft voyaging somehow through the strange
seas of time within the Eater. Yet it is addressed to
you, the lowest form I have ever witnessed. I must
not have fathomed its true import.**

"Let me have it!"

**Very well. I go now in haste. Your message
says:**

**Do not rebuild a Citadel. They will crush you
there. Believe you this of me, for I still live, and I
am your father.**

ELEVEN

They came straggling into Metropolis. The last distance they had covered on foot through a brisk warm wind, and that was when the fatigue came on. Killeen had managed to doze a bit on the Crafter's hull after the magnetic being had gone away. Then he had fallen asleep, like everybody else, in the Duster that brought them all back to the original landing plain.

The Mantis had come with them. It had necked itself down to a tight assembly of rods and oval compartments in order to fit inside the Duster. Now it wanted to stay beyond the range of hills ringing Metropolis until the right time to appear.

The magnetic being had said no more after delivering its strange last message. Killeen did not think about that or anything else. He was tired. He carried Toby piggyback for the last part because the boy had finally given out. The aftereffects of Toby's injury and the mech treatment came home and he could barely stay awake.

The Kings had gotten everybody fancied up for their arrival. Evidently Hatchet had always made an event out of his return from a raid. So as soon as people in Metropolis picked up the party's scent in their sensoria, Kings and Rooks and Bishops flocked to greet them.

As the party trickled in, not talking and not carrying much booty, the cheering died away. After they saw that Hatchet was not in the party, none of the Kings had much to say. Killeen just kept walking, carrying Toby through the dusty dawn light. Jocelyn and some of the Bishops came out and tried to talk but he carried Toby into his small hut and put the boy to bed.

By that time Ledroff and Fornax were speaking with the rest of the party but Killeen did not go out to them. He sat for a moment on his own bed, his thinking going like gravel sliding downhill. Then he was blinking awake hours later with blades of yellow Denixlight striking him in the face.

He judged the time by where Denix hung against a distant backdrop of dark stardust. Though he had not slept more than a few hours, he felt rested. What was left of the fatigue became a mildness that he could feel giving him a sure sense of purpose. He checked on Toby, who slept sprawled open and easy.

Seeing his son, he remembered when the spectacle of Toby's breathing had transfixed him in this room. It had been so long ago. Seeing Toby again, but this time knowing his son would come bounding up as soon as he awoke, was worth every bit of what had happened. And worth what would come next.

Then he went outside.

It went with Ledroff much the way Killeen had expected it. He listened, nodding every once in a while to show he was paying attention, but thinking ahead. There would have to be a Witnessing, yes, he saw that. No, he didn't want to say that he had shot Hatchet by mistake while he was trying to hit the other thing. Yes, he was sure of that. Of course he understood that this was a serious matter. Yes, the others were right, the Mantis was staying out of Metropolis. There was no threat from it right away. No, Killeen did not want to see the woman Hatchet lived with and explain to her how it had happened. That would come out in the Witnessing. He would speak for himself and didn't need Ledroff to say anything much or make a plea to the assembled Families. Of course he saw that this was a serious matter. Of course.

Ledroff had Killeen's hut searched. Just a precaution, Ledroff said. He confiscated the small flask of alcohol in Killeen's carrypack. Killeen chuckled quietly when Ledroff stalked out with the flask held contemptuously at arm's length. He understood that the Cap'n meant it to be both a humiliation and a way to undercut Killeen's status with others. What Ledroff did not know was that such things did not matter to Killeen anymore.

He went back inside but Toby wasn't awake yet. Killeen watched his boy for a while, thinking. His Aspects sent tinny voices lacing through his sensorium, plucking at his attention. He could feel their anxiety building.

Shibo came by. They rounded up some food for their

carrypacks and checked out their equipment. This habit came from the years of running; you got ready to move again, first thing after you stopped.

Toby woke up and wanted to go out. Reluctantly Killeen went along, but guided them away from Metropolis. He did not want to meet people and talk about what had happened.

They strolled into the nearby hills, saying little. Shibo confirmed Killeen's guess. While they had slept, she said, the Mantis had spoken to Ledroff and Fornax. It had offered to shelter them in Metropolis.

The Mantis knew something of human psychology. It framed its arguments as an even bargain.

The Mantis said it would protect Metropolis, using artful deception of its superiors. It would deflect Marauders away. It would only "harvest" old people, when they were near death anyway.

In return—and here the Mantis revealed its understanding of human pride—the Families would undertake raids on selected mech cities. What they stole would provide the Mantis with barter goods. These it could use to amass wealth in mech society. Finally, neatly tying the loop, this added power of the Mantis would enable it to in turn cover the presence of the vermin humans.

Killeen was numbed by Shibo's clear explanation. The proposition was clever. It let humanity retain some of its dignity. To a Metropolis still shocked by the loss of Hatchet, it would seem a godsend.

And Killeen could see no way to counter it.

They walked through low canyons between steep hills. Toby showed no fatigue and even dashed about, chasing the vagrant small animals who lived beneath scrub bushes.

Shibo said little, just reported what people were saying. Ledroff and Fornax had told several of the Mantis's presence beyond Metropolis, and rumors spread everywhere.

The Witnessing to come would first take up Hatchet's death. Then it would move to the discussion of the Mantis's proposal.

Killeen said sourly, "I think I can predict what they'll decide."

"Yeasay," Shibo said forlornly.

From up a nearby arroyo came a woman's shout. "Hail! Killeen, Shibo—is that you?"

From behind a knot of bushes came a mech. Killeen automatically reached for a weapon and then saw that it was the manmech, last seen back at the mechplex.

"I have journeyed far, pursuing you," the womanly voice called.

The mech was dusty, dented, and marred. Broken links hung from its treads.

Shibo gaped. "How . . . ?"

"I attached a tracer to Toby's ankle. See?"

The mech gestured with an extruded arm at Toby's boots. A tiny patch no larger than a fingernail was stuck there. "I know the ways of mech transport. I followed your trail until I saw that you had returned to your Duster. It took a while to find an air-hauler I could assume command of. But I did, and have followed you. Ruff!"

Toby laughed. "The dog mech."

Killeen shook his head wonderingly. "I'm afraid things've changed since we saw you."

The woman's voice was incongruous, coming from the mech's speaker. "I sighted a large mech as I approached. I believe it could be quite dangerous. It moves among these hills. You should alert the human community here—"

"We know," Toby said. "It's the Mantis."

The manmech went on enthusiastically, "Very well then. Still, I must follow my time-honored injunction. I remind you, humans, that I need only the correct key to deliver to you information."

Killeen shook his head tiredly. "Don't think old lore's much use now. See, we—"

"No, wait," Toby said. "Dad, 'member what that thing in the sky said?"

"What—the magnetic mind? Listen, I didn't understand much what it said either, and—"

"We figured it said somethin' 'bout old things," Toby said earnestly. "A city or somethin', right?"

Killeen frowned. "I doubt it, but . . . let's see, what'd it say . . . ?"

Shibo said precisely, "Do not build a Citadel."

Killeen smiled without humor. "Good advice, but too late. Citadels draw Marauders. Metropolis isn't any Citadel, but it's already built."

Toby added, "There was somethin' else. Right—it said, 'Ask for the Argo.'"

Suddenly the manmech cried, "Ruff! The sanctioned key! Thank you! Thank you!"

They all stared at the mech as it spun with joy on its treads, barking.

"Argo! Argo! This word is my key. It licenses me to deliver my message at last."

Killeen asked, "Argo? Some old human city?"

"Oh no! Argo is a *ship*. Long ago my brothers and I concealed it. I know the place. I know where the Argo lies!"

Toby said wonderingly, "A ship . . ."

Killeen consulted his Face, Bud, and asked, "For oceans?" He shrugged. "No big water left on Snowglade."

"No! It navigates between stars. The craft was completed long ago. I helped bury it. It can sail toward the Mandikini."

"In the sky?" Shibo asked doubtfully.

"Yes! Humanity made the Argo especially to accept only human-tinged commands. I and a hundred of my brothers were charged with carrying information of its location. If humanity ever needed a long-voyager, and could not fashion one themselves, we were to speak. But only to the descendants of those who made the Argo—such as are you, since you know the key word, the ship itself!" The manmech finished with a resounding bark.

The three humans stared at one another, startled.

The manmech spun again, rattling and churning. "Ruff! I stand ready! Ruff. Message ends! Ruff!"

He had no warning. The attack came as he walked back into Metropolis with Shibo and Toby. They were talking to the manmech, which ground along on noisy, grating treads.

Toby chattered at his side, eyes alive with bright visions.

In a distracted moment, Killeen's own Aspects struck at him.

He wavered, stumbled, and fell in what felt to him to

be a pinwheel dive forward into a thin patch of aromatic grass.

A tide rushed in him. All his Aspects and Faces yammered at once. Quick hot spikes of protest shot up from an undercurrent of low moaning fear.

It was a chorus that swelled into a lifting, surging wave. Each voice lapped over others. They invaded his arms, legs, and chest with icy rivulets. His muscles jerked. The hammering shouts coursed through his veins and struck coldly into his tightening gut. He opened his mouth to cry out and they jammed that, too, lockjawing his aching hinge joints.

They had seen what he was thinking.

Aspects and Faces were old, conservative, wedded to Snowglade.

A wave of shrill fear broke through him. His heels drummed against the grass. Milky white flooded his eyes, blotting out Toby and Shibo, who were reaching for him, their mouths moving soundlessly like fish behind glass. Killeen fought against the swelling ancestral yammering.

He tried to slip away from them, escape down into his sensorium. They followed everywhere, striking chilly spikes into the crevices where he fled.

Don't risk us! *a dozen voices cried.* **Never leave the homeworld!**

He writhed. He felt his body only distantly, through a narrow gray tunnel. His feet and hands scrabbled at the soil. These came as slow percussions, as though he was numbed by creeping cold.

And still the high-pitched babble washed through him. Burnt-yellow anxiety spurted, yowling. Below it groaned a mad bass undercurrent of foreboding.

Coward! Do not flee!

The shouts came to him through watery light.

Rebuild the sacred Citadels. The Holy Clauses demand it!

Killeen struggled against a downsucking wave of anger. He was drowning in a sea of insects.

They splashed against him and crawled into his nostrils. Tiny shouts plucked at his skin. Pincers stung his flesh. He tried to breathe and inhaled a tickling, tinkling chorus.

Fool! Ingrate!
Traitor you are!
Centuries labored we here. Dare flee it now?
Think not of us?
We belong here. Snowglade is humanity's true home.
Run now you would with tail between legs?
Coward!

He felt himself weakening.

Tiny feelers plunged through his sinuses. Antennae choked him.

His lungs filled with a black army.

Then his furiously kicking heels nicked something solid.

The waters were a living mass of tiny scrabbling legs.

He rolled in a crashing insect wave. He struggled for air and his legs sought the firm rock beneath.

Caught it again.

Pushed down. Stood.

Wriggling masses lapped at him.

Plucked at his skin.

Swarmed and cried and splashed.

He was standing in the wash of a pounding storm that blew in from far offshore. The waves of tiny voracious minds came steadily, shouting at him, licking mouths in every droplet. Moist tongues lashed at him. But he dug in his heels and the next wave did not overpower him. He fought against the swirling currents. Then the riptide tried to draw him away, tugging at his feet.

If he had been standing on sand, the rushing insect waters could have undermined him, cut away his footing.

But it was rock. Hard and solemn stone.

And it carried the stiff, brittle feel of the Mantis.

He backed toward the shore, always keeping his eye on the incoming toppling combers of mad mouths. They sucked at him with bloody lips. He stepped carefully, always gripping the rock with his toes, feeling his way, the stone his true anchor.

The currents lashed and fought and then finally ebbed. He struggled ashore against a strong tide. Then he puffed and coughed, spitting out the motes, blowing his nose clear of sticky mucus. As the slimy stuff struck the rocks it cried out sharply in vain tenor despair.

Cool droplets of tiny biting pincers oozed down his legs and puddled on the crisp warm sand. He shook the screaming insect minds from his hair, cricked them forth from the corners of his eyes. Their wails dwindled.

He looked at a yellow glow high up the sky. It dried him.

Then he was staring faceup into slanting blades of pale pure Denixlight.

Shibo said, "He's blinking. Are you . . . ?"

"Yeasay. I'm here."

"Aspect storm?"

"Yeasay. I . . . something . . ."

He felt the solid stone still pressing against his heels. He glanced at the circle of anxious faces peering down at him.

"It was . . . the Mantis," discovering this and saying it in the same instant. "It came, gave me a standing place. Leverage. So I could fight them down."

"Mantis?" Shibo asked wonderingly.

He was still panting and the air cut clear into his lungs. Memories of the horde seeped away. "It . . . knows about . . . what it calls 'sentient information.' Can keep subsystems . . . Aspects . . . in line."

"You can stand?"

"It did somethin' more, too. When the Aspects opened up, the Mantis could reach them. And farther in, too. Undid some stuff I got in there. I can feel it . . . different."

"You need rest." Shibo wiped his brow with a cloth and he was surprised to see it come away sopping wet.

"The Aspects, they . . . saw what I was thinking."

Shibo frowned. "Did Mantis?"

"Don't think it had time."

"You think there's . . . hope?"

"Yeasay."

Shibo's face of planes and angles showed relief and lingering puzzlement.

I can solve that puzzle, he thought. The abrupt idea seemed both odd and yet certainly right, obvious.

Then Toby was hugging him and sobbing with long-stored tears that seemed to patter down on Killeen from the limitless sky. Arms wrapped around him. Hands helped him up. The manmech barked. They crowded around, talking and patting and asking.

TWELVE

There was not much time to rest before the Witnessing. Killeen lay for a while thinking and then people came knocking tentatively at the door of his hut.

They were Bishops. Killeen talked to them in turn, not being too specific but telling them the outlines of what he had learned. He spoke calmly and with assurance, feeling a certainty he never had before.

But not true assurance, he reminded himself. When he momentarily wondered what to say, he would ask himself what Fanny would have done. Often he was not sure but he got through the difficult points somehow.

He could see in the faces of the other Bishops a surprise that evolved into interest and then agreement. A grudging agreement for some of them, but he sensed that it would stick. As word had spread about the Mantis, about Hatchet and what the man had been doing, everyone in the Families was sobered. Some Rooks came by, too.

After they had eaten some baked sharproot, Shibo and Toby and Killeen went for another walk around Metropolis, just exercising the boy's legs. They left the manmech sitting inert, its solar panels repowering. Killeen was afraid the Mantis could interrogate it from a distance if it was running normally. The information about the Argo was best kept secret for a while longer.

Killeen deflected people who came up to him and wanted to discuss things. A clammy fog shrouded the growing fields to the south of Metropolis. They walked among towering fragrant corn. Toby had never seen cultivated plants so high and couldn't recall even the long rows of tomatoes where he had once played near the Citadel. The Eater rose and cut through the thin fog, bringing a crisp savor to the air. Killeen went back to the hut and slept easily until the Witnessing.

The Kings spoke against him.

They had worked on their arguments, using testimony from the Kings in the raiding party to good effect. They made a simple case, plainly thinking that the facts would be enough.

Fornax presided, since he was the Cap'n who had been in power longest. The Kings were deferential to him. They would choose a Cap'n soon after the Witnessing, but until then Fornax was in nominal control of the Cap'nless Family. And he would be a good ally to have later.

Once the opening charge was made, and the Kings were done, Cermo and Shibo spoke in opposition. Following tradition, Killeen sat in the middle of the crowded bowl carved from a hillside. Each speaker took turns at the center of the bowl. Except for the perimeter guard, the bare scooped rock held all known humanity.

Shibo said few words but conveyed much. She was respected. Though she gave the same picture of Hatchet's killing that Cermo did, her words weighed more heavily. In the Witnessing, all that mattered was the final vote of the assembled Families. Every person convinced by Shibo's simple eloquence was a gain.

After her, Ledroff spoke as Cap'n of the defending Family. He was vague, saying that Killeen was reliable and not the kind of Family member who would ever attack a Cap'n unless it was in some way unavoidable.

Killeen thought this did him no good at all, but he was not prepared for Fornax.

As presiding Cap'n, Fornax was nominally neutral. But

as the wiry man began, Killeen saw that his every sentence was slyly shaped.

Fornax's lined face wrinkled with skepticism even as his mouth formed wry, scornful phrases. He treated gravely everything the Kings claimed. Then Fornax passed over the Bishops' version as mere opinion.

He did it subtly, choosing his words to soften the facts and round them to his end. His face, turned up to the rings of faces, carried a sorrow at what he had to say.

Killeen could not tell if the expression was real. He did know that Fornax could reasonably expect to exert much power in Metropolis as the senior Cap'n. Though a King would still run Metropolis, the new King Cap'n would necessarily be less powerful because he or she would be fresh. The more Fornax appeared as a wise figure, the greater would be his influence among all the Families.

Fornax sat down and it came to Killeen by tradition to say the last words.

Killeen felt himself alone. Yet he did not doubt what he should do. Against Fornax's eloquence he had no wordy defense. The gathered Families looked at him with expectant faces.

"I speak flat and plain. You know what happened. Point to all this is *why*. You can't know that without feeling it yourself. So I call on the one way you can see that and feel it and know it for what it was. Not through talk can anyone do that. Only this way."

He stepped back a pace as though admitting someone else to the flat slab of tan-flecked gray rock. This was the speaker's spot; Hatchet had spoken often from that already worn place.

I know you're listening. Killeen made each word separately in his mind. *You must have stored it. Bring it. That's the best way.*

Something shimmered at the speaker's spot. A whirlwind frenzied the air.

And abruptly Killeen was *there* again.

The mechplex. The vast shadowed plain dotted by gray-moist contortions.

In awful, gravid grace the events unfurled. The Fanny-thing shambled closer to the figure which Killeen only slowly saw was himself.

Hatchet stepped forward. Unhitched his harness and then his pants. Let them drop. Reached out. Drew the scaly thing toward him.

She cupped him with a blunt, budded hand.

With a quick soft jerk he entered between the canted thighs.

They worked together. A soft sucking sound came from them.

And the fragile world of the sensorium shattered. Killeen's shots came as rushing hard claps that reflected from icewall layers, hammering at the images of falling bodies and maddened frosty air.

And then Killeen was back.

He let his breath ease and slow, watching the bowl of stunned faces. He had made no attempt to use his sensorium to reach the Mantis, not since the party had left it in the hills beyond.

Yet he had sensed what to do. He saw the long journey ahead and knew it whole, though each step his feet sought was fresh as it came to him.

He said nothing as a shaken Fornax stood. Long moments drifted by as the people recovered. They said little. Talk trickled over Killeen like mild warm rain. He answered the questions with only a few words but that seemed enough. The voices tapered away.

Fornax called the question. Killeen sat.

He could not vote himself and did not look up to see the oldfashioned raising of hands. They could as easily have taken a vote through the sensorium, but it still echoed and seethed with the presence that had passed through it like a chill wind.

Fornax counted, grimaced. His face a grave mask, he summoned up the ancient formal terms, "By a factor three do the assembled Families absolve he who stands in trial. I so validate said judgment. I do welcome the once-pariah back to the manyfold. I do salute the once-cast-out as reborn into the Family of Families. Rejoice!"

The ritual embrace from Fornax was stiff and unfriendly and told Killeen more about the man than words could.

As he stepped back in the still silence the Mantis voice came.

> A good ending. Now that I am summoned forth by your needs, let me speak.

The Mantis voice was a sure, steady thread in their sensoria.

> I offer you all protection from the buffeting you have received for so long. I express my sorrow at your suffering.(Unintelligible.) I shall keep you here and prevent further attacks. Know this as tribute to the essence of what you are.

Killeen nodded. He had known this would come. One more step.

The Families stirred. Fear and hope dawned upon them in equal measure and fought across their faces.

> Your ways must be preserved and exalted in the manner of art. You are valuable. Your quick and savory lives are themselves your highest works. Give this to me and I shall preserve the best in you now and forever.

A fevered breeze rippled through them.

The Mantis paused.

Killeen rose and spoke to the bowl with a powerful voice.

"Some would live in such a place. There is an old word for it. *Zoo*. And some would not."

The Mantis countered:

> Without my skills, the Marauders will have you. I am but one element in a complex beyond your imagining. I cannot stop the Marauders, for they proceed from a longer logic. Forces align against you.

"Not everything's against us," Killeen said dryly. "The magnetic mind, it made you speak true 'bout that."

The Mantis voice returned, cool and sure. Killeen
could see by the transfixed eyes of the Families that they
heard.

> True, I cannot conceal what was forced from me.
> Organic intelligences do range elsewhere in the
> zone of the Eater (as you call it) and measures are
> proceeding to see that they do not unite. You are
> such an element. Though diminished now, your
> potential is harmful. Thus vectors intersect and
> bequeath for you a future of perpetual onslaught
> from the Marauders. (Unintelligible.) Only if you
> consign yourselves to my aid shall you survive.

These thoughts came with the solidity and massive
presence of words written in granite.

The rude scooped-out depression seemed suddenly a
small place, a bowl into which the Mantis voice poured,
encompassing the human tribe and defining its puny
position.

People stirred, fitful expressions of wonder and fear
flickering among them like summer lightning. They all
knew from their sensoria that this intelligence was massive,
complex, vastly calm. From it came tremors of large intent,
an impression of solidity and complete, unblinking honesty.

Killeen waited for the effect to wear upon the Families
for a long moment. He remembered his father's old words,
back at the Citadel: *Thing about aliens is, they're alien*.

The Mantis might be honest and it might not. Any
sense of that was a human projection. He had to remember
that. He could not assume that he understood the machine.
Or that it fully comprehended them.

> I ask now that you agree to accept my shelter
> against these harsh winds which shall continue
> to buffet you. Agree, and I shall enter into a
> partnership with you Families. I may be able to
> rescue other humans still lost in the plains of this
> planet—though I must tell you there are few
> such. Agree, now, and we can begin.

Killeen waited again for the effect of the forceful thoughts to disperse. Then he raised one hand in a fist.

The Families noticed him standing there, still at the speaker's spot. He stood silently and looked steadily ahead, waiting until the tension and focus he felt could spread through his own sensorium and into theirs. Scattered remarks died down. The bowl quieted. He could hear Snowglade's soft winds stroking the hills. Humanity watched him. He now had to speak of his own vision. He had to make it real to them.

"To follow the Mantis way is to ensure that there will be no true destiny remaining to us now, or our children, or to that long legion which will come forth from us. You can take the Mantis's shelter, yes. You can hide from the Marauders. Raise your crops. Birth sons and daughters and see them flower, yes. That would be human and good. But that way would always be hobbled and cramped and finally would be the death of what we *are*."

Killeen swept his gaze through the ranks of watching eyes, seeming to catch each in turn for a brief moment.

"There is another course. A larger way. One that believes—as you did here today, in your vote for the Witnessing—in the enduring worth of simple human dignity."

In the sudden alarmed and yet excited looks which greeted his words he saw in the Families, for the first time in his adult years, a heady opening sense of possibility.

THIRTEEN

He had expected the Mantis to respond with an icily reasoned attack. Or some strange mindstorm. Perhaps with an assault on Killeen himself.

He had certainly not expected utter silence.

The Families were apprehensive as they left the bowl. No one knew what the Mantis's lack of reply meant.

Killeen felt a vast sense of relief as he walked back from the Witnessing.

Toby chattered at his side, eyes dancing with bright

visions. Killeen had awakened those thoughts in the Families and the experience had drained him.

Speaking, he had felt for the first time what it was to drive forth into the unforgiving air your own self, projected through the weblike sensorium but riding finally on the resonant tones of pure voice. Words were blunt, blind things to use in aid of the clear way he himself saw the world. He wrestled with them like strange tools, forcing their soft meanings to drive hard facts into the minds of the others. Words not only meant things, they made the mind feel and stretch, the blood pound faster.

He had sketched for them his way, the tale of the Argo. From the Families had come an answering song, a muttered assent peppered by questions, doubts, naysays which bobbed like flecks on a dark ocean. They did not all agree. At best a fraction had the resolve and spirit to follow where the ideas led, to take the first few steps marked in uncertain sands.

But some had it. Some had heard.

He had never thought it could be so exhausting. He had great respect for what a Cap'n had to summon up. His mouth was dry and his legs ached as though he had been marching for hours.

Then he felt the pressing weight of the Mantis mind returning to his sensorium.

Despite your phylum's limitations, you are capable of surprises.

"Thanks most kindly and fuck you," Killeen said.

The people walking nearby heard the Mantis as well. They all stopped, heads tilted back. The Mantis seemed to crowd the very air with its presence.

Even given my great abilities, your invitation is at root impossible.

"It's an expression, not a proposition."

I see. I have interrogated historical compilations from our cities, circling Snowglade. Among the

messy archives of (admittedly, nearly indecipherable) human lore, there are faint traces of such a
craft named Argo. It may have been built to
reach your Chandeliers. Apparently, when we
began to spread over Snowglade and carry out
the necessary changes in it, your forefathers
elected to store the fast-vanishing human technology.

"You understand my offer?"

Your threat, yes. (Unintelligible.) Indeed, if you
attempted to reach the Argo by yourself, I could
easily stop you. I can cause Marauders to block
your path.

Killeen smiled coolly. "Sure. Stoppin' us is easy. Just
kill us."

Which is precisely what I do not want, of course.
I had believed that I could complete my art in
one human generation. I see now this cannot
be. You are deeper and stranger than I suspected.

Shibo broke in, "Always be some stay here, in zoo. You
use them."

But do they represent the full range of your odd
talents? This I do not know.

"You'll find out. Just let some of us go."
A hollow pressure rang through the sensorium, repre-
senting some alien reaction Killeen could not interpret in
human terms.

I will do more than that. I shall even help you.

Killeen did not take part in the cheering that broke out
among the Bishops and Rooks nearby. Wary, he wondered
what the Mantis's true thoughts were, and motives.

* * *

"Mantis present now?" Shibo asked.

"I can feel it." Killeen rubbed his face. He had a headache that ran like strips of fire along his brow. He asked her to press the spots behind his ears at the base of his skull. That was the old Bishop way of releasing the pain and it soon brought easing. His senses seethed and sought, awakening. To him her hands were purring ruby-hot.

"It'd always be like this if we stay here," he said as the warmth crept over him. "Mantis'll be there in the background."

"Watching?"

"Wish it was only. Naysay noway we can stop it."

"Senses us?"

"We could get rid of it if we shut down our sensoria. Went blind."

"Don't want."

"Me either. I . . . I'll try . . ."

Carefully he focused his attention on the points where the faint buzzing presence entered him. He pushed it away. Gently, carefully. Then harder. The subdued hum vanished.

"I think it'll go if we want."

She nodded. "I feel too."

"Still around though."

"Yeasay. But it goes."

"I'd've never got through the Aspect storm without it. I'd be in a trance, same as that woman Hatchet used have as his translator. Her Aspects must've panicked on a raid."

"Crafter couldn't fix her?"

"That's what I figure. Mantis gave me just enough help. It's some use."

"I don't like though."

He knew what she meant. Life under a benign umbrella would always hint of distant eyes.

Slowly she let her eyes stray from the stars visible out the window. She looked at him aslant, speculatively. A thin knowing smile illuminated the smooth planes of her face.

"The interlock commands I had. The sexcen modifications. They're gone."

She said nothing, just smiled.

He kissed her neck, face, mouth. All tasted of the air

and soil but the mouth was stronger, deeper, moist. His knees dropped him to the rough dirt floor. His teeth searched for the pullstring of her jumper. The weave was harsh and his beard scraped a purr from it. The cloth came free and slid easy and she locked her legs over his back. The small room was twilight cool and had no bed. They rolled over twice on the fragrant lumpy dirt. His saliva soaked through the cloth before he got it all off her using only his mouth. He would not give up his hold on her, or she hers. They rolled again, this time against the wall, stubbing toes, bumping knees.

She wriggled away. A popping sound, snaps. She slid free of her exskell.

Then he encountered in the gathering dark her hip, her marvelous compact breasts. His tongue discovered her back, sharp shoulder blades, furred nape of the neck. Kneading. Rubbing away the riverrun layered silt of tension and fear that had built up in them both. He felt thick years of it shimmer and dissolve. Her teeth plucked delicious pain from his lips. His chin bristled in her hair. A wind blew down from her great nostril mountains. Layers peeled away and he felt deep within an old Aspect of his, a woman, sliding down his arms and into his fingers. He had not felt it this way before, with Veronica or Jocelyn. A soft womanly weight came into his touch. Going layers down. Access. Slow nudges. Rolling down slow tremors together, they moved in a hovering hush. Her legs enclosed him. Cradled heat burst into his mouth. Grab, release, return, circle. A liberating toss of the hip brought bone to bone. Bellies opened and a shoulder fell through to the vexed heart. The woman in him felt her trip-hammer pulse quicken, ebb, come again. A hushed audience seemed to attend each movement, the slick slice of him and her together ramifying up into higher chords. Fit snug. Passages widened as muscles stuttered. He grasped and suspended himself, felt her spiral up. Heat lifted her hair.

Twists and twinges set off sure long motions and he felt in the instant the meaning of the grotesque statuary he had seen back in the mechplex. The tortured coiling thing reflected his need for this and yet in its relentless plunging power and opening fissures managed to get the whole thing profoundly wrong. The Mantis would never know them. There was a press of essences beyond the digital romance. A deep-buried spirit filled organic life. It came from origins in the way the universe was made, and generated out of itself the life each mortal being felt throbbing in every sliding moment. The Mantis had robbed such moments as this from the suspended minds of the suredead but it could not surecopy this; Killeen knew this fact solidly and forever in the mere passing twist and twinge of a second. She felt it too, gave him a flex and thrust that brought moist skirtings into him. She loosened a knot in his wrist so it snapped up into his elbow, whizzed through his shoulder, wakened a hollowness behind his right ear. She kissed him, sinking teeth into soft gums. Their tongues slid rough over each other, finding the slick underside. Hothearted, she nicked him higher. Something had unlocked him and he felt the secret source of the power he had that day in the bowl, the push behind his solid words. Life regenerate. As he was his father had been and Toby would be: tongue into ear, moist brush of seabreeze. His father lived. He passed the movement back to her and her teeth drew red lines down his throat. A bead grew from a slow delirium firepoint. Centripetal violence clasped them both. It hit him hard.

EPILOG

ARGO

ONE

The Argo lay buried beneath a knobby hill that looked completely natural. The entrance portals were under a deep gully half-filled with gravel. Killeen had been the first to go in because the portal was keyed to accept only an authentic human handprint. It had some way to check his genetic coding, too, searching for key configurations that showed he descended from the humans who had pioneered Snowglade.

The mechs had figured this out but that was all. No mech simulacrum would have made it in. It was easy for him though and no safety triggers or alarms went off. The portals led through tunnels to a huge enclosure under the hill.

Killeen spent time afterward on the brow above the steadily expanding excavation, looking out across a shallow broad stream and the plain beyond that rose into blue mountains. There were snowy peaks in the mountains and the water ran down from them painfully cold. This place was halfway around Snowglade from the speck that was man's Metropolis and here he could see the advance of the mech climate. He had to wear doubleweave jacket and leggings or else his feet would ache. He and Toby spent hours down by the stream listening to the sound of it on the pebbles and boulders that lay smoothed and night-black in the channels. The water streamed clear and swift with a

tinge of blue in it. Toby picked thin plates of ice from the
eddies at the bank and skipped them like stones across the
broad fast water and then yowled at the stinging cold in his
hands.

The mechs liked the cold. Legions of them went by the
stream and up to the hill and the dust they raised filmed the
sharp air. The large shell-shaped enclosure they had now
uncovered was streaked with the rust of ages and the slow
settling of it had powdered the ship within. Killeen and
Toby had watched the mechs carefully cut the dirt away
from the enclosure's interlocking framework and then peel
it back to reveal the hard stark whiteness of the Argo. Long
columns of mechs marched in complex formations to rake
back stone and soil systematically, searching for remnant
traces of whoever had left the ship. They treated it like an
archaeological site of a long-dead culture.

The Argo was buried in a metal-rich area so no simple
detector could pick it out from above. Whoever had left it
had intended it to stay a long time and had provided against
quakes and seepage. Several times mechs had prospected
this area for ore but had never found the ship.

The squads of mechs raised more dust that fell on the
Argo and for the first two days that was the only thing that
touched the broad bone-white skin of it. The ship was like
two palms cupped together. The palms joined seamlessly
but fore and aft translucent cowlings covered complex
extrusions. The mechs seemed to know what these things
were and treated them very gingerly as they rolled back the
cowlings.

Then the Mantis had ceased its directing of the mech
army and come to the small encampment of humans. It
needed two people who could enter the ship's locks. Again
only a human hand could trigger the right response.
Killeen could tell that the Mantis had tried a number of
ways to unlock the mechanisms but had failed and was
momentarily mystified. He thought the Mantis was surprised that humans had once devised something a mech
could not quickly crack, but when he said this in passing
the Mantis replied:

No. A long time has elapsed since elements of me saw such work from your kind, but it is not unknown to us. The first of your phylum who came to the Center were not so skilled when they arrived. (Unintelligible.) They quickly learned some of our arts, however. You yourself encountered one of their duplications of a great work from your own far past, I believe.

"Whatsay? I don't—"

I was tracking you at the time. You had an unfortunate encounter with a Marauder, class 11. I had been unable to dissuade it from attacking you. (As I noted before, I must work within my society's contexts.) You took refuge in an artifact which we had preserved from that longpast event, when several of your phylum re-created the thing they called Taj Mahal. It was marked with the emblem of the human who led that party, a group now gone elsewhere in the Center.

Killeen remembered staring long and hard at that monument so he could place it in permanent storage. He called that up now and studied the artful curves, the solemn white glow of the stonework. Then he saw the square marker set in black. *NW.* So that stood for some forefather who had shaped and built as mechs did. "They made the Argo?"

No. They came well before the Chandeliers and were the first humans here at the Center. Later came other humans. The Argo, as nearly as we can glean from these surrounds, was the product of the early Citadel makers. They foresaw a time when your phylum might need a means of escape. They had witnessed our works towering in other parts of the Center and knew that time would bring us to occupy and shape Snowglade (as you call it) to higher purposes.

Killeen snorted. "Killin' Snowglade's a higher purpose?"

You must understand that my interest in you does not mean I believe your destiny is somehow on the level of ours. This, too, will be apparent to you as you learn more.

Killeen smiled without humor and said nothing.

He was learning to sense something of the complex interweaving states the Mantis possessed. It was a mistake, he knew, to believe that behind the Mantis's words lay anything like emotion. *Thing about aliens is, they're alien,* his father had said, and he would not forget it. Still, any feeling for what state the Mantis was in could be useful.

The Mantis was a faint presence on the edge of his sensorium when Killeen entered the Argo for the first time. Cermo-the-Slow and a Rook had made the first entrance and found nothing they could understand. Now micromechs crept stealthily into the Argo, trying to understand the ship.

From the Mantis Killeen picked up a chromatic shifting that seemed to correspond to anticipation, excitement, interest. He and Shibo prowled oval corridors dimly lit by red running lights. The Mantis could identify some modular sections from old mech records. Pieces of the Argo came from mechtech sculpted to human needs. Others had been shaped from ancient human designs, perhaps reflecting the technology which humanity brought to the Galactic Center long ago.

Killeen felt spurts of recognition from some of his oldest Aspects as he inspected the Argo. Old human technology brought warm memories welling up. Man was tied to his artifacts.

The Mantis commented:

Precisely. Often your works long outlive you. We, who propagate forward forever, do not tie any of our deep concerns to artifacts. They are passing tools, soon to be rubbish. This is one of the many intriguing distinctions between you and us.

When the Mantis spoke through his Arthur Aspect, Killeen had to guard against replying with more than a distracted assent. The Mantis was a thin wedge driven into Arthur, and might pick up Killeen's own protected thoughts. Deception was difficult.

He was aided, though, by his other Aspects. The Mantis had not co-opted them. Their pleased chatter as the Argo's mysteries unfolded served to mask Killeen's more canny, assessing thoughts.

The Aspects' muted cries would once have plucked at his attention, diverting him. Now he found he could suppress them to mere shadowy flickers on the wall of his mind. He had learned that in the Aspect storm. To his surprise, he now suffered no stark dreams when he slept, or had to struggle to smother his Aspects and Faces when he awoke. They still rode far back in him, though, and came quickly when summoned. He had only occasional glimmerings of the way they had struck at him in the storm. The waves that had broken over him, a biting acrid fluid of squirming bugs and spiders—that image he could swiftly force down.

Yet it came back to him in an oddly different way as he moved through the murky passages of the Argo. Micromechs scrambled everywhere. Their insect energy inspected and checked and fixed the long-dormant mechanisms of the slumbering craft. They seemed like waves washing over the carcass of a deep-sea beast, now beached and forlorn.

Yet the Argo stirred. He could feel at the tapering fringes of his own sensorium a skittering, bright presence. The Argo's inner networks were reviving.

Laboring mech squadrons flowed like dark streams around the pebble that was the small human camp. There were many varieties of mech which humans had never seen before. Tubular forms, blocky things, splotchy assemblages with razor-sharp tools. Somehow these methodical machines knew to avoid humans and gave their open fires and tents wide berth.

In all, slightly more than a hundred people had come on the long trip to the Argo site. Mostly Bishops and Rooks, they had been frightened by the Duster that had flown them and the commandeered Rattler that had brought them here from the landing field. The Mantis had been the first startling encounter for them, when it met them beyond the hills that ringed Metropolis. But perhaps because of the prior presence of the Mantis in their sensoria, they got used to its assemblage of pipes and nodules.

Still, the motley collection of humans needed constant reassurance. Killeen found this irksome. People continually peppered him with questions whenever he returned from the Argo site to their camp.

What was that gas that had enclosed the ship, the one that made you talk funny if you inhaled some of it? (Helium, Arthur informed him. An inert protection against rust.)

Why was the Mantis getting bigger? (It added components to direct the swelling mech crews.)

Why was it so cold here? (They were nearer the northern pole. But Metropolis would eventually feel such bite, as the mech changes progressed.)

Food was running short; couldn't the mechs hurry? (Making a centuries-dead ship work again took time. And Killeen would ask the Mantis to have some mechmade food brought in. Not tasty, but filling.)

Why was the manmech coming with them? (Left behind, far from its work site, it would be run down by a Marauder. It carried some fragment of the old human ways. And it wanted to come.)

He was glad Fornax and Ledroff had declined to go. Having either along would make this impossible. Both men had listened to Killeen's proposal and had promised to ponder it overnight. But in the morning retreat had lined their drawn faces. As the three of them had spoken, the two Cap'ns had eyed him with new recognition. Speaking softly, not rushing things, Killeen had bargained for the people who wanted to go and see what the Argo was.

So the time had come three days later when the long column wound out of Metropolis. They might all return, of course. There was no guarantee that the Argo even existed anymore or that it would work. They had only the map of the manmech to guide them. But a hundred-strong they gambled.

Ledroff had stayed with the remaining Bishops. Already he was more occupied with maneuvering against Fornax, to become Cap'n of the entire Metropolis. But neither Cap'n was strong enough yet to stop the party that wanted to go to the Argo and so they had stood and watched, blank-faced.

The loss of Hatchet, the revelation of what he had done, the sudden jolting Mantis presence—these had rocked Metropolis and made Killeen's maneuvers possible. Hatchet had kept silent about his deals with the Crafter and what he saw on raids. Unlike the ancient Family rituals of tale-telling following a raid, Hatchet had confined talk to stories of their stealth. The Mantis's depiction of what Hatchet was willing to do, the awful moment with the Fanny-thing—this had forever dirtied Hatchet's memory.

Killeen had all along phrased everything as mere possibility, as an exploration. Yet he knew when he marched out that he would never see Metropolis again. Even if the Argo had been a mere tale, he would not have gone back. Better to roam slow-dying Snowglade than to cower in a cage.

Still, he understood the sense of the majority that stayed. Fornax and Ledroff would make competent keepers. With the Mantis's protection, Families could grow.

Humanity had always been dominated by the stay-behinds, Arthur had told him. It was a prudent strategy for the race, a heavy hedge on every daring bet. So none of the departing party had scorned the timid; wordlessly, with intuition born of hard trial, they understood.

The people gathered together on a bleak hillside to watch the Argo's first flight.

It lifted with a rumble from the staging area around the burial site. Human hands had flown it into orbit long ago. The Argo had linked the Citadels with the Chandeliers. The ship used mech parts, linked solely to human commands. Its sensorium answered to telltale signatures of human thought processes and rejected mechspeak in any form.

So, though humans now knew nothing of things mechanical, once again human hands had to fly her.

Shibo had been the obvious choice. Her exskell could perform the deft, quick moves of piloting. And through her sensorium the Mantis could link the Argo's ship-mind to her exskell.

Killeen sat beside her as she made the ship's motors thrum and storm and thrum again. She had trained for days, with the Mantis's help. Once routes and channels were laid down in her sensorium, the ship's intricate self-sentient structures took over. They could interlock with her mechanical movements through the exskell.

Her hands flew swiftly among the command modules, her exskell buzzing. Anything done by word-level simple transmission of instructions would have been impossibly slow.

She took it well. A dim rivulet of the flow came to Killeen through the margins of his own sensorium. Raw touches and cutting smells and sour tastes, all scrambled and scratch-quick. Her face tightened with effort as she moved over the oblique board before her. At each step the ship verified that she was indeed human; an ancient security measure.

Her eyelids fluttered, her lips drew thin and pale.

"Heysay?" he whispered beside her.

"Getting it." Words slipped from between clenched teeth.

"Leave off if you feel—"

"I *can*. I can do it."

She seemed to be listening to far voices. Killeen felt the swirl of information funnel through her like an accelerating wind.

The ship whined higher. He felt a wobbling sensation.

"We're clear," she said, so faintly he could barely hear.

A drifting sensation swept over him. It was only a dim echo of what she endured but it told him of the data inputs from a thousand sensors. He felt himself lift and tilt and glide.

He had the sudden perception of looking down, straight down. A carved hillside hung below like gnawed fruit.

—*Yeasay!*— Cermo-the-Slow called faintly from below. —*They're flyin'.*—

"You're wonderful," he said simply.

She sat at the board like a queen, the first human to master this strange artifact since the days of the Chandeliers. He knew the importance of it but could feel only the personal: his sudden love for her. Bursting liberation. Having control of his own mind and being able to give of himself without constraint.

Unbidden, Arthur's small voice, free of the Mantis, chirped:

> You are now tapped in to her pheromones. These are molecular notches which must link up to excite the full level of male-female attraction. The Mantis undid the inset which the Family Bishop imposed on all. Do not mistake this for anything ethereal or intellectual. Fitting of such neural notches is unrelated to the lady's social standing or your opinion of her. Mating proceeds not to express the higher functions within, unfortunately, but to please the great genetic pool lapping around us. I must say—

Killeen cut him off.

He and Toby walked beneath the twilight sky that evening, more to keep warm by moving than to see the endless workings of the mechs. The scuttling forms labored without sleep, refitting the Argo, gathering supplies, doing their own inexplicable research.

"How's the Mantis get so many 'em workin' for it?" Toby asked.

"It's like a . . . a Cap'n for mechs," Killeen finished, realizing that in fact he knew nothing of what the Mantis was.

"Think it'll really let us go?"

"It better."

"Don't see why it should." Toby frowned. Killeen saw in the boy's face a struggling to understand that confirmed what had happened to him inside the mechplex. His son was changing with every passing day, thrust forward by the gravity of events to an early adulthood. A certain blithe assurance was gone from Toby, would never return. He would worry each odd point of the world now until he had it, understood it, could fit it in the scheme of things.

"We used the only weapon we had left," Killeen said. "Vulnerability."

"Don't get it."

Killeen hand-signaled to Toby to shut down his sensorium.

"All 'em?"

"Yeasay." When they had only stunted, conventional senses, Killeen said, "If it kept us all in Metropolis we wouldn't be the same."

Toby blinked. "Huh?"

"Boxed in, we wouldn't be true humans anymore."

"Turn into porkers?"

"Yeasay. So fat, hafta get mechs in, cart us 'round."

"All those people we left, they gone get fat, you figure?"

"Maybe. Not that that'll bother the Mantis much. Way I figure it, Mantis'll track us, too."

"How?"

"Those micromechs."

"Ummm."

Toby stopped walking, hands in jacket pockets, his breath fogging the still air. "Heysay hear somethin'?"

Killeen saw the Mantis approaching from the Argo. "Kindle your systems. Don't want it suspectin'."

As his sensorium brightened he felt the hard outline of the Mantis intrude. He said as if in ordinary conversation, "Thing is, son, there's something we lose . . ."

Laughter. That is the signature of your inner sense. That will die in the Metropolis.

Toby started, eyes big.

"Damn it!" Killeen shouted at the consuming dark around them. "I said before, don't come in like that. We have a code, a right, privacy among ourselves."

Yes—and that, too, is part of that "something" you feel you would lose. This facet is related to

your interior processing. I do not understand
how this is so. It relates to your habits, of that I
am sure. You must sleep to filter your experience
of the world. This is typical of lower, naturally
evolved forms.

Toby's mouth twisted, his eyes narrowed. Killeen saw
that rather than being scared, the boy already considered
the Mantis an irritant. He understood this but knew it was
dangerous. They were getting used to the Mantis. *Thing
about aliens is, they're alien.*

"So what you do, huh? Don't sleep?" Toby demanded.

We process information in parallel systems while
remaining conscious. Such clearing mechanisms
as sleep and laughter we do not need.

Toby said derisively, "Must get on your nerves."
Killeen said, "Don't have any. Nerves, I mean."
Toby shrugged. "Can't be much fun."
"Prob'ly isn't," Killeen agreed.
Toby chuckled. "Prob'ly don't know what fun *is*,
right?"

Not precisely, no. It has to do with your downtime processing mechanism, of that I am sure.
You accumulate your curious dynamic tensions
through conscious operations. Some of these
discharge during your downtime processing,
your sleep. (Unintelligible.) Others escape with
the venting of the reflexive sounds—

"Laughin'?" Toby asked in disbelief.

Yes. There are also accumulations of identity-sig-
nifiers. You must continually maintain your self-
knowledge, your interior image of your essence,
in order to keep your subprograms working
properly. We have similar systems, of course.
Yours, though, appear to be keyed to your
sexual identity. Internal questionings accumu-

late. Only by reaffirming your sexual self, by
uniting with an opposite member, can you resolve and discharge these accumulated signifier
problems —tensions, I suppose you would call
them. Curiously, this can occur with only a small
sample of the available candidates, often merely
one candidate. For example, your father has,
once I released him of some crude internal
programming, formed with Shibo a—

Killeen said sharply, "Don't go talking dumb 'bout
things you don't know."

I see. Yes, I take your point.

A fitful tang pervaded Killeen's sensorium. He had the
distinct impression that the Mantis was politely backing
away from the subject. Killeen felt a mild outrage at a mech
intruding into things so fragilely human, talking to a boy
about his own father's sex life. He said, "You mechs got no
balls."

Not in the sense you mean.

Toby laughed. "What's *that* mean?"

I will not discuss the implications of our lives, for
you are a lower thing. Do not mistake your value
as a phylum for more than it is. We have studied
others of your sort, elsewhere in the Galactic
Center.

"Where?" Killeen asked intently.

Do not think you can easily deceive me about
your intention to find your father. I understand
these primitive motivations.

"Dammit, I want know where other humans are."

The original ones, the builders of the Taj Mahal—I do not know. But the later group, from which you descend—they are spread in several spots. I enjoin you, however. I have adjusted the Argo. (Unintelligible.) It cannot sail inward toward the Eater. We will not tolerate lesser forms interfering there. You must chart outward. There you may find humans. There are other forms in that region, as well.

"Sure you don't want come along?" Toby asked, suspicion tightening his mouth.

I wish the laughing, dreaming vertebrates to retain some freedom. Otherwise they will not remain in the wild state. As curator of such forms I shall preserve them.

"We're gettin' away," Toby countered.

You will remain within reach of the Center. The Argo cannot voyage far. It can reach at most a few hundred stars in the Center. If I wish more specimens of you in the natural state, I can come and harvest some. To leave you here, wild, would be to see you become extinct.

"Don't look like you could catch anythin'," Toby said with thin bravado. Killeen gave him a warning glance.

You do not know of what you speak. I require from you, however, a pledge that you will not seek the one who spoke to you through the magnetic creature.

Killeen looked back to where the Argo lay in a glare of working lamps. What strange code made the Mantis believe he would honor a promise to a mech?

"Sure, I pledge," he lied.

* * *

He and Shibo took their food to eat down by the stream. It splashed over ebony rocks and Killeen hoped that this murmur would make them hard for the mechs to overhear.

"Good food," he said. "Never ate such."

"Soft," she answered. They smacked their lips with relish, eating with their hands the first product of the Argo's automatic kitchen. The ship converted raw materials into warm, spicy, aromatic wonders of layered and moist richness. The tastes kindled in Killeen old memories of his mother's cooking.

"Tonight we bed early," she added, looking at him with a distant mirth. He saw that she intended to have some fun with their talk.

"Yeasay. Tomorrow night we either sleep among the stars or we sleep forever."

"Tonight I get on top."

"Taking over already?"

"Ground rocky."

"Ah. You were always on top with the other men?"

"Which?"

"You must've had some."

"None."

"Sounds like you're lying."

"Yeasay." Her slight smile brimmed.

"Keep right on lying. I want it that way. Fill me with lies. Yeasay. Were they all Knights?"

"Never had any, on top or on bottom."

"I understand. Were they ugly, like me?"

"Never had any. I was ugly, too."

"We were made for each other. Uglies attract uglies. How many?"

"How many what?"

"Knights you had."

"There weren't any and I didn't count."

"Yeasay. Do Knights take their boots off first?"

She laughed. "I wouldn't know."

"I heard Knights were always run-ready."

"One on top keeps boots on."

"Why?"

"Might need run fast."

He looked shocked. "Even inside shelter?"

"I wouldn't know. I'm always on march."

"On the march nobody's inside."

"Not inside me anyway." She grinned.

"With all those big Knights around? You must be fast."

"I fast all right."

"Hafta be." He looked at her steadily and tipped his head slightly toward the big floodlit work zone where the Mantis moved among its mech army. "Big problems take quick reflexes."

"Little ones too."

Killeen glanced toward the Argo. "I count plenty little problems."

"Have to be fast, is all."

"No rush, I guess. Can take care little problems later."

She nodded. "Everybody knows that."

"Yeasay, even the manmech."

She nodded again. "Want be on top, be fast, wear boots."

"You're learning."

"Good teacher."

"Seems like you learned somewhere before."

She gave him a silky, sideways glance. "Never learned your moves, naysay."

"I like that. Keep lying and I'll keep liking it." He finished his food and licked his hands and the plate.

"I'll try."

"Yeasay. Tonight you can get on top." He grinned.

"Not sure I want."

"Why not?"

"Have wear boots."

"You get the point."

"That's what I want."

TWO

In the long stretching moment before the Argo lifted off Killeen felt a dim red pressure.

It was the mass of humanity at his back, on decks below. Their sensoria linked and intermingled like sliding soft fluids. Never had he felt them this way. Skittering tension shot through them but there was a calm smooth undercurrent too.

The long years on the march had hardened them. They could wait, knowing that their lives depended on their speed, and yet not permit this knowledge to tighten or distract them. Those who had not learned this had fallen somewhere back along the bleak and desolating train the Families had now left behind. So the Mantis, who had surekilled so many in that panicked state, would not sense in the sensorium today a premonition of what was to come.

Good. He nodded to Shibo. "Yeasay."

"Ummm. I like being on top."

He laughed. She began the launch.

The couch enveloped her. This was a last precaution against mech control. The laminated layers of the couch responded only to human inputs. Shibo worked within it, arms extended to the canted surfaces before her. Her hands moved in an exacting blur. Her exskell hummed and buzzed like an earnest animal.

He felt the ship gently lift from its mount. Thrumming strength beat through the air.

The wall opposite them wobbled. It gave a panoramic view of the site. Legions of black mechs ringed them.

The Mantis stood at the base of the ruined, scooped-out hill. Its myriad knobbed joints made it seem like a half-finished construction beside the broad blue stream.

Shibo took them up. The Argo leaned over, preparing for full boost. A rumbling came through the deck. He watched her intent face and saw there no trace of fear or doubt.

Behind him Toby called out, "Heysay yeasay. Go!"

Calls answered him down through the bright tapestries of the sensorium. All this legacy now rode on a single turning moment that came rushing toward them. Yet he found no panic or unsteadiness among them. They were an instrument honed by harsh years and ongoing tragedy and nothing could deflect them now.

—Boots on?— he asked them. They answered the code word with raucous and joyful affirmations.

The Mantis sent from below:

I wish you good voyage. You shall hear from me and my tributaries again.

"Yeasay!" Killeen answered.

"Go!" Toby called.

Shibo threw the Argo into full thrust. A hammering roar burst upon them. The Argo arced up and away. Sudden weight pressed them into their couches.

The ship rammed up into the hard sky.

And then it failed. Engines fell silent. The craft flew on, whistling and weightless.

They began falling. The view-wall cleared as their exhaust blew away. Far below, the mechs were a black ring.

Killeen felt a sudden vacancy of a kind none of them had ever known. The fall seemed infinitesimally slow. Every sense in him cried in shrill panic.

The Argo plunged aft-down toward bare rock. The plain rushed at them.

Killeen bit his lip to stifle a cry. He knew he could not let his fear leak into the sensorium but it threatened to overwhelm him. He saw Shibo pause in her feverquick movements, judging, pacing, listening to the ship's own small ancient minds.

The Argo veered. No lifting pressure slowed them but they did drift in their fall. Toward the hard blue stream that snaked like a cutting wire through the weathered stone.

—Now.—

Shibo's call came at the same instant that a brutal hand slammed them hard.

Killeen saw the stream below, its surface a reflecting

glare. The Ship's exhaust played upon it, driving waves. The Argo turned toward the shore.

The Mantis saw them coming and had only an instant to move. It lifted a turret weapon—

And was blown to fragments as spurting exhaust showered down on fragile structure.

Struts and rods and polished chromed complexes—all jerked and dissolved and scattered like useless random junk on the burnished rock.

The Argo hovered for a long moment. Its hot gases played with loving, lingering detail on the scattered, melting parts.

—Let's see you recover from that!— Killeen thought, and his bottled-up rage burst the words crimson through the sensorium.

—Feel what it is to die. Even if you come back, if you're saved somewhere else and can be regenerated, feel it *now*.—

Hails and gleeful cries answered him all through the Argo.

—Feel it! For Fanny. For what you did to her. For every one you surekilled and forced to live again as your grotesque artworks. Feel it!—

A punch drove Killeen down into his couch.

The Argo lifted at tremendous acceleration. It shot up from the plain and into an empty sky, leaving a towering yellow exhaust trail. Streamers of hot gas pointed back like an arrow toward the still-exact circle of black mechs. Severed so surgically from their master, none had fired at the lifting ship.

Killeen let the heavy weight press him without resistance. He had prayed that the Mantis could not read his emotions any better than he could read its. The Mantis's cozy use of Arthur's Aspect had made it seem almost human. Killeen would never know how close to the truth that was. Could a vastly intelligent mind, reduced to their level, mimic humanity?

It made no difference. The Mantis had violated the dignity of living things and by human standards that was enough to know. Nothing else mattered.

* * *

Little problems. That had been their code for the micromechs who infested the Argo. Who now ran mad through the ship, attacking it, cutting and searing.

And as they moved from their hiding places the Families cut them down.

The humans poured from their couches.

Boots on. Their running equipment gave them the power and agility to move through the Argo, even though the ship was under hard boost.

The micromechs were engineered to work in steady gravity. So Shibo rammed the Argo to high thrust, then backed off, then ran it high again.

The surges tumbled the micromechs from their holds on cables, pipes, circuitry. Bishops and Rooks swung through suddenly full-lit corridors, nerves quickened for the hunt. They shot and stabbed at the small creatures. Sudden surges slammed them against bulkheads but they kept on, relentless. The hunt sang in them. Micromechs scurried and fled and tried to hide. Boots stamped them into oblivion. Hands ripped them in half.

Where they did flee the humans had allies. The manmech pursued them, wise in the ways of these small microbots. It ground them under steel treads. Toby followed it down the lurching, careening corridors of the Argo. He shot micromechs but took more pleasure in pounding them with the butt of his e-beam gun, feeling the crunch of collapsing metal, of shattered microcircuits.

They hooted and called and yelled, this fevered mob, as they spilled like an avenging flood through the big ship. Old blood-songs sprang to their lips. Glee and rage echoed savage and pitiless through the metal warrens.

By the time the Argo had achieved a staging orbit the micromechs were smashed and riddled.

"Got 'em all," Toby said. His eyes were big and bright. "W'out Mantis tellin' them what's up, they're not so smart."

Shibo nodded, distracted by her work at the board. They began boosting at steady acceleration on a course the Mantis had plotted. She was going to follow the course, find out where it led. She understood by feel only a minute fraction of the ship systems, but now she could rely on them. With the Mantis control gone, they were free.

Killeen asked, "Any casualties?"

Toby sobered immediately. "Jocelyn got hit in the leg."

"How's she?"

"They're workin' on her."

He grimaced. Every loss was irreplaceable, final. Now that they were his responsibility, they cut even more deeply. He saw that he was always going to have doubt afterward, questions, second thoughts, regrets. Always.

"We got 'em all, though," Toby said confidently.

"Maybe."

"Naysay, we did. Honest."

"If the Mantis had some fixed so they'd hide when things went wrong, we'd miss 'em," he said mildly. He didn't want to take the steam out of Toby so fast—the boy needed a victory—but he might as well start now in showing how you had to look at every side of mechs if you wanted to guard against them. That was the way the world was. The boy had to learn.

"Well . . . maybe," Toby allowed. Then he brightened. "Want we look some more?"

"No, get some food. Any mechs hiding, maybe they'll come out in a li'l while. Keep somebody watching all the time."

"Yeasay. The manmech'll be good for that."

"It work out okay?"

"Sure. Wish it'd cut out that barking, though."

"You don't like it?"

"Well, that's not so bad. Sounds funny with the woman voice, though. Was there really an animal made that noise once?"

Killeen smiled. "So I hear. Worked for us."

"Did all the animals?"

"Some. What my Aspects tell me is, we got more and more of them working for us. Or we ate them, which is another way of working for us I guess."

"*Ate* 'em?"

"Yeasay. First food humans ever had, I s'pose."

Toby's forehead wrinkled in doubt. "Thought we jus' ate plants."

"Aren't animals left on Snowglade big enough for eating. We would if we could find some, prob'ly."

"Sounds funny. Not sure I'd like eating somethin' that was movin'."

"We'd cook it first, the way we do most plants. Aspects say there was a time when we took animals and put them in fact'ries. Made them grow fast and didn't let them get out or move much, so they'd grow faster. Then we'd eat them."

Toby looked at Killeen in flat disbelief. "We'd do *that*?"

Killeen opened his mouth to say something and suddenly saw in his mind's eye the grotesque scenes in the mechplex.

The pumping legs. Racks of bulging, muscular arms. The vaults of glazed human parts. The Mantis-made sculptures. And finally, the shambling monstrous Fanny.

Had humans ever done that to lesser forms? Used them for parts of manufacture or casual amusement?

He found it hard to believe humans would do that to animals. Box and gouge and use them like machines. As though they were not part of the long chain of being that united life against mechanism.

Killeen remembered the gray mouse that had peered up at him so long ago. Between them had passed a glimmering recognition of joined origins and destiny. Cruel need might force Killeen to eat the mouse—though he could not imagine the act—but never would he hurt or degrade it. Not the way the Mantis had eaten the essence of Fanny and made it into something terrible.

No. He did not think humans would ever have done that.

You could not trust everything the Aspects said. They were repeating history they had heard and that could be wrong. Or they could lie.

"Don't worry 'bout that. Just go get something to eat. And watch yourself in the tunnels out there, huh? Could be mechs still hidin'."

Toby's frown vanished in a glimmering. As the boy went out of the control room Killeen could see him cast his questions aside and take up again the eagerness of the hunt. He would find the manmech and together they would prowl the corridors. Through the complicated scheme of the ship would resound distant enthusiastic barking, glad cries, and the hot energy of pursuit. Something in him looked forward to that, for reasons he could not name.

* * *

Snowglade was a brown, rutted ball.

That shocked them, even though they had fled and fought over innumerable broad wasted plains of it. Among the Families there had always been the long-held memory of old Snowglade: of great lakes shimmering blue, of green glades, of moist high valleys warmed by Denix radiance.

The globe that swam in the view-wall was a dried husk. Not the ample fruit which the Aspects remembered and spoke of recovering. Snowglade was the pit of that fruit, now eaten. The mechs had buried its ice, cooled its plains, smothered its brimming life in dust and desecration.

Mechworks dotted the night side of Snowglade with their pale, blue glow. Traceries looped and cut the night with amber, ruby, burnt yellow. It was their world now.

Killeen listened to the startled exclamations as the people passed through the big control bay. They took a while to understand what they saw and the ideas did not come easily.

Once they did, there was always a moment of indrawn breath, of amazement at the scale of what they witnessed and what it meant. Snowglade was a blasted ruin. The fabled green paradise of their forefathers was lost.

He remembered Toby when he had been the merest infant. If you let him go for a second, or even partially subtracted some of his support, the small brown thing would quickly respond. His arms would reach out to grab, his hands clench. Even his feet would seek purchase and his toes would grasp.

The Arthur Aspect had told Killeen that this was an instinctive response. If matters of gravity changed, if support failed, the young sought to grab their parent and hold on. The baby did not know it did it. It simply did.

Killeen wondered if they were doing that now. Reaching out from the dead parent planet. Grasping, even as they said farewell.

Life carrying out impulses implanted in the very way the world worked. Not following a program of its own, but a design won from experience itself, from being immersed in the world and inseparable from it.

Grasping for something it did not fathom.

* * *

Shibo had stayed with the ship system until her eyelids drooped, her exskell whined, her hands strayed randomly. Then she slept.

When she awoke, Snowglade was a dwindling dry mote. The Families were securing the ship by hook and by crook, figuring the works of it. This was the first technology they had ever seen designed for human use. Tinkering with it, solving puzzles no more complex than a doorknob, opened long-dormant ways of thinking, avenues sealed by the ancient identification of machines with mechs and mechs with death.

Killeen took courage from this. If they could master this ship they had a chance. Not a good chance, perhaps, given what might lurk up here in the swallowing black. But it was a beginning. And they had faced hard nights before.

Shibo told him what she had learned of their course. "Outward from the Center, that much I see. Winds of matter blow here. We catch some that. Don't know how but the ship does. So we go out."

It was enough for the moment to know that the Mantis had not placed them on some deadly path. There was time enough to learn more and in that could lie their future.

"We can't take everything the Mantis did as wrong," he said to Shibo and Cermo when they all met before the view-wall. "It might have sent us somewhere useful."

"Glad we killed it," Cermo-the-Slow said, his face twisted up in distaste. "The Fanny-thing . . ."

Killeen nodded. "It did not know human dignity. How could it?"

Cermo shook his head. "Should've."

"When you back us down and we haven't got anything left, you can't take our dignity," Killeen said. "We'll die for it. Kill for it. Hatchet forgot that and so he died. Everyone in the Families understood that as soon as he or she saw what Hatchet had done. That he would do anything, sink as low as he must, if that meant his Metropolis dream could continue."

"Yeasay," Shibo said.

He went on. "The Mantis made a mistake, showing everybody what Hatchet had done. I asked it that because it thought that would somehow move us. Make us do what it wanted. Make Metropolis into a zoo. But instead it united us."

Killeen said this slowly, carefully. Cermo had to understand it because Cermo had to tell the others, to speak for Killeen when voices rose in opposition behind his back. As they always would.

There was much he wanted to tell Cermo and Shibo and the others but could not yet, in the confusion of so much newness.

"We got it," Shibo said. "Mantis gone."

Killeen gave her a wan smile. "Maybe. Prob'ly not, though."

"But I burned it."

"Mantis, it's spread out some way. You blew it away so fast maybe it didn't get all itself moved, sent other places on Snowglade. Some got away, though. That's what it did times before, when we thought we killed it. Maybe *nothin'* can kill it."

Shibo said, "Next time—"

"Hope there's no next time," Killeen said fervently. He loved Shibo and didn't ever want to subject her to a risk like the one they had just run. "We were lucky. Damn lucky."

And in destroying the Mantis they risked Metropolis, as well. If the Mantis did not reassemble itself quickly, Marauders might find and attack the humans left behind.

There was no way around that fact. It was the price of their freedom and they would have to live with it.

To Killeen's surprise Arthur broke in, his small precise voice seemingly unchanged from the time when he had been possessed by the Mantis.

Hormones are great weavers of illusions. That was most clever, using the natural response of yourself and her to mask your speech. Little problems, indeed. Quite probably the Mantis could not penetrate it to understand what you meant. Still, I do feel you could perhaps have negotiated with it a more safe resolution of—

Killeen cut off the Aspect with a gruff grunt. Shibo lifted an eyebrow at him, as if suspecting what went on. He grinned.

Cermo-the-Slow asked about some details and Killeen answered with only part of his mind. He was tired but he did not want to rest. There was so much to understand and so few clues. He would have to listen to his Aspects more than ever, but always on guard against their incursions, their willfulness.

He wondered idly if the Mantis had such problems. What was an anthology intelligence? Wasn't Killeen, with his Aspects and Faces and own self-doubts, a collection of minds? As he grew older, parts of himself came into view like fresh landscape.

That was what the Mantis missed. Mech civilization was beyond humanity's grasp in many ways, but of one thing Killeen was sure. The machines lived forever in some sense, their myriad selves gathered up and reprocessed in some collective mind. The impulse to do that must have come long ago from the same despair that afflicted humans—the sure knowledge of a personal, final end.

So the mechs had made immortality their greatest aim. Renegades who wanted to preserve all their minds were condemned. Somehow, mech civilization had decided that only a fraction of a single consciousness was worth saving. So it promised a salvation of sorts. Killeen had listened to the rantings of his own Nialdi Aspect and knew that the idea of some God-granted life was a powerful drive. Humans had believed that, too. Mechs had made it real. They had sought and found a way out of the crush of matter and time. Their world was one of perpetual obedience to a single order, because to disobey meant true oblivion.

And that was where the Mantis had missed the essence of the thing. Killeen knew this in a way he could not express, any more than he could say out loud what he felt when he put his arm around the shoulder of his son. But he knew it all the same.

Death's sure and steady measure was not pure evil. It brought an intense poignant richness to every moment. To mortal men each day came once and forever and struck sure into the heart. The machines would never know that. They lived in a kind of still gray death, where no one moment meant anything, because all moments were alike.

Only the dreaming vertebrates knew that life held more than that.

Which was why the Argo voyaged up. They moved across dark vaults beneath shimmering stars, the great sky river, perhaps to some tranquil end and perhaps equally to final black oblivion. But outward. Outward.

He was passing down a corridor on the way to see to some trouble when Cermo-the-Slow and three Rooks stopped him to ask about still another problem. There had been no time to call a meeting of Families, a Witnessing of all the events which had befallen them so quickly, a time to sort it all out. But when they had all settled on a solution to the problem Cermo grinned and said, "Yeasay, Cap'n."

The four of them matter-of-factly departed. Killeen stood looking after them blankly. This was a ship and she was under his helm. But he had not fully thought of the fact that this was the first time in a long drumroll of centuries when the conditions of the title were again met. Killeen blinked and even mouthed the word out loud. Then, slowly, he nodded.

ABOUT THE AUTHOR

Gregory Benford is the author of several acclaimed novels, including *Heart of the Comet* (with David Brin), *In the Ocean of Night, Across the Sea of Suns,* and *Timescape,* which won the Nebula Award, the British Science Fiction Award, the John W. Campbell Memorial Award, and the Australian Ditmar Award. Dr. Benford, a Woodrow Wilson Fellow, is a professor of physics at the University of California, Irvine. He and his wife live in Laguna Beach. His new novel will be published by Bantam Spectra in hardcover in early 1989.

The groundbreaking novels of
GREGORY BENFORD

☐ **In the Ocean of Night** (26578-4 • $3.95/$4.95 in Canada) From far beyond the shores of space, a mystery emerges as vast as the limitless sea of stars. This is one man's encounter with that mystery. *The Magazine of Fantasy and Science Fiction* called this "A major novel."

☐ **Across the Sea of Suns** (26664-0 • $3.95/$4.95 in Canada) Human and alien technology have brought forth a new age of enlightenment for humanity. As earth falls prey to attack, from the far reaches of space comes an alien message of astounding importance, revealing great wonders and terrifying danger. *The Washington Post Book World* said "Adult characters, rich writing, innovative science, a grand philosophical theme—it's all here."

☐ **Heart of the Comet** (with David Brin) (25839-7 • $4.95/$5.95 in Canada) chronicles the daring mission to the heart of Halley's Comet by a team of brilliant—and very human—scientists. *The Los Angeles Times* called it "A glittering new work of hard science fiction." *The San Diego Union* said it is "Better than Dune . . . tremendously imaginative . . . a breathtaking effort from two of science fiction's brightest stars."

Buy In the Ocean of Night, Across the Sea of Suns and Heart of the Comet wherever Bantam Spectra books are sold, or use this handy page to order:
